WHAT HAPPENED
IN
ROOM 13

TONY ASHRIDGE

BALLYCOPELAND BOOKS

Tony Ashridge

BALLYCOPELAND BOOKS UK

Cover Design: Izabeladesign

Cover Images: Deposit Photos

tonyashridgeauthor@gmail.com

http://ballycopelandbooks.uk

PRAISE FOR
WHAT HAPPENED IN ROOM 13

I was gripped throughout – a brilliant novel. The shocking revelation at the beginning really hooked me in and kept me turning the pages. Tony Ashridge doesn't disappoint as the plot gathers momentum, delivering unexpected twists at the end.
Sylvia Blackmore

Intelligent and humane writing, What Happened in Room 13 is definitely a page-turner with a firecracker of a plot twist. The reader is kept guessing until the end.
Tim Holbert

Compelling and believable, sometimes shocking in places. The sub-plots and twists, gentle at first, lead to a big surprise, inspired by true events awaiting the reader.
Sue Turner

This is a smartly told murder-mystery tale, masterfully blending fact and fiction – the writing is sharp and sparing with humour and dramatic interludes throughout.
Anousha Pawar

An original novel, Tony Ashridge writes with such an inventive spirit. This is a mind-blowingly good, buoyant and mischievous crime-mystery tale: enjoyably creepy at times, which certainly keeps one turning the pages.
Bridget Hanson

Skilfully evocative, this book is multi-layered with richly-woven plots, inventively sustained. Sad, funny and frustrating in places. Scandal, fury, accusations and revenge are all part of the drama. Never a dull moment A corker of a book – totally unputdownable.
W. G. Mendoza

For Sheryl

The sins of the fathers
are to be laid upon the children.

William Shakespeare,
The Merchant of Venice

Prologue

1583

The pounding at her door seemed unusually persistent. There was an urgency about it; such was its tenacity. Wearily, she made to pull-open the large iron bolts. Who could this be, so late on a cold, wet windy November night?

Opening the door, she was confronted by a mysterious man dressed in dark clothing, his hat and muffle concealing all but his eyes.

'Art thee Mrs Walt'rs the midwife?' he asked with ferocity in his voice.

'Aye that's me. How can I beest of s'rvice to thee on such an evening as this?'

'I cometh from the lrd's house. We has't a baby needeth deliv'ring. Thee shall beest hath paid handsomely f'r thy w'rk this night. Secrecy is requir'd. But thee needeth to cometh anon. Immediately h'rewith.'

The offer of a good financial incentive was enough for old Mrs Walters to immediately gather her coat and little bag of tools for the job in-hand. Then, mounting the waiting horse, which had been saddled for pillion, they both galloped-off along the woodland track to cover the three miles heading to Crawthorne Hall.

On their arrival, she was led, blindfold by her escort into the house, up a flight of stairs and into a room. Her blindfold was then removed to reveal a sumptuous bedchamber. There lay a young woman whose features were concealed by a mask. Even so, Mrs Walters could clearly see that she was in much distress and close to giving birth. Approaching the bed, she turned to see a man emerge from the shadows dressed in black velvet and also wearing a mask.

'Well, madam, I assume thou art the midwife?' He turned away from the East wing window through which he had been gazing out at the still grey lake to one side of the great house. He had been contemplating his plans and now stood waiting for her to answer.

'Aye I am, sir.'

'Th're's two sov'reigns f'r thy troubleth, madam.'

'Thanketh thee, sir,' she replied.

This all seemed too good to be true, for two sovereigns would pay a skilled worker for two months' service. The midwife began to wonder exactly what was expected of her on this night. He spoke to her again, as though reading her mind.

'But,' he added, 'thee wilt bid no-one of what thee seeth and heareth tonight. Doth thee und'rstand?'

'Aye Sir.'

Mrs Walters was a shrewd old woman and, looking at the scene before her, assumed that the pregnant wench was most probably Lord Crawthorne's secret mistress – and that he was the man in the mask – clearly prepared to give her good money to keep her mouth shut. No doubt, the new-born baby, once delivered, would be smuggled-out of the house along with the mother – probably left destitute – discarded like unwanted rubbish? But this wasn't unusual in these times – he was a wealthy man.

Local gossip was rife with stories of his debauchery. Some spoke of his unnatural tendencies towards his own sister. He was also known for pleasuring himself with his servants who, in turn, being desperate for employment would give him what he wanted, hoping that they might find favour. Some, naively, hoped that bearing-him a child would act as a bond between them. In truth, a bastard child was the last thing that Lord Crawthorne would endure.

'Anon, beest about thy office,' he told her gesturing impatiently toward the bed.

The midwife felt awkward about him being in the room. It was not respectful or, indeed, good manners for a gentleman to witness the birth of a child. 'Wouldst mind leaving the bedchamb'r?' she asked.

However, Lord Crawthorne ignored her and paced agitatedly about the room. Mrs Walters thought it wise to say nothing more. She approached the bed.

'Don't w'rry, mine own loveth, i'm h're anon. We'll anon has't yond baby of yours safely deliv'r'd,' she said, trying to reassure the young woman as best she could.

Mrs Walters feared she may not survive the birth, indeed she feared for her own safety. After all, what could be stranger than being covertly brought to the manor house in the dead of night, blindfolded and placed in the company of a masked woman and a decidedly unpleasant masked man then told to deliver a baby. As she readied herself for the task in hand, the midwife couldn't help but notice the room had not been prepared to receive a new-born: there were no blankets and no water.

Mrs Walters complied with the lord's wishes despite her suspicions. The continued presence of his aged servant standing nervously in one corner did little to inspire the midwife's confidence. However, within a short time a healthy baby girl was delivered. As for the woman who had just given birth, the midwife's concerns only deepened as, cradling the infant in her apron, she was about to present the child when the man spoke.

'Nay. Thee might not but not giveth up the baby to h'r. Giveth to me.' She stood floundering as he roughly snatched the child from her, looking closely at the new-born. 'Behold thee has't b'rne me a monstrous issue,' he snarled.

'Giveth h'r to me mine own broth'r,' the mother of the child cried with desperation.

'Tis god's beshrew. A punishment upon us,' he replied heading for the door.

Following him into the hallway, Mrs Walters the midwife gasped with horror as the masked man – the person she believed to be the master of the house – Lord Crawthorne, 3rd Baron Crawthorne – strode towards a roaring fire. Without hesitation he threw the new-born into the flames, holding her there amidst burning coals with his booted foot. The midwife screamed, trying to pull him away, joined by the mother's piteous cries as she was held back in the bedchamber by the servant. The child, struggling amidst its torments, rolled from the flames upon the hearth.

'A beshrew on thee, thy sons and thy son's sons. May thee roteth in hell,' cursed the old midwife, who dabbled in the black arts.

In spite of the cursing midwife and the pleading of the agonised mother, the man seized the new-born, thrust the baby under the grate, finally murdering her by heaping live coals upon the body.

The child's agony had been short-lived and within seconds she lay motionless in the fireplace outside the now-sombre bedchamber in the eastern wing of Crawthorne Hall.

Chapter 1

2008

It was a small room measuring only about three metres by two metres: just enough space for a single bed along the back wall. A little radiator and wash basin had been plumbed-in at one side. Apart from a small bin half-full of screwed-up tissues and other debris, there was nothing else – no home comforts. The floor and walls were blandly, clinically tiled. It was a functional, utilitarian space fit for purpose, like hundreds of others in De Wallen in central Amsterdam.

She was clad in a black bikini and wore stilettos as she stepped over to pull apart the heavy red curtains which provided her entrance to the display window on the other side of the room. Slipping through the gap in the material, she mounted her stool before taking up a provocative pose ready to tout for business, to lure customers inside with a promise.

Laetitia was a new girl on the block – recently in from Eastern Europe. She was slim, young and desirable to the punters who would wait impatiently around her window, like dogs, for their fifteen-minute slot. Beautiful long, fair hair and sparkling blue eyes, she was in high demand.

In the evenings as the atmosphere in the sordid streets darkened with menace, swarming crowds would gather like locusts as they invaded this red-light district of the city with its three hundred booths selling sex. There would be tourists – families with children, young men on stag weekends, business men, loners – people from all walks of life – traipsing up and down the pavements – most looking to be entertained by the spectacles: some serious about finding relief, comfort and thrills. It was a supermarket for the punters who preyed on human misery.

George Crawthorne had told his wife that he had a little business to settle in Amsterdam. Although officially retired some years ago, he did genuinely fly over to the Netherlands from time to time to settle certain financial matters that he liked to keep secret from the tax man – especially his little side-line in diamonds – he'd become something of an expert since he first started dabbling in the early 1990s. Until recently, this little hobby had helped to subsidise his extravagant lifestyle.

George Edward Crawthorne, 15th Baron Crawthorne was now in the money once again. He'd recently sold the run-down, dilapidated family home near Hailsham, East Sussex, which he'd inherited from his father. He'd nearly always lived there: in the main house as a child and then occupying the West wing after his marriage to Isabela. The only times in his life when he'd lived away were to attend boarding school and university for his education; and later-on in his forties when he'd worked at the British Embassy in Hong Kong for three years. It was true to say that he'd felt a tad guilty about relinquishing ownership of the estate which had been handed-down over the generations. However, he'd been unable to pay the Inheritance Tax and there was no other choice. So, when a hotel group made him an offer he could not refuse, he'd jumped at the chance.

Now he had paid-off all his gambling debts, moved to a more modest eight-bedroomed house near Chichester in West Sussex and was set on-course for a leisurely retirement. There were just a few matters that he had to deal with before he could finally move-on in his life – one of these concerned his clandestine involvement in the diamond trade.

George's other main interest in Amsterdam centred around the delights on offer in the red-light district – conveniently situated and easily accessible for day tourists like him. On his last visit he'd come across a prostie in one of the four booths in Oudekerksplein 2, a little street in the heart of the De Wallen district of the city. Since then, he hadn't been able to stop thinking about her. She had said that he was a nice man: she'd made him feel special, wanted, valued. He just had to see her again.

*

Taking the morning flight from Gatwick, George had landed at the giant Schiphol Airport around ten thirty; then taken the train to Centraal Station. After coffee and a leisurely stroll along the side of a canal heading southwards, he had soon found the familiar backstreets which at around midday were relatively quiet from the seething masses which inhabited the nightlife of the area. The advantage of visiting at this time of day was that the prosties were desperate for custom; the disadvantage was that many of the windows were not yet occupied – even the girls needed time-off to sleep. He was taking a chance. Maybe she was there and maybe not … he just had to hope.

As often was the case with George, his luck was in and there she was, poised on her stool in her window. He sauntered up and gawped at her, lust arousing him. There was no compassion in his heart; he didn't ever stop to wonder about her degradation; he had no idea of her disgust and the bile that rose up in her as she looked out on the overweight old man on the other side of the window. All she could do was to smile tantalisingly and beckon him with a finger. She seductively licked her lips slowly with her tongue slithering between them from one side to the other.

Laetitia leant forward, closer to the window – he could just see one of her nipples as he looked forward to indulging his fantasies. He could wait no longer.

Approaching the little door, George waited while she opened it from the other side.

'I was with you a few weeks ago. Do you remember me? George?'

'Of course I remember you, George,' she lied. 'How could I ever forget!' The irony was lost on him.

'How much, then?'

She showed him the price list for her many services. Like a customer anticipating a luxurious lunch in a high-class restaurant, he browsed the menu of delights and then decided to opt for today's special. Only when they had agreed the price would she finally drop the security chain and let him in.

Fifteen minutes later after a cursory 'thanks' out of empty gratitude he emerged back on to the street one hundred euros poorer. With a feeling of delirious, heady pleasure he looked at his watch. He was on-time for his meeting in Damrak, one of the main streets adjacent to the station, just a few minutes' walk from where he had just enjoyed his liaison with Laetitia. Walking up past the sex museum he came upon the pizzeria that he had suggested for their rendezvous and, yes, there he was, sitting at a window table near the door. His grandson signalled in recognition as George entered.

'Hello, Charles. I'm glad you managed to find it.'

'My hotel is just up the road, so it was easy.'

Handsome from the depths of his deep brown eyes to the gentle expressions of his voice, Charles always reminded George of himself when he was younger. However, that is where the similarity ended, for his grandson possessed an intensity, honesty and gentleness which was lacking in the Crawthorne family dynasty. George, like his forefathers, possessed a certain cruel streak; he was impulsive and reckless, often driven by desire, selfishness and greed. Charles, on the other hand, was caring and considerate, always thinking of others – or so it seemed. He was the product of the marriage between Helen Crawthorne and Richard Eden, a lawyer. George worried that Charles wouldn't go far in the world – he was too honest and trusting – and his choice of career was a mistake as far as the Crawthornes were concerned.

A waiter came along and dished out menus which they started to browse.

'How are you, Charles? I'm glad to hear you've been accepted as a trainee manager,' George Crawthorne lied. His grandson had just landed a job with a prestigious hotel in Surrey.

'Yes, that's my first step. I'd like to work abroad eventually but thought I'd get some experience nearer home first.'

The waiter returned and took their orders – then they continued their conversation. Charles told his grandfather about his time in Amsterdam, so far. He was staying in a cheap hotel with a crowd of friends for two nights: his chosen way of celebrating his twenty first birthday. Richard, his father, was footing the bill. George kept off the subject of the nightlife in Amsterdam although did wonder whether his grandson and friends had chosen to visit this city for the same reason he did today – albeit under the guise of meeting some financiers.

'How's your dad, anyway?' he always asked this question, despite the differences between his son-in-law and himself. In truth, they did not get on well together – George had always felt that his daughter could have married someone with true wealth – after-all, his family was titled – he had hoped that she would attract an American tycoon – but she had fallen for Richard, who had been a law student at the same university – and they had been inseparable from that time onward.

'He's fine. Mum and Dad should have just got back from their cruise.'

They carried on like this for just short of two hours. Charles had other things planned for later in the afternoon – he was going to visit Anne Frank's House – he'd always wanted to see the famous bookcase on the stairway which had disguised the entrance to the secret World War Two annex where the family had lived in hiding for over two years. After this cultural interlude he would be joining-up again with his friends, boozing the night away.

As for Lord Crawthorne, he needed to catch his late afternoon flight.

'Anyway Charles,' he said. 'When are we going to see you in Aldwick Bay? Your grandmother would love it if you would come and visit us soon?'

'Maybe when I've settled into my job,' replied Charles.

'By the way, I assume they give you accommodation in the hotel?' continued George, genuinely interested.

'Yes, there are staff quarters,' replied Charles. 'The hotel relies heavily on foreign workers so it's an added attraction to offer live-in accommodation. I'll have to wait until I'm actually working there to see if there are any downsides to that arrangement.'

'Well, we'll have to meet up again soon. Perhaps even here in Amsterdam?'

Charles smiled to himself. It seemed a ridiculous notion that his grandfather should suggest coming all the way to the Netherlands when it would be so much easier to meet back home in England. After all, once in his new job, he would only be about eighty miles away from where George lived in West Sussex. However, he wasn't as stupid as his grandfather seemed to think: he had a shrewd idea about one of his grandfather's real motives for being in Amsterdam. It was obvious that George had a wandering eye for the opposite sex: like all his predecessors in the Crawthorne family. Licentiousness seemed to be a family trait and George's affairs with women were legendary.

Charles had always felt sorry for Isabela, his grandmother, wondering why she hadn't ever walked-out on her philandering husband. He had assumed that, despite her husband's faults, his grandmother somehow loved George enough to stay: she was probably dependent on him anyway, having never worked for a living herself. Still, he guessed that he would never get to know the real reason.

After a short walk heading North up Damrak Street, George entered the Centraal Station and caught a train bound for Schipol Airport just as it was leaving. He was in a buoyant mood and, being approached by a woman with a small child who was walking from carriage to carriage begging for money he delved into his pocket withdrawing a five euro note. Her eyes widened in astonishment and she smiled gratefully, which gave him pleasure – but not nearly as much pleasure as he had enjoyed earlier that day at the hands of the lovely Laetitia.

George sat back content, with a smug smile on his face as he thought of his grandson, Charles. When he had left him at the pizzeria, he'd taken out his wallet and given him two hundred euros as spending money during their stay in Amsterdam. He had then handed something else to Charles.

'This is from your grandmother and me. Happy twenty-first birthday.' It was a cheque for one thousand pounds.

'Make sure you come and see us soon.'

*

While George Edward Crawthorne, 15th Baron Crawthorne sat comfortably in the business class section of the aircraft bound for Gatwick, the board members of the consortium who had purchased his former home in East Sussex, were just finishing for the day. They had been meeting on-site with their architect, surveyor and interior designer to discuss the work that was going to be carried-out to the main house. The building would be completely renovated and refurbished at great expense – each bedroom alone would have a budget of a quarter of a million pounds – providing top quality accommodation for what was to become a four-star country hotel.

There was excitement and joviality in the air as the group strolled away from the unoccupied former manor house which, within two years, would be open to the public and re-named Crawthorne Hall Hotel. The sun was going down and dusk was settling as they dawdled in the car park making conversation and saying their goodbyes.

Last to leave was the interior designer, a highly strung creature by the name of Belinda. She was just about to shut her car door when she happened to glance up at one of the upstairs windows in the East wing overlooking the lake. In her mind she was imagining the transformation that she would make to the room; remodelling and converting it into a luxury hotel suite with rich furnishings and drapes. In many ways, this guest suite – which would be known as Room 13, was the most challenging in her portfolio due to the interplay of shadows and shapes in certain lights. Belinda was a perfectionist and still couldn't make up her mind about the final colour scheme. As she continued to ponder, looking up at the window, she suddenly saw a figure looking back at her. He was wearing a mask and seemed to be staring straight at her. It was then that he started beckoning with his finger.

Chapter 2

Bob Bennett was serving his second prison sentence for reckless arson.

This time he had been travelling on the empty top deck of a London bus and, having finished with his copy of the *Evening Standard* had decided to dispose of it in the way that he knew best. In the absence of a waste bin, he had decided to crumple-up the pages of his newspaper on the seat beside him. Taking out his cigarette lighter, Bob held the flame, fascinated at the way in which the burning paper took on a life of its own, dancing and licking its surroundings until he felt its scorching heat. He had watched, mesmerised, as the small fire settled on the fabric of the seat. Within seconds a fierce blaze was engulfing the upholstery and he could smell burning plastic as dark smoke plumed up towards the ceiling.

He was oblivious to the abrupt braking of the bus and the appearance of the driver, holding a fire extinguisher. By that time, Bob had edged towards the front of the bus where he was grabbed by two passengers and held-down on the floor while the fire was brought under control. After a lot of angry shouting and rough handling he had lain still until the police had finally turned up, handcuffing him, then taking him into custody.

The rest, as they say, was history. Bob now looked at his surroundings: a single cell sparsely furnished with a basic storage locker and metal wardrobe, bolted to the wall. He had a chair, a small table and a waste bin. The wall was adorned with a pin board on which he had mounted photos, pictures and drawings of his favourite locomotives: Bob had always been an ardent railway enthusiast.

He thought back to his school days in Chichester when, from the age of thirteen, he used to travel each day by train. At the age of fifteen, on one of his daily commutes Bob and his friends had discovered discarded newspapers which had been tucked under the seats by passengers over time and had been missed by the overworked cleaning staff at the railway depot. The boys had decided to make a bonfire, so scattered loose pages into a pile in the carriage aisle. Bob, as ringleader, did the honours, setting the newspapers alight but was surprised at how rapidly the flames gathered momentum and leapt up, taking hold and spreading over the seats. The train was pulling into a railway station and, as it slowed down, the gang opened-up two of the doors and jumped-out, running along the platform and out through the exit barrier before they could be caught. Two pensioners who had been standing waiting to board the train looked into the carriage.

'Look what they've done now!' one of them complained.

'These school kids – I blame the parents,' added her friend.

The boys naively thought that they were immune once again from being caught – that is, until the next morning during the school assembly. The head teacher gathered together all pupils who used the train and then issued an ultimatum: the culprits were either to admit who they were and suffer a good caning at his hands, or he would leave it to the police, which would inevitably result in prosecution. So, the boys opted for the former punishment, testifying to their suffering by displaying the rows of bruises on their buttocks in the boys' changing rooms during the P.E. lesson later that morning.

Bob had grown to love fire-raising and particularly enjoyed finding new places to cause havoc. As a teenager he had set alight bins in toilets and public places. He didn't ever stop to consider the dangers and the harm that could come from his activities. He saw himself as harmless and, in character, was without malice: he did not for one minute think that his actions could result in death or injury. It was only when, finally, the long arm of the law caught up with him that he knew he was going to have to pay for his campaign of arson. It had been during his time as a student working as a dustman in Chichester.

After having too much to drink one night Bob was passing the council depot when he noticed that the security gate had been left ajar by the watchman. This seemed to be negligence as far as Bob was concerned: anybody could just squeeze in and do some damage at will. To prove his point, he crept around the yard, always keeping to the shadows, until he reached his crew's refuse truck. Levering-open the driver's window, it was an easy matter to then reach in and open the door. Within minutes he had gathered-up enough old newspapers inside the cab and set them on fire.

Unfortunately for Bob, he hadn't reckoned on planning an escape route and it was a simple matter for the night watchman to padlock the gate and call the police. After his night's drinking Bob was in no fit state to go anywhere and waited for the police to arrive and arrest him. True to form, the watchman pretended that the gate had been locked and claimed that the drunken student must have climbed over the twelve-foot fence.

As this was his first offence, the court was lenient in imposing a community order for one hundred and fifty hours of unpaid work as a way of Bob making amends for the thousands of pounds worth of damage that he had caused. Being highly intelligent Bob had managed to find employment and gained a position with British Railways despite his criminal record. However, unable to shake-off his fascination with fire he continued with a series of arson attacks. This had led to his current three-year stint in a Category C resettlement prison in Surrey. Here he had access to a psychiatrist who purported to be able to provide therapy for Bob's diagnosis as a pyromaniac: someone who loves fires and the damage they cause. However, Bob was far from happy. His family had disowned him and he had no-one he could call a friend.

Bob rarely had contact with the outside world and so, when he was offered a weekly slot with an official prison visitor, he jumped at the chance, glad for the opportunity of relieving the day-to-day boredom of life in the slammer. So, he found himself being led to the prison visit room one Thursday afternoon in early May for his thirty-minute appointment. Dressed in his jeans, the standard clothing for inmates receiving visits, he approached the small table with a familiar looking female figure sitting waiting patiently for his arrival. He gazed around at the hubbub of activity around him with a handful of children in the play area and prison officers dotted around; some scowling as they scrutinised the prisoners and their visitors. There were strict rules and conditions in place regarding movement and contact: any breach of these would result in instant termination of the visit. Once seated, prisoners were not allowed to move out of their chairs. Bob sat down.

'Hello. I thought it was you.' He proffered a resigned smile.

'I *knew* it was you, Bob. How are you?' Elaine looked concerned.

'I'm swell – never been better!' Bob Bennett had always been known for his sarcasm. 'What about you?'

Elaine thought of the last time she had seen Bob. They had both been staying in a homeless shelter in Sheffield when the police had come to arrest him.

'Me? Well, I've trained as a seamstress but I'm also an official prison visitor in my spare time. So, when your name came up recently, I volunteered for the slot.'

'That's very altruistic Elaine. I never took you to be the charitable type.' He had only ever known her as a money-grabbing hyena and wondered what there was for her to gain by visiting prisoners.

'I've met some interesting people. Some very bad people, in fact.' It was as though she could read his thoughts.

He assumed there was money in it for her somewhere along the line. Perhaps she had tapped into a bank robber's stash? Or was she smuggling-in drugs? He knew her well and he wouldn't trust her an inch. But why him? How could she possibly hope to benefit from visiting him here in this hellhole?

'So why me, Elaine? Come, on, level with me.'

'For a start I wondered whether you'd like me to bring you anything?'

'Nothing I can think of. It would be nice to have more cigarettes and food, but you're not allowed to bring those in.'

'How are you finding the conditions in here, Bob?'

'Awful. True to say that we all have our own cells – they call them rooms. The worst bit is the actual living conditions though. There are five hundred prisoners in here and we are treated like animals, trodden underfoot all the time: not so much by the screws, more by the system. It's a road kill situation. There's no sanitation in the rooms so we have to use chamber pots and slop-out each day, taking it in turns to queue-up at the sluice room. I won't go into any more details but it's degrading – hasn't changed since Victorian times.'

'I didn't know that. It must be dreadful.' She sounded as though she was going through the motions.

'Yeah – there's a lot of us in here who are angry about it all. Things like poor ventilation – in the summer I sometimes have to sleep on a wet towel to keep cool. Also, we have to contend with stinking clothes which are hardly ever washed. I won't even get started with describing the food!' He smiled, showing a sense of humour. 'Well, you *did* ask!'

'All I know is that there are a number of prison reform groups campaigning at the moment, so things should get better – but, yes, all these things take time I'm sorry to say. But I'm more than happy to take any complaints to the prison authorities if that would help?'

'Thanks for the offer Elaine. I'm sure that you know my life wouldn't be worth living if the prison officers heard that I'd made a complaint. Thanks, but no thanks.'

'By the way …' She hesitated. *Here it comes at last*, he thought.

'Yes?'

'I hear that Ronnie Howell is in your wing. Do you know him?'

'Everyone knows Ronnie.' He was top-dog in the wing – a convicted armed robber with strong psychopathic traits. The inmates called him Mad Ronnie Howell due to his unpredictable temperament and his fondness for extreme violence. Even his closest allies were afraid of him.

'Well, I want you to get a message to him within the hour.'

14

This wasn't a request – it was an instruction; and Bob knew better than to refuse. Clearly Elaine was mixed-up with some hardened criminals on the outside.

'So, what do you want me to tell him?' Bob had lowered his voice.

'Tell him that tonight's the night. He'll understand the message. Got it?'

'Yeah, I've got it.'

'Well, repeat it then.'

'I need to tell Ronnie Howell that tonight's the night.' Bob was finding this tedious but he knew better than to argue with anything involving the top-dog.'

'That's right. Don't forget it.' She sounded like his old history teacher.

With the message delivered, Elaine suddenly lost interest in Bob. She'd played her part as errand-girl and didn't want to spend a second longer sharing in the misery of law breakers who had been stupid enough to get caught. She watched as Bob was escorted back to his prison cell sensing a certain tension and edginess in the room as she stood and made her way out, back through the security checks and past several sets of doors before she finally found herself back in the car park. She took a deep breath, savouring the sweet fresh air of freedom outside.

That night in the recreation room in Delta Wing a group of prisoners, led by Ronnie Howell had finally had enough. The management always paid lip service to the so-called government reforms but nothing was ever done to improve the conditions. The inmates were no longer prepared to go on being treated inhumanely. Reaching breaking point, their resentment and anger had finally bubbled-over and during a staff hand-over of duties, they seized on the chance to overpower three prison officers, grabbing a set of keys. Ronnie, being particularly vicious by nature, had managed to get hold of a kettle of boiling water to which he had added sugar to intensify its burning effects: he'd then thrown it into the face of one of the screws.

That was the signal for the one hundred inhabitants of the wing to go on the rampage, opening-up locked cell doors to release prison mates. A loud siren was wailing monotonously throughout the wing accompanied by the flashing of lights. Some of the prisoners had climbed up on to the metal gantry with its corridors, railings and stairways leading to the cells and communal areas. Suddenly everything was out of control.

The next day there were articles in several national newspapers and on main channel news about a riot in a Surrey prison. Inmates had taken over a wing where they were protesting about the insanitary conditions. There was a photo of a group of men holding a banner, which bore the words *Treated Like Animals*. One of the ringleaders had set fire to the roof: fire fighters were still trying to bring the blaze under control. A prisoner by the name of Ronnie Howell, a convicted bank robber, had escaped during the commotion – it was suspected that the riot had been orchestrated as a smokescreen, drawing attention away from the fleeing inmate who had last been caught on CCTV climbing into a black Lexus saloon car in a side street. The prison was now in lockdown.

Chapter 3

Elaine Reynolds had a past.

Growing up in her home near Manor Park in Sheffield had been tough. Her dad had left when she was just three years old and her mum had remarried. Mack, her stepfather, had been a bastard to Elaine, merciless and sadistic. Her mum had always been insecure and feared that he would leave her, so would close her eyes to the abuse suffered by her only child at the hands of her husband. Plastered after spending the family income support money on a heavy drinking session, he would become aggressive and violent on his return home, gratifying himself by taking out his frustrations on his step-daughter. His wife would turn away as always, duck-shoving her motherly duties and responsibilities. Even then, Elaine had sworn never to have children of her own – a promise she managed to keep.

When Elaine's mother had died – knocked off her bike by a boy racer as she returned from the local shops one misty morning in May – she had little other choice than to stay with her stepdad. With no other family, the only other alternative would have been to go into local authority care. At least she had some kind of freedom outside the house when she was away from this scumbag broozer: something she would not have in a children's home. So, she spent her time in the evenings hanging around street corners with other kids in the neighbourhood, often bored and looking for something to do.

Elaine had always been overweight and had a plain look about her, unattractive to boys – until she found something that they wanted from her – and something that she could freely give. All her life she had been a loner, mostly tolerated by other people. Then all at once she had her own admiring followers: mostly teenage boys. She lapped-up the popularity, now in control, setting the agenda. Alleyways, parks and bus shelters became her habitual hangouts.

She didn't care what the other girls said: the snide and bitchy remarks which followed her around – but it made her smile when even the most prim and proper of her classmates would ask her the same question as everyone else. *What's it like?*

Not that she spent much time at school. She truanted often and her lazy, sick, filthy, loud-mouthed stepdad who drank his life away let her do whatever she liked – provided she didn't get in his way. He had his life and she hers. So, she dragged herself up, at times resting in warm places but always wallowing in dirt; never straying far from the gutter.

Then everything changed.

He had come home from the pub ranting and raving as was his habit with his booze-addled brain. Plates and dishes had gone flying into the wall as he lost control of his temper. He'd mislaid his betting slip and was accusing her of taking it from him. Grabbing hold of her she'd been winded by the first punch and knocked half unconscious by the blow to her head, lying there in a pool of blood until he'd finally passed out and she could clean herself up.

The next day Elaine was playing hooky from school when she decided to risk going home to fetch her coat – it had started to rain. She had hoped that he would be down the pub: he was unemployed but had just received the child benefit money. But instead, here he was, up a ladder in the back yard trying to adjust the TV satellite dish mounted on the wall near to the gutter – he probably needed to check the odds for his accumulator bet on the horses that afternoon.

Watching him for a moment, a sudden urge took hold of Elaine. Years of hate and loathing for the scumbag now balanced on the ladder above, welled-up inside her. All at once she acted on impulse and without thinking of consequences she pushed.

She was already sauntering down the back alley as she heard a crash, a thud and shouting. Then silence.

Mack had damaged his spine – he would never be able to walk again.

Elaine, at fourteen years of age, found herself living in a children's home at the other side of Sheffield. She would be living there or in a similar place for at least two years – possibly more if she stayed until she was eighteen. Then, she'd have to leave and make her own way in the world – although she knew that the local authority was supposed to give some kind of support up to the age of twenty-five: all this had been explained to her.

However, despite now feeling incarcerated in her new setting under the control of others, which she hated, Elaine consoled herself with the news, shortly after moving in, that no-one had connected her to Mack's fall from the ladder. It was established that she had been truanting from school on the day of the accident but witnesses were thin on the ground and no-one had seen her anywhere near the house.

So, she began a new life, soon attracting the attention of Nigel, the night manager; a predatory creature, who would make her attend to his needs and whims. She learnt to endure humiliations and violations worse than the beatings that she had suffered at the hands of her abusive stepfather – that was until Nigel's sudden and unexpected accident when he fell down the stairs breaking both legs: there were no witnesses to see it happen.

Before long, she'd decided that she couldn't stand life in a children's home any longer so she had just walked out of the door one day and never gone back; living on the streets; plying her trade with men; sometimes staying-over in hostels for the homeless. There she had met-up with losers like Bob Bennett and it was then that she had made up her mind that her sole ambition in life would be to make a million pounds any which way she could – and then move abroad. The only question was *how* to make this happen. She thought of her past life and the skills that she had honed over time – and the inkling of a plan had come into her head. But first, she needed to re-invent herself – moving away from her roots.

She'd decided to leave Sheffield for good. First stop: Scotland.

Chapter 4

George Edward Crawthorne, 15th Baron Crawthorne had always been a chancer – it was in his nature. Since selling Crawthorne Hall he had assets worth well over ten million pounds but this was small-fry compared to the wealth accumulated by most of his contemporaries – a number of his schoolboy friends had made their first billion by the age of forty, so he was lagging behind greatly. His fondness for women and gambling had always been a problem from a financial point of view: he lived an extravagant playboy existence as well as enjoying the pleasures of family life. It all came at a price.

He was on a scheduled flight travelling from the giant Schiphol Airport in Amsterdam, heading home via London Gatwick, having picked-up his latest consignment of diamonds – he'd decided to make a few more of these so-called business trips just to top-up his income before finally throwing in the towel. As expected, he'd had no problems passing through customs – this was a well-rehearsed routine that he'd perfected over many years.

It had all started when he'd been in Amsterdam on business in the early 1990s. After partaking of the pleasures offered in the De Wallen district of the city, he'd been sitting in a sleazy bar chilling-out when he'd been approached by an African man.
'Helo muhn, do yu wuhnt to muhke zome euhze muhee?'
'What sort of easy money?'
'I've got zomedieng duht might interezt yu.'
'Yeah?' George wasn't stupid – it was highly improbable that a complete stranger in a bar was going to come along offering him a genuine chance to make some money – that is – unless he was offering knocked-off goods? Now *that* might be a different story. His new companion took something out of his pocket and held it up. It was a tiny gemstone.
'What is it?'
'Thiz, me frieend, iz uh one cuhruht uncut diuhmuhd.'
'A one carat diamond? It's very small.'
'Yow eenglizh?'

20

'Yes.'

'In eowr cownchre diz iz word uht leuhzt zix hundred powndz - it'z from sieruh leuhe.'

George was in a good mood. He'd won three hundred pounds at the casino the previous evening and then gone on to sample the delights of a young woman by the name of Teodora in one of the many nearby brothels. He had been thinking of buying his wife a present to assuage his guilt – and this might just fit the bill.

'So how much are you asking for it?'

'Two hundred guilderz uhnd it'z eowrz.'

George as usual was feeling reckless. 'Two hundred guilders? That's about seventy pounds in my money.' He liked to gamble – and there was an outside chance of this one coming in: he'd probably put-on odds of one hundred to one of it being genuine. But the good news was that, like him, Isabela wouldn't know the difference between a real diamond and a fake. He paused – deliberately.

'Wel, uhre yu interested?'

'What's in it for you – that's what I want to know?'

'Look muhn. Yow bue it, tuhke it home, zel it. Yow muhke muhee. Theen yu come buhck – here – to diz buhr. I huhve muhne more'

George was finding it hard to decipher the African's broken English but it seemed that he was saying that this was a sweetener – like an introductory offer: that he could come back and buy more if he found he could make money on it. He decided that it would be worth a gamble.

'I'll give you one hundred and sixty guilders for it.'

'One zeveentefive uhnd it'z eowrz.'

'One seventy-five it is.' They shook on the deal and money was exchanged.

*

When Lord Crawthorne had arrived back at the family-home he'd found his wife Isabela in the drawing room with friends. He'd briefly drawn her to one side and presented her with his new acquisition – the tiny diamond. Knowing her husband and his philandering ways, she had assumed that the gift was, in part, to ease his guilt: she rightly guessed that he had been with another woman – she could smell it on him. Throughout their marriage, from the very beginning, he had enjoyed sexual encounters with other women. In his younger days his wit, his intellect and his charm were attractive attributes to the opposite sex. After all, she herself had been there once, beguiled by Lord George Crawthorne in her younger days. This dashing, handsome man used to tell her that she was the most sexy, voluptuous creature that he had ever set-eyes on.

'Isabela, I love you so much I could take a bath in the way you look at me,' he had once said in their courting days. Then once they were wedded, he had quickly become tired of his new wife, looking for excitement elsewhere, just going through the motions of marriage for the sake of appearances.

George had always been assertive and sure of himself, oozing power: a great aphrodisiac to those at the centre of his attentions. One in particular, by the name of Sheila who happened to be his personal assistant – in more ways than one – had become his mistress. Isabela had finally confronted her husband after finding receipts in his jacket pocket for stays in the Burford Bridge Hotel in Surrey. After that discovery, she and George had agreed to remain married, in name only, leading separate lives privately.

So, no, she didn't want his diamond – or any other gift for that matter. Politely thanking him, she had given it a cursory glance, then shoved it into her jewellery box before returning to her game of bridge.

The following week Lord Crawthorne was in London on business so took the opportunity to have the stone valued: he was offered four hundred and fifty pounds by one dealer and five hundred and thirty by another. He suspected that it was worth much more.

This was just the start in George's shady dealings with diamonds. Over the years he had gradually become more deeply involved with the big players in the game – diamond smugglers with long-reaching arms across every continent of the world. The stones he dealt with were known as *conflict diamonds* – mostly originating from war-torn Sierra Leone but also from the Democratic Republic of Congo and Angola. Rebels and revolutionaries would take control of the mines, using the millions generated from selling their diamonds to fund their terrorist regimes involving the slaughter and brutalisation of many innocent people – even genocide.

Essentially, the diamonds, bought and sold cheaply, were smuggled from country to country, evading taxes at every border. George would travel to Amsterdam three times a year – where he would be given a small bag containing about fourteen stones to secrete on his body ... he'd been told that *diamonds are a smugglers best friend* as they were so small and so easy to hide – he would secrete them in his underpants. However, at the turn of the millennium, the whole operation had become trickier – the authorities had introduced a certification system to check the origin of imported diamonds. The stakes had never been higher: if caught, he would be looking at a long jail sentence. But, more worrying, the owners of the diamonds would want their goods back.

Now, fifteen years later, George looked out of the window as the Boeing 737 landed at Gatwick on a dark, dismal evening in October. After fifteen years of this lark, he wanted *out*. But would the money man let him? He would have to explore his options.

After a long walk from the gate, taking about twenty-minutes, he finally reached the customs hall. As always, he passed through the channel for EU citizens and through the green channel – *nothing to declare*. Then, out through the arrivals lounge, up the elevator and across the bridge to the multi-storey, finding his black Range Rover where he'd parked it earlier that day. He texted a number to say that he'd arrived on time.

On his way back home towards Chichester, George took a detour, stopping in the car park of the small recreation park in Brighton where the exchange always took place. After ten minutes he heard a motorbike approaching. Shortly afterwards there was a double thump on the roof of his Range Rover.

He wound-down the window, passing over the velvet bag wrapped in plastic, from inside his trousers. A leather gloved hand took the bag and George could see a helmeted figure in his rear-view mirror checking the contents by torchlight. He knew that this was just a cursory look – the real experts would need time to evaluate their goods properly. Shortly afterwards there was another thump on the roof and a large A4 envelope was passed through the semi-open window.

After the motorcyclist had roared into the distance George opened the envelope, flicking through the large bundle of used notes from the paymasters. Then, breathing a sigh of relief, he headed along the A27 road towards Chichester and home.

Chapter 5

2009

Paul Marsh, a convicted paedophile, was currently serving a two-year sentence in a Category B prison in the heart of Sussex. It had taken eight months to bring his case to trial when the police, pressing forward their evidence at the crown court, had convinced the jury that the accused was not only storing and supplying child pornography, but that he also had intent to groom minors, including his two stepsons. Amongst the other evidence, the prosecutor had detailed text messages which had been sent to, and often reciprocated by the victims.

Now he found himself locked in his small cell, bored out of his skull with only a tiny television and the radio which he had been allowed to buy with his prison wages. There were two small wardrobes and bunk beds: this accommodation was designed for sharing. His cell also enjoyed the luxury of a sink and toilet hidden behind a partition.

Paul was only allowed to use the shower room in the block once a week, but this was notoriously a risky business. The showers were open, with no privacy; used by other inmates at the same time. It provided an opportunity for others to wreak their revenge and frustrations, proving their status and hence gaining power over others. This was achieved through violence and intimidation. So far, Paul had escaped lightly with two broken teeth and bruised ribs. Prison officers had been conveniently looking the other way at the time and, when questioned about his injuries, Paul gave them the conventional answer – he said that he had slipped.

As a convicted paedophile Paul had been placed in F Wing, which was the vulnerable prisoners' unit, known as the VPU. This enabled him to have a certain degree of protection, being with the other nonces and beasts serving their sentences for sex offences. It also offered therapy designed to help their particular perversions and included the services of a psychiatrist. However, even in the confines of this special wing there was a hierarchy amongst prisoners with the violent perpetrators of crime at the top of the tree. This included those convicted of rape, kidnap and torture. The lesser offenders tried to keep away from the head cases.

Right now, Paul, who was at the bottom of the pecking order, was anxiously pacing up and down in his cell. The previous day his cell mate had been taken out and transferred to another prison where he would be prepared for release. Paul had no idea who would be replacing him – it was a random system: he could find himself sharing with a new inmate, an old lag or someone on a transfer. Paul hoped that the newcomer did not smoke cigarettes – or anything else, for that matter. Although it was against the rules to smoke in the cells, this was ignored by everyone, leading to an existence in an enclosed space, constantly breathing in a fug of smoky stinking miasma: a far cry from the fresh air that Paul used to enjoy when coaching boys' football.

Worse still, would be if Paul found himself sharing his cell with a violent offender. Nonces like him were regarded as the lowest of the low in prisons. Recently, with prison overcrowding, a number of mainstream prisoners were being held in the vulnerable prisoners' unit in F wing. Hardened criminals had children and families of their own and hated perverts who harmed the weak and the innocent. Paul was a coward and did not cope easily with bullies, sadists or even other prisoners with mental issues: there were plenty of inmates like that who he tried to avoid on a daily basis.

As he continued to dwell in his thoughts and speculate on what was to come, Paul heard a key being turned in the lock. The door opened and he was greeted by the sight of a prison officer accompanying a thin, lanky man with a shaved head. In his arms, the prisoner was carrying some bedding with an issue of prison clothing. On top was balanced a plastic plate, mug and cutlery.

'Here's your new home, complete with en-suite,' the prison officer announced sarcastically. He was supposed to introduce the two jailbirds but he couldn't be bothered: there was a cup of tea with his name on it waiting for him in the staff room. So, with the door firmly shut and locked he sauntered down the corridor, swinging his keys in rhythm as he looked forward to his break.

Inside the cell, the two prisoners looked at each other warily. The newcomer dumped his belongings on the top bunk which had a bare mattress and was obviously destined for him. He could have started an argument, insisting on having the bottom bunk in order to exert some authority; but he was weary of the macho expectations and petty confrontations in this world of incarceration, so settled on the obvious. Anyway, it was not in his nature to be aggressive. Briefly glancing around in the confines of his new home, he focused on the dark haired, beer bellied man before him but said nothing. So, nervous and tense, Paul decided to speak first.

'Hi. My name's Paul Marsh.'

The other man folded his arms and seemed to relax a little.

'Hi. I'm Bob Bennett – but everyone calls me *Dangle*.'

.

Chapter 6

They had now been cell mates for two months.

Bob Bennett had been transferred from his previous place of incarceration after the riots and the fire which had destroyed a large part of the prison roof. CCTV footage had identified Bob as one of the ringleaders. So, he had been transferred as a way of splitting-up the troublemakers. Mad Ronnie Howell was still at large and it was rumoured that he had now moved into the thriving diamond business – offering protection, muscle-power and intimidation as one of his specialities.

On this particular day Paul Marsh had just been escorted back to his cell from the hospital wing after spending three days recovering from his latest kicking in the showers. His loud mouth and tactless sense of humour had attracted the wrong kind of attention from a hard-headed bunch of yardies and, as always, the prison officers had seen nothing.

He was finding it difficult to endure prison life – a far cry from his time married to his second wife, Sandy and two step-children. Unfortunately, during his marriage with her, he had found that old habits died-hard: he'd been unable to give up his obsession for child pornography – feeding his mind with increasingly extreme images which he shared with a group over the internet. The court had also found him guilty of grooming Sandy's boys, which had led to a hefty sentence. He should have been more careful – his current predicament could have been avoided. But now, here he was, feeling depressed and lonely – with no-one prepared to visit him he had no regular first-hand news of anything going on in his former world – old friends had dissociated themselves from him and he had now received a letter setting out the divorce proceedings which would shortly be taking effect.

Paul was feeling down and depressed – desperately unhappy as he had returned to their cell, the door being ceremoniously closed behind him and the key turned in the lock. Bob Bennett had been lounging around on his bed reading, looking pleased with himself.

'Hey, partner, is that three days already? I was getting used to having the place to myself. How's it going anyway?' Bob, remained slumped on his top bunk bed.

'Not good.' Paul was overcome with dread and fear, scared of what might happen next, now that he was back on the so-called vulnerable prisoners' unit. It seemed to him that a number of other mainstream prisoners on the wing hadn't been vetted properly – some of them were having a field day sporadically attacking the sex perpetrators whenever the opportunity arose. Paul was afraid of leaving his cell now, knowing that he was easy meat.

'They've given me that job in the prison library, anyway,' Bob continued, still with half-an-eye on his book – an encyclopaedic volume entitled *Trains and Locomotives*. 'So, I'll be tootling along there this afternoon. It'll give you a bit of time to sort out your head after your life of luxury in the hospital wing – was the food any better there?'

'Not really.' Paul had painfully clambered on to his bottom bunk and lay there staring at the mattress above him.

'No more news about your divorce then?' persisted Bob thoughtlessly. He had actually missed the company of Paul over the past few days. He had enjoyed having one less body in the small cramped room with its smells and odours, but time passed far more slowly with only your own self to talk to: Bob was making up for lost time. However, he started to realise that Paul was in no mood for conversation, so let it pass, going back to admiring the colour-plated locomotive photos in his book.

But then Paul started to stir and with it came an unexpected line of questioning which unsettled Bob.

'So, what made you become an arsonist, Bob?' his cell mate ventured. They often reminisced with each other as a way of stemming the boredom of looking at four walls and to take their minds away from the stench of the lavatory on the other side of the small partition. However, they had never discussed their respective obsessions: Bob with his penchant for fire raising and Paul, his fascination with children.

'I could ask you the same kind of question, Paul – like what made you become a paedophile – a nonce. But I don't think I'd like to hear your answer. That's all sick-stuff.'

'So, you mean that setting fire to things – potentially burning people alive – that's perfectly acceptable, is it? Come on Bob, please tell!'

'What are you? Some secret psychiatrist smuggled into my cell?'

'Don't forget that I was here first.'

'Okay, Einstein. I suppose you could say that it all started with a spark.' Bob grinned, displaying his usual baby-faced look with a demeanour of innocence. Then he resumed. 'My dad, Graham Bennett worked as a health and safety officer for British Rail: but he didn't have the same exacting standards when it came to his own home. He knew well that it was foolish to overload an electrical socket by having several devices plugged into one adapter.'

'And?'

'He was overworked and just wanted to relax once he was at home. Together with his pregnant wife Nancy, my mother, he had a lot on his mind. So, he never got round to sorting-out the faulty wiring. Then my baby sister was born. They called her Portia: she was six days old when it happened.'

'I think I know where this is going.'

'In a nutshell, I was three years old, asleep in my room when an electrical fire started one night – apparently under the stairs. The house was ablaze in no time. I only remember being carried out and then standing, watching the fire take hold of the building. There were bangs and loud crackling. Thick black smoke was billowing out of the roof. Neighbours had alerted the fire service but they'd been unable to rouse my poor mother. My dad was out working overtime.'

'That's terrible. Did your mother survive.'

'No. I never saw her again. But every time I light a fire, I think about her – and my newly born sister. They died in that fire and I never forgave my dad for his negligence. He never forgave himself either.'

Bob paused as he thought back to the memory which has been etched into his brain, nagging away at him like a little worm wheedling away in his head. 'Anyway, it's your turn – come-on, I've spilled the beans. What is it that made you into what you have become?'

'Like you, I find it hard to talk about. My father was head gardener at a big country house called Crawthorne Hall. Have you heard of it?'

'Nope. Not me.'

'It's near Hailsham in East Sussex. They were always entertaining – wild parties – weird things went on. There was one particular room that I used to be taken to … it was in the East wing overlooking the lake.' He stopped talking, overwhelmed by painful memories. 'Look, Bob, I really don't want to say any more – it makes me feel sick just thinking about what happened in that room. It ruined my life. They made me swear never to tell anyone.'

'Look Paul, you're an adult – not a child anymore – it's up to you whether you tell me anything. Whoever *they* were.'

'I can't begin to tell you about the abuse and degradation that I suffered, Bob – and I'll spare you the details. However, there is one thing that I want to get off my chest.'

'Okay. I'm listening.' Bob was intrigued.

'Along with the parties came sado-masochistic games and practices – that's where they brought in the children – like me. But there were also a bunch of people who were serious gamblers. They'd play through the night – mostly cards – betting high stakes.'

'So? A lot of people gamble. What was so special – or terrifying – about what happened in that room?'

'On one occasion – it's etched on my memory – when I was just ten years old – I was in that room in the early hours of the morning ...'

'Why were you, a ten-year-old, up at that time of night?' Bob interrupted.

'My dad used to hire me out – often for unsavoury purposes, as I told you ...' He hesitated.

'Sins of the fathers,' muttered Bob.

'What?'

'Haven't you ever heard the saying that *the sins of the fathers are to be laid upon the children*?'

'Nope.'

'It comes from Shakespeare – *The Merchant of Venice* – it means that children often suffer for the bad things their parents do.'

'You and your posh education!' Paul was only half-listening.

Bob persisted in making his point. 'In my case, it all started – my obsession – because my dad's negligence caused the fire in which my mum and baby sister died. In your case, your dad rented you out. We both suffered because of our dads' actions or inactions. It damaged us irreparably.'

'I get that, Bob. But on this occasion, it was different. I didn't feel that I was in any sort of danger – I was just fetching and carrying – mostly topping-up glasses with vodka and other booze. They seemed like regular, ordinary guys: a bit posh – but most of the visitors at Crawthorne Hall were toffs, so that was no surprise. Anyway, by around four o'clock in the morning the gambling session was coming to an end. Gradually, one-by-one people had given-up and left the room. Two men were finishing a game of poker when a furious argument broke-out. The loser was accusing the other man of cheating. Then an old-fashioned revolver was drawn, a shot was fired – blood splattered everywhere.'

'So, you're saying that as a ten-year old, you saw someone being shot with a gun?' Bob wasn't entirely convinced. A lot of cons made-up stories – it was a way of passing the endless time in prison – maybe this was just a made-up yarn? Maybe Paul had told this story so many times that he even believed in what he was saying. Bob, a cynic, would reserve judgement – for now.

Paul continued with his tale. 'The man, who had been standing-up ready to leave, put his hand to his chest – blood was seeping through his clothes and covering his fingers. Then he sank to the floor and slumped down. I'll never forget it. I still wake-up having nightmares all these years later.'

Bob became more interested in the story. 'Who was shot?'

'I don't know who he was – I have a vague memory of a smartly dressed man in a suit with a big moustache – that's all I remember.'

'And who pulled the trigger?'

'Paul hesitated, not wishing to disclose the name at first. Bob looked expectantly at his cell mate.'

'Well?' he said coaxingly.

'It was the old Lord Crawthorne.'

'Are you sure?'

'Of course, I'm sure. He sent me to fetch my father.'

'The head gardener, you said?'

'Yeah. Then I stayed at home in the lodge – I was knackered and went straight to bed – it was raining. When I woke up later that morning, I noticed my dad's filthy wet muddy boots by the back door.'

'And is that *it?*'

'Not quite.' Paul looked wretched as he cast his memory back thirty-five years. 'When I went out into the grounds that morning, I was passing through the kitchen gardens when I noticed a freshly dug mound of earth which hadn't been there the previous day. I've often wondered ...'

'Whether there's a body buried there!' Bob was amused by his cell-mate's cliched conclusion. 'Come on, Paul, you don't seriously believe that a dead body was buried in a vegetable patch!'

Paul looked hard at his companion. 'Actually, yes I do – near one of the apple trees. My dad made me swear not to tell anyone – then a couple of days later he suddenly appeared with a Scalextric set as a surprise present for me – although it wasn't my birthday. Then a week after that my dad, who was usually skint, was presented with a new Ford Cortina by Lord Crawthorne 'for loyal services'. So how do you explain that lot of coincidences, Bob? It's been doing my head in for years – and now that you've weaseled-it out of me, it's brought all those bad memories back with it. As if I wasn't feeling bad enough after everything that I've had to endure here in the clink.' He was clearly upset.

'Say no more.' Bob had been glad to be spared details of the horrors suffered by Paul as a child at the hands of the Crawthorne family – and he had to admit that if, as Paul said, there had been murder in that room, then what had become of the body? He noticed that Paul's face had paled after his revelation that morning. He was truly concerned for his cell mate.

Bob spent the afternoon out of the cell, issuing library books to small groups of prisoners who took turns making use of this popular prison resource. One of the worst aspects of prison life was the sheer boredom and so, even fairly illiterate inmates, were drawn to spending their many hours of confinement reading. Some of the most popular books out on loan were crime novels – which nourished a common interest amongst the prisoners.

Often, black market and smuggled goods were exchanged for particular books in high demand. Even in this aspect of their incarceration, there was, as always, a pecking order with those at the top of the prison hierarchy having first choice of reading material – even if that meant coercing someone to relinquish their required book by means of threats, violence or intimidation. As always, Paul Marsh and others like him were last in the queue and had to be happy with the leftovers. However, now that Bob was working in the library, he would be able to obtain books to take back for them both.

Returning to his cell later under escort, Bob had two library books tucked under his arm: the first was a book on photography for his cell mate – this had been one of Paul's passions when he had been on the outside. Bob had chosen for himself the Charles Dickens classic *Great Expectations* – he always liked reading the bit about Miss Havisham when she went up in flames near the end of the story.

As he entered his prison cell, he immediately sensed that something was not right and it took a few seconds for him to realise what was wrong. Dropping the library books, he shouted at the prison officer, who was in the process of closing and locking the door.

'Boss, it's Paul. Quick, open the door, boss. Help me!' He was shouting at the top of his voice and thumping on the inside of the door with his fist. Then, realising that the prison officer was not reacting fast enough he pressed the emergency call button. Kicking the door repeatedly he carried on shouting. 'Open up! Help me!'

The door finally swung open and three warders appeared, all of them staring ahead. Paul was dangling from the frame of the top bunk, a laundry bag tied around his neck, ripped and fashioned into a makeshift noose. His eyes bulged and his tongue protruded from the asphyxia and suffocation that he had suffered from his relative low point of hanging on the bed. His face looked swollen and his skin had a bluish-purple hue with pinpoint bleeds around his eyes. Bob had often heard about hangings but had never witnessed the aftermath of anything so horrifying: he was set to remember this scene for the rest of his life. He was physically and emotionally distraught, looking at what had become of his cell mate – one more casualty of the prison system. This scene was about to undo the many months of psychiatric help that Bob had been undergoing throughout his recent stint inside.

While the prison officers were assessing the scene and phoning through for more help, Bob stumbled round to the other side of the small cell partition and vomited profusely into the bowl of the toilet. He remained kneeling on the floor where he cried and cried until he heard the sound of more footsteps and hurried voices as prison personnel, including medics came crashing through the door. At that moment, Bob Bennett swore that if he ever had a chance, he would pursue Paul's story and try to find out some answers. However, here, incarcerated in prison, he hadn't a clue as to how he might even begin such a quest.

Chapter 7

It had been a hell of a day for Gareth Evans.

There had been nothing but trouble with his building company's latest renovation at Crawthorne Hall. They were running behind schedule – big time – and there was now the real possibility that penalty clauses in the contract would come into force if there were any further delays.

The problems had started from Day One with scaffolding collapsing on to Lucio Battisti, the project manager: that had landed him in hospital for two weeks – it was lucky that he hadn't been killed. Then there were the missing tools, the sudden leaking of pipes for no apparent reason and the fire which had self-ignited in the attic. Fortunately, a vigilant sub-contractor had spotted it and dealt with it quickly using a carbon dioxide extinguisher. Then Belinda, the highly strung interior designer had started seeing-things – talking about a masked man hiding in one of the rooms. They'd conducted a search but there was no evidence of intruders – no squatters in sight and no would-be saboteurs. Maybe the house was just jinxed?

Straight after work, Gareth had stopped-off at a service station on the A22 where he had changed clothes and freshened-up ready for a fund-raising evening at the glamorous Glinfield Manor House near Eastbourne. He'd been invited in his capacity as Chairman of the local Chamber of Commerce. Also, as managing director of a successful reputable building company he had been earmarked for an award for his service to charity work in the area. It had been a prestigious black-tie event attended by local dignitaries and a sprinkling of celebrities. The champagne had been flowing although Gareth, aware of having to drive himself home, had sensibly restricted his intake on this occasion. Normally Alma, his wife, would have taken on the role of chauffeur allowing him to get sozzled, but she was away on business for the next few days.

On this particular evening, Gareth had not enjoyed the fund-raising event – something which he attended every year. Normally, he would be the life and soul of a fund-raiser like this; telling jokes, making people laugh and generally networking – making new contacts as well as consolidating old ones. He had, since early childhood, enjoyed being at the centre of attention. He thrived on it. Gareth was a social animal – but on this occasion he was a damp squib. The problems at Crawthorne Hall were getting him down – he just didn't feel like himself at the moment – as though a miserable version of himself had crept in through the backdoor of his being and was now trying to take charge of his thoughts and emotions. All in all, Gareth was feeling down and depressed; his mood exaggerated by his earlier intake of alcohol.

As he fired-up his grey 2009 Aston Martin V12 Vantage, parked alongside the Ferrari belonging to a well-known actor, he noticed that his petrol indicator was nearly on empty – that was strange as he'd topped-up the tank on his way to Crawthorne Hall that morning. Perhaps he was going mad after all – imagining things – or perhaps he was just overworked and overtired. Either way, he decided to fill-up on the way back home to Bognor Regis where he lived. Maybe he'd have the car checked-over to make sure there were no leaks.

Eventually Gareth pulled into a service station near Berwick – it appeared to be open. There were no other cars on the forecourt as he filled the tank and went to the kiosk to pay, being careful to lock his doors.

'That's forty-seven pounds fifty,' chirped the cashier, a dour looking woman in her late thirties; lank brown hair, huge breasts and a little pudgy.

Gareth flashed his credit card.

'I like the wheels!' continued the woman, whose name was Elaine according to the badge on her corporate uniform.

'It's a new Aston Martin V12 Vantage,' replied Gareth perking-up, glad to find someone admiring his pride and joy. He had been beside himself with happiness when he'd recently taken ownership of the car which had cost him well over one hundred and thirty-five thousand pounds – something that he had neglected to tell his wife.

'How fast can it go?'

'Top speed of two hundred miles an hour.'

'I bet it can't – all car makers are liars!'

'I bet it can.'

'Anyway, what are you – a secret service agent or something?' Elaine Reynolds nodded at his attire; tuxedo and black bowtie. It wasn't every evening that a toff pulled in to top-up with fuel.

'I might be.'

'Where's your 007 number plate then?' she joked.

'I'm undercover,' he quipped.

'I bet you are!' She was quick witted. She had a northern accent.

'Are you from around here then?' Gareth was intrigued.

'No. I'm from Sheffield originally – how can you tell?'

'I like the humour.'

'I could see you needed cheering-up. Hey, I'll tell you what.'

'Yeah?'

'I'm closing up in ten minutes. How about you giving me a lift home Mr. Secret Service Agent? You can show me your nice big car – and save me the cost of a taxi.'

Gareth picked up on the innuendo and just couldn't help himself – she had massaged his deflated ego and he was curious to explore where this might lead. This was completely out of character: his brain was not in his head at this moment in time.

After waiting for ten minutes the passenger door of his shiny grey coupe opened and Elaine Reynolds, now with a waft of dewberry perfume fragrance lingering around her, sank into the pure luxury of the leather clad upholstered seat inside the car with its rich, sweet earthy smell.

'Where to?'

'Just down the road near South Bersted – I'll give you the directions when we're getting near.'

Gareth, keen to show-off his five-hundred and seventeen horsepower car, accelerated to ninety miles an hour within ten seconds.

'What do you think? It can do nought to sixty in less than six seconds?'

Elaine knew all about Aston Martins. She hung around with some serious guys who dealt-in expensive prestige cars – usually stealing them to order. As a petrol head herself, she took a genuine interest in the nitty-gritty of car specifications.

'Well, what do you expect from a big six litre engine – but I still don't believe it can go much faster,' she teased.

Gareth was impressed by her knowledge. Taking the bait, he slammed his foot on the accelerator and the powerful car rapidly lurched forward as though it had been stung by a bee. They were soon travelling at one hundred and twenty miles per hour along the A27 road heading West. She was clearly impressed.

'Wow. Come on baby! Let's see what you can do!'

Within a short space of time, they had reached her flat. She pointed towards the upper part of a run-down Victorian house in the untidy backstreet where the car had finally come to a standstill, purring as it idled patiently in the road. Without so much as a 'thank you,' she opened the door and wriggled out.

'Are you coming in then?' She turned to Gareth.

He followed her as she approached the front door to the house, unlocking it and passing through the hallway, then up the balustraded staircase. Gareth wondered whether his car was safe outside – he hoped he would still have wheels when he next saw his beloved Aston Martin. Anxious that a passer-by might accidentally damage the paintwork or deliberately vandalise it, he decided he'd have a quick cup of coffee and then be on his way.

As soon as he entered the messy apartment, Elaine took hold of his bowtie and pulled him towards the open bedroom door with uncontrolled exuberance, clearly in control, with her own agenda. Gareth, like a puppy being led down a rabbit hole, found the whole thing amusing. To him it was a game in which she was the wild card – and he wanted her in his hand.

'Here, Mr. Secret Agent,' she whispered in her rich, husky voice. Helping him off with his jacket she nimbly unbuttoned his white, silky dress shirt, feeling the warmth of his chest with her hands; brushing his nipples with her fingers. Then, as he started to undress, she too began to strip-off; afterwards reclining on the bed, stretching and splaying out before him. He was aroused and quickly joined her, soon on top, heaving and grunting with her underneath breathing deeply and squealing in pleasure. It was all urgent and immediate – wanting her right now.

Gareth was flying high – no matter what the consequences he just had to keep going forwards – he couldn't see the landmarks anymore – his old life was falling away before his eyes – a new life had begun and his head was spinning. They began a rhythmical, furious coupling, moving and gyrating together until they finally lay, seemingly drained and exhausted.

Curiously enough, Gareth felt no self-recriminations or guilt for his actions – all he could think of was how alive and exhilarated he felt – this was far better than anything he had ever experienced in bed with Alma. They lay there together for a while.

'You're good. You're very good. I like it,' was all that she said, sprawling-out on the bed like a dish of promises.

'I like it too,' replied Gareth, his ego finally restored. He felt like a different person: invincible, revivified, able to do anything with impunity. At that moment Gareth Evans fleetingly thought of Crawthorne Hall where he had recently been spending so much time – and the legendary line of barons who had lived there – who had reputably indulged in so many pleasures during their lifetimes. Gareth then thought about his unexpected encounter with Elaine that evening. Already he was intoxicated with her. In his mind he had started to imagine himself as a secret service agent with women throwing themselves at his feet. He felt refreshed, renewed, relaxed. He wanted more.

'So, tell me your sexual fantasies, mystery man.' She hadn't even stopped to ask his name.

'That's for me to know and you to find out.'

Twenty minutes later she was on top and they were fast approaching another crescendo – he felt as though his head would explode with pleasure. At no time did he think of his wife Alma who, after her business trip was currently stranded in JFK Airport in New York. She was missing her husband.

Chapter 8

It was a magnificent detached Georgian Grade II listed residence tucked away in one corner of the exclusive Aldwick Bay Estate near Chichester in West Sussex. George and Isabela Crawthorne had been delighted with this exceptional house, recently renovated with a unique blend of character features, period elegance and modern fittings: a far-cry from the crumbling fortress which they had once called home in the West wing of Crawthorne Hall. It was a handsome, part-rendered brick and flint building surrounded by extensive landscaped gardens: ideal for entertaining guests. Lord and Lady Crawthorne were socialites, well-known for their parties and gatherings.

Arranged over three floors, the majority of rooms had views over the gardens, with the English Channel in plain view from the upper storeys. Isabela had been particularly impressed with the superb reception rooms: especially the magnificent double aspect first floor drawing room which had access to a west-facing terrace. Leading from the rear of the house, a pathway led to a remote-controlled wrought iron gate built into the high wall. Beyond that, was the private shingly beach, shared with other residents of the Aldwick Bay Estate. Here, a number of bespoke beach chalets had been built: one of these now belonged to Lord and Lady Crawthorne.

The house had been named *The Knapp* by the previous owners. They had originated from Knapp in Dunn County, Wisconsin, a place steeped in Wild West history, involving European settlers and native Indians: that would explain the totem pole in the back garden, fashioned from the remains of an old oak tree. George looked forward to having it cut-down. He had nothing against totem poles: if he'd found Nelson's column in his back garden, he'd have felt the same way.

There were several other features in the house which had a certain Native American theme: most notably, the wooden statue affixed to the newel post at the bottom of the main stairway. It was a delicate carved piece which obviously meant something to the previous owners – probably reminding them on a daily basis of their roots back in Wisconsin, USA? Maybe they were superstitious and looked on this as a kind of good luck charm? It had been fixed with its face looking towards the front door at anyone entering or leaving the house: always on-watch as if guarding the innermost rooms and conclaves within *The Knapp*. Isabela had instantly named it *The Knapp Goddess*. George, who had never been superstitious – even living for so long in Crawthorne Hall with all its so-called ghosts – thought that *The Knapp Goddess* was an ugly piece and intended disposing of it at his earliest convenience.

George had in his hand a box of keys meticulously labelled by the previous owners and started to dish-out a set for his wife. She fixed the main outside door keys together on one of her existing keyrings. Noticing a large, single mortice-lock key with its fob labelled *The Knapp Beach Chalet, Aldwick Bay,* she shoved that one into a pocket in her handbag for safe keeping. Then she carried-on with some of the unpacking, pleased that they could at last relax and concentrate on creating their new home together.

Everything seemed perfect. That is, until Isabela and George became acquainted with Albert Warnford, their new, rather peculiar next-door-neighbour, who seemed to be bent on driving them to distraction.

The removal vans had only just left when Lord and Lady Crawthorne were disturbed by the heavy cast iron door knocker being rapped loudly several times. Standing on the doorstep was a tall, thin man aged about seventy years old with a shock of white hair and a ruddy, pinched face. He had an intense, almost fierce look about him which seemed to say, '*Don't mess with me!*' This contrasted with the tight-lipped smile which he attempted as he announced his name – a smile which didn't quite reach his eyes.

'Hello, I'm Albert from next door.'

'Pleased to meet you. I'm George Crawthorne. Excuse me a minute, I'll just fetch my wife.' He stepped towards one of the reception rooms where she was unpacking. 'Our next-door neighbour has stopped-by to say *hello*.'

She sauntered through to greet their visitor. 'How do you do? I'm Isobela. So nice to make your acquaintance.'

'I'm Albert from next door. Albert Warnford. Welcome to the neighbourhood.' He smiled stiffly with the hard line of his compressed lips.

'Thank you, that's so kind of you,' replied Isobela.

Then all of a sudden, Albert's smile dissipated as he moved on to the real purpose of his visit.

'You've probably gathered that this house is in a real state – I wanted to let you know that there are some real health and safety hazards.'

'Oh?' said George, taken-aback by the tone of his neighbour's voice. Lord and Lady Crawthorne were not used to being spoken to like this – by anyone.

'Yes. I'm talking about your garden. For a start – you see that tree?' He was pointing to a tall Eucaliptas in the front garden.

'I see it,' replied George having recovered his composure. It stood beside two gnarled apple trees.

'Well, it's dying. All it needs is one strong gust of wind and that tree could blow down. You'd be liable if it fell on to my house – it could kill someone. It's a real health and safety hazard. You need to sort it urgently.'

All at once, the euphoria of the moving day was rapidly starting to evaporate as this surly, miserable old man started ranting at the Crowthornes. They were shocked by his rudeness and coarse behaviour. There was no reciprocity in his words or his manner.

'Thanks for letting me know,' replied George politely, seething inwardly, about to close the door.

However, Albert Warnford had not finished. He had a metaphorical foot in the door and was determined to say his piece.

'You also need to know that the ditch at the front of your house is liable to flood in the winter as it's blocked in parts. This is the best time of year to clear it out. When it overflows it runs down into my garden and spills out over the road. All you need is to have a freezing spell and it's like an ice-rink out there. People can slip and break their legs. A car could skid – it could cause a nasty accident. You'd be liable. Thought you need to know.'

Lord George Edward Crawthorne and his wife just stood there wondering what planet their next-door neighbour lived-on – and whether they had made a dreadful mistake choosing this house? Having just moved-in, here was this old man standing on their doorstep trying to arrange their schedule – suggesting strongly that the ditch should be cleared in case it caused flooding in the winter. His lack of decorum was almost laughable but it did occur to George that the man might be mentally ill. He seemed to live in a parallel universe, slightly different to everyone else – a universe that was a reality only in his head.

'Maybe you can make it one of your priorities?' Albert Warnford suggested, scrutinising George with a watchful menace in his gaze.

As he marched-off up the sweeping driveway, then along a garden path and back through the lychgate they closed the front door and stood aghast looking at each other.

'What is he – a health and safety nazi?' suggested Isobela to her husband.

'Maybe he's unwell, my dear,' replied George. I'm sure it will all work out in the end. Some people react badly to change – he's probably just anxious about us as new neighbours.'

'That's very generous spirited of you,' replied Isabela. 'Personally, I think that he's just a nasty piece of work.'

In truth Albert Warnford believed that he was King of the Road. He'd lived in Aldwick Bay for thirty years – longer than most other residents. As such, he felt that he had a stake in everything that was going on around him. He saw himself as the big cheese; the head honcho, the grand poohbah; the top banana on the tree – a self-appointed commander-in chief; policing the other residents in his particular road as though he were living in some sort of authoritarian fantasy. He hadn't reckoned on a real titled Lord and Lady suddenly moving in next door to him. He was jealous and worried about being knocked-off his perch by the landed gentry who had suddenly made an entrance into his life. His rudeness was a prelude of things to come as he grappled with ways of taming Lord and Lady Crawthorne to his way of thinking.

Albert had enjoyed an easy time with his former next-door neighbours. An elderly couple, they had been only too willing to take his advice; let him into the privacy of their lives; praise him highly for the little jobs that he always did for them so willingly. He dug their ditches, pruned their trees, unblocked their sewers, cut their lawns. All this gave Albert a raison d'être – a purpose for living during his retirement years. He could never keep still, always needing something to do and was glad to find a way of filling his hours. Being involved in other people's business was like a hobby to him.

In his working life Albert had built-up his own double-glazing empire: a hard task-master if ever there was one. He would always push to the limits, setting ever-increasing sales targets for his colleagues, never taking 'no' as an answer: presumptuous and pushy, even promoting unethical practices to clinch deals with customers. In the sense of bringing in lucrative sales, Albert did a marvellous job – but at a cost. He was loathed by many of his associates and the target of ridicule by his enemies. In reality, he did not relate easily to others on a personal level: secretly insecure, he always took on an aggressive stance whenever he felt threatened.

By nature, a bully, Albert had decided as soon as he saw the removal men leave, that this was the time to strike; to set the agenda; to show his new neighbours that he was the big enchilada on the Aldwick Bay Estate: that nothing happened around here without his say-so.

Chapter 9

They say that opposites attract. This was certainly the case with Albert and his wife Kathy, who was the yin to his yang. She was calm, accommodating, pleasant to other people – and very long-suffering: everything that her husband was not. Over the weeks and months that followed the Crawthornes' move to Aldwick Bay, George and Isabela noticed that Kathy Warnford seemed to spend most of her existence in her house while her husband appeared to enjoy being outside – often to be seen prowling around his two-acre garden or making his presence felt around the neighbourhood. On the rare occasions when Kathy was seen, she would normally be in the company of her husband: whenever she was out, it seemed to the Crawthornes that she was always under escort as though she were Albert's and Albert's alone. However, whenever either George or Isabela had spoken to her, they had found her to be a very kind, gentle and considerate human being.

One Sunday afternoon in September Lord and Lady Crawthorne were in their garden entertaining guests. The champagne was flowing and everyone was in good spirits, chattering away.

'I do admire your lovely new home, Isabela,' remarked her friend Elizabeth, wife of the local member of parliament. 'And what a lovely view of the English Channel from the terrace.'

'Thank you. That's very kind of you to say so. We realise that it is rather modest compared to Crawthorne Hall – but as you know, the cost of its upkeep had become unviable. Then there were the death duties. We had no option but to move out of our wing after the passing of George's father.'

'I quite understand. It's so difficult nowadays to keep hereditary homes in the family.'

It was at this point that loud music began to blast-out from a shed in Albert Warnford's garden. Isabela recognised the music immediately – it was named *Promontory* – the theme-tune for the 1992 blockbuster film *Last of the Mohicans*. George, embarrassed, made his excuses and strolled over to the fence, beckoning to Kathy Warnford who he spotted sitting in a garden chair. He politely asked her to have the music turned-down and she, in turn, went in search of her husband to pass on the request.

Later, with more guests having arrived, the caterers were serving afternoon tea in Lord and Lady Crawthorne's back garden when a dog started barking incessantly from next door. Albert's daughter was visiting with her Staffordshire terrier Bruno.

'Bruno, Bruno, come here, boy,' she shouted, throwing a ball down the garden.

The loud voice, like an intermittent chainsaw in intensity continued to disturb the genteel peace of the Crawthornes' garden party for the next twenty minutes, causing great distraction and ruining the event.

'Here Bruno. Fetch! FETCH!' the daughter bellowed at around a hundred and ten decibels.

'Bruno! Bruno!'

The dog was barking again, waiting for a ball to be thrown. Then, for the third time that afternoon the ball came over the fence: this time narrowly missing one of the Crawthorne's antique eighteenth century Meissen cups – part of the extensive tea set which they had inherited. It had a dainty 'deutschBlumen' floral design – bone china and was very delicate – easily broken. Sir Arthur Bromdale, one of the guests picked-up the missile and lobbed it back into the garden next door.

'Thanks.'

'You're welcome!' Sir Arthur looked over the fence and smiled at the young woman in her thirties who was stroking a vicious-looking dog. She was bending down and he drooled lingeringly as he gazed at her cleavage. Casting his eye over her lecherously one last time he then returned to top-up his glass and make small-talk with his hosts.

After that, the noise dissipated and a civilised air took hold of the gathering once more.

Later that evening, after the last of the guests had left, George Crawthorne spotted his nemesis, Albert, coming through the lychgate and down the little pathway at the front of the house. He had no wish to speak to his neighbour after the events of that afternoon. He also wished to avoid further confrontation with Mr. Warnford after being presented with a catalogue of complaints earlier that day. However, on this occasion Albert had come along to show-off his latest acquisition. It was a hessian sack – and it was moving.

'Do you want to take a look at this George?'

'What is it?'

Albert opened the sack. To George's surprise, wriggling and writhing inside was a massive grass snake, well-over a metre long. The grey-green creature was hissing and striking-out defensively with its mouth while the two men looked-on.

Although the two neighbours didn't hit-it-off personality-wise, they shared a common interest in nature and wild creatures. George, when he was younger, had been responsible for managing the gamekeeping at Crawthorne Hall and was very knowledgeable on many matters concerning wildlife. Albert was an accomplished fly-fisher and something of an expert ornithologist.

'Where did you find it?' asked George, still staring down into the open sack held by his neighbour.

'It was in my pond – probably looking for frogs. I got it out with a litter picker. It's a strong bugger.'

The creature was still struggling to be free and Albert re-tied the top of the sack.

'That's amazing. I didn't know that grass snakes could be found in a beach environment. What will you do with it?'

'I'm going to take it down to Cullimer's Pond in Chichester and let it go. I love wild creatures but they can be a pest in the gardens.'

'Yes, in my old home it was usually deer destroying trees by eating their bark.'

'Not a lot that you can do about them apart from making sure you have a good, high fence. The worst pests for me though are the magpies.'

'Why's that?'

'I hate the way they kill little birds – and steal eggs. But I have a way of dealing with *them*,' Albert said proudly.

'So, what do you do?'

'I put down bait and catch them in a cage.'

'And then what? Do you take them somewhere and let them go?' asked George naively, thinking of his neighbour as an animal lover.

'No, I wring their necks,' he replied nonchalantly.

Chapter 10

2010

As soon as they set eyes on each other there was a chemistry attraction, drawing them together.

Charles Eden, junior manager at the prestigious Langley Hall Hotel in Surrey had been chosen to move over to its sister hotel, recently opened near Hailsham in East Sussex. It was company policy to always draught experienced staff to new hotels in order to provide continuity of service and standards, ensuring that the expectations of its loyal clientele would be more than satisfied. The owners, aware of Charles' background as grandson of Lord Crawthorne, thought that it would be an added bonus to appoint a manager with family connections. In their brochure they had outlined the history of the old place, capitalising on some of the stories of resident ghosts – many guests were intrigued by such snippets.

Charles had been in the general manager's office when Amy, a new trainee manager had first walked in. Smartly dressed in a grey trouser-suit with honey coloured hair tied back in a low-bun style, she gave an easy, confident smile, which went all the way to her beautiful deep brown eyes. Straight away Charles felt a connection.

'Hello, Amy. I'd like you to meet Charles Eden, our new Front of House Manager,' announced Colin Howard the General Manager.

'Hi Amy.' This from Charles. Out of habit his eyes had fallen to her hand to look for rings – there were none.

'Hi.' She replied cheerfully, colouring slightly when she met Charles' lingering gaze. He averted his eyes.

'Charles recently joined us from Langley Hall. He's going to work through our induction pack with you – starting with all the health and safety aspects of the job first, of course.' Colin sat at his desk while the other two stood – but it was an informal and friendly meeting – almost welcoming. 'He'll be your mentor, arranging for you to spend time working in all the main areas of hotel management.'

'Okay,' she replied.

'Maybe you can start Amy in bookings and reception?' suggested Colin, turning to Charles. 'Then I'll leave you to arrange experience in the kitchens, restaurants, bars, housekeeping and maintenance.'

Charles nodded in agreement.

'Do you have any questions?' continued Colin Howard, turning once more towards Amy.

'Not for the moment.'

'If you do, just ask Charles. He'll show you what to do about a uniform, your work shifts, living arrangements, etiquette with guests etc. Most of it's in here anyway.' He picked up two A4 packs which had been sitting on his desk and handed one to each of them. 'These induction packs should answer most of your questions.'

They'd headed over towards the main hotel entrance after that, finding some chairs in the little office adjacent to the reception desk.

'I'll fetch us some drinks before we start on the induction packs,' announced Charles. 'Coffee?'

'Yes please.'

'Just a moment.' he disappeared, returning with a tray set-out with cups of coffee, a jug of milk and sachets of sugar.

'So, Amy,' he stirred his cup. 'Where's home?'

'Oh – I grew up in Surrey.' She took a sip of cooling coffee, then posted half a digestive after it.

'Whereabouts?'

'I lived in Dorking in Surrey – have you heard of it?'

'Yes, Langley Hall Hotel – where I've been working up to now – that's near Dorking. I know it well.'

'I went to the Ashcombe School in Dorking; then studied hotel management at Bournemouth. How about you?' asked Amy looking at him with those deep, unfathomable brown eyes. She seemed to be genuinely interested.

'Grew up in Chichester; took a hotel management course at Essex University; worked for just over a year as a trainee manager – and now, here I am.'

'Just like that!'

'So how long do you think you'll be working here before moving on?' Charles was curious to know how she saw her new position here at Crawthorne Hall.

'I'm planning to give it a year or so – enough time to learn the barebones of the business and to give something back in return.' She spoke assuredly.

'I guess that anything else would be frowned upon after all the training and experience that I would have received from working here?' she added.

Charles loved the way she spoke; soothing and calming with smooth, sweet, mellifluous tones.

'That sounds about right,' he replied. 'And then? What would you be looking to do?'

'No doubt about it. I want to work abroad – to see the world.'

'Me too.' He smiled – so did she.

'Anyway, that's for the future. For now, I can't wait to get started!' She beamed at him enthusiastically. It gave him a warm, fuzzy feeling inside.

'Well, welcome to Crawthorne Hall Hotel,' he replied. 'If you'll follow me, I'll give you the *grand tour* with a chance to ask any questions – then I'll leave you to settle-in. How does that sound?'

'Perfect!'

'This way then. First stop – the East wing – it's a good place to begin, as it's the oldest part of the house. I can fill you in with some of the history – and introduce you to some of our ghosts. So, I hope you're not squeamish!'

She wasn't sure whether he was joking or being serious. 'How old is Crawthorne Hall then, Charles?'

'It dates back to the thirteenth century but became family home to the Crawthornes in Tudor times – a New Year's gift from Henry VIII for services rendered.' He didn't mention his own connection to the Crawthorne dynasty: she would find out about that in the fullness of time.

*

Over the weeks that followed, Charles was struck by Amy's caring nature – nothing was ever too much trouble. A good organiser and always ready to help those around her, she was clearly a people person: calm in a crisis and honest when dealing with guests and staff; unafraid of tackling difficult situations. Amy had a happy, outgoing personality and soon settled down to life at Crawthorne Hall Hotel. She worked closely with Charles as her mentor and they soon became close colleagues.

However, it wasn't until Christmas when they found themselves dancing together at the staff party, that their personal relationship had finally ignited. As he held her, she seemed to melt into his arms – he felt her warmth as they moved to the steady rhythms of the music. Afterwards, they were walking back to the staff accommodation wing – it was mild for the time of year – although with a wispy wind. As gentle rain fell, she looked up at him with her lovely eyes and said the most unexpected thing.

'Charles, tell me something you've never told anyone before.'

'I really like you. I've never said that to anyone before.' They carried on walking while they laughed and joked together.

'No, I meant secrets – tell me a secret that you've never told anyone before.'

'That would be difficult – me being an open book with no secrets.'

She was silent for some moments waiting for him to be serious.

'Come on Charles, there has to be something.'

There was plenty to choose from – family secrets – he'd told her many stories about when he had been a boy, staying at Crawthorne Hall.

'Okay. I feel a bit disloyal about this but when I was a child, I used to explore the secret passages and once spied my Grandad George in bed with a younger woman – and it wasn't my Grandma Isabela.'

'You'll have to show me some of these secret passages.'

'They were more-or-less bricked-up when the house was refurbished and the bedrooms remodelled.'

'A pity.'

'Now it's your turn – tell me something you've never told anyone before.'

'I've never met my real father.'

That was a conversation-stopper if ever there was one – but what Amy had just revealed served to pull them closer together – it showed that she trusted him enough to share her secret.

Nearly back at the accommodation block Charles reached in his pocket for his door key, accidentally pulling it out with a ten-pound note which he hadn't needed to spend after all as the drinks had been free. The note, caught by a gust of wind, flew up, catching in the low branch of a tree. Getting up on a wall, he reached-up to retrieve it.

'Be careful you don't fall,' called Amy from below.

'I already have,' he said turning to look at her, '… madly for you.'

Charles was walking on air – he had a feeling of elation and joy that he had never experienced before. That night he knew that he would not sleep well as he could not stop thinking about her. In turn, Amy knew that she just had to be with this man – something had ignited between them and was drawing them together as though they belonged to one another. From that moment it seemed that nothing could extinguish that flame. Love was born.

Chapter 11

Bob Bennett had just absconded from Ford Open Prison where he had been on a resettlement programme after his latest stint in a Category C prison in Kent. After serving two years for arson, extended for his part in a prison riot, he'd been moved to his new accommodation to prepare him for re-entering the outside world. He had cleverly convinced the prison shrinks that he was a reformed character but they had not reckoned on his spontaneity and recklessness which remained ingrained in his character. Feeling fed-up one sunny afternoon in May he had simply walked out of Ford Open Prison, an institution set in the beautiful West Sussex countryside.

Quickly making himself scarce, he had hidden inside a removals' lorry, which seemed very apt for his purpose. Eventually waking up on a pink velvet couch, he had emerged some miles down the road in the seaside town of Bognor Regis with the sound of gulls in the sky, the smell of fresh salty air and the sight of glistening water lapping the seashore. It was here that he decided to start begging for a living – an occupation that he was well-versed in and knew to be much more lucrative than the crummy jobs that the prison service had been training him to take up.

On his first day, he had enticed a stray-looking dog to sit with him outside the local Waitrose food supermarket. Dogs often evoked sympathy amongst gullible punters. The sight of a helpless animal led people to be more generous in their giving. This particular dog, which only had one eye, seemed to fit the bill for Bob. He'd named the dog *Tod*.

'Hello, boy,' said Bob, who had always been an animal lover. The mangy brown and black dog sniffed around. Bob, sitting on a blanket which he'd retrieved from a dustbin, moved to one side allowing the dog to lay next to him. Nearby he'd placed a large canvas holdall, which he'd blagged from a charity shop earlier – something to contain the few belongings which he had started to gather since escaping from the open prison. The dog started to nuzzle at Bob in an affectionate way and was rewarded with some broken biscuits from a packet donated by a punter earlier in the morning.

'You're a friendly fellow,' Bob had said to his new pal. 'But you're Tod Sloane – all alone, just like me. I think I'll call you Tod.'

As they had both continued sitting there, with sympathetic supermarket customers dropping donations of money or food from time-to-time, Bob noticed a sleek, silver BMW saloon car pull-up under a shady tree in the adjacent car park. A scruffy man got out and, pulling-on a holey beany hat, grabbed a filthy looking sleeping bag and shuffled-over in the direction of the supermarket entrance. He stopped in front of Bob.

'Oi mate, this is my patch. Piss-off,' he said angrily in no uncertain terms.

Bob simply shrugged. 'Well, it's my patch now. Go and find somewhere else.'

While he'd been in prison, Bob had read in a newspaper about a family man who made a lot of money posing as a homeless beggar. He drove to Oxford each day, parked his new VW Golf and changed into rags before busking and begging in the streets. Right now, Bob was sure that this unwelcome stranger was one such phoney. Begging was a lucrative career – in the right places and with the right people.

'Cheeky bastard,' the man spat-out. 'I'm warning you.'

'And I'm warning you,' retorted Bob unfazed. He was quite used to standing his ground in prison – and anywhere else for that matter. He wasn't afraid of this man.

The man kicked-over Bob's polystyrene coffee cup in which he had collected the loose change which he had been given by sympathetic passers-by. Tod growled menacingly.

'Are you going to move, or not?' Bob's new rival tried once more, although his resolve was waning – especially with Tod now snarling threateningly.

'Not,' replied Bob. 'By the way, I see you have a nice new Beema over in the corner of the car park.' He nodded in the direction of the BMW. 'Must have cost you a pretty packet? Shame if anything happened to it. Could get damaged – might even catch fire? Now, run along mate and leave us alone.'

The man hesitated and then decided to return to his car, pulling-out at speed, on the way to finding pastures new in which to beg.

Bob carried-on sitting outside the supermarket for the rest of the day, amazed at the generosity of many members of the public. There were no further incidents although he was slightly amused when, towards the evening, the Salvation Army set-up further along the road, playing brass instruments, drumming along in rhythm as they cheerily set-about collecting money for the homeless. At no time did any of them offer either help or money to Bob. They didn't even seem to notice him sitting there, trying to eek a living through begging. He shook his head at the irony of the situation before shambling along to the local park to find an unoccupied bench for the night. He was pleased that his new friend Tod decided to trail-along behind him – a dog was always useful in warding off unwanted company in the dead of night.

Over the next two days Bob continued to occupy the pavement space outside the Waitrose supermarket store. He was amazed that, so far, he had not spotted a single law enforcement officer. The only further trouble that he encountered was from a group of teenagers – boys and girls – who thought it was funny to mock him for being homeless. However, like the BMW man, they were easily dissuaded from their revelries by the presence of Tod.

On Bob's third day of begging, Lady Isabela Crawthorne was exiting the Waitrose store when she noticed a homeless man sitting loitering near the trolleys. Despite looking grimy and creased with exhaustion, he sat reading a book about railways while stroking a mangy-looking dog with one hand. As Isabela fumbled clumsily in her bag, she pulled out two bananas and offered them to the beggar.

'Sorry, I don't eat bananas,' Bob slurred, slightly inebriated. He'd had a bad night trying to sleep on a park bench and had managed to find a bottle of cider to keep him company, along with Tod the dog. He looked up at her with glazed eyes, pleased that someone had taken the trouble to stop and engage with him

She hesitated for a moment, making up her mind. Should she offer something more fitting to the tastes of this vagabond now that he had turned-down her bananas?

'Don't worry. I might have some spare change here somewhere.' She delved into her purse and fetched out a note. Bob's eyes lit up as he looked up at this lady, a true angel with a twenty-pound note tantalisingly fluttering around in her hand. Lady Crawthorne had no real money sense.

'Thank you,' he said. 'I have some food here that I don't want. Would you like to buy some from me?'

'How much?'

He could see that she was three knives short of a cutlery set when it came to giving her money away. These rich do-gooders were all the same. So, he thought he'd chance his arm. 'Five pounds?'

'Oh, alright.' She liked him. He seemed to be a polite young man who'd probably come upon hard times. Isabela liked to think of herself as a charitable person: she was, indeed very kind hearted and generous by nature. So, finding a five-pound note she handed it to the homeless man. Bob wished he'd asked for ten. He hoped she liked the bread, fruit and sausage rolls that he had just sold to her. Personally, he preferred booze to all that crap.

Lady Crawthorne dumped her new acquisitions into her cavernous plastic shopping bag then zipped-up her handbag which she hooked over her arm. Checking her watch, she then hurried off – she had a bridge party later that afternoon.

She didn't notice that something had dropped out of her bag. It fell into Bob Bennett's lap like manna from heaven. Who said that Christmas only comes once a year?

Chapter 12

George Crawthorne was in a reflective mood, sitting on a bench overlooking the sea at Pagham in West Sussex. He often came here nowadays, staring out to sea, thinking about his life and what might have been. Looking into his inner self he thought about his achievements in life – his successes and failures. He even considered his wife, Isabela, who he had lulled into marriage with his charms, only to treat her badly – betraying her with his numerous affairs and his lies. Then there was his involvement in the diamond trade. He was involved with some pretty heavy guys who could do some serious harm if he crossed them – yet he couldn't carry-on in that business for much longer – he was getting old. George wondered whether, if he had his time again, he might do things differently – if he had the chance to be a better person would he take it?

Thinking about all the real excitement in his life he decided that he would change very little: like all the women who made him feel so alive. Laetitia in Amsterdam, for one – a true beauty, lubricious and always eager to please him. Then there was his long-term girlfriend, Sheila who had once been his personal assistant. He still saw her regularly – there were many good reasons for their continued relationship – including the secret that she had sworn him to … the secret that he would take to the grave.

It was still early evening and the September sun was beginning to retreat already. Gulls were still circling in the air and the tide was on the turn; blue-green water retreating over a percussion of pebbles at the shore side. He could feel a cold onshore breeze picking-up and he felt a shiver. As the light faded, George rose and wearily trudged along the beach, which stretched into the distance like a horseshoe bending around the coastline. The tide was going out, now giving way to patches of sand on the shingly beach. With every step the sand shifted, leaving a trail of shallow craters following George as he headed up towards his exclusive beach chalet in Aldwick Bay: it was really more of a cabin, fashioned in oak. He passed a seaweed covered groyne with gurgling and gushing waves lapping away at its side. Then he took the narrow concrete pathway which ran alongside six bespoke little wooden buildings, each one far larger in size than Laetitia's little room behind her window in that sleazy Amsterdam street.

George thought about that last liaison with Laetitia and determined that he must soon return to her again. Feeling the need for comfort he remembered his bottle of single malt whisky stashed away in the corner cupboard inside the beach chalet. He decided to fetch it there and then; to drink away his melancholy – perhaps even numb his inner pain for a while.

Reaching *The Knapp* beach chalet, he noticed that the door had been unlocked – there was a gap where it hadn't been closed properly. Entering the little wooden building, he could see something slumped on the floor. In the dim light of a street lamp, he could clearly see a body. Warily stepping inside George grabbed a chair and shoved it hard on to the offending trespasser who was now occupying his property.

'WHAT THE HELL ARE YOU DOING IN MY PROPERTY?' he shouted at the top of his voice. George was furious and unafraid.

The figure, roused from his slumber, looked up, terrified.

'Don't hurt me. Please – don't hurt me.' He looked to be around fifty years of age, bedraggled with long hair and beard. Dressed in an old raggedy overcoat, he appeared unwashed, smelling like he'd never met a bar of soap. Hung-over and drugged-up there was a distinct stench of piss and whisky surrounding him as he lay there on the dusty wooden floor clutching a bottle. Lord Crawthorne was livid.

'THAT'S MY BEST MALT WHISKY, YOU BASTARD. I'M CALLING THE POLICE.'

Still holding the chair in one hand, George fetched his mobile phone out of his pocket. However, at the mention of *police*, the vagrant looked even more disconcerted – as though he were more afraid of that threat than the imminent possibility of Lord Crawthorne flooring him with the chair. He scrambled to his feet, grabbed a large canvas holdall and bolted out of the door.

'That's right, clear owf you sodding bastard.' George replaced the chair. He was angry and annoyed that someone had been sleeping in his beach chalet – maybe they had been here for some days? However, most of all he was furious at the loss of his twenty-five-year-old malt whisky.

There had been a lot of news coverage recently about the numbers of homeless people targeting beach huts and chalets for shelter with the onset of winter just around the corner. Clearly it was preferable to sleeping rough in shop doorways but this was trespass. He had assumed that the man had broken in and went to examine the lock: it was intact. Lord Crawthorne was puzzled. He was just about to take out his key to lock-up when he noticed something shining on the tiny table top in the far corner. It was a key – and attached to that key was a fob with the address label *The Knapp*

Beach Chalet, Aldwick Bay. Guessing that the vagrant had stolen the key from Lady Crawthorne, he wondered whether any of her other possessions had recently gone missing – maybe jewellery or money? George decided that he would mention this incident to the police commissioner, just in case there had been a spate of thefts in the area. If so, then this man might be responsible.

Meanwhile, first thing in the morning he was going to get hold of a locksmith to fix a double padlocked drop-in security bar: that would stop all these scroungers in their tracks. He also knew a man – a former poacher associated with Crawthorne Hall – who dealt in animal traps. He'd get some of those and leave them strategically poised inside the beach hut – maybe using a bottle of whisky as bait. Lord Crawthorne liked being in control: there was no way he was going to let a beggar get the better of him.

*

In the early hours of the morning blue lights were flashing as an emergency vehicle raced along the main arterial road towards the sleepy Aldwick Bay near Chichester. Approaching the beach, the crew were aware of the unmistakable acrid smell of belching black smoke which announced the location of the fire: it had been reported some fifteen minutes earlier. There had been an unprecedented number of incidents recently in the area and this one was rampaging through a row of wooden beach chalets Encouraged by the persistent breeze the nascent flames had leapt up, sweeping rapidly through the dry, flimsy structures.

The moon was low in the sky and there was a scattering of diluted stars above the inky, shifting water. Sitting on the beach in a drunken stupor, a sedentary and solitary figure had propped himself up against a seaweed covered groyne a little way from the burning beach chalets. Bob was feeling lonely again after his new friend, Tod the dog, had deserted him in favour of a bitch on heat. He held a nearly empty bottle of malt whisky in one hand: booze had always given him a safe harbour in the tempestuous sea of troubles that had plagued his life; but it never completely quelled the pain. There must be something better than this existence. But the future seemed bleak.

As he feasted his eyes once more, roused by the dazzling display of burning beach chalets like funeral pyres with their flames blazing high, in his addled brain he was convinced that he had just seen a figure slowly emerge from the furnace, walking towards him. As it approached, he saw that it was a wretched-looking woman, cadaverous and frail with spindly arms long and bony; scarcely able to carry her limp, lifeless baby. Her dull hair fell over her face in heaps although he could just make-out her eyes, which seemed to stare into oblivion. For the ten thousandth time in his life, he thought back to that night as a child when his mother had died, consumed by the fire which had destroyed their home. Nightmare images were once again bombarding his mind. He tipped the last of the whisky into his mouth hoping to dull the painful memories that haunted him, then cast the bottle carelessly to one side.

The apparition didn't stop: it walked straight past him looking only ahead, over the darkened-night shingly beach, illuminated faintly by the pale moon. It carried on walking, reaching the reawakened tide. Then, continuing on into the cold grey waters, heading steadily away towards the horizon, the figure waded deeper and deeper until there was nothing but the murmuring of the languorous waves.

Bob Bennett's attention was suddenly diverted once again towards the activity on land surrounding the burning beach chalets. The emergency vehicle had arrived. He scrutinized the crew as they leapt from their fire tender, quickly locating a hydrant: hoses were unreeled and attached, water gushed out, dousing persistent flames, taming them. They hissed and spat back sullenly, but were soon defeated, diminished and extinguished.

He watched the last of the dancing, flickering flames and he smiled contentedly. Then, with his canvas bag at his side, he shuffled-off along the shore, melting into the darkness of the night.

Chapter 13

2011

Just one kiss she said, enticing me to bed.
Warms to her seduction, man of the womb.
Soft, curved, delicious; she was born to be seditious.
Man becomes a tool through his chasm deep and full.

The Kiss by JB & MM June 1990 *

Gareth Evans, Managing Director of Evans Construction Ltd., had it all – the lifestyle, the house, the money. He'd aspired to having the perfect family. Then it all went wrong: he'd thrown it all away. But he'd become reckless – he didn't care because he'd been blown away by Elaine – the woman ten years younger than him who he'd first met in a service station on his way back from Glinfield Manor House near Eastbourne where he'd been attending a black-tie fund-raising event.

Soft, alluring, feigning, enduring, fantasising, pretending, unaware – acting out his sexual fantasies. She had a penchant for dressing up as a maid *all soft and curved and round.* He would hold her tightly in his arms, she feigning resistance until she succumbed to him – *warm, close, related* as their final pleasure would pulsate – drawing each other together.

The problem was that Alma, his wife, had found out. How could he have been so careless? She had become suspicious by the sudden appearance of a second mobile phone – he'd jokingly told Elaine that it was a 'burner' for his secret service missions. She told him that she would be his 'handler' and called herself 'E'. So, their secret texts had been sent with caller IDs of 'E' and 'G'.

However, one night he'd forgotten to turn off his spare phone before he went to bed. Alma and he had just finished going through their usual once a month love-making ritual and he'd fallen asleep. Then in the morning he'd been in the shower when a text message pinged through. Alma, curious, had discovered the offending phone tucked into his shoe and she'd read the latest message.

E: I loved what you did to me with that passion fruit last weekend – smother me again when you can get away x

'What the hell is this?' Alma was standing, phone in one hand as Gareth emerged dripping from the shower; hair still wet, towel around his waist.

'Oh that. It's a joke,' he was dismissive.

'From who?'

'Just someone at work. Don't worry – I know what it looks like – but it's just a prank.'

'So, who's this *E*?'

'It's Elizabeth.'

'I haven't heard you mention her – and anyway, what's with the spare phone?'

'It's my new office phone – I've issued them to the other senior staff to avoid using personal devices for work purposes. It has been a popular move.'

They had been married for twenty-five years, having just celebrated their silver wedding anniversary in St. Lucia. She knew him better than anyone – and at this precise moment he was lying to her. She stomped down the stairs, her cotton kimono draped around her. Then, sitting on one of their bar stools, rain lashing the window panes, she scrolled through his text messages. Still fresh and dripping from the shower, he wasn't quick enough to commandeer back his precious burner phone.

'So, what's all this then?' she called as she read a number of the texts on his so-called business phone.

E: I wonder what sex is like in an Aston Martin x

'Is that your boss or this person called Elizabeth? Then there's this one.' She read it out.

E: I heard you've been a very bad boy – Auntie is cross with you!

'I told you, it's a joker from the building site office,' he claimed lamely as he inched down the stairs to join Alma.

'You fucking liar. Do I really look that stupid?' She continued to scroll down the messages, becoming more upset by the minute as the seriousness of the situation hit her like the after-draught of an express train hurtling through a station – it was too late to avert the disaster that was once their marriage.

'Can I have my phone back? Alma, please?' Gareth, ever-optimistic preened his ego, hoping he could talk Alma round, explaining the inexplicable.

'Piss off. And don't you dare touch me.'

He started to realise that there was no clear path out of the situation. She wasn't stupid and, by the time she read the rest of the text messages, he knew that it would be well and truly over between them.

'I don't think I'm a bad person.' He was now vying for the sympathy vote.

'Bad people never do.'

Dressing quickly, she picked-up her handbag, dropped the phone inside and, without another word unlocked the front door, soon disappearing down the windy driveway in her car.

Chapter 14

There's something rather magical about going where the wind takes you: the cares and stresses of everyday life ebb away, and the present becomes everything.

Charles was having the time of his life. Just him and the girl that he'd fallen in love with, sailing seamlessly over the choppy waters of the English Channel on their way from Bexhill to Pevensey Bay, where they were planning to have a light lunch. Crawthorne Hall Hotel owned a sailing boat which they hired out to guests: managers could use it free of charge when it wasn't being hired-out. Amy, now steering the Enterprise sailing dinghy with its distinctive blue sail, caught the full breeze which carried the little vessel, propelling it onwards. Swells broke against the hull, sending waves of ice-cold water over the side. They both laughed, exhilarated by the briny air. Charles Eden, despite being grandson of Lord George Edward Crawthorne, hadn't been sailing before and was awestruck by the power of the elements – the wind and the sea – it somehow seemed to put everything in perspective – he found it freeing.

'Well, what do you think of it, Charles?'

'I think it's amazing – like you,' he couldn't help adding.

'We'll have to allow more time for the return journey as we'll be working against the wind – and the currents are strong.'

As Amy negotiated the bracing breeze, adjusting the sails, she looked ahead to the shingly shoreline which fronted the quiet pebbly beach where they were going to stop-off for a couple of hours before making their way back. She smiled at Charles, who seemed mesmerised by the bobbing of the undulating sea as they talked about nothing and everything, Amy constantly keeping a watchful eye on their progress.

'I love this fresh air. It's like having your lungs bleached clean!'

'Yes, sailing is a good antidote to all that air conditioning in the hotel – constantly breathing in everyone's regurgitated germs!' Still looking ahead, Amy saw the beach approaching rapidly. She started slackening the sails. 'Hey, Charles, when I say 'NOW' can you jump out of the bow with that rope – it's called the 'painter' – it's for tethering the boat. Then try to steady the dinghy so that it doesn't scrape up the shingle – we don't want it getting damaged.'

'Okay, I'm ready.'

'NOW!'

He jumped as instructed. Then turning around, holding the bow to stop the momentum, he brought the dinghy to a gradual halt. This was far more difficult than his car – which at least had brakes. Amy, meanwhile had brought down the sails completely, so they were no longer driven by the wind. She leapt-out on to the shore and they both hauled the boat a few metres up the beach.

Fifteen minutes later, she'd fetched the plastic picnic hamper which she'd been keeping stowed-away. Handing Charles two plastic beakers, she drew out a bottle of Lanson champagne.

'I'll let you do the honours!'

Popping the cork, he half-filled both beakers.

'I couldn't risk bringing glass champagne flutes. Anyway, Charles, happy birthday! I hope you liked the surprise!'

'It was great! I really enjoyed the experience. You're brilliant at handling that boat – you say you've only been sailing for a few years?'

'Yes, I took it up when I was a student – I joined the sailing club and took a couple of trial sailing lessons, then did some training in Poole harbour – including going to sea for two days at a time.'

'Not in a tiny dinghy, I hope!'

'Course not.'

'Have you ever capsized?'

'Cheeky!'

'Well?'

'Only as part of my training. I know what to do if it ever happens.'

'So, what's the worst thing that's ever happened to you on a sailing vessel?'

'That's an easy one. We were just setting-off on the two-day adventure when I looked on the mast and saw a robin perched half-way up looking at me.'

'And?'

'Only it wasn't a robin – when I looked more closely it was a rat – which ran down and across the deck heading in my direction.'

'What happened?'

'One of the guys saw-it-off with the help of an oar – he flicked-it into the water. We guessed that it must have been attracted by the food that we'd brought onboard.'

'Anyway, what qualifications have you got?'

'Why? Are you vetting me just in case I'm incapable of getting you back to Bexhill safely?'

'Well?'

'After doing all the basic sailing courses, I then worked for my Day Skipper certificate, which took five days. I've also got the Level Two certificate for seamanship skills – sail handling, ropework – things like that. I thought I'd learn to do it all properly – unlike some idiots.'

'What do you mean?'

'Sometimes novices think they know it all – a while ago I was down in Bexhill and saw some of our guests having a hard time controlling our dinghy.'

'That's a shame.'

'They obviously hadn't a clue – one of the sails was upside down for a start!' They both laughed.

'By the way, I thought this would be a good time to give you your birthday present.' She delved into the picnic hamper, drawing-out a large envelope, which she handed over to him.

Opening it, he pulled-out some papers and a glossy brochure. Then, looking up at her, he smiled widely. It was a course of sailing lessons.

'Amy, that's brilliant, thank you so much!'

She was glad that her present had pleased him.

Although it was Charles' birthday, they had arranged to meet Amy's parents that evening. Mr. and Mrs Hughes were staying in a prestigious Eastbourne hotel and had invited Amy and Charles over for a celebratory meal. It would be the first time that he had met them and he was slightly nervous, but wanting to please Amy, he'd decided to forego the intimate evening with just the two of them that he'd planned. It was rare that they both managed to have a day off together like this. However, there would be other evenings for romance.

'How many boyfriends have you taken to meet your parents then, Amy?' he'd said when she asked him to have dinner with them.

'Only the important ones,' she'd told him.

When he heard that, he'd felt a warm glow deep inside.

After their stop-off in Pevensey Bay, Amy and Charles started back on the five nautical mile jaunt back to Bexhill. By this time, grey clouds were scudding across the sky and shafts of sunlight were occasionally bursting through a backdrop of late afternoon drizzle. Charles loved the confident way in which Amy handled the Enterprise dinghy – she'd told him that it was really built with a crew of two in-mind. So, he thought she did pretty well to steer it single handed with all that was needed in harnessing the wind. It seemed to him, a bit like trying to tame a beast – and she certainly had everything under control.

Approaching the shingly shoreline at Bexhill, Charles decided to use his initiative. Thinking about how Amy had asked him to jump into the sea earlier to stop the dinghy from scraping up the beach, he prepared to do the same again – to show that he had learnt something about boats today, albeit a small insignificant detail.

'Right Amy. I've got hold of the painter.' He'd remembered the name of the tethering rope.

'Great. But you need to get closer to the shore this time as the water is much …' She didn't finish her sentence before Charles leapt-out. She had been starting to warn him that the sea was deeper here than at Pevensey Bay. Too late, he'd jumped.

Charles, having drunk half a bottle of champagne, had misjudged the speed of the boat. Looking down, he thought he was jumping down into about six inches of water. Instead, as soon as he entered the sea, the painter rope in his hand, he found himself plummeting down into about nine feet of water – then suddenly buoyed-up by his life jacket, he surged upwards again, spluttering, surprised – and a little embarrassed.

For a moment, Amy had been worried – he could-have bobbed-up directly under the hull, hitting his head dangerously – but fortunately for him, he had resurfaced to one side, out of danger.

Coming to his senses, Charles had helped to haul the boat on to the shore where Amy had taken down the rigging and stowed it away. Then they'd negotiated it on to the boat dolly – a metal three wheeled trolley – and pulled it over to its allotted place before setting-off back to the hotel to change and prepare themselves for meeting her parents later that evening.

Chapter 15

'Hi Harry!' Amy had been calling her dad by his first name ever since she'd moved away. 'I'd like you to meet Charles.'

They had just arrived at the Grand Regent Hotel. Amy's parents were sitting in the bar waiting for them.

'Charles. This is Mum and Harry.'

'Hi.' Charles smiled amiably.

'Happy birthday, Charles!' Harry stood and shook hands. 'Pleased to meet you. Can I get you a drink?'

'Just a beer for me, please.'

Harry seemed to Charles to be a pleasant, cheery, welcoming type. Aged in his late sixties with greying hair combed back, he wore slightly old-fashioned horn-rimmed glasses and had a serious look about him. Being in the hotel business, Charles and Amy were used to playing a little game in which they tried to guess people's personalities and characteristics from giveaway body language and their appearance. In Harry's case, Charles guessed that he was probably a stolid, reliable, loyal and sincere kind of guy – perhaps a bit on the quiet side. He hoped he would get on well with Harry – and his wife.

'I'll have a white wine spritzer, please,' Amy said as she kissed her mother and then sat down. 'Hello, Mum.'

As Charles sat down, too, he was struck by the attractiveness of the older woman now facing him. Young-faced with a blonde bob-style haircut and large rimmed glasses, she was wearing a clingy, but classy low-cut green dress which showed-off her well-kept figure. He thought it was slightly provocative, yet at the same time there was a quasi-conventual quality about it. He noticed that she wore an unusual silver brooch fashioned as a snake.

'How's your break in Eastbourne going, Mum?'

'Lovely – as always,' she replied in a dulcet voice – sweet and soothing. Charles instantly liked Amy's mum. She looked across at him with her green eyes, which seemed to twinkle as she spoke. 'I don't know whether Amy has told you, but Harry and I come here every year for our wedding anniversary – it's where we spent our honeymoon.'

How romantic, thought Charles wistfully. *I hope that when I get married, I'll carry on doing something like that for years.*

Before Charles could carry on with the conversation, Harry returned with the drinks and then the head waiter suddenly appeared.

'Excuse me. Mr. and Mrs Hughes?' interrupted the head waiter. 'Your table is now ready. Would you like to follow me, sir?' He addressed Amy's dad.

At that, they all stood and followed him through to the adjoining room where they were seated.

'So, Charles, Amy's been telling me about your day.' Mrs Hughes was sitting opposite to Charles, just finishing her plate of scallops. Throughout their first course, she'd spent most of her time catching-up with her daughter's news.

'Yes, it was brilliant,' Charles replied enthusiastically. 'It's the first time I've ever been sailing.' He looked across, noticing her well-manicured carmine-red fingernails as she forked the last of the scallops into her mouth.

'I think he's got the sailing bug – like me,' interrupted Amy.

Although Charles found Amy's parents very warm and approachable, he couldn't help feeling that somewhere along the line he was in for a grilling – but maybe that was just him being paranoid? As for Amy's mum, she was still trying to work-out whether or not Charles was worth getting to know. She had no real idea of how serious he was about her daughter – so she decided to delve further.

'Tell me Charles, what did you think, the first time you met Amy?' said Mrs Hughes with a demure smile. She looked at him with arched eyebrows and slightly pouting lips, an amused, playful expression on her face.

'Oh Mum!' protested Amy. 'What a question to ask!'

'Well?' she persisted, unperturbed.

Charles hesitated for a moment. 'It's not so much what I thought as what I felt meeting someone so fun-loving, not taking life too seriously.'

'That's where she takes after her mother!' she joked. Charles thought he detected a slight northern lilt in her voice.

He didn't mention the way Amy's smile had radiated a warmth which had brightened-up his day when he first met her. That, as he got to know her, he'd loved the way she was so kind and caring to those around her – that now, he always felt good just being around her. Neither did Charles tell Amy's mum that he was, at this moment, overjoyed to be on the same planet as his beautiful girlfriend; who he had fallen in love with and hoped to marry one day. Charles could have told her that sometimes, he could hardly catch his breath when he was with Amy, that there was a longing in his heart for her. He hated the times when they were apart. All these thoughts were private and personal – not to be shared with this stranger who he had only just met an hour earlier.

Their main course had now arrived – T-bone steak for Charles, Duck à l' Orange for Amy and Beef Wellington for Mr. and Mrs Hughes.

'So, what brought you to Crawthorne Hall Hotel, Charles?' Harry asked brightly, supping his beer.

'I used to work in its sister hotel in Surrey,' he replied.

'Which one?' Harry asked amiably.

'Langley Hall Hotel'.

'Yes. We know it well. We often go there for special occasions ...' Harry paused then addressed his wife who was in conversation with Amy. 'Hey, darling, Charles used to work at Langley Hall Hotel.'

'Yes, dear. I know,' she replied – slightly patronisingly it seemed to Charles.

'No-one tells me anything!' joked Harry.

'I wanted to start my career in a place with good prospects. Then I was lucky enough to be transferred to Crawthorne Hall when it opened as a hotel,' continued Charles with sincerity.

'It's certainly building-up a good reputation,' commented Harry conversationally. 'You've only to look at the online reviews.'

'We always do,' replied Charles. 'It's one of my jobs to deal with complaints! You should come and stay – try us out!'

'We thought of that, but felt it might compromise Amy – staying in the same hotel where she works.'

Charles, still chewing, swallowed then grinned. 'Fair enough!'

'So, Charles, have you got a large family?' Amy's mum came pitching-in again.

'I wouldn't call it particularly large,' replied Charles nonchalantly.

'Tell me, where did you grow up?'

'Um ... near Chichester. I lived there all my life until I went to uni. Do you know it?'

'We have been over that way,' interrupted George. 'But it was a long time ago. We went to see an old friend.' He didn't elaborate. 'I remember stopping-off in the city centre – it's a lovely place.'

'We bought that Chinese vase – do you remember?' added Amy's mum.

'Was it an antique?' Charles asked curiously.

'Yes, we always look for pieces when we are away – we're collectors of-sorts.'

'My grandad has recently moved to an area near Chichester – Aldwick Bay.'

They had all finished their main courses and had agreed to forego a dessert and move through to the lounge area for coffee.'

'I hear it's very nice in that part of the world,' she replied. 'Some big houses in that area.'

'Yes, I suppose so,' he replied, 'but I think his new place is a bit more manageable.'

'Oh?' she sounded curious, now waiting for further explanation.

Charles reddened – he felt that he'd divulged too much – he didn't like to advertise his family connection to Crawthorne Hall. There had been much controversy in the family over the years with tabloid newspapers and magazines circulating stories of ghosts going bump in the night, raucous parties, sex scandals and even suggestions of murder in the Crawthorne's household. Charles was not proud of these allegations which had given his family a bad name, albeit deserved in some instances.

'I never told you, Mum,' Amy interrupted. 'Charles' grandfather used to live at Crawthorne Hall before he sold it to the hotel chain. Charles is Lord Crawthorne's grandson.'

Both Amy's parents glanced fleetingly at each other in a curious way and it was as if a shadow passed over their faces – *slightly spooky,* Charles thought.

'What's this? The Spanish Inquisition?' Amy was taken-aback with the way in which her parents – particularly her mother – were quizzing her partner.

The lounge area was a huge palace of a room decorated with a combination of traditional grandeur mixed with modern design flourishes. A stunning, sweeping spiral staircase to one side, rose up to the first floor with its guest bedrooms. Harry found a table with a small settee and two armchairs, a little way from the resident pianist who was going through his set-pieces: currently playing Claude Debussy's Clair de Lune. Then he and Charles went to find the Gents' toilets, leaving the two women to chat.

'So, is it serious between you two, Amy?'

'Well, we're *an item* – if that's what you mean? Next year we're going to look for a placement together.'

Her mum's eyebrows pulled together as she briefly wrinkled-up her nose

– the look she used to show distain when she did not like something. It was as though she had just tasted a bitter herb or smelled something not quite pleasant. In this case, though, there was clearly something about what she had just heard. Amy guessed that her mother had heard – or read – about some of the goings-on in the old Crawthorne Hall and disapproved of her only daughter being mixed-up with the notoriety and scandal associated with the Crawthorne dynasty. Amy was confused – and a little angry.

'So, it *is* serious then?' she repeated the question.

'Look, Mum. You seem to have taken a dislike to Charles. Apart from him being my boyfriend, and it being the first time you've ever set eyes on him, it does happen to be his birthday. You could have made more effort.' She was sad and disappointed with her mother.

'I just don't think he's right for you. I think you should distance yourself from him.'

Amy could hardly believe what she was hearing.

'Mum! How dare you say that to me! Anyone would think he was related to the Kray Twins or the Yorkshire Ripper! You're treating me like a five-year-old-child. I can make up my own mind about my boyfriends.'

'Look Amy, you need to get onboard with this!' Amy was surprised by her assertive tone.

'With *you*, dictating who I should or should not be with? Let me tell you this – I love Charles and we're going to be together – it's inevitable. So just suck that one and be happy for me for once!'

Just then, the two men appeared and sat down in the two armchairs. Harry nodded to a waiter and suddenly the lights were dimmed as a small posse of hotel staff, surrounding a lit birthday cake made their way towards the Hughes' table singing *Happy Birthday … to Charles*. A number of other hotel guests joined-in good humouredly and then, after blowing-out the candles, a bottle of champagne appeared. After serving the cake and drinks, the hotel staff made themselves scarce, leaving Charles flushed, but happy that Harry had been so kind and considerate.

'Thanks. That's a really lovely surprise.'

'Our pleasure.' Harry looked like he really meant what he said. 'Raise your glasses everyone. Here's to Charles.' They clinked glasses – the two men oblivious to the conversation that had just ensued between the two women.

Amy and her mother looked at each other with barely disguised anger after their disagreement. Wishing to avert a hiatus, Amy decided to avoid being drawn further into a ridiculous argument; so, carried-on engaging pleasantly, being determined to make this a memorable day for Charles. The men seemed oblivious to the antagonism between the two women

Shortly afterwards, having said their goodbyes, her parents headed upstairs to bed while Charles and Amy walked to his car and drove back towards Crawthorne Hall Hotel, already starting to anticipate the early morning shift the following day. Suddenly Amy's mobile phone sang in her pocket, an irritating jangling sound. Looking to see who was calling, she recognised her mother's number so ignored it. Then, less than a minute later there was a bleep. Amy looked at the text message that she had just received. It was from her mother.

MUM: *Sorry if you think I was mean. Mum xx*

Amy was still cross with her mother but decided not to be churlish – it was tempting to ignore the message – at least until the morning. So, she sent a brief message back before turning-off her phone.

AMY: *I really didn't mean to joust with you. See you soon. A x*

'Who was that?' Charles spoke without turning, keeping his eyes firmly on the road.

'Just my mother.'

There was a pause, both of them in their own thoughts. Then Charles spoke again.

'Thanks, Amy for a great birthday – full of amazing things and surprises!'

'Just how everything should be in life!'

'Only if they're nice surprises!' He paused again, deciding whether to say what was bothering him. 'Hey Amy, I'm not sure whether your mum has taken a dislike to me though? Have I offended her? Have I missed something?'

'I think we all have,' said Amy, just as perplexed and puzzled as Charles.

Chapter 16

2012

I'm the luckiest guy in the world!

Despite making huge financial losses during his company's renovation work at Crawthorne Hall, Gareth Evans had bounced back, having worked through periods of depression since the break-up of his marriage. Although his quickie divorce with Alma, his wife for twenty-five years, had knocked him sideways at first, he had now adopted a rather cocky attitude to life. It was almost as though he had undergone a personality change since that night when he had first met Elaine. There was a certain underlying note of bragging and boastfulness which now underlay his character.

He realised that in the breakup of his first marriage he was the victim of his own cavalier attitude, resulting in all the heartache and anguish that had ensued from his betrayal. In the end he had just wanted all the messy divorce proceedings to be over and so faced up to the inevitability of the truth, admitting his adultery but never showing any sign of regret for his actions. Being a pragmatist, he'd walked away from his marriage with Alma, finally closing the book with a flourish to be with Elaine. After re-marrying a year ago, he had moved on and he intended to enjoy every moment of his new life with his new wife – albeit on a reduced budget.

'To what do I owe this pleasure?' Elaine had walked into the bedroom that morning stark naked, exposing her large, bounteous breasts as she clung on to the wooden tray containing two full English breakfasts with crumbly buttered croissants. Coffee had been freshly brewed and the aroma wafted around the bed. Between her teeth she held a single red rose.

'Just to take your mind away from your ex-wife's re-marriage today, honey.'

'Oh, don't remind me! It's Alma's wedding day.' Gareth was still recovering from their round of passion the previous evening. He lay content, musing over the mounted picture on the opposite wall: it was a copy of the seductive painting called *The Kiss* by Gustav Klimt, a painter who often explored the themes of love, intimacy and sexuality in his works of art. Gareth had first spotted a copy of the painting whilst he had been working on the refurbishments at Crawthorne Hall Hotel. The picture, chosen by Belinda, the interior designer, had been hanging up in Room 13 when he had been accompanying the project manager, making a snagging list of work still to be carried out. Just as they had opened the door and walked-in, the picture had fallen off the wall – he couldn't help but notice it. Recently he'd seen a copy in a local gallery and had bought it as a first wedding anniversary present.

'A pity we didn't get an invite,' Elaine mused.

'The story was that their romantic vault only holds up to eighteen people. Anyway, she hates us both. Even if there were three thousand guests, we still wouldn't be on the list.'

'Never mind, babe, I'll make up for your disappointment.'

She slipped under the quilt beside him, her hand deliberately brushing slowly against his groin. They kissed then started on their breakfast. He grabbed the half-open, half-flat bottle of Bollinger champagne beside the bed and topped-up their flutes, still sitting on the bedside cabinets from the previous evening. Gareth had given up certain luxuries from his previous opulent lifestyle – but he saw champagne as a necessity, not an extravagance.

After breakfast her head disappeared under the bedding and he could feel her tongue gradually creeping down his body, slowly writhing its way over his chest and downwards until he began to gasp: he had never felt more alive. It was nearly an hour later by the time they were finally ready to dress, shower and look to the day ahead.

'So, what was this lavish breakfast all about, today?'

'My way of thanking my wonderful husband for his latest present,' she smiled, thinking of the new red Mazda MX5 sports car that he had just given her for her fortieth birthday. Still mad about cars, she had always desired to have something a bit sporty and this certainly fitted the bill. It would go well with her ever-increasing collection of expensive jewellery and designer clothes – a far cry from her humble beginnings back in the day.

'You said something about going out in it later today?'

'Just to get a few things for our holiday – I need another pair of sunglasses and don't want to waste time in Spain looking for them.'

'Do you want me to come with you?'

'That's okay. You have the packing to finish. Anyway, I might find some new sexy underwear while I'm out and it will be no surprise if you see it before I have a chance to wear it!'

Gareth started to become aroused just at the thought of it – Elaine certainly knew how to turn him on.

'Well, I need to tidy up the garden a bit, too – the front lawn needs mowing.'

'Oh, while you're at it, that back gutter is still overflowing – last week it was pouring down over one of the security lights.'

'Yeah, I was going to do that – there's supposed to be heavy rain again next week. Is there anything else, madam?'

'Did you check with the taxi company for tomorrow morning?'

'Yes, I got a text early this morning.'

'I thought that was from your handler.' She still made jokes like that.

'You know that you are the only handler for me!' He enjoyed the banter.

It was a hot, sunny August day as Gareth watched his wife driving off in her car. She was beaming away and happy. That, in turn, made him happy. *It's only the giving that makes you what you are,* he thought to himself.

Later, having finished the lawn he decided to attend to some of the other outstanding jobs. The problem with his new lifestyle was that he didn't have a couple of gardeners as in his previous home so had to contend with some of the tedium of mundane time-wasting jobs. One of the regular chores included getting rid of moss which rapidly accumulated on the roof due to the large overhanging oak trees shading the house over the summer months. Heavy rain shifted clumps down into the gutter, blocking the drainpipes. Gareth's neighbour was always complaining about the water gushing over and running into his garden – he wished he had the time to worry about such insignificances in life. However, on this occasion Gareth decided to show willing – especially as he was giving his neighbour the key to the house while he was away on holiday.

Gareth was scraping away, thinking about his vacation – this time tomorrow he'd be on a plane heading for the sun, the sea and the nightlife; staying in Elaine's apartment in Marbella. As he stretched out just a little further to grab another handful of moss, he seemed to upset the balance of the ladder. A shadow passed across the sun as he held on to the guttering, trying to prevent himself toppling sideways: but too late. There was a sudden, wrenching movement as the ladder quickly gathered momentum; Gareth unable to stop himself from falling. He looked for somewhere safe to land, but all he could see was the ground racing towards him with concrete patio slabs fast approaching. He jumped to avoid the impact.

Chapter 17

Bob Bennett, was a reformed character.

Now aged forty-nine he'd decided it was about time he settled-down after an adventurous and often unglamorous life which had so far often featured the police, prisons, homelessness and insecurity. He'd finally handed himself-in at Chichester Police Station after the Aldwick Bay beach chalet fire. Then, back at Ford Open Prison, he'd had another six-month stretch added on to the sentence as punishment for absconding. During that time, he had finally persevered in kicking his long-term addiction for booze: the tyranny of the bottle had masqueraded as safety and belonging for too long. Bob had finally plucked up the courage to admit that he actually needed help. After that, bent on no longer driving himself towards an early grave, he had resolved to do something purposeful with his life before it was too late. However, he was still a work in progress after reaching such low depths and it would take a lot of determination to change. For the first time in years, he was seriously considering taking a job and working for a living.

With the help of a set of forged documents, testimonials and references – courtesy of an old lag who owed him a favour – Bob had turned-up shortly before Christmas at the four-star Crawthorne Hall Hotel, nestled in the heart of the ancient and semi-natural Wartling Woodland near Hailsham, East Sussex. With no money to his name, he'd managed to blag some decent second-hand clothes from the Salvation Army hostel in Eastbourne where he'd stayed for a couple of nights. He had always heard that the *Sally Army* were keen to help break the cycle of homelessness so, when he heard that one of the staff was going on a routine trip to collect left-over food from hotels in the area, he'd asked to hop onboard the van. At every stop, armed with his fake credentials, he'd asked whether there were any vacancies for casual workers in the run-up to the festive season. Having had a shower, a shave and a clean change of clothes, he looked the part: an experienced hotel worker seeking a steady job.

As soon as he'd set-eyes on the Grade II listed Crawthorne Hall, a luxury country house hotel with its olde-worlde sense of charm set in sixty acres of glorious parkland & gardens, Bob knew that this was where he wanted to be – for the moment. He had a sharp memory and remembered his old cell mate Paul Marsh telling him about this place – he had often wondered about Crawthorne Hall – did Paul really grow up here, son of the head gardener? Or was it all just a pack of lies? You could never trust a jailbird.

The van swept along a tree-lined avenue full of redwoods which seemed to march towards the distant Magham Down. Then all at once the magnificent Elizabethan country house appeared; its full beauty slowly revealed as they drove through the avenue of trees that framed the approach. Next, they'd stopped outside the main entrance. By this time, Bob had expressed his interest in finding employment so, instead of the usual ritual of taking the tradesman's entrance round the back, the Salvation Army driver, whose name was Keith, had boldly suggested going straight to the reception area to enquire about vacancies.

Once inside, Bob was immediately taken aback by the elegance of the palatial entrance hall: floor to ceiling walnut panelling sweeping up a magnificent staircase creating a kind of splendour and warmth – it almost brought tears to Bob's eyes as he thought about his privileged upbringing, his grammar school education and the prospect of a successful career in engineering: that is, before he'd thrown it all away as a result of his obsession with fire-raising – something that he would definitely keep quiet about if he wanted any chance of landing a job. No hotel would want to employ a known ex-con and arsonist.

'Hello Amy.' Keith addressed a smartly dressed young woman in her early twenties. She wore a black trouser suit with white blouse. Bob was immediately struck by her spools of beautiful, shiny blonde hair which spilled around her shoulders and back. In his life as a prison inmate and on the road as a beggar, vagabond and homeless man, he could only ever dream of being so close to a soft, warm woman like this with her intoxicating smell of fragrant soap and subtle perfume. It brought-out the carnal instincts harboured for so long within his being. He found her very charming and alluring, instantly longing to push her up against a wall then and there.

'Chef should have something for you round the back as usual, Keith. Just drive round.' She had a voice like an angel with a lovely lilt – he couldn't quite make out the accent – but it was posh – somewhere from the home counties – maybe Surrey?

'This is Bob. I thought I'd stop by with him on the off-chance. He's been staying with us at the Lifehouse hostel in Eastbourne and is looking for a job. He has excellent references and a wealth of experience in hospitality.'

'Hi, Bob.' She looked-up with her lovely deep-brown eyes which seemed to smile at him.

'Hi.' Bob put-on his politest grammar school voice. 'I'd be very interested to know whether you do indeed have any vacancies.'

Amy was surprised at his refined mode of speaking – it was an asset for hotel workers to be able to talk to guests with good enunciation – so many of the staff were from abroad with English as a second language – the hotel needed some balance when it came to two-way communications. First impressions were so important in the hotel trade and Bob had certainly passed the first test as far as she was concerned.

'Well, Bob, we do actually have vacancies and, if you can wait for ten-minutes I'll try to locate one of our team – to have a chat with you.'

'Thank you so much.' Bob smiled, trying not to reveal too much of his yellow teeth or stinking breath.

Maybe if you wait outside – go and enjoy the sunshine – I need a quick word with Keith.'

Bob withdrew like a lamb going out to frolic in a meadow – he had a spring in his step – mainly because he'd instantly become infatuated with this creature behind the reception desk. She picked-up the phone and punched-in a number as Bob walked through to the outside.

Sauntering down the main entrance steps and breathing in the sweet fresh air he thought about how different all this was to his miserable existence in prisons over the years. This really felt like freedom: quite a contrast to the fear and intimidation of life behind bars with its dank, smoky stench of incarceration. He'd always hated that. *If I'm lucky enough to get a job here, I'm never going back to that life*, he promised himself.

'Well Keith. What do you have to say? Do you know anything about Bob – apart from him being homeless and down on his luck?'

'All I can tell you is that he appeared on our radar a couple of months ago – he'd been travelling from place to place – had spent the summer over in the Kent region. He's obviously well-educated – tells me he had a bad experience as a child and could never settle down to a career when he left school. He seems to be a fairly gentle, harmless guy.'

Just then somebody answered Amy's call. 'Hello. Charles? ... Someone's just walked through the door looking for a job. How do you fancy doing an informal interview ... about ten minutes? Okay I'll see you in ten.' She replaced the receiver.

'Hey Keith. You probably heard that. I've got a colleague coming along to meet Bob.'

'Great news! Thanks Amy.' Keith was animated by the thought of having helped a homeless man take his first steps back into employment: even being granted an interview was a positive achievement.

'Our interviews usually take the form of a fifteen to twenty-minute chat for casual workers. Can you stay that long?' she added.

'Of course – especially if you make it worth my while – by finding him a job!'

'That will be up to my colleague.'

'By the way, I think Bob likes you – I think you dazzled him with your stunning good looks and lovely personality.' He said this with sincerity – there was no hint of sarcasm. After all, Amy was a very attractive young woman – in many ways.

'Flattery will get you everywhere,' she joked.

After completing a successful interview Charles had welcomed Bob with open arms. Stuck away in the middle of nowhere it was hard to find enough staff – especially in the run-up to the busiest time of year. With a promise of a regular basic wage, living accommodation and occasional tips Bob was given a three-month trial. Ironically, he was well-used to trials – but more of the County Court variety after being convicted for arson on several occasions during his adult life. As for hotel employment, the nearest he'd got to that line of work was a spell in a prison kitchen and enjoying the hospitality of Her Majesty during his times in the clink.

*

Now nine months into his job, Bob had settled remarkably well. He had a natural innate intelligence, enabling him to be adaptable and versatile, turning his hands to most tasks, quick to learn new skills. He was employed as a general casual worker: sometimes based in the kitchen, helping with hotel housekeeping; even starting to master the etiquettes of silver service waiting in the dining rooms. He had undergone rudimentary training, including the mandatory health and safety aspects of the job.

Although Bob enjoyed the variety of it all, the part that he loved most of all was helping-out in the kitchen with the *flambé* cooking – and the occasional winter barbeque. After his spells of incarceration over the years, he also liked servicing the bedrooms – cleaning-up after the guests and preparing rooms for new inmates (as he liked to think of them) – only nowadays, it was he, Bob, who had access to the door keys.

Often, after clearing-up the mess, he would take black sacks full of rubbish to the burning area, which was to the side of the hotel in one corner of the kitchen gardens. He would sort-out the flammable from the recycling waste and then, finally to his personal pièce de resistance: start a fire, watching with great relish and huge satisfaction as a flame would grow, taking on a life of its own, devouring everything around it. He was happier than he had been for years. Bob Bennett, the arsonist back to doing what only he knew how to do best.

Chapter 18

The funeral took place on the second Tuesday of October.

Frances P. Grangewood was in her early fifties, short brown hair and slight in build. She had a ruddy complexion and a cheery disposition: an asset in her chosen career in the funeral business. Her husband, George, ran his own family firm *Grangewood and Sons Funeral Directors* in which she was responsible for the financial side of affairs. However, from time to time she helped with the more practical aspects of the trade – sometimes acting as pollinctor, preparing the corpses ready for their journey onwards to their final resting places.

On this occasion she had taken a call from the celebrant who was due to perform the obsequies at today's cremation service. He was supposed to be officiating at the early morning slot. It was the funeral of a middle-aged man – a tragic death, by all accounts. The celebrant was running a high temperature and regretted he was in no fit state to carry out his duties: he asked if she could step in for him? She said she would: she owed him a favour. Besides which, it was easy money.

Standing outside the crematorium chapel Frances watched as mourners fluttered together like blackened butterflies on a sunless day. She hated this place, especially at this time of year; bleak and unwelcoming. A large fountain nearby sputtered away with its icy coldness giving no comfort to weepers nearby. A stubborn grey mist lurked over the well-manicured lawns which lay divided by trees, shrubberies and plant borders, shrouding the place in gloom and despair. Chilled, she checked her watch again. Good, the funeral cortege should be here in ten minutes.

As Frances waited, she listened to the comments of the gathered throng. She had heard most of these sentiments a thousand times before.

'He was such a lovely person,' a middle-aged woman was talking to a frail elderly woman aged about eighty.

'It was a real tragedy for him to die at such a young age. We'll miss him greatly,' was the reply. Frances guessed that this might be the mother of the deceased.

'His death was a shock to the whole family,' muttered an old man.

'We know who to blame,' added the elderly woman with bitterness, almost to herself. There were a few nods from two younger people standing close to her.

'Just as his career had taken-off again – such a pity,' said one. Frances guessed this was probably a distant relative or a colleague?

'I went to school with him – I'd known him for most of my life,' commented the other. This one was obvious.

There were other snatches of conversation, too, drifting over from huddles of mourners.

'He hadn't been married long to his new wife – a real shame that it was all cut short.' A well-dressed woman in a smart dark grey suit was addressing a younger man.

'Apparently the surgeon said he was brain dead,' replied her companion.

However, it wasn't just the conversations that always fascinated Frances: it was the body language, too. She sensed an air of animosity about the place today. There appeared to be factions at play – individuals averting their eyes from those they didn't wish to acknowledge; groups turned away from others. The tension amongst the mourners was tangible and real.

Just then there was a muted hush as the sleek, black hearse, followed by a single solitary limousine, appeared through the pillared gateway. Frances' eldest son appeared, attired in a morning suit, top hat held by his side as he walked solemnly up the slope with the cortege following behind.

Two huge, bald-headed men wearing smart dark suits and sunglasses stood amongst the guests. They were accompanying a diminutive figure dressed in black, also wearing sun glasses. In his sixties with long greying hair and matching beard, he could have easily been judged by the casual passer-by as an insignificant and non-descript person, blending-in with the crowd. This perception suited him as it was far from the truth. Although standing at a little under five feet and three inches this lean, mean little man wielded a giant influence within the criminal enclaves in the South of England and in parts of Europe. A tactician of remarkable skill and a deal-maker extraordinaire when it came to organising drugs deals and providing arms in exchange for diamonds, he was also the main man behind the muscle power needed to keep his foot soldiers in-line. Mad Ronnie Howell, still wanted by the police, had come a long way over the past few years.

Ronnie watched as a single door at the back of the limousine was opened for her. She emerged dressed in her black widow's weeds, her long hair hanging like a veil, moving in the wispy breeze. At her request, Ronnie had come along – not to pay his respects for the deceased, but to demonstrate his support for *her,* one of his most loyal camp followers. This was an honour, indeed: that he had spared his valuable time to attend the funeral. He knew that her late husband's relatives harboured deep feelings of hate and disgust towards her, the black cloistered widow, now following the coffin into the crematorium chapel.

Elaine had found him, splayed-out like a rag doll, thick red liquid seeping out of a wound, he'd barely been alive. Gareth had fallen from a ladder straight on to concrete patio slabs, head cracking open like an oversized coconut as it took the force of the impact. The paramedics had rushed him to St. Richard's Hospital in Chichester where he'd remained in a critical condition for five weeks – that is, until Elaine took it upon herself to have the life support machine turned-off. The family had not been consulted.

By the time the funeral took place, there was tangible ill-feeling, animosity and festering resentfulness towards Gareth's widow. This was exacerbated by her dramatic, theatrical arrival emerging as a solitary figure from a shiny black limousine, wearing black veil, black sunglasses – everything black apart from her signature red stilettos.

After the committal service Gareth's father, looking frail but still with his full head of hair and greying moustache, approached his daughter-in-law outside in the crematorium as the mourners paused to look at the swathes of flowers from well-wishers which had been placed by the chapel wall.

'I hope you're happy with yourself.' His tone was bitter with sarcasm; his words acting to fan bitter antagonisms into flames.

'What do you mean?' Elaine rounded on him.

'You know very well – you didn't tell us that he'd had an accident – and you didn't bother consulting with the family before you had the life support machine turned-off – how can you live with yourself?' He could barely keep the anger out of his voice. Both he and his wife were distraught at the demise of their favourite son, Gareth, blaming their scheming, conniving bitch of a daughter-in-law for wrecking his first marriage to Alma, and then being instrumental in his death. In their minds, Elaine was shrouded in suspicion although they were unable to substantiate their misgivings towards her. For them, there were no good days – only bad days as they struggled in the bleakness of their grief.

By this time their raised tones had drawn attention to the scene playing out next to the garden of rest. Others had shuffled nearer, including Gareth's mother. She had a look of disgust on her face.

'And what are *you* gawping at?' spat-out Elaine full of indignation and fury, addressing her mother-in-law.

'There's no need to be rude,' Mr. Evans pitched-in, defending his wife.

'I'm not prepared to joust with you,' Elaine replied, shouting loudly at her in-laws. 'Like you, I'm going through a horrible time,' she added convincingly. 'I don't need anyone telling me what I did wrong.'

Was this contrition? Mr. Evans doubted that very much. 'I know who you are,' he said ambiguously.

'And what's that supposed to mean?' She took a step towards her father-in-law, fearless. '*Never* give an opinion to me about *anything* again. Got it?' She pointed her forefinger angrily in his face as she spoke, then turning around she walked-off in the direction of the car park.

'Why does she have to be vile like that?' her mother-in-law muttered, almost to herself.

'She's despicable,' Mr. Evans voiced loudly as Elaine, accompanied by her friend Zoe, stepped into a beat-up mini 1000 and sped-off in the direction of Bognor Regis. Ronnie Howell and his two minders followed at a discrete distance behind them on their way to the ironically-named *The Good Knight's Rest* pub. It was a run-down establishment located right next to a noisy road near the centre of the town. A pneumatic drill was busy at work, repairing the highway outside the pub as they arrived.

When Ronnie and his henchmen arrived, they were aware of low background music – mostly drowned-out by the sound of laughter. At first, Ronnie thought it was a hen-do.

'Have you heard the one about the three nuns?' It was Elaine – sounding far from heartbroken over the loss of her husband.

'Which one?'

'The one about three nuns who have to answer a question before they're allowed into heaven.'

Ronnie moved towards the sound of the voices which cackled away – it sounded to him like a coven of witches at work rather than a funeral wake.

'Who was the first man on Earth?' Peter asked.
'Oh, that's an easy one,' the first nun said, 'It was Adam of course!'
'Music chimed, the gates opened and the first nun entered heaven.'

The group had now quietened-down as they listened to Elaine who, like her deceased husband, had always revelled in being the centre of attention. Ronnie noticed that there were four women and one man enjoying the revelries – he remembered seeing them at the funeral. Elaine continued, speaking in a loud voice, a large glass of pink gin in one hand.

'Who was the first woman on Earth?' Peter asked the second nun.
'Oh, that's an easy one,' she said. 'It was Eve of course!'
'Music chimed, the gates opened and the second nun entered heaven.'
'Finally, the third nun stood before Peter.'
'What was the first thing Eve said to Adam?' Peter asked her.
'Oh, that's a hard one,' she said.
'Music chimed, the gates opened and the third nun entered heaven.'

They all laughed – just as Ronnie finally made his appearance. He beckoned to Elaine, who followed him to a quiet corner of the bar.

'Discretion, Elaine. How many times have I told you?' There was a steely tone in his low voice. Instantly Elaine was cowed like a small puppy being admonished.

'Sorry Ronnie. I wasn't thinking.'

'You never do when you have an audience. You don't wanna go drawing attention to yourself, Elaine. Apart from anything else, that could put me in the spotlight – and I don't need the publicity. Got it?'

'Course. Sorry, babe.'

'Right, so keep it down – I need to know I can trust you. I done you a favour – came along to that miserable gathering of relatives. Now I'm gonna piss-off. I'll see you back at your gaff laters before I fly home.'

With that she re-joined the revellers, only this time there was hushed whispering by the small group. Ronnie, satisfied, nodded to his minders and all three exited the pub. Mad Ronnie Howell had more important matters to settle before his flight back to Amsterdam. It concerned the burial of a police informant under a motorway construction site. The victim was currently waiting in the boot of Ronnie's car ready to say his last goodbyes.

.

Chapter 19

Nervously she waited in the reception area of Crawthorne Hall Hotel, gazing around at the grandeur surrounding her. She was seated on one of the three thick, luxuriant sofas which were positioned around the flagstone fireplace, forming a semi-circle. Looking ahead, high above the fire mantle the chimney piece was adorned by a pair of mighty antlers and below that, a man, about the same age as her, engaged in a peculiar activity on such a warm spring day. He was lighting a fire.

'Hello, are you here for the interview?' He had a bright, cheerful demeanour and she took to him straight away.

'I'm here for the housekeeping job,' she replied, smiling, feeling a little less nervous now that she'd found someone to distract her. 'Can I ask you a question?'

'Ask away.'

'Why are you lighting a fire on such a warm day?'

'That's a good question,' he said teasingly. He didn't bother to explain further.

'Well?'

'Well, what?'

'The fire.'

He had struck a match and set-it against the crumpled newspaper covered in thin slivers of kindling wood which he'd been carefully arranging to maximise the draught. Immediately the flames grew, flickering and dancing as they took-hold. He added larger pieces of wood from the pile stacked beside the hearth.

He turned to look at her – an attractive middle-aged woman; long coral-brown hair, pale skinned – very thin as though undernourished.

'This old place can feel a bit damp – especially at this time of year when the main heating is turned down,' he explained. 'Look at the high ceiling.'

She glanced upwards at the void, punctuated only by a huge chandelier which seemed to be making rainbow colours dance across the ceiling.

'There's a lot of space to heat – and a lot of wood to burn. But once the fire's lit it gives a good, welcoming feel – makes a good first-impression on the guests – it's comforting and cheering – some might even say revivifying. Burning logs in the hearth massages the senses.'

'That all sounds very poetic, you obviously enjoy making a good fire,' she said.

If only you knew! he thought.

That was when their conversation came to an abrupt end as the approaching sound of footsteps echoing across the marble floor caused them both to look around.

'Hello. Penny Hawkins?'

She nodded. Bob re-focused his attention on lighting the fire.

'I'm Amy Hughes – one of the managers.' She looked at the middle-aged man who was still nursing the fire. 'I see you've met Bob. If you'd like to come with me, we can have a chat about the job.'

Penny rose from the comfortable settee and followed Amy towards a door which lay to one side of the reception desk with its green granite top.

'Good luck,' Bob called over to her and she turned, smiling briefly at him before disappearing into the office where Amy tended to conduct her interviews for this grade of job.

'So, why are you interested in working here?' Amy came straight to the point as soon as they had sat down.

'A friend recommended it to me.'

'Would that be Mr. Gareth Evans – the one who has given you a glowing personal testimonial?' She looked at the application form in her hand.

'Yes.'

'Sorry to hear of his death. I understand he headed the building company which refurbished the hotel. However, I didn't know him personally.'

'It was his funeral yesterday. He and his first wife Alma were close friends – before I divorced my husband and moved away.'

Penny was, to some extent a walking cliché: her husband had cheated on her after twenty years of marriage and, with a good solicitor, had cleaned her out financially. She had survived by taking on domestic jobs and working in a nursing home but had run into debt. She'd decided to rent out her house and take a live-in job for the foreseeable future until she was back on her feet again.

'And what skills can you offer us here at Crawthorne Hall?' Amy continued.

'Well, as you can see from my application form, I have worked in a residential home for the elderly – that's involved cleaning, bed-making, ironing, laundry, helping with meals – really almost anything you can imagine in that setting,' replied Penny brightly.

'I know that it can be very demanding in a care home environment. Do you enjoy that sort of work?' asked Amy smiling encouragingly.

'I'm quite happy with it,' answered Penny without hesitation. 'I was a stay-at-home mum for years and didn't ever have a chance to train for anything else! Although I have a basic food hygiene certificate.'

'That's good. I can tick that off my list of questions!' commented Amy. She paused and then added, 'Would you be prepared to train – for instance silver-service waiting?'

'Yes. I'd like to broaden my repertoire.'

'Tell me more about yourself, Penny.'

After the interview Amy suggested that Penny might like to take a look around while she discussed a few details with the general manager. They agreed to meet-up thirty minutes later. So, Penny decided to go exploring; firstly heading out for some fresh air. She took a pathway which skirted one side of the lakeside, snaking around little copses with trees still dormant. Being springtime, daffodils were already scattered about the lakeside, poking their heads up here and there beside grassy knolls and wild areas bursting with new growth. She paused for a moment, realising that her movement had disturbed something out near the middle of the lake: then she caught sight of a heron as it rose with the slow methodical beating of its wings. Swans had begun to nest nearer to the edge, untidy piles of twigs, branches and bulrushes being jealously guarded by the large birds. There were many ducks, too, which started following her progress along the trail, hoping to cadge food.

Penny emerged from the pathway on the eastern side of the hotel. She paused for a moment with a shiver and tightened her coat. She had a feeling almost as though she was being watched – which would be very likely as there were many guest bedrooms looking out on this side of the hotel with its view over the water. Coming to the kitchen gardens as she rounded the corner, she watched two of the hotel's gardeners gathering brussels sprouts, cabbages and savoys. Amy had earlier explained to her that it was part of the hotel's mission to grow their own food organically as far as possible. She carried on along a pathway, past a burning area at one corner with its accumulation of grey, powdery ash; then a number of fruit trees – plum, pear and apple – before eventually finding a side entrance beside an outdoor swimming pool. Looking at her watch, she realised that time was running out and so she wended her way through a maze of downstairs corridors, up and down sets of steps, past an oak panelled dining room – until she eventually found herself back in the reception area.

This time there was no sign of the man called Bob. As she sat back on the same settee, Penny, flushed with adrenaline, gazed around her, now more relaxed than before. She noticed the carefully arranged flowers on a mahogany pedestal table adjacent to the fireplace – far enough away not to be disturbed by the heat which had built-up. Amongst the mixed blooms were a number of beautiful pink lilies: perfect shades to complement the woody hues of the panelled walls. Stepping over to admire them she could see that their stamens had been pulled to prevent the pollen disturbing the perfect sheen of the table. She really hoped that she could work here where such close attention was paid to detail.

She felt that the interview had gone well – particularly when she spoke about how she liked meeting new people. Oddly, Amy had mentioned Gareth Evans again at that point, asking about the interviewee's connection with him. Penny told her about how she and her then-husband had first met Gareth and Alma Evans as members of an exclusive dining club in Chichester some years previously. Amy seemed impressed that Penny had an informed idea of fine dining from first-hand experience. At the end of the interview Penny had been asked whether she had any questions. There was only one.

'It's important to me that I have live-in accommodation.' She had already outlined her personal circumstances and Amy seemed genuinely sympathetic with her plight. 'Can you please confirm whether or not you could offer this?'

'I'll see what I can do,' Amy had replied. Unbeknown to Penny, this was one of the reasons why it had been necessary to speak to Colin Howard, the General Manager, as he had to be in agreement to any member of staff being appointed who wished to include living accommodation in their contract.

After waiting for another ten minutes, Amy's footsteps came echoing back across the marble floor. Strutting over to where Penny sat, she looked straight-faced at first – but this soon changed into a kind, warm smile before she uttered the words that Penny had been hoping to hear.

'Well, you're in luck. One of our foreign workers has just returned to France – so yes, we do have a room. I've just checked with my senior manager. Sorry about the delay but he was dealing with a booking. Anyway, the good news is that we'd like to offer you the job plus room.'

'That's wonderful! Thank you so much.'

'Do I take that as a yes?'

'Yes, Thank you again.'

'The job will be at the rate advertised – but there are plenty of opportunities to work overtime. We'll obviously make a deduction for your accommodation – I'll go through all of that with you.'

'Thank you. I'll look forward to working here.'

'I'll get someone to show you around and then when you come back to me, we'll arrange a starting date.'

About an hour later Penny was just getting into her battered old Fiat when a lanky man approached her from the other side of the car park – he seemed to be dragging his feet behind him on the gravel.

'Did you get the job then?'

'Yes. I'm starting next week.'

'Congratulations. I'll see you again, then. By the way, what's your name?'

'I'm Penny … Penny Hawkins.'

'Nice to meet you,' he said in a friendly fashion. 'I'm Bob Bennett.'

Chapter 20

Everyone has a dark side – some of us are better at hiding it than others …

Elaine was still on-course to fulfil her dream of becoming a millionaire by the time she retired – whenever that might be. Looking at her, it would be easy for the casual observer to think this woman was a little crazy to have such dreams – here she was, just a plain, pudgy, non-descript character drably dressed, who hobbled around – often using a stick or even crutches at times to get around. Most people in passing her in the street wouldn't give her so much as a second glance. If they did, then they might feel sorry for her – but it was all a ruse, a smokescreen which hid the real person behind the façade that was Elaine Evans. In reality she was a very rich woman. She had hit the jackpot twice before and was now waiting for her latest pay-out, which would make it a hat-trick – leading to that elusive million.

One of Elaine's problems was that she had no sincerity when it came to relationships with regular guys like Gareth. She enjoyed the initial intrigue; the chase and excitement. She genuinely liked the physical side of sex, taking pleasure from men and what they could do to her – especially with their tongues … but after a while the initial excitement would start to dull and she'd look for new thrills. Besides, Gareth had served his purpose – him with his flashy Aston Martin when they had first met. Elaine's emotions were on no ordinary plane: she either loved or loathed. It hadn't taken her long to realise that Gareth was really a loser and that she wasn't in love with him. Maybe it had just been a trick of the light – a moment which had passed and gone.

Her only one constant lover through the years had been Ronnie. Although small in stature, he was a tough cookie who oozed power, which she found to be a great aphrodisiac. They had first met in an Edinburgh pub when she had been in her early twenties.

He'd been sitting in a corner with a group of hard-men talking in low voices. Some kind of meet – they had all gone their separate ways when he'd seen her sitting alone on a barstool. He'd assumed, rightly, that she was there on the pick-up.

'Hello, can I get you a drink?'

89

'I'm drinking gin – they have sixty-two varieties in here. You can surprise me.'

He joined her, taking up the empty barstool next to hers, signalling to the bartender.

'Another malt whisky for me and one of your specialist gins. What do you recommend?'

'We've got several specials tonight. How about our *cactus and lime gin?*'

Elaine nodded and the drinks were served.

'Anyway, I'm Ronnie. Are you waiting for someone?'

'That's a very leading question, Ronnie. I could say that I'm waiting for my nine-foot boyfriend – or I could say that I'm on my ownsome waiting for someone to pick me up – but that wouldn't be true on either count. By the way, I'm Elaine.'

'Hi Elaine.' He held his hand out and they shook. His touch was warm and slightly lingering.

'So, what brings you here?'

'The truth is that I've just moved to the area to be near my boyfriend – he's in Saughton Prison.' She watched him carefully – he didn't appear to want to back-off. She liked that.'

'What's he in for?'

'What makes you think he's a prisoner?'

'I'm a mind reader.'

'He was careless with a pair of scissors.' Elaine took a sip of her gin – it was good – very good.

'Silly boy.' Ronnie had a deep growly voice – it reminded her of a grizzly bear.

'Very.' She decided to change the subject. 'Anyway, are you local?'

'Me? Depends what you call *local*. I'm working over this way for a while.' He gave no more away

Within an hour of meeting, they were back at her place – a tiny bedsit with damp and mould creeping up the walls.

'No. Not yet,' she'd teased pulling his shirt over his head and pushing him hard onto the bed. He sank down into the mattress with Elaine falling gracefully on the bed next to him, then straddling his hips. He'd made to sit up, but she pushed him back down.

'I'm in control.' She'd spoken like a strict schoolmistress, slightly smug, telling-off a recalcitrant pupil. 'So, you be a good boy and don't move your hands. I'm gonna drive you crazy, then stop, then do it all over again until you beg me to finish this.'

Ronnie had found this talk very arousing. Even in his younger days he had always been a control freak, always leader of the gang: he was used to snapping his fingers and having lackeys jump to his every whim. It made a refreshing change to just lay back and be pleasured by a woman like this.

'I'm just gonna do every naughty thing to you,' she continued, 'until your mind and body explode.'

That was just the beginning.

Now, twenty years later, Ronnie was lounging around on Elaine's sofa in her living room. They were in the house which she'd inherited from her recently deceased husband Gareth. An hour earlier they'd arrived back from Marbella. As Ronnie headed to the kitchen to fetch himself another beer from the fridge, Elaine, came down the stairs with a smirk on her face.

'Clench those buttocks, Ronnie!' she laughed as he disappeared out of sight. Although he was a nasty, murdering bastard, Ronnie Howell had always had a soft spot for Elaine and allowed her to tease him like this. Very few people were able to talk to him in this manner.

Just then, there was a loud rapping of the front door knocker. She went to see who was there. Sauntering over into the hallway she could make out the shapes of two men standing on the other side of the glass-panelled door, which she inched open. A large-framed man in his mid-forties with thinning brown hair spoke first.

'Hello, Mrs Evans, I'm Detective Sergeant Tom Crompton,' he announced flashing a warrant card. 'And this is …'

Elaine contemplated slamming the door in their faces but, instead, decided to brave it out.

'Don't bother, I know who you are,' she said, looking at his companion. 'I remember you from before. You're DC Cheema.' Elaine had a good memory – he was the dark, handsome police officer who had interviewed her … and consoled her … after she had found Gareth splayed out on the patio; an upset ladder to one side of him and blood spewing out from a gash in his head.

'How are you?' asked DC Mac Cheema.'

'I've been better.'

'Haven't we all,' commented DS Crompton. 'May we come in?'

She showed them through to the lounge where they seated themselves.

'I have to be blunt Mrs Evans,' began DS Crompton without any preamble. 'We understand that a few weeks before your husband's fall from the ladder, you took out a life assurance policy for two hundred thousand pounds – with double indemnity. Is that correct?' He looked directly at her, relaxed and purposeful.

Elaine was taken-aback and started reddening – she had been quite unprepared for such a question. Instantly concerned that it could be the thin end of the wedge, with more searching questions to come, she decided that attack was better than defence in this situation.

'What happened to sensitive policing? I've recently lost my husband – I'm still grieving and you start asking me about insurance policies. No wonder people hate you.' She spoke in a tongue-in-cheek, cocky manner: jokey with a tinge of seriousness.

'Please answer the question Mrs. Evans.'

'Well, yes, I did. But I don't understand why you're asking me this?'

Ronnie, loitering in the kitchen finally emerged, joining Elaine and the two policemen. She had assumed that he'd have slipped out of the back door as soon as he realised that it was the police – after all, he was still at large – a wanted man. However, he was confident of his disguise – the long grey-haired wig and glasses for a start. He was never going to hide his small stature so was content to front-it-out. Besides, the passport he was currently carrying identified him by one of his aliases – it was a good enough forgery to fool the Filth.

'This is Martin, a family friend,' Elaine muttered by way of an introduction, gesturing fleetingly with her hand. Ronnie came to stand by her side.

'I see you've just come back from holiday,' mentioned the detective sergeant, scanning the two cases, lids open, at one side of the room – their debris of sun-cream, swimwear, dirty underwear sprawled-out alongside sachets of hotel coffee, soaps, shampoos: it was all a dead giveaway which even a rookie cop would spot immediately. In the case of DS Crompton, he was a veteran with a long list of criminal convictions to his name – he had only just started smelling-out the bare bones of Elaine Evans and already he could sense that something was amiss – he had a nose for these things – he had already done some groundwork and was aware that Mrs Evans had history.

'I have an apartment in Marbella. I needed a break after all the trauma with Gareth my late husband – and the funeral. Is that a crime?'

'And you accompanied Mrs Evans?' he asked, eyeballing Ronnie.

'She needed some company.'

I bet she did, thought DC Mac Cheema.

'While we're on the subject, is that the apartment that you inherited from your late husband, Callum McFinn?'

'So, what if it is?' she replied stroppily.

'The same husband who died six years ago after falling from a ladder when you were living in Edinburgh?'

'Yes, it is. I still have nightmares about it – the way I found him.'

Her face became etched with confusion; the words strangled by a sob as she spoke. Elaine was wondering what she was going to say to wriggle-out of this situation – away from the insinuations that were being made about her part in the death of Callum. She decided to take a more subdued approach as it was obvious that the police knew more than she had at first realised; now bringing her first deceased husband into the line of questioning. So, she adopted a sad façade: desolate-looking eyes prickling with tears; sighing deeply and miserably with painful memories.

Ronnie, of course, knew all about her first husband – it had been him who had first put the idea into Elaine's head – the plan to net nearly half a million pounds through his unfortunate accident – only it hadn't been an accident. Ronnie started to shift uneasily, unconsciously moving slightly away from Elaine as she stood, still facing the detectives. There was a pause before DS Tom Crompton dropped his last bombshell for today.

'Can you confirm that a few weeks before the death of your former husband Callum McFinn, you took out a life assurance policy for two hundred thousand pounds – with double indemnity in the case of accidental death – and that you subsequently made a successful claim for four hundred thousand pounds?'

The look on Elaine's face said it all. It reminded Crompton of the time he'd found his young son stealing biscuits from the top shelf of the larder at home – totally caught on the hop, guilt written all over his face. He'd seen that look many times and decided not to pursue this any more for the time being – he had more fish to fry and criminals to bring to rights – a whole case-load. Elaine Evans could wait for another day and give him a chance to build-up a profile on her – he also had further discussions scheduled with the insurance fraud investigators before finally interviewing this fine lady in more appropriate surroundings – meaning the local *nick*.

'Thank you for your time Mrs Evans.' He nodded at Ronnie. 'I'll leave you two to finish your unpacking. We'll be in touch.'

The two policemen moved towards the front door, DC Cheema opening it on his way out followed by Crompton. Before leaving, the detective sergeant turned one last time towards Elaine. He had a serious, no-nonsense expression on his face.

'May I request, Mrs Evans, that you do not leave the country. If you have need to stay away from home overnight, we must have your contact details.' He proffered his official card. 'This has my mobile and landline numbers and the address of the police station if you need to get in touch.'

'And how do I get in touch with the Independent Office for Police Conduct to make a complaint about harassment of a recently widowed member of the public?' Setting aside her grieving widow persona, Elaine could not resist the opportunity to goad the police.

He ignored her underlying jibe and just answered the question. 'The normal procedure is to contact the police station either in person, by phone or on our website – there's a form which may be completed. All the details are on the card that I've given you.'

'And if I don't trust my local police station – say, they were trying to fit-me-up for something I hadn't done?' She was still on the offensive.

Still keeping a professional distance and not taking the bait – her insinuation that somehow, he was conspiring with other officers against her, he simply answered the question once again.

'You can contact the Independent Office for Police Conduct direct – they have a website on which you can complete an online form – but I need to tell you that the form will be forwarded to the local police station in the first instance.'

'Then, you'll be hearing from me, Mr. Detective Sergeant Tom Crompton.' She spat-out the words bitterly and with disdain, taking-on the persona of someone who had been gravely wronged and offended by these heavy-handed Nazi police with their blackbelts in intimidation.

'And you, Mrs Evans, will definitely be hearing from us. We will be in touch.' He was unphased as he headed towards the unmarked police car waiting at the side of the road.

Chapter 21

'Is there anyone there?'

The remnants of the hen party – six young women in their mid-twenties – were seated at one end of the bespoke Jacobean-style solid oak table designed to seat up to twelve guests. The oak-panelled Baronial Room was also home to a genuine seventeenth century oak dresser with two cupboard doors at the centre with intricate carved floral decorations and carved panels at either side flanked by turned columns.

After the drunken frivolities of the evening, half of the guests had staggered back to their shared rooms, crashing-out with heads spinning, now ready to sleep-off the effects of the alcohol until morning. Penny was on duty in the privately hired dining room and now sat patiently in a recess at the other end of the room, unnoticed by the six hotel guests. It was her responsibility to clear-up after the partying and to then lock the Baronial Room for the night – there were too many valuable items to risk leaving the door unsecured.

Above the door, a deer's head looked out blankly across the room at the six women. In one corner near to where Penny was secreted, stood a full-sized replica medieval suit of armour complete with helmet, shield and sword. Two of the guests sat with their backs to an antique Gothic style sandstone arch fireplace with carved columns, which was set on a grey-stone hearth. Bob had not lit the fire this evening as the heat would have been too intense for those sitting close. Instead, a fake electric fire with flickering flames had been placed there – just to give the room some atmosphere. It was all tastefully arranged and didn't detract from the ambience of the surroundings. However, even though the central heating was full-on, there was a certain chill about the Baronial Room – a penetrating draught which had persisted throughout the meal and the hens' merriment; especially when the door was opened to bring in more food and take away used dishes.

Above the table, suspended from the ceiling by chains was a gothic-themed wrought-iron circular ceiling fitting with seven candle-lights. The room had an intentional subdued gloominess about it which enhanced the authentic atmosphere which the hotel had tried to recreate. Wrought iron wall lights together with lit candles strategically placed on the table lent a certain romantic element to the occasion.

'I know.' Freya, looking around at her gloomy surroundings had an idea – a fun way of finishing-off their evening. 'Why don't we have a séance?' Freya was the best friend of Esther, bride-to-be. They were sharing Room 13.

'What do we do then?' Tamila, holding a bottle of prosecco in one hand wasn't really bothered with any of it but would happily join in if someone told her what to do.

'We need some paper or card and a wine glass,' Freya announced. Her family sometimes played this as a party game: she knew how it worked. Carole found some card which was left over from one of their earlier silly games of daring. They tore it into small squares about the size of beer mats; then wrote the letters of the alphabet on twenty-six pieces and spread them in a circle around their end of the table. Then, using ten smaller pieces, she numbered them from nought to ten and arranged them in a line.

Rita and Tamila sat on one side with their backs to the fireplace; Freya, Carole and Brianna sat opposite with Esther, the bride-to-be, at the head of the table. Penny, still sitting patiently in the little recess looked at her watch and hoped that this wouldn't take too long – she was tired and just wanted to get back to her room – and bed.

'So, continued the knowledgeable Freya, this is called a Ouija board.'

She then added two larger pieces of paper, one at each end with the words YES and NO.

Before long, all six friends sitting at the table each had a finger placed on top of the inverted wine glass.

'Boring,' slurred Carole, much the worst for drink.' How long have we got to sit like this? I'm hungry – how about sending out for a pizza?'

'Shut up,' Esther scolded. 'Give Freya a chance.'

'Everyone quiet now,' Freya continued.

Suddenly there was a tremendous sneeze from Brianna and everyone laughed. It was difficult to take this seriously after the amount of alcohol consumed that evening. Penny stayed still, quietly listening to the goings-on. She'd never seen anything like this before and thought it was all a load of nonsense. However, she soon noticed a shift in the mood and everyone had become more subdued. Penny had surreptitiously poked her head around the corner by now, her interest piqued. It was at this point that the glass seemed to twitch. Probably someone pushing it hard, she guessed.

'Is there anyone there?' Freya called. The glass twitched again.

Esther was scrutinising the glass, unsure what to make of this game. She decided to play along. 'Is there anyone there?' she called out, repeating Freya's words.

Carole started to laugh and then suddenly stopped as the glass, slowly at first, began moving, then gaining momentum, heading towards the YES sign at one end of the table. All six fingers were still on top going along with it. Penny wondered what would have transpired if it had headed to NO instead: she was convinced that one or more of the guests were pushing the glass along. Maybe it was staged – a set-up previously organised to give the bride-to-be a fright?

'What is your name?' commanded Freya.

The glass spelled out L-U-C-K-Y.

'Is your name Lucky?' Freya was confused, wondering whether the spirit had heard the question correctly.

Y-E-S

Freya was still not convinced: it sounded like the name of a dog or a cat. If so, surely, an animal, even in the spirit world, would be unable to talk – or to spell? It was all very bizarre. Perhaps the other hens were rigging the game after all? However, she decided to persist.

'Can we ask you a question?'

Y-E-S.

'What is my job?' Esther called out with a furtive giggle and a sliding glance through her veil of hair at her best friend Freya.

The glass hardly paused as it spelled out N-U-R-S-E.

It was the correct answer. Freya gave a half-smile, still wondering whether her friends were steering the glass to give the correct answers. Glancing around, the other hens seemed genuinely impressed, taking it all more seriously now.

'Can you name a country that Tamila has visited?' Brianna joined in.

J-A-M-A-I-C-A came back the answer from the glass.

'Where did you live when you were alive?' asked Rita, assuming that he was talking to a spirit.

E-N-G-L-A-N-D was spelt out.

'How many husbands will I have?' Esther asked.

O-N-E came from the letters touched by the glass. Esther smiled.

They carried on asking these kinds of questions for about fifteen minutes. The room was chilling as night drew in and Penny was beginning to feel cold huddled in the shadows. By now, she dared not move for fear of frightening the women – they still had not realised that a member of staff was secreted in the recess at the other end of the room.

'How did you die?' Rita pitched-in.

'*You're not supposed to ask those sorts of questions – it upsets the spirits,*' whispered Freya. But it was too late. There was a pause and then the glass started circling around wildly. It stopped for a moment before resuming its previous pace, heading towards the letter 'S' and then 'H'.

'*What does sh... mean?*' Esther whispered, puzzled. But then the glass started moving again, slowly at first, indicating the letter 'O' followed by 'T'.

'Were you shot?' Freya ventured, thinking of his name 'Lucky' – an inap:ronym, if ever there was one.

'Again, the glass started going into a frenzy. Penny looked-on, shocked, unbelieving. There was no way that these young women were faking this – they would not be able to control such violent movements of the upturned wine glass. Then it suddenly stopped.

Esther was a little frightened by now and decided to change the subject, asking a question that she was anxious to have answered. 'How many children will I have?' she glanced at Freya and they both smiled, intrigued to find out what the spirit was going to say.

There was another pause from the glass, longer than last time and then it started moving slowly but forcefully to three of the letters closest to where Esther was sitting. It spelt the word D-I-E.

Esther went ashen and pulled her finger away as if she had just burnt it on a hot pan. Freya followed suit and then the others. The glass remained on the table, inanimate, next to Esther who had suddenly sobered-up and looked petrified. She decided that she didn't enjoy this game and wanted to go back to their room. It was at that point that Carole decided to puke-up, over the now-disturbed cards on the table. She headed for the door, in-need of a shower and bed: the others soon followed leaving their mess in their wake.

Penny picked-up the internal phone and made a call. It was answered immediately.

'Hi, Bob. It's Penny.'

'Hi. How can I help?' Bob was lounging on the top of his bed in the staff quarters – he was finding it difficult to sleep. He kept thinking about his old prison-mate Paul Marsh. Sometimes he had nightmares about the way he had found Paul hanged in their shared cell.

'Sorry to waken you.'

'I wasn't asleep.'

'That hen party – they've left the Baronial Room in a real mess – I could do with some help – there's vomit everywhere.'

'Five minutes and I'll be there. Don't worry, we'll soon have it cleared-up.'

Passing along the back of the hotel, Bob Bennett paused by the huge, overgrown Bramley apple tree at one corner of the kitchen garden. Deep in thought, he shook his head before continuing on through a side door and into the Baronial Room.

Chapter 22

He was sitting on a low armchair in one corner of the room; a used breakfast tray in front with crumbs sprayed around – a slick of butter smeared to one side of a small plate, remnants of marmalade adhering to the edge of a silver-plated knife.

There was a gentle knock on the door. Then the brass handle turned and it opened inwards. An attractive middle-aged woman stepped into the room and she smiled.

'Good morning, sir. You asked for your room to be made-up?'

'Yes. I'm going to be based in here all morning and this lot needs tidying-up – so you can work around me.'

'Very well, sir.'

It was normal practice to keep the doors open while servicing the rooms but Penny had been told to treat this guest with kid-gloves. He had already made a number of complaints and demands since his arrival the previous afternoon. He was a critical old man, a fault-finder. Unfortunately, he had been given Room 13 – there always seemed to be problems associated with this particular suite with its little annexed sitting area and luxury bathroom with jacuzzi. Beautifully furnished and designed, Room 13 had cost nearly two hundred thousand pounds to fit-out with its antiques, bespoke wallpaper and unique accessories. However, it was surprising just how many guests shied away from staying the night in this luxurious, spacious corner of the hotel. It was mostly about superstition – who would want a room with such an unlucky number?

As a result, there was an element of self-fulfilling prophesy at play whenever Room 13 was inhabited. Over time, due to lack of occupancy little faults and problems had a habit of developing and growing in the absence of regular room servicing. After checking-in earlier, the single male guest had walked-in to find a leaking radiator drenching one corner of carpet beside a window. Then, once that had been fixed, he'd discovered that the thermostat wasn't working properly. The third complaint was about two lightbulbs that needed replacing.

On this occasion, the occupant had deliberately asked to stay in Room 13 – just for old times' sakes. Lord George Edward Crawthorne, 15th Baron

Crawthorne, had not been back to his former home since he had sold the estate to the hotel consortium. He had come to see his grandson, Charles Eden and, although living only sixty miles away, had decided to stay the night. He had fond memories of this particular bedroom as he had often used it to entertain the ladies in his younger days. Being in the East wing, it was far enough away from Isabela's prying eyes and he could be assured of some modicum of privacy. He had even brought his long-term mistress Sheila to this room right at the beginning of their relationship. It was here that they had shared their secret.

Of course, Room 13 had notoriety in its own right – starting with that old legend concerning his predecessor, the 3rd Baron Crawthorne and the alleged murder of his illegitimate baby in Elizabethan times – it was rumoured that the mother of the child had been his own sister. Then there was a whole list of goings-on which had supposedly happened in this room – debauchery, wild parties, high-stakes – and even murder. George Crawthorne had always thought that most of the stories were nonsense – embellished over the ages to frighten any would-be listeners by the light of a fire on a cold winter's evening. The stories of ghosts, too – George had never believed in such things. But he supposed that it all came with the territory – every old house was haunted with memories anyway.

Lord Crawthorne was feeling randy. Lying in the four-poster bed that night, he had whiled away time looking at the Klimpt painting which had been mounted on the opposite wall: it had been driving him wild with desire. The painting depicted an embracing couple kneeling in a grassy patch of wildflowers as they made love. George regretted that he hadn't arranged for a little female company that night. He wasn't sure whether this was something that the hotel concierge might have arranged for him – at a price. Nevertheless, it was too late now – or was it? Still sitting in the chair and dressed only in his black towelled bathrobe he looked up and gave a shark-like smile as the chambermaid moved the empty tray.

'Thank you.' He placed his laptop on the table, booting it up. Then he attended to a small beige canvas bag, opening it and taking-out a wodge of banknotes which he started to sort. The woman, long dark hair, skinny, aged in her forties, started to make-up the bed.

'Would you like me to tidy the top of your bedside cabinet, sir?' Penny called over to the white-haired gent: he reminded her of a shrivelled prune sunken back in the chair inside his gown. She was referring to the array of magazines and papers scattered on the surface beside the bed – she was wary that disturbing them might invite yet another complaint from their guest.

'No that's okay, I'm in the middle of working on those.'

'Sure.' She continued with her work.

He watched her as she worked. Black-uniformed with white apron. Hair tied-back – probably thirty years younger than him. She had a fresh lemony smell about her, intoxicating to his senses. He imagined her whimpering in pleasure, giving herself to him.

'So, what makes an attractive woman like you work on such low wages in a place like this?'

She felt a tingle of discomfort at the question – it was a tad inappropriate – but she didn't wish to be rude to him.

'I like working here – and it pays the bills,' she replied, finishing with the bed and moving on to tidy the sitting-area.

George liked the way she talked – a soft, well-spoken voice – he thought it was sexy. He had an inkling that the chambermaid was flattered by his interest in her. Penny, now polishing an antique art nouveau statue of a woman, caught dust in her eye. George, still gazing over at her imagined that she'd just winked at him. Looking down at her black-stockinged legs he felt stirrings in his groin. She was certainly a very tantalising woman and he decided to carry-on with the banter, trying his luck.

'The trouble with the hospitality industry is that it's so badly paid. I should know. My grandson works here and he earns a pittance.'

'Who's your grandson?'

'Charles Eden. Do you know him?'

'Yes, he's one of the managers.' She'd stopped dusting and scrutinized the hotel guest – so this was Charles' grandfather, the lecherous Lord Crawthorne. His reputation as a womaniser had gone before him.

'See this money?' He held up a wodge of notes.

'Yes.'

'There's a thousand pounds here. I know a way that you could earn this much in ten minutes – and easy work at that.'

She didn't like the sound of this but, somehow, she found herself lulled into asking the question that he was expecting of her.

'How?' As soon as the word was out of her mouth, she regretted it.

'Drop your knickers and it's yours!' He said it in a jokey way, but she knew he meant it. He was asking for sex. Penny felt a sense of panic rise up in a spiral through her body, up to her brain. Her face reddened and she just knew that she needed to get out of this room, away from this horrible man as soon as she could.

She started towards the door.

'I could say that I caught you stealing my wallet while I was in the bathroom. You could lose your job. I'm a powerful and respectable citizen. Who do you think they'd believe, a hotel maid or a peer of the realm? All I'm asking for is ten minutes of your time and the money's all yours. Is it a deal?'

She stopped by the door. 'I can't let you blackmail me.'

Lord Crawthorne was well-known for his persistence – he never easily took *no* for an answer – particularly when it involved sex. He'd tried playing Mr. Nice Guy. It was time to put-on some real pressure so, quickly moving over to the door where she was starting to turn the handle, he placed a hand on her shoulder.

'Now listen to me you silly little bitch, I've made you a fair offer,' he sneered showing the cruel, meaner side of his nature.

She shrugged-off the hand, pulled the door open and burst out into the corridor where she found Bob Bennett in the middle of emptying bins into a large black sack. Lord Crawthorne stood at the open door of Room 13, a smirk on his face – he'd found the whole episode amusing.

'Hi Penny. Is there any rubbish to collect from that room?'

'There's plenty of rubbish in there, Bob, but I don't think you have a black sack big enough for it!'

She sped-off, looking distraught, heading towards the stairs, the door of Room 13 now closed. Bob, realising that his friend was distressed about something, rushed after her, finally finding her sobbing in a corner of the hotel kitchen.

Penny looked up as he came through the door.

'Are you stalking me?' she just wanted to be alone at this moment.

'It's a valid hobby,' he replied facetiously with misplaced humour.

'That's not funny Bob – not after what I've just had to endure from Charles Eden's grandfather: the filthy old pervert.'

'Sorry, I was just trying to cheer you up. Here', he said, handing her a mug. 'I've made you some tea.'

Bob spent the next fifteen minutes listening to Penny. She was now shaking.

'I feel like I've just jumped out of the fireplace into an empty grate,' she told him. 'I mean – where's the support mechanism when incidents like this happen? What did I do wrong, Bob? I didn't intentionally encourage him. And what would have happened if he'd stopped me getting out of Room 13?'

'I can't answer that, Penny. However, I think you need to hear something – none of this is your fault.'

'Well, what should I do?'

'To start with, we must tell someone. I'll go with you.'

'What about my work – I haven't finished the rooms.'

'Don't worry about that. I'll take you along to Amy. She'll know what to do. Then I'll finish your work for you.'

She started crying again. 'Thanks so much, Bob, I'm glad I've got a friend like you.'

'That's what mates are for!'

Chapter 23

They watched each other like dogs at the start of a fight.

George Crawthorne, the 15th Baron Crawthorne, with no compunction, embarrassment or shame, was now sitting in an upholstered red velvet chair opposite Colin Howard, General Manager of the hotel.

'Thank you for coming along to my office Lord Crawthorne. I'll come straight to the point. There has been a formal complaint about you from one of our employees.'

'Oh?' replied George feigning innocence. 'I'm not aware of upsetting anyone – unless it was felt that I'd been a bit rude about the state of my room when I arrived: Room 13. The radiator had leaked water in one of the corners – then the thermostat was faulty – and two of the lightbulbs needed replacing. Mr. Howard, for a four-star hotel charging four hundred pounds a night, that is not good enough – and you know it. Besides which, I had been specifically looking forward to staying in that room as it holds so many fond memories for me. It was one of my favourite rooms when my father owned the house. So, yes, maybe I was cross and probably upset one of your staff. If that's the case, then I'm sorry.'

'No, Lord Crawthorne, it's on another matter.' He knew very well that George was perfectly aware of what he was talking about. This was, indeed one very crafty and canny old man.

'Well, it has been alleged that you propositioned the chamber maid.'

'What! How dare you say that!' he replied, full of bluster and outrage. 'I suggest, Mr. Howard, that you choose your words carefully – this is slanderous talk.' He gave the general manager a fixed stare, his bulging eyes full of anger and fury at such an accusation.

Colin Howard looked back at this old decrepit creature with his scraggy tortoise neck, loose and wrinkled. He was not intimidated in the presence of a lord of the realm.

'Then, do you deny that you offered one of our chambermaids a thousand pounds for sex – and then tried to blackmail her?'

'Oh, that!' George laughed dismissively, casting an amused, contemptuous glance at Colin Howard. 'That was a joke. We were talking about low wages in the hospitality industry.' He hesitated for a moment.

'Please – go on, Lord Crawthorne,' Colin was aware that the old man was now scratching around in his head trying to come up with a plausible story.

'Thinking of footballers and other such high earners,' George began cautiously, 'I remember saying that some people can earn a thousand pounds for just ten minutes' work. Then I said *I bet you could find a way of earning that kind of money, too.* I was trying to be encouraging to the nice young lady. I'm sorry if she took it the wrong way.'

A slippery customer indeed, is our Lord Crawthorne, thought Colin, looking intently at George.

'I know the member of staff well,' he said. 'She is a reliable and truthful employee and would not have put-in a complaint unless she was convinced that she had been wronged.' *Unlike you, mate – a very unreliable witness if ever there was one,* he thought.

'I think you'll find it was me who was wronged. I came out of the bathroom and found her with my wallet in her hand. Don't forget that she has freely admitted that I had a large amount of cash on me – and she had also had a conversation with me about her low pay. It is me who should be reporting her to the police. But we are both men of the world – I'm sure that we don't want any more fuss over this. You could do without bad publicity – things like me going to the police; it leaking to the press – even the bad review I might give the hotel on breakadvisor.com.'

'All I can say Lord Crawthorne is that you are due to check-out of Room 13 by twelve noon. You are more than welcome to report anything you wish to the police, breakadvisor.com, or anyone else. However, please remember that we can also take action of our own – and our aggrieved member of staff could still decide to report her allegations to the police.'

'So, all said and done, what, out of interest would she hope to gain from doing that? Maybe they would come and give me a reprimand for telling her jokes!' Lord Crawthorne was arrogant and cocky in his manner, not appearing to take the situation seriously. He was secretly pleased with the results – a stalemate, he guessed.

Howard had no more time for this. 'I hope you have had a good stay, Lord Crawthorne. Thank you for coming to see me.'

He could have added that the old git would never be allowed to step forth into his hotel again. But he thought he'd save that for another day – perhaps for the next time that this nasty piece of work tried to make a booking – if he was stupid enough to try. For Colin Howard was unimpressed by the peer's behaviour towards a member of his staff. As far as he was concerned this was no longer the family home of the Crawthorne dynasty and they would be treated like any other paying guests – and expected to conduct themselves accordingly.

Once Lord Crawthorne had swaggered out of his office Colin phoned through to reception. It was time for him to have a sharp word with Charles Eden, one of the rising stars amongst his young managers. What on earth had possessed him to allow his grandfather to come and stay at Crawthorne Hall?

Chapter 24

'Look, what are you doing here Grandad?' Charles was furious.

They were standing together on the picturesque boathouse bridge looking back towards the hotel, framed by the giant redwoods.

'You mean here – at the hotel?'

'Yes, *you*, here at the hotel suddenly turning-up like a meteor in the sky.'

Charles was still recovering from the embarrassment of being hauled into the general manager's office and being severely reprimanded for his grandfather's appalling behaviour earlier that morning. He wanted to know what had possessed Lord Crawthorne to drive from Aldwick Bay in West Sussex – a mere sixty miles – just to stay the night, cause havoc and nearly have his grandson sacked for bringing his workplace into disrepute. Charles was innocent of any wrongdoing – he could not be responsible for his grandfather's behaviour, but nevertheless, it seemed that blame was being unfairly apportioned to him.

'Why did you come, Grandad?'

'Nice to see you, too,' Lord Crawthorne replied sarcastically.

They started walking along the part of the hotel grounds known as the Acer Glade, towards an arched bridge with a Japanese Maple tree beside it.

'I can't believe you've come such a short distance just to stay the night and then go home again!'

'Obviously I'm here to see you – you are my grandson – I'd go anywhere for you. You know that.' George wasn't going to tell Charles the real reason for his visit.

'Very flattering.' Charles had calmed-down a little.

They took a winding, narrow path which veered around to the right following a gentle incline up a rhododendron walk – but it was too early in the year for flowers.

'Look Charles, I thought I'd surprise you.'

'You certainly did that. It wasn't a very nice surprise – all those accusations about what went on in your room.'

'Maybe it's just an unlucky room after all – that Room 13,' joked George. 'Anyway, it all backfired – I hadn't realised you'd be working all those hours – this is the first time that we've actually had a chance to talk face-to-face. I wanted to know how you're getting on with your job.'

'Very well – until *you* decided to turn up. Now I'm not so sure.'

'So, what's your next move? You've been here for over eighteen months now. It doesn't do to stay too long in your early career.'

George Crawthorne and his grandson Charles were now on a path heading towards an old oak-framed summer house. They sat on a wrought iron garden bench near to an avenue of lime trees which led back towards the main hotel complex.

'Well, actually, I'm applying for a job on a cruise liner – hoping to start in May.'

'As what?'

'As a hotel manager.'

'Are there any career prospects in a job like that?' He said it with a strong air of pomposity.

'I've looked into it. After my first nine-month contract, I'd be eligible to apply to be a senior hotel manager. Then the next step after that would be Director of Hospitality.'

'And from there, Captain of the Fleet!' quipped Lord Crawthorne.

Charles didn't think this was very funny. His grandfather was definitely in a strange frame of mind – somehow, he didn't seem right. Perhaps he was having some sort of breakdown – but, no, not the invincible Lord Crawthorne. Surely? Or maybe it was true – all the rumours about how Room 13 affected people's minds.'

'I've got all the right qualifications for the job – and it will give me a chance to see something of the world. It all depends on how I get on with ship-life as I've never been to sea before.'

'I've heard that these cruise ships are like floating hotels. I'm sure you'll be fine Charles,' commented George Crawthorne more soberly. 'So long as you don't get lonely.'

'There's not much chance of that, Grandad. I meant to tell you, I've just got engaged – and she'll be coming with me.'

'Oh. This is news to me. Who's the lucky girl?' George Crawthorne gave his grandson a strange, cowled look. Charles felt a surge of panic for a moment, wondering whether his grandfather had propositioned his fiancé, Amy, as well as Penny during his stay at the hotel. However, he answered the question.

'Her name's Amy. She works here. I'd introduce you but she's gone sailing for the afternoon – a little later than she'd planned as she found herself dealing with an upset chambermaid this morning. You'll be long gone by the time she's back.' Charles knew that, after the alleged incident that morning there was no way that Amy would want to meet him anyway.

'Well, maybe another time.' George hesitated. 'Are you sure about this, Charles?'

'About what?'

'You're still young, with your life ahead of you. Do you really want to get tied-down at your age? Sometimes you have to not want what you want.'

It seemed that Lord Crawthorne was back in his strange mood.

'What on earth are you talking about Grandad. You're making no sense to me.'

'I'm just saying that it's easy to get carried away with our emotions – to fall for someone and assume she's *the one*. You should be playing the field at your age.'

'Really?' Charles was becoming weary of his self-opinionated grandfather. What business of his was it anyway?

'Yes, travelling the world and forging a career for yourself is a good idea – but it's too soon to be settling down. Some things are best left until the future. I'm sure you want her with all your heart – but sometimes you need to let your head rule your decisions.'

Lord Crawthorne always seemed to assume that he had a stake in how his family led their lives. He was well-known for trying to get his own way, never happy with 'no' as an answer. Charles no longer wanted to continue with this conversation.

'Look Grandad, I don't wish to be rude, but I think you should keep your nose out of my private life. I've told you what I'm doing – applying for a job on a cruise ship and travelling the world – along with my fiancé.'

'Then I hope you'll be very happy,' George said quietly.

They arrived back at the main hotel entrance just before noon – the official time for checking-out. As they'd walked back from the summer house, the mood had lightened considerably, with Lord Crawthorne talking about his new toy.

'It's called a Horizon Elegance 20. It's twenty metres long – an entry-level yacht. It certainly beats the old beach chalet – we still haven't had that rebuilt since the fire.'

'Where's the yacht moored?'

'In Chichester Marina. You must come and see us soon – we can go out on it.'

They had reached Lord Crawthorne's Range Rover: he'd thrown his overnight bag into the back of it shortly before going to speak with Colin Howard.

'Well, good to see you, Charles. Don't take what I said earlier too much to heart.'

'I won't.' Just then as they stood there, Charles remembered something that he had intended asking his grandfather. 'By the way, I wondered whether you could do me a favour?'

'Of course.' George Crawthorne brightened up at the prospect of being able to be of service to his grandson.

'There's a bloke working here at the hotel by the name of Bob Bennett. He claims to have known Crawthorne Hall's old gardener's son – Paul Marsh. Does that ring a bell?'

'I do remember Daniel Marsh and that he had a small son – they lived in the lodge.'

'Right. Well, apparently, Paul Marsh committed suicide, but shortly before his death he reportedly spoke of an alleged murder here at Crawthorne Hall. Sometime in the 1970s. Is there any truth in it, Grandad?'

'I heard rumours,' George replied, 'but your grandmother and I were living away in Hong Kong at the time. I have no idea of what went on at Crawthorne Hall while I was away.'

'What sort of rumours?'

'About an argument concerning cheating in a game of poker. Some people claimed to have heard a shot. I returned from Hong Kong in 1976 – about two years after it had supposedly happened. My father admitted firing a gun to frighten the man. Apparently, he drove off into the night and didn't come back to Crawthorne Hall after that.'

'Well, that's not what I've heard.'

'Come on, Charles, this is ancient history. Why bring this up now?'

'Because Bob Bennet was told that the man was shot dead – and possibly buried here in the grounds of Crawthorne Hall.'

'That's scandalous talk, Charles.'

'In a nutshell, he believes that there could be a body buried in the kitchen gardens – in fact he seems obsessed about it. Is there any way you could pull a few strings to persuade the owners to bring in a digger?'

'I don't think they'd listen to me, Charles. I'm not the most popular guest around here. I wouldn't be surprised if they try to stop me returning as a guest.'

'Quite understandable. I'm cross with you, Grandad – your behaviour was abysmal and you're lucky the police weren't brought in.

'Is that all. May I go now?' Lord Crawthorne felt that he had indulged his grandson for long enough.

'Just one last question, Grandad.'

'Well?'

'That poker player who was supposed to have been cheating – what was his name?'

'I don't know.' There was something cagey in his manner. Charles had a feeling that Lord Crawthorne knew more than he was letting-on. Penny Hawkins had been spooked by what she had witnessed in the Baronial Room the previous week and had told Bob everything that had happened. Bob Bennett, in turn, had passed this information on to Charles, hoping that he might be able to shed some light on whether there was any truth in the name that had come up in the Ouija session.

'Does the name Lucky mean anything to you?'

Lord Crawthorne momentarily jerked as though he had been stung by a bee. Then he quickly regained his composure.

'Sounds like a one-eyed cat to me – or even a dead cert for the Epsom Derby,' he joked. Then, clamping-up, he looked at his watch and quickly changed the subject.

'Look, it was good to see you Charles, but I must be orf. I have some House of Lords business to attend to on my way home.'

'See you sometime – before I go travelling around the world!' Charles replied. He didn't know what else he could say.

They shook hands. Then George Crawthorne pressed something into his grandson's hand.

'Just something to treat yourself – call it an engagement present if you like.' He slid into the car, then, engine purring, he slowly pulled away and disappeared down the long driveway.

Charles Eden, now somewhat relieved to see the back of his interfering grandfather, headed through the main door into the reception area wondering how long it would take to repair the damage caused by Lord Crawthorne's unwelcome visit to the hotel. He felt frustrated that his grandfather had tried to take control of his future aspirations, yet was not prepared to be more helpful and forthcoming over the matter that he had raised on Bob Bennett's behalf. There was an air of suspicion about how much his grandfather really knew on the matter of that poker session all those years ago. Why had he suddenly needed to rush-off like that?

As Charles walked into the little office behind the reception desk, he stopped to glance at the piece of paper which his grandfather, Lord Crawthorne had given him. It was a cheque for five thousand pounds.

Chapter 25

'Mrs Evans, I'd like you to tell me one more time about the death of your first husband, Callum McFinn.'

Elaine had now been in the police interview room for nearly an hour playing a cat-and-mouse game, with little progress being made. She had opted to be accompanied by the duty solicitor, Wendy Mason who was now sitting beside her. Facing Elaine was Detective Sergeant Tom Crompton alongside DC Cheema.

'As I told you earlier, I'd gone shopping.'

'On the afternoon of Saturday the fifth of July at around two o'clock.' Crompton read from his notes.

'Yes. And I got back at …'

'Around four o'clock …' he interrupted again.

'You know all this.'

'Please move on, detective. Remember that my client is here on a voluntary basis,' the duty solicitor chirped from the side, a supercilious expression on her face.

Elaine went on to explain about how she had been distraught at finding Callum, her wonderful husband, sprawled-out on the patio, the ladder from which he had toppled, now to one side, its upper-end embedded in the smashed greenhouse roof. She had rushed-over to his motionless body, blood puddled-around his head. Checking for signs of life, she'd found none. Then she'd called the emergency services.

'Is there anyone who could corroborate your version of events Mrs Evans?' This from Cheema.

'We didn't have much to do with the neighbours. The police at the time knocked on the doors of surrounding houses, but no-one had seen him fall. And no, I have no-one to corroborate anything. For goodness' sake – it was six years ago – I went through all this with the Edinburgh police at the time.'

Lucky for you, thought DS Crompton. He still had his deep suspicions about what had really played-out when Callum Mc Finn met his death.

'Then moving on, Mrs Evans. Your recent husband, Gareth. Where were you prior to finding him after his 'accident' on the ladder.'

'I'd been shopping – in Bognor Regis – we were going on holiday the next day and I needed a few things.'

'Please move on Sergeant,' urged Wendy Mason the duty solicitor – she had a date-night planned and needed to be out of here pronto, sometime during the next thirty minutes.'

'Continue, please, Mrs Evans.'

'When I got back – around three-thirty, I found Gareth on the patio.'

'He'd 'fallen' off the ladder? Just like Callum six years earlier? Quite a coincidence, I'd say.'

The solicitor whispered something in Elaine's ear.

'No comment,' Elaine piped-up, taking Wendy Mason's advice.

'Only this time, your husband was still alive – just.'

'No comment.'

In Elaine's mind she played-out the two scenarios – only this time she reflected on the true, unedited version of events. How, in both cases, she'd come up with the idea of gutter cleaning while she was out, knowing that her husbands were gagging to please her and would most likely to be doing her bidding. Deep-down, after suffering an abusive childhood, she secretly despised all men, using them for her own gains – even Ronnie Howell, her long-term lover. They were like toys to her, putty in her hands – she knew how to manipulate them, knowing that the vast majority of them seemed to keep their brains in their pants. What wouldn't a man do for gratification – whether it was to boost his ego or to feel good about his sexual prowess. To her, men were like little boys – but she was a dangerous babysitter.

On the two afternoons in question, parking discretely – a little way from home – she'd surreptitiously made her way back. Then striking lucky, she'd simply given the ladders a quick shove and a push, making herself scarce, then returning later in the car to find that tragedy had struck – twice.

She hadn't even bothered to change her MO – modus operandi – her method of operating. It was literally a copycat crime – why mend something if it ain't broke? It had worked the first time with her nice, but dim husband, Callum, so why not again? Perhaps, on reflection, this had been a tad stupid and naïve.

Her fleeting reflections were rudely interrupted as Detective Sergeant Crompton suddenly changed tack.

'I understand from your insurers Mrs Evans, that you received four hundred thousand pounds after the death of your first husband. Is that correct?'

Again, Wendy Mason whispered something in Elaine's ear.

'No comment,' Elaine piped-up, taking her solicitor's advice.

'And that you have submitted a claim for a further four hundred thousand pounds after the death of Gareth,' continued Tom Crompton. 'Is that correct?'

Once more, the duty solicitor whispered something into her client's ear.

Yet again, Elaine came up with the standard response.

'No comment.'

Detective Constable Cheema then took a turn. 'Also, as a result of the deaths of your husbands, you have inherited a holiday apartment in Marbella and have also inherited the house in Bognor Regis, in which you currently live. Is that correct?'

'No comment.'

'For the record, Mrs Evans,' added Crompton, piling-on the pressure, 'did you push either or both of your husbands from a ladder?'

'DS Crompton, that is out of order, tantamount to accusing my client of committing a crime for which there is no evidence. I think she has answered enough of your questions this afternoon,' Wendy Mason interjected. 'It is clear that you are just going over old ground and making unsubstantiated aspersions regarding my client's character. Enough is enough. Unless you wish to press charges, I'm advising my client to leave. Perhaps you need to remember that she is here purely on a voluntary basis.'

The two women made to get up. It was the moment that Crompton had been waiting for. As a veteran detective he always liked this bit – he enjoyed the drama of it all. Still sitting, he held his hand, gesturing for them to stop.

'Please remain seated, ladies.' This sounded patronising – just as it was intended to be. 'There is something that you need to know. We have a witness.'

Chapter 26

2013

Natasha Warnford had fallen pregnant and decided she didn't want Bruno anymore.

The little Staffordshire Terrier, previously badly-treated, had come from a dog rescue centre. She'd originally bought him to keep her company in her tiny apartment – and all had gone well for a year. Treated like an only child, Bruno had been lavished with her attention and in return he was gentle, affectionate and loyal to Natasha. However, the trouble started when she met Jed, with whom she became besotted.

Bruno didn't like having to compete for Natasha's attention and took an instant dislike to Jed, growling threateningly and snapping at her new partner whenever he was around. Worse still, the novelty of having a dog had worn-off: Natasha no longer wanted to spend time taking Bruno for walks or playing with him – all she wanted to do was to spend every spare moment with Jed. Then she found she was having a baby. The dog had to go – so she enlisted the help of the person in her life who always took care of her and her problems. She'd picked-up the phone and asked her dad to make the problem go away. She knew she could rely on him.

Albert Warnford had just returned home from the vet's after having Bruno put-down. As he pulled into his driveway, he spotted Lord Crawthorne sweeping-up leaves and decided to approach his next-door-neighbour about something which had been bothering him for some time. However, as usual, he'd started the conversation with a few pleasantries before revealing to George the real purpose of coming to speak to him.

'Hello, George. How are you?' He made to shake hands with Lord Crawthorne as though greeting a business partner.

'I'm fine. Just tidying-up out here,' replied George, stating the obvious. 'The gardener is on holiday.'

'I've just taken my daughter's dog to the vet,' continued Albert. He didn't mention that he'd just had Bruno killed. 'I stopped-off at the betting shop on my way back and got some really good tips for the three-thirty Cheltenham Gold Cup race next Friday. I can place a bet on for you if you like?'

Lord Crawthorne's ears pricked-up. He had been a professional gambler for a number of years after coming back from Hong Kong in the late1970s. 'What's the name of the horse?'

'*Big Girl's Blouse.*'

George tried to conceal his amusement. He knew the owner, Lord Grantby – the old nag was a rank outsider which should have been put-out to pasture two years ago. The word was that *Diamond Lady* with odds of nine to one, was worth considering. Lord George Crawthorne himself would, as usual, be making a trifecta bet – choosing which horses would come first, second and third. It was a high-risk gamble which demanded all his expertise and skill in predicting how the horses would finish the race.

Apart from dabbling in the horses, Albert Warnford claimed to have invented a system for predicting football results, betting regularly on the number of teams who would win, draw and lose each week, based on historical data for each team. He had all sorts of algorithms programmed into his computer and, amazingly, earned several thousand pounds a year through his method. However, it didn't stop there. He would make bets on the weather – will it snow on Christmas Day? Political events – how long will the Prime Minister stay in office? Anything of topical interest was fair game as far as Albert's betting habits were concerned. However, it was the horses that piqued his interest above all other forms of gambling and at that moment he relished the thought of placing a large amount of money on *Big Girl's Blouse* to win the Cheltenham Gold Cup: the pinnacle of the jump season.

'Thanks for the tip.' Lord Crawthorne smiled at his neighbour.

'I'm down to win twenty thousand pounds if my horse wins,' boasted Albert, who decided to go on to another subject before confronting George with the real reason for this little chat. 'By the way, how was your stay at your old home. Has Crawthorne Hall changed much since you lived there?'

'How did you know I'd been back there?' George was puzzled.

'Isabela mentioned it to Kathy. She said that your grandson works there – Charles Eden?'

'Ah!' George deliberately evaded answering the question.

'I've heard that it has a good reputation – so I'm taking Kathy there for our wedding anniversary in April. I'll let you know how we get on.'

George, accustomed to Albert's softening-up technique – his conversational pleasantries as a fore-runner to spitting-out some complaint or gripe, knew that it wouldn't be long before the blow was dealt. He could sense that it was coming.

'By the way,' began Albert.

Here we go again, thought George. *What's he going to moan about today?*

'I've been checking your fence and I see that two of your panels are five centimetres over my boundary.'

'Well, as you know, the fence was erected by the previous owner. Did you tell *him* about it?'

'I've only recently noticed it. Anyway, I'd like you to take it back so it's no longer impinging on my garden.'

'Does five centimetres really matter?'

'Yes, it does – to me. I don't want it on my land. And Lord Crawthorne?' Albert was deliberately reverting to addressing his neighbour in a formal manner.

'Yes?' George was almost speechless, still processing what he regarded as a ridiculous request.

'If you won't move your fence, then I will.' In a flash, his cordial mood had become serious and threatening. It was as though a switch had been flipped: he'd dropped the friendly façade, leaving only a snarling, miserable, unpleasant, humourless, long-faced, unsmiling dastard.

Chapter 27

'Over my dead body!' George and Isabela were relaxing on the L-shaped leather sofa in the saloon area of his Horizon Elegance 20 yacht, now moored in Chichester harbour. George was telling her about Albert's latest gripe.

'So, you mean that you're not going to move the fence. How un-neighbourly,' she said sarcastically.

'I really think that this could be the proverbial straw that breaks the camel's back,' he replied. 'I'll face him in court if necessary. No way am I having the garden fence moved! What nonsense!'

'So, you'll just ignore him?'

'For the time-being. I'm seeing my solicitor tomorrow over in Chichester anyway – I may mention it to him.'

'Are you seeing Jacobs?'

'Yes. Some business concerning Crawthorne Hall. Look, Isabela, can you remember when we moved back from Hong Kong in the late seventies and there were rumours circulating about my father shooting someone who had been cheating in a game of poker?'

'Of course. I think the police had been involved at some point.' Lady Crawthorne knew more than she was prepared to admit – she didn't see the sense in raking-up the past – it was in nobody's interest. So, she just shrugged and looked disinterested, waiting for her husband to say more.

'Well, Charles – now that he's working at Crawthorne Hall – has got it into his head to delve into the story. He seems to think he's a self-styled journalist – wants me to help.'

'How can you do that?'

'A chap who works with him claims that a body is buried in the kitchen gardens. He wants me to find a way of having it excavated. I have an idea – but need some legal advice first.'

They carried on talking for a while and then George retired to the master bedroom – they had decided to stay for the night. He was pleased that his wife had settled so well to the idea of spending some of their evenings on the yacht. She had been genuinely overcome with emotion when he'd renamed the Horizon Elegance *Isabela* in her honour. He hadn't mentioned that it was part of a ruse to literally get her onboard with the idea of sailing.

This boat was his insurance policy – a means of getting away quickly if necessary. He was soon planning to visit Amsterdam to let the firm know that he was retiring. It was possible that the announcement would not be welcome – Lord Crawthorne might need to disappear for a while in those circumstances until the heat died down.

Back in the saloon, Isabela's mobile phone was ringing. It was Charles.

'Hello, Grandma.'

'Hello, how's my favourite grandson?'

'Very well.'

'I hope your grandfather behaved himself when he was over at Crawthorne Hall Hotel last week?'

'Of course,' lied Charles. He didn't want to cause a problem between his grandparents.

'Sorry I couldn't come with him – I was up in London with your mother for the weekend – shopping. He says he was bored and decided to see you on the spur of the moment. Pity, I'd have liked to see the old place – after all, we did live there for many years.'

'Maybe another time, Grandma. Anyway, did he tell you that I got engaged?'

'Yes. When are you bringing her over? We'd love to meet her – I understand that she had gone sailing when George visited you.'

'That's right, he didn't get to meet her. I'll check my work rosters and get back to you. There's only one problem, though, Grandma. When Grandad came over, he seemed to disapprove of my decision to get engaged.'

'Look, Charles, you know full well that he can be very self-opinionated. You don't need to listen to anything he has to say – or anybody else for that matter when it comes to matters of the heart.' Charles warmed to her concerned tone – he found his grandmother reassuring. They had always had a close relationship.

'So, what's your advice, Grandma?'

'Look, Charles, I'll never cease to be amazed by the vagaries of human nature – no-one else in the world can tell you what you can or cannot do with your life. *That* is my advice. Whatever anyone says, you're free to do whatever you want. Something I've learnt through bitter experience, is to never turn your back on true love despite all the sacrifices and pain – and above all – look out for your own family.'

'Does that include you, Grandma?' They both laughed.

'Who is it?' George had just appeared from the master bedroom on his way to fetch a glass of water.

'I'll pass you to your grandfather. Remember to call when you have a date. Bye.' She handed her mobile over to her husband. 'It's Charles.'

'Hello, Charles. How are you?'

'Very well. Just catching-up with Grandma.'

'I've been doing a little bit of prodding since we last spoke – on the matter of commissioning a spot of digging over at Crawthorne Hall.' Lord Crawthorne was straight down to business with his grandson.

Charles was a little baffled, wondering what his grandfather was alluding to. He remained silent for a moment – then he suddenly realised that this must be about the proposed excavation of part of the hotel kitchen gardens. 'I was under the impression that you weren't seriously interested in helping me, Grandad?'

'Well, I mulled it over and decided that it might be a good idea to dispel all these rumours for once and for good. Our family name has been tarnished for too long on account of frivolous gossip. I want to lay this to rest so have made a few discrete enquiries amongst some of the hotel's board members. But that's as far as it's gone for now. I'll let you know if I get the green light on any of it.'

'Thanks for that.' Charles was slightly embarrassed – he had misjudged Lord Crawthorne assuming that his grandfather wasn't going to help him.

They carried on chatting for a while and Charles was made to promise once again to visit his grandparents as soon as both he and Amy were free. He was just about to end the call when Lord Crawthorne changed the subject.

'By the way, Charles, I heard from my next-door-neighbour today that he has booked to stay at Crawthorne Hall Hotel in April. I thought I'd just warn you!'

'Is that the ignoramus you were telling me about?'

'I won't say another word! I'll leave you to make your own judgements!'

'What's his name? I'm in the bookings office right now – I'll check the date when we're expecting him.'

'His name's Albert. Albert Warnford.'

There was a pause from the other end of the line while Charles checked the reservations list.

'Oh. I've found it. Twenty-Seventh of April for two nights. He's booked one of our superior rooms. Is there any particular reason why he's chosen to stay at our hotel?'

'Yes, he told me it's his wedding anniversary. But I expect he's also curious to see my old home!'

'Unfortunately, he booked late,' continued Charles from the other end of the line. 'So we gave him the last available suite for those two nights. He's staying in Room 13.'

Chapter 28

The net was fast closing-in around Elaine Evans née Reynolds – and she knew it.

Detective Inspector Angelia Wilmot sat in her office reading the latest email from the Criminal Prosecution Service, known as the CPS. To one side of her, a thick file lay open with neatly clipped-together papers spilling-out. She took her time before addressing the two police officers sitting at the other side of her desk. DS Tom Crompton and DC Mac Cheema were waiting to hear her verdict on the investigation so far.

'Well, there's good news and bad news,' DI Wilmot was telling them.

'Ma'am?' This from Crompton.

'The good news is that under the Fraud Act of 2006 we have more than enough evidence to convict her on the charges of defrauding the State over her benefit claims.' She handed-over a sheet of paper relating to this side of the investigation.

For years Elaine had been defrauding the State Benefits System. Since claiming a disability allowance some years ago while she was unemployed and almost destitute, she had carried-on hoodwinking the system – even though she had completely recovered from her medical problem. She'd contracted a rare disorder known as Guillain-Barre symdrome in which the immune system attacks the nerves in the body, eventually causing paralysis. In Elaine's case, she had been admitted into hospital as an emergency at the time. However, like the vast majority of people who suffer this condition, she was now capable of returning to an active and healthy lifestyle but had omitted to mention to the authorities that she was no longer disabled.

For the sake of appearances, Elaine usually remembered to carry a walking stick with her when she was out; she could often be seen limping around the neighbourhood where she lived, knowing that Social Services could be watching her every move. It was well-known that people suspected of defrauding this government agency were liable to be under surveillance – maybe even being filmed. Therefore she was careful – or so she thought.

Elaine was a good actress – but not quite oscar-winning material. She made mistakes: one of her most recent blunders was at Gareth's funeral when she'd forgotten her walking stick. So, playing the grieving widow, she'd limped out of the limousine when she'd first arrived and carried-off the deception convincingly enough. However, carried-away by the euphoria of the occasion once the coffin had disappeared at the end of the service, she'd emerged from the small chapel with a spring in her step. This had been noticed and there had been low-level mutterings and grumblings amongst a number of the mourners.

The Department for Work and Pensions had contacted Elaine to ask how she had paid for the funeral after she had tried making a claim towards the expenses. In truth, she'd used cash out of the huge A. W. Beasley safe which she kept in the kitchen larder of her house and which was bolted into the concrete floor. Elaine did not believe in using banks. Besides which, her benefit payments would soon stop if her fortune in used notes and jewellery was discovered.

However, unbeknown to Elaine, the Department for Work and Pensions fraud investigators had been tracking her for some time now. It was obvious that Mrs Elaine Evans, previously Elaine McFinn née Reynolds, was a rich lady who enjoyed a good lifestyle. She had recently upgraded her Mazda MX5 to a BMW Z4 sports car. That was when the police finally moved-in.

Crompton looked at the information detailing the charges, which included the fraudulent claiming of money from the Government through dishonesty, including failing to report a change in circumstances. This crime was known as fraud by false representation under Section 2 of the Act.

'We can bring her in and charge her for the benefits fraud,' continued DI Wilmot. 'She'll be bailed of course, but at least it will give us some control over her movements. I have a feeling that this is one very dangerous lady and we need to do everything we can to protect the public.'

'So why not just nick her for manslaughter – then she'd be put on remand out of harm's way?' Cheema ventured.

'Because, DC Cheema, as you well know, the Crown Prosecution Service would not be prepared to support us on the insufficient evidence that we have so far.'

'Ma'am, we need more resources – if this was a full-scale murder-hunt we'd have well over thirty officers on the team: we have only five – and one of those is a uniformed PC.'

'We're working with what we've got. There are much bigger fish to fry and more criminals to catch – the force is stretched to the limit – and we have no actual proof that Mrs Evans has actually committed a crime. That's for us to prove,' replied Wilmot curtly.

'But we all know she's as guilty as hell.'

'I don't need you to remind me, DS Crompton.' Then she paused before adding, 'Why don't you indulge me a little and recap on where we are, so far, on the case?'

The police love an interesting death and the detective inspector visibly settled back in her chair, hands folded over each other, as she listened to Crompton regaling her of some of the main facts in this case.

'Okay, Ma'am. We've checked with the police in Edinburgh and I've been to see where Callum McFinn – Elaine Evans's first husband – fell to his death from a ladder six years ago. There were no witnesses. DC Cheema and DC Walker have been making house-to-house enquiries at properties backing-on to the Evans' house in Bognor Regis. Still no witnesses. However, we've had a breakthrough. It appears that, badly injured as he was, Gareth Evans regained consciousness briefly on his admission to hospital just at the point of handover between the ambulance crew and the accident and emergency team.'

'And?'

'Gareth Evans allegedly said that Elaine had pushed the ladder.' He flipped through his notes. 'Yes, here it is. He told one of the hospital doctors that *she pushed me ... my wife ... Elaine ... pushed ... ladder.* Those are the last words that he ever uttered.'

'Did anyone else hear him say that?'

'Yes, one of the paramedics.'

'Look, Tom, you know that wouldn't hold up in court – any lawyer would say that Gareth had been delirious when he uttered those words. I think we should change tactics.'

The two men listened to what new ideas their senior officer was going to bring into the investigation.

'I want you to continue to look for witnesses – I'll put in a request with our Scottish counterparts to do the same. But I think we should hone-in more on circumstantial evidence now. I'll ask the Chief for manpower to sift through CCTV footage in the area of the Evans' house and in the shopping area between one o'clock and three thirty on the afternoon of Gareth's accident. It shouldn't be difficult to spot a bright red Mazda MX5 soft-top convertible coasting around on a hot sunny day with the lovely Elaine preening herself inside. Tom, I'll leave you to monitor progress.'

'What charges are we looking to work towards, boss?'

'I think the best way forward is to look for evidence under the Homicide Act of 1957 – conduct on Mrs Evans' part involving intentional harm resulting in death. But we have to place her at the scene if we are to hope for any chance of a prosecution – proving the times of her whereabouts that afternoon will be of the essence in taking this case forwards.'

'Okay, boss.'

'And Cheema.'

'Yes, Ma'am?'

'Assuming we get this to court, we'll need a report on the defendant's medical condition – her state of mind. She'd be bound to use her abusive childhood as a defence and we need to prove that she is perfectly rational and calculating. I want you to delve into this – see what you come up with.'

'Ma'am.' This from Cheema.

The meeting was almost finished. Tom Crompton and Mac Cheema were just getting up to leave when DI Angelia Wilmot reminded them of one outstanding task that she knew they were looking forward to undertaking.

'By the way,' she said. 'You need to know that I'll be concentrating on liaising with the insurance company fraud investigators – they're as keen as us to find evidence. They're still hanging on to their four hundred grand – and don't forget that Elaine Evans has already been paid that amount on her first husband's death. You never know – they may come up with something that we can use.'

'Anything else?'

'Yes. Before you get your teeth into proving an unlawful and dangerous act of manslaughter, remember that you have a little job to do on the matter of fraudulent claims under the 2006 Fraud Act.'

'Don't worry, Ma'am,' replied DS Crompton. 'We'll get on to it first thing in the morning. We'll look forward to nicking her won't we Mac?'

'It will be our pleasure.'

Chapter 29

'Fuck! Fuck! Fuck!' His face was taut with anger.

'What on Earth's wrong, Albert?' Kathy Warnford was losing patience with her husband.

This was supposed to have been a lovely, luxury break to celebrate their wedding anniversary but there had been nothing but problems since they had arrived at Crawthorne Hall Hotel two nights ago. She loved this Grade II listed hotel with its olde-worlde sense of charm set in sixty acres of glorious parkland and gardens. However, what had spoilt her anniversary break was the company that she kept – namely her cantankerous, whinging, complaining husband. She'd married a young, clever, handsome double-glazing salesman and forty-five years later she'd ended up with a self-centred domineering, tetchy old pensioner; now swearing his head-off as though it were all her fault.

Bob Bennett had first come across Albert two days earlier when he and Penny had walked down the country lane from the hotel to *Barkers*, the local general provisions store, which doubled as a post-office. She had a parcel to post for her son's birthday and Bob had decided to keep her company. They had become best friends – particularly after the incident with Lord Crawthorne in the bedroom – Penny now held great respect for her colleague and thought of him as a bit of a hero and protector.

Arriving at the shop they were surprised to find the front door boarded up with plywood and inside, the post office section was partitioned-off with plastic tape.

'Hello, can I help you?' The bored-looking young assistant looked-up as they entered.

'Yes, I'd like to post a parcel, please.' Amy pulled the package out of a white plastic bag.

'Sorry the post office section is closed – there was a break-in last night.'

Bob looked-over the counter and could see that the intruders had smashed a phone and the till had been prised-open. Red paint had been sprayed on the wall and over the CCTV monitoring camera.

'Was much taken?' His curiosity was aroused.

'Dunno. I usually work at our shop in Hellingly, but I'm standing-in for the owner for a few hours.' She gave no more of an explanation.

'Do you know when the post office is likely to re-open?' Penny was concerned about her parcel reaching her son in-time.

'Everyone's been asking the same question. Should be tomorrow.'

Penny picked-up a few toiletries – staff were not permitted to use those provided for hotel guests. She was just about to pay for them when a white-haired man in his seventies with a fierce look on his face suddenly burst through the shop door, pushing his way in front of Penny.

'Do you sell batteries? My bloody camera's packed-up?' He glared at the shop assistant.

'Yes. What sort do you want?'

'A packet of AA sized-ones.'

'Excuse me!' interrupted Bob, scowling hard at the old man.

'Do I *know* you?' The pensioner replied rudely, clearly dismissive of Bob.

'We were just being served when you barged in front of my friend,' Bob replied. He stood there with a lanky-legged slouch, eyeballing the intruder.

The young girl made no effort to intervene. The man ignored Bob.

'I'm talking to you,' Bob was becoming riled. 'I said that you pushed in.'

'Bugger-off,' answered the old man contemptuously.

'Leave it, Bob.' Penny didn't like scenes. She had a feeling that this ignorant customer might be a hotel guest: if so, it wouldn't be wise to get involved in an argument. She decided to defuse the situation.

'I've just remembered, I need a few more things, Bob, anyway.' She moved over to the other side of the shop grabbing hold of a packet of black tights and some hair ties.

'Sorry, we're out of AA batteries,' the sales assistant announced, continuing with serving the unpleasant man.

'Shit. Where can I get some?'

'Our shop in Hellingly may have some – about three miles away.'

As he stood there thinking about it his eyes settled on a stack of Lottery play slips. He grabbed one and filled-in some numbers.

'I'll have one of these.' Then he stepped over and grabbed a broadsheet newspaper. 'And this.'

'Anything else, sir?'

He grabbed two chocolate bars. Then paid and started exiting the shop, glaring at Bob on his way out.

Bob just shrugged.

Kathy Warnford had been waiting patiently in the car for her husband. They were on their way to Crawthorne Hall Hotel – it was nearly time to check-in.

'Did you manage to get your batteries?' she said amiably to her husband.

'No, I sodding didn't,' he answered abruptly looking at his watch. Then he handed-over one of the chocolate bars that he'd bought in the shop. 'Happy Anniversary.'

'Thanks,' Kathy replied. *At least he remembered this year,* she thought to herself – *although a card would have been nice.*

Her husband scowled as he drove the short distance along the lane to the luxury hotel. He was not in the best of moods.

Later-on that afternoon, Albert Warnford was sitting on one of the sofas near to the flagstone fireplace in the huge reception area of the hotel. He was reading his newspaper – annoyed that the hotel provided the same one free of charge to residents.

If only I'd known, I could have saved myself some money, he was thinking.

Kathy had gone swimming and they'd agreed to meet here before going into the lounge for afternoon tea. As Albert Warnford sat there, a tall, lanky man with a little beard appeared with a bundle of kindling wood and newspapers. He instantly recognised Bob as the person who had started to confront him in the shop earlier.

'You're not doing that right,' he called over.

'I beg your pardon, sir?'

'That's not the proper way to make-up a fire. You were obviously not in the boy scouts.'

Bob ignored the guest's comment. *The man's an idiot,* he thought. *If only he knew that he was talking to an ex-arsonist. If anyone knows how to light a fire, it's Bob Bennett.* He grinned to himself.

Albert Warnford saw the grin. 'So, you think that's funny? Wait till I complain to the management about your rudeness towards me in the shop this morning. That'll soon wipe that smirk off your face,' he spat-out nastily.

Bob was all-but ready to floor the cantankerous old git but, aware that it would mean instant dismissal and an assault charge, decided to retreat to the kitchen and come back later to finish laying the fire.

Two hours later, Charles was at the reception desk when he received a call complaining about the loudness of music in Room 13 which was disturbing guests in three adjacent rooms. He tried calling the Warnfords to ask them to turn-down the volume but there was no answer. So, this was the nightmare next-door neighbour that his grandad had warned him about. He was certainly living-up to his reputation.

Charles strolled up the main flight of stairs which led from the reception area. Moving along the corridor, the sounds from the old creaking and groaning floorboards underneath the plush carpeting, were swiftly drowned-out by the thumping of music as he approached Room 13. He knocked twice.

'Excuse me, this is the duty manager. May I come in?' He had his master key at the ready – it was always possible that there was a good explanation for the excessive noise – maybe some emergency situation? But he knew instinctively that he was making excuses for what he believed to be merely an inconsiderate guest. He'd seen it all before – the selfishness of people who didn't stop to think of others around them – other guests who had also paid good money for a relaxing break – not a holiday from hell.

The door opened just as Charles had been ready to push his key into the lock.

'Yes?' Albert Warnford, white haired and scowling stood there in his flannel dressing gown looking like an angry polar bear with a toothache. In his hand he held an opened packet of salted cashew nuts courtesy of Room 13's mini-bar. Tchaikovsky's 1812 Overture, arguably the loudest piece of classical music on Earth with its use of artillery in the percussion section, was still blaring-out full-blast.

'Excuse me. We've had complaints about the volume of your music. Can you please turn it down?' Charles was trying to shout over the noise.

'Wait a minute and I'll turn the music down – then I can hear what you're saying.' Albert, still chomping away at the cashew nuts, didn't realise the irony in his response to the duty manager's visit.

Charles repeated the message. He guessed that the old man would be unlikely to comply straight away – his dad had warned him about this awkward character.

'I've paid an extortionate amount for a two-night stay in this suite – are you telling me that I can't have my music on when I want?'

'Not at that volume, sir.' Charles remembered his grandfather, Lord Crawthorne, telling him that Albert Warnford was in the habit of regularly disturbing his neighbours in Aldwick Bay with loud music from his shed. He had another think coming if he thought he could get away with it here. The management would send him packing if he couldn't behave himself as the hotel had a zero-tolerance policy for anti-social behaviour by guests.

'I had to turn the music up loud anyway to drown the noise from that screaming baby next door.'

Charles was puzzled. 'I'm sorry, sir. What baby is that?'

'I told you. The one next door. Ever since we arrived it has been making a racket – crying its head-off.'

Both men paused and listened. There was no sound of a baby's cries.

'Maybe it's gone to sleep?' Albert Warnford suggested.

Nothing would go to sleep with the music at that volume, thought Charles. But he kept his own counsel. Instead, he said, 'I'm sorry Mr. Warnford, but there are no babies in this part of the building. The other rooms are occupied by elderly guests.'

'Are you saying I imagined it?' Just then Albert noticed the badge on the young manager's jacket which announced that he was CHARLES EDEN, FRONT OF HOUSE MANAGER.

'So, you're Lord Crawthorne's grandson.' He scrutinised Charles for a moment. 'Alright, I hear what you say – but I'm not happy about it. There is definitely a baby around somewhere and it's disturbing me – someone needs to sort it out – maybe I'll phone down to reception myself next time it starts-up with its wailing. I'm making a note of the feedback that I'm going to give the travel website when I get back home – and so far, your hotel has scored two stars out of five. I'll be looking for improved service and manners from your staff, Charles Eden. For a start, there's a faulty bulb in one of the lamps in our room. I'd like it fixed straight away – it should have been checked before we arrived. Also, it's very cold in here – even with the thermostat on MAX''

I'll send someone up right away, sir.' Charles didn't tell him that he had checked the room personally ahead of the arrival of Mr. Miserable. Everything had been in perfect working order at the time.

However, things had a habit of going wrong in Room 13 and he had a feeling that this would not be the last that he heard from Albert Warnford during his romantic wedding anniversary stay at Crawthorne Hall.

Chapter 30

Albert and Kathy had spent the following morning relaxing in the nearby elegant seaside resort of Eastbourne. After strolling along the wide promenade fronting a stretch of the quintessentially British shingle beach, they then headed down the nineteenth century pier where they stopped for lunch. It was a pleasant, sunny day and Kathy had at last begun to enjoy their little anniversary break – her husband seemed to be in a better frame of mind.

Afterwards, passing an Indian take-away restaurant Albert suddenly had an idea for making their occasion special later that evening.

'You remember that super holiday we had in India when we were newly married, Kath?' She nodded. 'How about having an Indian meal tonight with all the works?'

'I don't think the hotel's likely to have Indian food on the menu.'

'Then we can order it in. What do you say?'

Kathy wasn't at all keen. She had come away for some pampering and had been looking forward to having a nice meal in the dining room with silver service. Throughout her marriage she had always been the skivvy to Albert – cooking, serving, clearing-up all his meals while he sat reading his newspaper or mowing the lawn. She felt that on her wedding anniversary it was a rare opportunity for someone to wait on her for a change. However, Kathy knew that if she told Albert what she was thinking he would spoil the day by trying to convince her to do as he wanted – he was used to getting his own way. So, Kathy did what she had always done throughout her forty-five-year marriage – she just agreed to keep him happy.

Albert, after all, saw himself as the boss: the ultimate decision maker, having the final say in all things in their marriage. Or so he thought. He looked on his wife as *the little woman*, weak and vulnerable, thinking of himself as the alpha male, the protector. This suited Kathy to a large extent as it meant that Albert, ever seeking to prove himself, would always sort any problems that came their way. However, he did have a tendency to create problems that hadn't previously existed: it was as though he was hardwired to look for trouble. It was in his DNA.

On their way back to Crawthorne Hall Hotel after an enjoyable day in

Eastbourne, the Warnfords soon found themselves driving in congested, slow-moving, traffic as they approached the town of Polegate. Crawling along, a white Ford transit van suddenly accelerated paste them, cutting in to a gap in front of their car. Albert was livid.

'Did you see that, Kathy? What a stupid idiot. He could have caused an accident!'

Smouldering with an overpowering anger, he threw the car into third gear and jammed his foot hard down on the accelerator, narrowly missing an oncoming vehicle. Then finding a straight stretch of road, he sped past the van, which had now been hogging the road in front of them for the past five minutes.

'Get out of my road, stupid git,' he called through the partially open window as his BMW E60 Sedan flew past the white Ford transit along the now crowded street. He eased his grip on the steering wheel although now once again in one of his stinking moods, he continued cursing for some minutes. Kathy had been rummaging around in the front glove compartment looking for mints when she had chanced on a packet of Viagra.

'Hey, Albert – I didn't know you took these?' She held up the blue and white box. It had been his little secret: now that the Viagra had been discovered, he felt that his manhood was somehow under threat. At this, he felt his characteristic volatile temper beginning to flare-up once again. Starting to drive recklessly to vent his anger he now pressed his foot firmly on the brake as he drew up to a red light at the Polegate level crossing. The white Ford transit van crept slowly to a halt behind him: three burly men then climbed-out and walked over to Warnford's car. There was a knock on the window of the BMW and a huge left hand grabbed Albert by the throat.

'Don't you *ever* do that again – do you understand?' A massive leather jacketed figure stood outside the car and pointed threateningly at Albert's throat with his right index finger. He had long hair and wore a huge Zappa moustache. Even in the half-light, Albert could make out the letters L-O-V-E tattooed near the taut, white knuckles of the angry fist. Like all bullies, Albert Warnford was also a coward and he started to make a high-pitched whimpering sound, like a trapped animal trying to escape from a menacing predator. At that point, a train rushed past the level crossing and, realising that the lights were now changing to green, the hulk, accompanied by his friends, climbed back into his van and pulled out, once again overtaking the BMW. He was satisfied that he had made his point to the rude loud-mouthed old man. He left a shaking Albert trying to get a grip on himself amidst impatient horn blasts from frustrated drivers waiting in the queue. Kathy shrunk down in her seat cringing with shame.

*

That evening while Albert was in the bathroom luxuriating in the jacuzzi there was a knock on the door of Room 13. Kathy had just finished tidying up Albert's mess – receipts, bits of paper, tissues, half-used sugar sachets, biscuit wrappers. The bin was now brim-full with his rubbish.

'Room Service,' called someone from the corridor.

Kathy opened-up to find an attractive middle-aged woman with coral-brown hair standing there. She was dressed in a black uniform with white apron and was wheeling a trolley.

'I'm here to lay your table, Madam.'

'Come in,' replied Kathy. 'We'd like to eat in the little sitting room area, please.'

'Very well, madam.'

Penny busied herself, laying firstly a white linen cloth and then the cutlery and champagne flutes as instructed.

Strictly speaking it was against company policy to have meals delivered from outside caterers to the bedrooms of the four-star hotel: it was thought to lower the tone. Besides, the hotel was ultimately in the business of making money, not subsidising local eateries, providing a venue for their take-away services. However, Colin Howard, the General Manager, trying to appease the complaining customer in Room 13 had decided to make an exception for once: it was the old couples' wedding anniversary, after all. Also, it might persuade Mr. Warnford to write something favourable in his threatened hotel review.

After setting the little table, Penny finished-off by positioning the ice-bucket with its bottle of Taittinger champagne within easy reach of the diners. She turned-down the bed, placing a chocolate on each pillow. Then she left.

Meanwhile, Albert, still in the bathroom had opened-up the packet that he'd purchased over the internet and which Kathy had earlier discovered in the car's glove compartment: it contained four large light-blue Viagra tablets. He decided to double-up on the dose, swallowing two at once, just to ensure that he would be able to stay the course tonight. After that, donning a shirt, tie and pair of smart trousers, he swanned-through to join his wife in the bedroom, stopping briefly at the little fridge for a miniature bottle of whisky and a packet of nuts: just in-time to answer the door, where an Indian man stood with a plastic bag full of disposable polystyrene food containers.

Albert had ordered a surprise selection for their anniversary meal – all the dishes happened to be his favourites. They started-off with papadums, onion bhajis and seekh kebabs – accompanied by the champagne, of course – although Kathy didn't really like the stuff, so just had a few sips to keep him happy before switching to water. Meanwhile, Albert had felt stirrings in his crotch and started looking forward to a night of pleasure later.

The main course consisted of chicken tikka masala, lamb tikka bhuna, Bombay potato, naan and mushroom rice which Albert gobbled-at greedily while finishing-off the bottle of champagne, known as the devil's wine which, on this occasion combined with the food and the Viagra, seemed to live-up to its name.

As the evening had progressed, so had Albert's huge erection: he'd had to unzip his flies to make himself comfortable, sitting talking nonchalantly about this and that, reminiscing on old times with only the white linen table cloth covering his large, exposed member. Then, just as they'd finished eating, he suddenly had an urge to vomit, rushing to the bathroom, making it to the toilet bowl just in time to retch and heave – although he managed to avoid actually throwing-up – that drama was yet to be played-out in the early hours.

He ran the cold-water tap, dousing his head, trying to sober-up – although this was more than just drinking too much champagne and whisky. In his fuddled mind he wondered whether the cheap Viagra that he'd purchased was actually the real thing – or maybe a nasty cocktail of chemicals? Or was it the Indian food? Maybe he'd never get to know the answer. All he knew at that moment was that he felt dizzy, nauseous, his stomach felt like it was being pounded from the inside – and he still had that huge erection – which was now like a rod of steel. Despite being dunked in the ice bucket, his penis refused to go back to its normal size – almost as if it had a mind of its own.

Albert left his trousers on the floor of the bathroom. Groaning and moaning, he crawled into the bed wearing only his shirt and tie. Ever-patient Kathy, still sitting at the table, romantic scented-candle still burning, sighed to herself resignedly. *Happy wedding anniversary, darling*, she thought sarcastically, looking over at her dearest husband, now asleep and snoring like a dyspeptic bullock.

It was three o'clock in the morning when the internal phone rang in Penny's room.

'Hello?' She had been asleep, dreaming of lying down on a sun-soaked beach, the sea lapping against the shore.

'Sorry to call, Penny.' It was Amy, on the night manager shift. 'We have an emergency – I need you in Room 13 pronto – and bring Bob with you.'

'What sort of emergency?'

'It's a major clean-up job. You'll need the sanitisation equipment – tell Bob to bring some black sacks, too. Make it quick.'

When they arrived, the first thing they were aware of was the collision of bad smells seeping-out into the corridor followed by an overwhelming, heavy stench which hit them as soon as they opened the door. They were greeted by Amy.

'Mr. Warnford is very unwell.'

'Has the doctor been called?' asked Penny, trying hard not to gag.

'At this stage he'd rather just try to sleep-it-off. He's in the bathroom being cleaned-up by his wife,' replied Amy.

They all looked about them, trying to hold their breath. The place was a hellhole, a nightmare scene like a horrific stage farce in which they suddenly found themselves – with Albert Warnford as the principal player.

'I'd like you to strip and change the bed: then generally sanitise the place and get it smelling a bit sweeter,' continued Amy. 'Then go and get yourselves some sleep.'

Penny and Bob both looked at each other as Amy slunk out of the room back to the sweet-smelling atmosphere of the reception desk with its arrangement of fresh oriental lilies, with their lingering fragrance wafting through the air. They started to gather the fetid, rancid, earthy-smelling bedsheets, wet, slimy and soaking after being soiled by Albert Warnford, unable to control his bowel movements in his self-induced stupor. There was vomit, too, on the quilt, spilling-out on the carpet: a sickly curry aroma assaulting their senses.

'I can do this on my own, Penny.' Bob, having served time in several prisons with slop-out regimes, was used to these kinds of unpleasant, nauseating stenches. *He* could handle it. But he was concerned for his lovely best-friend Penny – he thought it was all too much for her to bear.

'No prob, Bob. We're a team. Let's get on with it.'

He liked her spunk.

So, they set-about bagging-up the rank bedding and clearing-up the vomit; then after sanitising the carpet Bob brought in a steam cleaner to deal with the offending areas while Penny re-made the bed with fresh linen and quilt cover. Then they both tidied-up the room: she taking away the dirty plates, glasses and cutlery while he bagged the empty bottle and cork, emptying the overflowing waste-bin and then giving the whole room a good dose of air freshener.

'Hello, Mr. and Mrs Warnford. We've finished. Your bed is now ready for you.'

'Thank you,' called Kathy from the bathroom. Albert managed a tiny groan.

When they arrived back in the staff accommodation block, Bob and Penny grateful to be at the end of their ordeal, crashed into bed in their two separate rooms and quickly fell asleep again.

Back in Room 13 Albert and Kathy were now in their freshly made-up bed. She was lying awake, looking up at the ceiling, counting the hours until she was back in the comfort of her own home. As for Albert, he was fast asleep, head still spinning from time to time as he experienced deeply disturbing dreams, wading through a cold treacly blackness. His huge, rock-hard erection had still not worn-off.

Chapter 31

It had been an extraordinary two days for Bob Bennett. After just one hour's sleep, he'd been woken-up by his alarm clock ready for his early morning breakfast shift. This had been followed by his ritualistic once-a-week rubbish burning job, which he always enjoyed.

Like many businesses the hotel paid a fee for wheelie bins to be emptied regularly. It was part of Bob's brief to sort through the garbage once a week, burning anything that couldn't be recycled and didn't need to go to the landfill site: this made for more space in the giant bins, and so saved money. He always looked for items such as shredded paper from the offices which had once held sensitive information about guests and other confidential hotel data. However, he usually threw-in other rubbish such as used paper tissues and the odd cardboard box. He'd then collect a pile of sticks to burn from the hotel grounds and stand back, content, as he watched the flickering flames springing to life and engulfing the whole lot. Bob, after all these years, still enjoyed a good fire.

On this occasion, as he was feeling the heat from his bonfire, he grabbed the black plastic sack full of the rubbish that he'd collected from Room 13 in the early hours of the morning. At the time, he'd dumped it beside one of the bins on his way back to his staff quarters, meaning to deal with its contents later. So, he started to delve through the large bag, retrieving – used tissues; an old newspaper damp with a distinct smell of vomit emanating from its pages; two used paper cups – he lobbed handfuls towards his fire, fuelling the flames once more. Then just as he was about to throw his fourth handful something caught his eye. His sharp brain, processing a small, crumpled pinkish-coloured piece of paper, suddenly seemed to be telling him to stop what he was doing.

Flattening-it out, Bob pocketed the lottery ticket along with some of the other treasures that he had salvaged from the rubbish that morning. It reminded him of his time as a student when he had worked as a dustman during the summer holidays. Then, he had been amazed at the valuable items that some people threw away simply because they didn't want them anymore. The dustmen would rummage through some of the bins: especially those from wealthy-looking homes; often striking lucky – maybe the odd piece of jewellery, an antique clock no longer working or some electrical appliance still in good working order.

As a homeless vagrant for years, Bob had regularly delved into dustbins – usually looking for food – but at times finding other useful discarded objects – maybe a razor or a pair of shoes. On one occasion he'd even found a stash of half-empty liquor bottles – he'd often wondered whether the owner was a reformed alcoholic who'd thrown-out their secret supply. He'd been an alcoholic himself at the time.

At the end of his shift, Bob cleaned himself up and strolled down into the village alone: Penny was working, making-up rooms for the new arrivals later that day.

'I see you've had your door repaired,' he said cheerfully to Joe Barker, the owner.

'Oh, so you saw the damage from the break-in?'

'Yes, I was in here the other morning when you were out – you had your assistant from Hellingly standing-in.'

'That's Janine. Yes, she was here for a few hours, while I was sorting-out stuff with the insurers.'

'What a pain!'

'You can say that again!' He hesitated. 'Anyway, what can I do you for Bob?' He said this deliberately, trying to be funny. Joe knew a lot of the hotel staff – they were always popping into his shop for personal supplies. 'Cigarettes?'

Bob nodded. Joe grabbed a couple of packets – Bob's usual brand and placed them on the counter.

'Anything else, Bob?'

'I'd better have a new lighter … and some toothpaste.' Bob grabbed a pack from the toiletry section. After being penniless for years, he always appreciated being able to afford to clean his teeth. He'd also recently tracked-down a dentist in Eastbourne who had worked wonders on his neglected old gnashers.

Bob had just paid for everything and was turning to leave when he suddenly remembered something.

'Oh, I bought this last time I came in but missed the draw last night. Can you check it for me please?' He handed the lottery ticket to Joe, who ran it through the machine.

'Hang on a minute, Bob, there's something not quite right here.'

'Like what?'

Joe's face had turned a beetroot red colour as he took out his phone and punched in a number. Bob wondered if he was ill after the trauma of the burglary two days earlier? He wondered whether the shopkeeper was about to have a heart attack? Maybe he had delayed shock?

'Excuse me – I'm the owner of a convenience store near Hailsham, East Sussex … Barkers,' he began. 'I need to check the numbers on a lottery ticket that one of my customers has just brought in … Yes, they are as follows: one, four, twelve, twenty-three, thirty-three and forty with a bonus ball of thirty-five.'

There was hesitation at the other end of the phone. Then he was asked to repeat the numbers. Then another pause.

Joe turned to Bob. 'They want to talk to you.' He handed-over the phone.

Bob wondered what this was all about. For goodness' sakes, he only wanted to know if the ticket had any winning numbers on it – he hadn't expected The Spanish Inquisition.

'Hello … Yes, it is. I bought it two days ago … In the shop where I'm standing at the moment … Why …? I'll give you my mobile number – he can ring me on that … Yes, I can be available – it's my day off …'

*

'Hello, Mr. Bennett,' I'm Desmond Heathcote-Drummond-Willoughby. His long, triple-barrelled name ran after him like a poodle. 'I'm the Lottery Senior Winners Adviser from our Watford headquarters. We spoke on the phone several times yesterday afternoon.'

Desmond certainly looked the part. Professional and efficient in his manner, he was smartly turned out with his thick head of well-groomed hair and bushy handlebar moustache. Sporting a flamboyant red-spotted bowtie and expensive-looking tailored suit, he was the sort of person Bob imagined might breeze around the country dishing-out large cheques to lucky lottery winners.

'Hi.' They shook hands.

'And this is Nick Cousins, one of our finance representatives.'

Almost in complete contrast to Desmond, the finance guy was a small man in his mid-forties, slight in build with slicked-back dark hair and black rimmed glasses. He also, was dressed smartly, wearing a blue blazer, and high-quality grey flannel trousers.

'I'm surprised that you've come all this way.' Bob was still dumbfounded by the news that he'd heard the day before.

'You are my number one priority at the moment Mr. Bennett. How are you?'

'Fine – although I didn't sleep very well last night.'

'Understandable, Mr. Bennett,' he continued breezily.

'Sorry I have nowhere else suitable for us to meet.' They were in his tiny cramped bedroom in the staff accommodation block – it was the only place he could think of which offered any modicum of privacy without being overheard. Bob had told no-one of his news, including Penny. The only person who had any idea was Joe Barker from the shop – he'd been sworn to secrecy with the promise of a reward for his silence.

'Do you know the odds of winning the jackpot, Mr. Bennett?'

'No, I haven't a clue – and please – do call me Bob.'

'The odds are two hundred and ninety-two million to one, Bob.'

'Wow!'

'There's more chance of being killed by a vending machine, dying from tap water or being attacked by a shark in Britain. In your case you hit upon the winning combination matching six numbers and the bonus ball. Incredible luck, if I may say so – although, to be fair, I've seen a lot of extremely lucky people in my job.'

'Well, I still can't believe this is happening – it's like having an out of body experience.'

'Well said, Bob. Anyway, let's get down to business.'

The two visitors were now sitting squashed-up on the tiny, narrow bed while Bob sat in a plastic red chair facing them.

'So, what now?'

'Firstly, I need to validate your claim by examining your ticket to check that it is genuine.'

At this point, Bob stood-up and stepped towards a large poster of the famous *Flying Scotsman* steam locomotive. Apart from his passion for fire-raising Bob had been obsessed with trains for as long as he could remember – ironically even targeting them in some of his arson attacks in his past life. He nonchalantly peeled-back the picture, retrieving the lottery ticket from behind it. He'd placed it in an envelope and stuck it to the wall for safe-keeping.

Desmond Heathcote-Drummond-Willoughby made no comment – he'd witnessed all sorts of hiding places for winning lottery tickets – the most bizarre was when he'd visited a chap who had his precious piece of paper secreted in his snake tank – the hissing reptile wasn't happy to be disturbed as its owner had groped around under a rock for the ticket.

'Well, you'll be pleased to know, Bob, that I can confirm this is genuine. Also, to update you on what we've been doing since you confirmed your numbers yesterday. We've been carrying-out our checks to make sure the ticket hasn't been cancelled, forged or stolen.' He paused for a moment.

'Go on.' Bob sat there unblinkingly.

'The shopkeeper has confirmed the time and date when you bought it – although we weren't able to see CCTV footage as it was out of order at the time. So, with all that in mind, I'm now going to sit with you while you fill-in this claim-form.' He proffered this to Bob, who duly completed the answers to the questions, both visitors sitting patiently while he did so.

'I now need to see proof of identity please.' Bob handed over his passport and driving license. Desmond took a photo of each, then he continued. 'My last question, Bob, is whether you wish to accept publicity as a lottery winner or whether you want to keep this a private matter?'

'Definitely, I want to keep it private. I've told no-one apart from Joe Barker, the shop keeper – and he's been sworn to secrecy,' replied Bob.

'Now the hard part. You need to hand-over the lottery ticket to me.' Bob looked hesitant. 'I will give you an official receipt,' added Desmond, trying to sound reassuring.

'Yes, that bit's not so easy!' stated Bob, reluctantly parting with the piece of life-changing paper. In his mind it was like trying to tear a limb from his body – his hand was shaking as he finally released it.

'Thank you. Now, I'll hand over to my colleague … Nick?'

'Yes, Bob, I'm here to sort out the financial side for you. It's quite normal for us to set-up a bank account for winners. This is not the sort of amount that you can just deposit by walking into your local bank. I'm afraid I have more forms for you to fill-in.'

After two hours, the business was drawing to a close.

'Well, congratulations once again. You have our contact details if you have any questions whatsoever, Bob,' said Desmond Heathcote-Drummond-Willoughby as he made to leave. We'll give you any support you need – and also if you so wish, we can put you in touch with previous lottery winners who can give you advice.'

'I do have one more question,' said Bob – it had been nagging away at him all afternoon.

'Fire away.'

'When will the money be in the account – and when will I have access to it?'

'Rest assured,' answered Nick Cousins, 'it will be available within forty-eight hours – I'll phone you to confirm when it's all set-up. And before you ask – I confirm that the exact amount due is four million, four hundred thousand, seven hundred and eighty pounds. I hope your winnings bring you great joy and happiness. We'll be in touch.'

Chapter 32

Tom Crompton was going to go out for a slap-up meal that night: all this talk of murder had given him an appetite.

'Well done, Tom. Please congratulate the team and then let's get this thing in motion.'

At long-last Detective Inspector Angelia Wilmot had been given the go-ahead by the Crown Prosecution Service to charge Elaine Evans for the manslaughter of Callum McFinn in 2006 and Victor Evans in 2012. After hours trawling through CCTV footage, the police had been able to place her in the vicinity of the so-called accidents – they were able to prove, counter to Elaine's alibis – that after leaving home she'd doubled back. There was film footage of her skirting round towards the back garden – the most damning of this circumstantial evidence came from a local corner-shop in Bognor Regis which also showed her reappearance some five minutes later when she returned to her car. Traffic cameras showed her then heading back to town, finally reaching home again at the time when she said she'd discovered the injured body of Gareth.

Already Elaine had been charged and bailed under the Police and Criminal Evidence Act 1984, known as PACE for fraud offences against the Department of Work and Pensions. In collaboration with DWP investigators who had filmed Elaine driving, walking and shopping without any walking aid, she was going to be prosecuted for falsely obtaining over seventy thousand pounds in State benefits over time through falsely claiming Income Support, Disability Living Allowance, Independent Living Fund and Council Tax reduction. She had re-mortgaged her home to pay the court security bond: one of her conditions of bail. Finally, she had also been made to report weekly to the police station.

Elaine would most likely receive a custodial sentence for deliberate diversion of public money away from its intended purpose of supporting vulnerable people in the community. The government had zero tolerance for anyone defrauding the system and would, no doubt, also take action to recover as much of the money as possible. Similarly, the insurance company investigators were sitting on the side-lines waiting to retrieve the four hundred thousand pounds that they had shelled-out as a result of the claim on the life of Elaine's first husband. All actions relating to Gareth's life assurance pay-out had been frozen, pending the outcome of the police investigation.

At six o'clock the following morning two police patrol cars drove down a pleasant, leafy suburban street. The sullen, heavy night sky was beginning to lift, revealing a light drizzle of rain at the beginning of another dreary day in March as the cars parked out-of-sight, hidden from view just in case their target happened to be looking out of a window at that time – which was doubtful. The element of surprise was important in this dawn-raid in which the objective was to apprehend Elaine Evans, charging her with two counts of manslaughter.

Two uniformed officers – one male and one female, followed the alleyway round to the back of the house – the same one used by Elaine when she had sneaked-up on Gareth eighteen months earlier, shoving the ladder to one side – with him at the top. He'd caught sight of his wife as he tried to keep his balance – but that had not saved him from falling and suffering a massive head injury and trauma. However, he'd regained consciousness fleetingly: enough time to speak to the doctor – in simple terms – and implicate his wife in the incident.

The other two uniforms – again, one male and one female, walked down to the front of the house and stationed themselves by the door awaiting further instructions. Then, a third car arrived – this time unmarked – carrying DI Angelia Wilmot, DS Tom Crompton and DC Mac Cheema.

'Okay, you two. Let's do this one by the book,' said Wilmot as they parked.

'Ma'am,' replied Crompton.

Leaving their vehicle, they strolled up to the front door, Crompton ringing the doorbell continuously – a vague echoing sound followed by – silence. He banged the door three times with the flat of his hand. Still nothing from within. No stirring sound.

'Elaine Evans, open up please. This is the police,' he shouted.

A light came on across the road, and then another in the house next door. But there was no response from inside the Evans' house.

'Try one more time Tom.'

He did as she asked. 'Still no sign of life, Ma'am.' Then he radioed the two police constables at the rear of the property. No movement there – house still in darkness.

'We'd better use the Enforcer.' DI Wilmot nodded towards the male uniformed officer who held the metal battering ram which the police used for quick access into properties. In this case they'd been aware that there was a possibility of Elaine Evans doing a runner – absconding if she had wind of the arrest.

Within seconds the door was forced open, splintering from its frame: the three detectives rushing-in, leaving the uniformed officers at the entrance in case Elaine tried to escape. Crompton and Wilmot trudged heavily up the stairs, opening doors into unoccupied rooms. With gloved hands, they checked wardrobes and drawers – dresses and tops still on their hangers, jumpers and underwear neatly folded. They rifled through scattered possessions on her dressing table: cosmetics, hair brush, manicure set. Crompton found a couple of suitcases under the bed – both were empty.

'Guv, come and have a look at this.' It was DC Cheema from downstairs.

The other two detectives came back down the stairs, joining their colleague in the sitting room. He was pointing at a piece of paper on top of the dining table.

Detective Inspector Wilmot read the handwritten words:

By the time you read this I'll be dead. There is no other option left open to me.

'What is it, Ma'am?' asked Crompton surreptitiously looking over her shoulder.

'Looks like a suicide note from the lovely Elaine.' She carried-on reading quietly to herself while the detective sergeant carried-on poking around the room looking for anything that might shed light on the whereabouts of their suspect.

I considered not writing any of this because of how personal it is, but I like tying up loose ends and don't want people to wonder why I did this.

I had a bad childhood – raised by an abusive stepfather after my mother had been killed in a road accident. Then I went into care, abused by one of the managers – someone who was supposed to be there to protect me. My first marriage was short-lived – Callum, the love of my life tragically falling to his death. They say that lightning only strikes once – but that wasn't the case with me – my second husband, Gareth, also had a fall – leading to his death, too. I was devastated for the second time and hardly had the funeral day passed than the accusations came flying thick and fast – first my in-laws, Gareth's parents, then the insurance people and finally the police. Concocting some story – trying to fit-me-up for crimes that I didn't commit.

Tom Crompton and Mac Cheema had finished looking around and were now standing, waiting for their boss to finish reading the rest of the letter.

I'm an innocent victim here. The police have everything to gain from a conviction – promotions to be had, for a start. The insurance guys will do anything to avoid paying-out on my claims. As for the Department for Work and Pensions – I have a paralysing debilitating condition – some days are better than others. Their investigators followed me, took photos – an invasion of privacy – and then selectively portrayed me as able-bodied – saying I was a fraud. This is just one more thing to cope with in the hardest moment of my whole life.

I can't fight the system anymore. One person trying to make a stand in the face of insurmountable odds is too much for me to bear. I can't go on anymore. I'm going to kill myself. This isn't a cry for help – it's a statement of fact. Nobody has listened to me. Nobody has cared.

Elaine Evans

'Well, that's an unexpected turn-up for the books,' commented DI Wilmot once she'd read the note. 'What do you think, Tom?'

She handed the note over to Crompton, who finished reading it.

'I'd say that we have to follow the evidence. In view of our intended arrest this morning, it is most likely at the moment that she has absconded.'

'What about her belongings – her clothes and make-up still in her bedroom?'

'If she's rational enough to write a suicide note – one which paints her as the victim rather than the perpetrator – then she's canny enough to buy a few extra personal effects to make a quick getaway. It all sounds pre-planned to me.'

'Cynical indeed, Detective Sergeant!'

'As I said, I'll follow the evidence Ma'am, and in the absence of a body I'll reserve judgement.'

'Well said, Tom. For what it's worth, I totally agree with you. We'll message all units with a photo of Elaine Evans, asking for them to keep a look-out. We're treating her as a Misper in the first instance. As a precautionary measure I'll issue an APW too.'

Misper and APW were police acronyms for missing persons and All Ports Warning. Although Elaine Evans had been granted bail, she had not been required to forfeit her passport, much to Angelia Wilmot' annoyance.

So, it had to be assumed that there was always a possibility of Elaine Evans fleeing the country.

*

At a quarter past eight that morning the overnight ferry from Portsmouth to St. Malo in Brittany, France arrived on schedule with its two thousand passengers and six hundred vehicles.

The previous evening a lone female driving a silver BMW Z4 sports car had parked in a side street in Mile End, Portsmouth and then boarded the large ferry as a foot passenger. She was a fairly nondescript individual; slightly dumpy with lank, loose brown hair. Carrying only a large holdall and a shopping bag she had breezed through security, then headed to the reception desk where she picked-up the key to her luxury overnight cabin, complete with balcony: an essential requirement for what she had planned.

After the eleven-hour journey, with the passengers and vehicles disembarked, the overnight ship's staff signed-off and handed-over their duties to the daytime crew who then began cleaning and replenishing, ready for the next intake of passengers. It was not until nine-thirty that a room steward entered one of the deluxe cabins and immediately sensed that something was awry. The bed was still in its made-up state and looked as though it had been unused. On the floor beside an armchair, a large green canvas holdall with a gold zip appeared unopened, still secured with a padlock. A plastic shopping bag with provisions – fruit, a chocolate bar and sandwiches, had been left carelessly propped-up against the tiny radiator. A woman's grey double-breasted wool coat had been left splayed on top of the bed.

However, it was the sight of what lay on the little round coffee table which first set the alarm bells ringing for Madame Nicolette Allard, the room steward. Two opened boxes of Temazepam prescription sleeping pills; their blister packs discarded on to the floor with three yellowish-white round tablets scattered close-by. Then there was the half-used bottle of gin with its cork stopper missing. The curtains were blowing gently in the breeze and Madame Allard, with a feeling of trepidation, edged out on to the balcony, instinctively looking downwards at the waves lapping against the side of the ship. There was no sign of anyone down there in the murky, grey water.

It was then that she decided to raise the alarm.

Chapter 33

'I've finished with this place – but not with you. Will you come with me?'

They were sitting-in the old oak-framed summer house early in the evening. This was really out-of-bounds to staff during their off-duty times but the two of them had brought cleaning materials with them on the pretext of sprucing-up the place ready for the busy hotel season ahead. Sitting there, they had a degree of privacy, undisturbed for the difficult proposition which Bob had put forward.

Penny was in a state of shock – that Bob had not only won a lottery jackpot of over four million pounds, but that he wanted her to join him for his planned round-the-world trip. She felt a bit flaky and weird about the whole idea.

'Look, Bob, I don't mean to offend you – you're my best mate – a beacon of fun in a dismal world – and I'll miss you. But I can't just throw everything to one side on a whim.'

'And why not?'

'Because, for a start, I'm used to being independent. I'd be totally reliant on you; not my own person anymore.'

'I could give you a sum as a present. Then, anytime you got fed-up, you could leave. I'd give you plenty to live on.'

'That's very sweet, Bob and I really appreciate the thought.'

'Hey Penny, my lovely friend you're the only person who really knows who I am – about why I became obsessed with fire – my prison sentences – my homelessness. I've wasted so much of my life achieving nothing – I want to do something – see the world.'

'And so you can, Bob. Only not with me.' She sounded more positive than she really felt. After her skirmish with Lord Crawthorne in Room 13 and other near misses with randy guests, she wanted something better. However, her job at the hotel offered her security – and allowed for her to rent-out her little house.

'What about if I pay off your mortgage for starters. Then you could afford to go back to live in your own home anytime you decided you'd had enough of this job?' It was as though he'd read her mind.

'That's a very kind thought – and very generous of you, Bob.'

'That's the least I can do for my best friend,' he replied. 'But, come what may, I must go. You do understand, don't you? Please come with me.' He was persistent.

Penny started to waiver in her resolve. She did quite like having Bob around her. He was like a protector, always looking-out for her, giving her a sense of safety, security and belonging. Was she just going to let him get up and walk out of her life – or take the plunge and join him in his adventure? She needed to be true to herself, doing what she felt best, not just fitting-in with what Bob wanted her to do.

'Bob, you've been such a good friend to me.'

Gazing into her eyes he could see that she was starting to give the idea some consideration. He decided to try again.

'Look, Penny, I can't go back now – I've just got to keep on going forward. Come with me. We'd make a great travelling team together.' He made a last-ditch attempt. 'Penny *will* you come with me?' He looked at her with his mop of hair dangling like a curtain, partly covering those implacable eyes, innocently watching her, waiting for a final answer – and then a crack in her armour at last …

'Bob, one thing to get straight with you – which I'm sure you know already.'

'Which is?'

'That I'm not physically attracted to you. At least, not in any sexual, amorous way.'

'Of course, I know. I realised that as soon as I first set eyes on you that day in the reception area when you came for the interview. I was making-up the fire on that warm spring day and started talking to you – of course I saw a lovely, pale-skinned, slim woman sitting there and found you attractive. But it was your personality that I fell in love with – as a friend. You have always been like a sister to me and I'll miss not being with you.'

'Then, Bob, it's a good job that you are such a determined, persuasive, kind, funny and brotherly kind of friend to have around because you've tipped the balance for me. I still can't really believe any of this but I'm going to throw caution to the wind for the first time in my life. Yes, I'll go with you – if you will have me?'

'Wow! That's unbelievable! You won't regret it, I promise. We'll have a ball! But now the really hard bit.'

'And what's that?'

'I'm going to have to brave-up to telling Charles that I'm leaving.'

'You mean *we're* leaving. If we're going to be partners in this, we need to start in the way we intend to carry on – working together as a team.'

'Well then. Let's go and find him now before *we* change our minds!' replied Bob, beaming at her. He loved it when Penny was assertive like this.

*

'Hi Charles, we need to see you – fairly urgently.' They had finally found him in the little office behind the reception desk.

'Can't it wait?' Charles Eden was talking to Mateo, one of the wine waiters.

'Not really,' replied Bob.

'Give me a minute.'

Penny thought that Charles sounded a bit gruff – unusual for him. They stood waiting in the reception area, the large chandelier tinkling overhead, until Mateo emerged, wine menu and notepad in one hand.

'*He's not in the best of moods,*' he whispered surreptitiously as he sidled-out looking worn and brow-beaten – not a good omen for Charles' reaction when they told him of their decision.

They shuffled into the office and sat down on two rickety old chairs. Charles Eden was at his desk, which looked a mess – almost as though he was overwhelmed by the weight of paperwork sitting there in random piles.

Charles certainly doesn't look as though he's on top of his game this morning, thought Penny, not for the first time.

'Okay, what can I do for you?' He looked distracted as though his mind was elsewhere.

'I'm sorry to give you such short notice,' Bob began hesitatingly, 'but I have to leave Crawthorne Hall. Something of a personal nature has come up.'

'Can you elaborate?'

'I'm sorry but I can't say. I feel terrible about it,' replied Bob, answering the question.

And so, you should, you bastard, thought Charles. *After all we've done for you – giving you a job and a place to live.*

Charles was feeling really let-down. He had forged something of a friendship with Bob Bennett: he'd even gone along with him regarding his suspicions about the so-called buried body story. He'd recently approached his grandfather, Lord Crawthorne on the matter – stuck his neck out. And for what? Now Bob was leaving – probably no longer interested in his idea of excavating the kitchen gardens. What a mess this was turning into!

However, he decided not to say something he might later regret: so, he held his tongue. He'd always liked Bob: there was a soft, caring side to the man – who was a bit of an enigma – there seemed to be something about his past that he kept secret. Charles had never really been able to crack-open the mystery: all he knew was that Bob had got into a bit of trouble when he was younger – there had, apparently been some trauma when he was very young which affected him badly.

Charles wondered whether it was Bob's past that was in some way catching-up with him now? He would probably never know.

'Is there a problem here at the hotel? Is that why you're telling me you're leaving?' He wondered whether Bob needed help.

'Not at all, Charles. I'm very happy here – you know that. For me, my life was over before I came here – being homeless. This hotel saved me, picked me up, put me back together. Then, you've been so kind in trying to help me look into the story that my friend Paul Marsh told me shortly before his death. You have done your best for me and I truly appreciate that.'

Charles believed what Bob was saying. It sounded as though there was definitely some kind of personal reason for him to be throwing away his job – and with it, his live-in accommodation. Penny just sat there impartial, listening but taking no part in the conversation. The young manager wondered exactly why she'd come along with her friend: he had a shrewd idea that he would be finding out sooner rather than later.

'When are you planning to leave?' Charles decided to stick to the obvious.

'Well, I'll let you have my notice in writing first thing tomorrow – but I need to leave by the end of the week: Saturday 4th May.'

Bob would have been more than willing to stay for longer and felt bad that he was letting-down Charles and everyone at the hotel – deserting them when they were so short-staffed. However, he didn't entirely trust Joe Barker to keep his mouth shut: even with a big bribe. He was afraid that news of the lottery win would spread like wildfire; maybe soon reaching the ears of Albert Warnford, rightful owner of the ticket. If that nasty piece of work got to hear about it there would be big trouble indeed.

'And you, Penny. Are you just here to accompany Bob – or is there another reason?' Charles could no longer wait. He had a sinking feeling in his stomach and needed to know whether his gut instincts were correct. They were.

'I'm going to be leaving with Bob, I'm afraid.' There it was, out at last. 'I, too, owe the hotel a lot. You have all been very good to me.'

'And the two of you can't wait for a couple of weeks? You know that we have a very hectic weekend coming-up with a large wedding party reception. Can't you at least stay for that? We'll need all the staff we can rustle-up. It'll be a full-house.'

'We're really sorry, Charles.' This from Bob.

'I'm disappointed.'

Charles couldn't really say much more: he had troubles of his own which seemed to be building-up into a crescendo. For a start, he'd felt that, since his reprimand by Colin Howard, the General Manager, over Lord Crawthorne's proposition to Penny – namely money for sex – that his days were now numbered at Crawthorne Hall Hotel. So, he and Amy had decided to accelerate their plans to join a cruise ship – both as senior hotel managers. They, themselves would be starting their new jobs in two-weeks' time, flying-out to Venice on 13th May for their first nine-month contract. Right now, Charles couldn't wait to see Crawthorne Hall Hotel in his rear-view mirror. He would be counting the days to his own departure along with Amy, ready to start their new life. They both had a big surprise in store for the family when that time came.

Chapter 34

'Let me gouge his eyes out with a spoon, boss.' He spoke with an Eastern European accent.

The huge bald man looked threateningly at Lord Crawthorne.

'I'm sure there's no need for that, Luca,' replied Ronnie Howell in a soft, oily voice. The smaller man, currently using his alias of Martin Green had discarded his long grey wig and glasses. He now sported a neat little moustache and had a shaved head. Wearing a tailored suit, Mr. G, as he liked to be known by the foot soldiers, always carried an air of authority about him. Calm and gently spoken, he had been sent-in to use his powers of persuasion to remind their aging British courier that the only way out of the organisation was in a coffin.

They were sitting in a dingy private backroom behind one of the infamous coffee shops in the De Wallen District of Amsterdam. George had announced that this would be his last run. Approaching eighty he wanted to retire from the stone-smuggling business. He was giving them notice that, after fifteen years, he'd had enough. He was quitting.

'Come on George, you stop carrying for us, and you'll no longer be welcome in our city.' Ronnie Howell, known only as Mr. G in this neck of the woods, sat with his head tilted to one side – he had a neck deformity known as orthoptic torticollis. 'You'll have to stop having a sex life here. Laetitia's her name, isn't it? The one you've been seeing for the past five years. Ugly cow.'

'No, she's not.'

'Obviously too much Viagra's affecting your eyesight.' There was a stench of wine and spirits on Ronnie's breath as he moved his face closer to Lord Crawthorne. 'Either that or you haven't seen her since we taught her a lesson … we'd heard that one of our loyal couriers was about to leave us. You should see the state she's in, Georgie-boy. Isn't that right, Elaine?'

Elaine Evans was lounging on a wooden chair in the corner, manicuring her nails. Looking-up and nodding at Ronnie she then resumed her filing. Since absconding from the UK, helped by a lorry driver on the St. Malo ferry crossing, she had been living in one of Ronnie's residences near the city and had recently been given control of several of his brothels. She was a hard taskmaster, hated by the sex workers. Laetitia was one of her girls.

'What are you talking about?'

'She had a little accident with a bottle of acid – pity – the punters don't seem so keen on her all of a sudden.'

'You bastards.' Lord Crawthorne struggled to get up out of his chair but Luca held him firmly down, hands on his shoulders.

'The point is, George, that what has happened to our poor Laetitia could just as easily happen to one of your family – your lovely wife Isabela – or your daughter Helen. Maybe, even your wonderful grandson, Charles – I hear he's doing well in the hotel management business, by the way. Then again there's that long term girlfriend of yours – the one who used to be your personal assistant.'

Lord Crawthorne was shocked. He had not expected them to know so much about his private life: especially his secret girlfriend back home. It was imperative to keep her and Isabela – and the rest of his family safe from harm.

'If you or anyone else ever lays a finger on any of my family or anyone close to me, I'll make you pay. Don't ever underestimate me!' George was bluffing. He could do this without flinching – after all, he was a top-class poker player, used to putting on an act. 'Nobody threatens me. You can either accept what I'm telling you – or you can go fuck yourselves.'

George Crawthorne was becoming angry that it had come to this. Why didn't they just let him leave – after all the money he'd brought-in for them – taking packets of uncut diamonds through to the UK for all these years, risking his liberty. The least they could do was cut him some slack.

'Brave words, George. I've given you a fair chance but you don't seem to want to listen to me.' Mad Ronnie Howell's tone was the voice of reason. 'Look I have a proposition for you – just carry-on taking the stones over to the UK as you have been and we'll forget that any of this took place this afternoon.'

Lord Crawthorne had always been a hard nut to crack, always used to getting what he wanted – and right now he wanted out. He changed tack.

'I believe what you are saying, Mr. G,' he said calmly, eyeballing the lean, mean bald little man. 'It's just that I really need to do this.'

'And I, George, I really need to do *this.*'

Ronnie Howell nodded to his henchman, Luca who pulled the old man up – it was like uprooting a reluctant garden weed, along with the chair, which George was trying to hang on to with two hands. Luca shook him roughly until the offending item of furniture was dropped to the floor with a clatter. George, finally standing there defenceless, watched as Luca hesitated menacingly with a glint in his eye before kicking him deftly in the groin.

Lord George Crawthorne let-out out a long, rasping groan, then slumped down, folding in upon himself while trying to deal with the pain; suddenly feeling the urge to vomit.

'That'll put you out of business tonight,' the huge muscle-rippling, Luca muttered cheerfully; George at his feet on the dirty, dusty floor.

'Get your gorilla off me!'

'Now think about what Mr. G said – and show some respect.' Luca kicked George once more – this time in the ribs.

'I worry about him,' Mad Ronnie smiled lingeringly. 'He has a very short fuse. I'd hate to leave you alone in this room for,' he looked at his watch for effect, 'say ten minutes? How would you like that, Luca? Just you and our Lord Crawthorne left here as a playmate – show him what you are *really* capable of doing when I'm not around to control the proceedings?'

'Whatever you say, boss.'

'Please be reasonable,' George persisted, wheezing away, trying to catch his breath. It felt like he had a broken rib.

'That's just it, Georgie boy. I'm not a rational human being – particularly when I'm mad at people. That's what gives me the upper hand.'

It started to dawn on George that there was no easy way of resigning from what he had always thought of as a bit of a reckless pastime. He'd always had an adrenaline rush whenever he'd managed to walk through customs with a valuable stash of diamonds secreted on his person – then the clandestine meeting afterwards in the car park with him handing-over the stones in exchange for the cash payment for his services. However, in some deep-buried secret place in his heart he now wished he'd never become involved in the diamond export business: at last, the seriousness of his predicament was dawning on him. After all, he knew that, ultimately, the proceeds from selling the stones went to fund the warlords of countries in civil strife buying weapons, financing genocide and other crimes against humanity. In reality he was mixed up with serious organised crime – and it was not wise to antagonise them unnecessarily.

Lord Crawthorne decided to play-along with these two guys just to get out of here. Once he was safely back in Britain, he'd try to think of another way of retiring gracefully – he thought of his Horizon Elegance 20 entry-level yacht with its three berths – at this moment anchored in Chichester Marina – all kitted-out for making himself scarce for a while – with or without Isabela. She knew that he dabbled in diamonds, but hadn't the nouse to realise just how illegal his activities were – and the consequences if caught. All she cared about was having money to spend: she never stopped to think about where it all came from.

Mad Ronnie Howell, Alias Martin Green alias Mr. G. was exercising a high degree of self-control with this aged employee, as he didn't relish the prospect of diminishing profits in his UK diamond racket. He decided to try using the powers of persuasion one last time.

'Look, George, I know you're getting-on in life but you must realise there's no quitting in our business. I'm warning you that any attempt to leave us will make certain people very unhappy. You must surely realise that?' Then turning to his assistant. 'Luca, help Lord Crawthorne to his feet – if you would be so very kind?'

The huge man hauled George up from the floor.

'You appear to be somewhat dusty, George.' Then again turning to Luca. 'Brush him down, I think Lord Crawthorne is now ready to go.'

Luca complied as commanded. Then Mad Ronnie Howell took hold of George's right hand into which he thrust a small velvet bag.

'Now take the diamonds. You are still in our employment – got the drift?' He smacked Lord Crawthorne twice on the side of the face to accentuate his message. The usual arrangements for the exchange in the Brighton car park.'

'Okay, you win Mr. G.' George feigned defeat and contrition.

'I always do … Oh, and George.'

'Yes?'

'Make sure you don't get caught.'

Chapter 35

'I promise to love and respect you. Helping our love grow, always being there to listen, comfort and support you, whatever our lives may bring.'

Amy and Charles, after enduring mounting hostility from her mother, had decided to marry as soon as possible once they'd joined the cruise ship. Apart from anything else, this guaranteed them a shared cabin: company policy dictated that only married couples could live together in shared accommodation. So, unbeknown to anyone else, they had arranged for the quiet wedding – witnessed by just two friends – to take place in international waters on their second week of working on *The Sovereign Pearl*. It had involved some negotiation with the cruise line company as it was an unusual request for first-time staff members to make – and there was a lot of paperwork to be completed to comply with the Bermudian laws under which the vessel operated.

They had already completed the legal declarations and had now moved-on to the contracting words that they had each chosen for their civil marriage ceremony onboard *The Sovereign Pearl* cruise ship.

Amy read out her chosen words while the ship's captain, Luciano Baldovini who was officiating, looked-on.

'I promise to love and cherish you and always be your friend,' she said, looking at Charles. 'I promise to value our relationship and always be honest with you. I will be there to comfort you in times of sorrow and rejoice with you in times of happiness.'

They moved on to the exchanging of rings, starting with Charles. 'I give you this ring as a sign of our love, trust and marriage. I promise to care for you above all others, to give you my love and friendship: to cherish you throughout our life together.'

Amy reciprocated with her own words. 'I give you this ring as a symbol of our love and all that we share together.'

Then it was the captain's turn. 'Charles and Amy, you have both made the declarations prescribed by law and have made a solemn and binding contract with each other in the presence of the witnesses here assembled. It therefore gives me the greatest honour and privilege to announce that you are now husband and wife together.'

They kissed and one of the ship's many photographers stood-by, asking them to pose for the camera – he intended publishing a small photograph of the happy event in the ship's daily newspaper *The High C* – the guests liked it when there were weddings onboard – and it would be good for staff morale.

One of their new friends, Matheus the head wine waiter, turned-on the CD player to the tune of *Amazed* by Lonestar while the two newly-weds signed the register and received a copy of the marriage certificate.

'I'd like to be the first to congratulate you both on your marriage. May I wish you both a wonderful day today, a very long and happy marriage and all the very best for your future lives together. Congratulations Mr. and Mrs Eden!' announced the genial Captain Luciano Baldovini who then had to rush back up to the ship's bridge to check that the voyage was still on schedule with no untoward happenings onboard.

The Sovereign Pearl was following an eight-day itinerary around the Mediterranean starting-off in Venice. In the days that followed, the ship had stopped-off at Bari in Italy, Katakolon in Greece, Izmir in Turkey and then Istanbul. Their wedding had taken place on the sixth day while the ship was at sea – a very busy time for the ship's crew as it meant entertaining three thousand people, cooped-up inside a big tin can. However, being May, they had struck lucky with glorious weather – which meant that most of the guests were relaxing either on their balconies or in other outdoor areas of the ship while the little ceremony had been taking place.

Both Charles and Amy, being ranked as junior officers in their new roles as ship's hotel managers, had been issued with navy-blue uniforms – which they had been obliged to pay for – it would be docked out of their pay. They had decided to wear these for the marriage ceremony and would later surprise everyone at home by posting their photos on social media. Amy guessed that her mother would be furious – but the deed was done now and it was about time to accept the path that she had chosen in life – including her new husband, Charles.

Like the captain, both newlyweds were due back on duty within the hour. It hadn't been easy to find a time-slot for the ceremony – they'd had to fit-in their wedding around their shifts – and the captain's schedule. They didn't forget for one moment that they were on this ship primarily to serve their guests and would have to put-off any celebrating until they were at anchor the following day in Dubrovnik, Croatia.

*

Late that evening, at the end of their working day, they met-up again below deck in the staff quarters: a huge, cavernous area of the ship where over one thousand of the ships' personnel lived. The crew members: cleaners, waiters, laundry workers and maintenance staff, occupied the lower deck, Level B, which was below the waterline with no portholes or windows, sharing their two, three or four berth cabins.

Amy and Charles as staff members, which included management and officers, were housed on the higher deck. Known as Level A, this was just above the waterline. It was on this deck that the crew and staff facilities were based, which included the crew shops, bar and canteen. There was even a recreation area, swimming pool and outdoor space as many of the personnel were not allowed into the guest areas or public places on *The Sovereign Pearl*. Guests were generally unaware of the unseen army of people who kept the ship running smoothly twenty-four hours a day.

Standing together hand-in-hand on the busy outdoor deck at the stern on her first evening of married life, Amy looked at the reflection of the moon shimmering on the water.

'It's so stuffy in there tonight,' she said, 'even with the air conditioning full-on.'

'I hate the heat at times – it makes people do some crazy things,' Charles replied.

She laughed. 'Like deciding to get married on a cruise ship in the middle of the ocean, you mean?'

'Well, we came to see the world – together – and that's what we're going to do, Mrs Eden!' Charles took her hand.

'I can't wait to visit the old city of Dubrovnik,' she said, her deep brown eyes shining in the half-light. 'I'd love to walk along the ancient walls – it would be a memorable moment. Maybe a good photo opportunity too – being our first full day of married life?'

'It's a pity we won't be able to spend more than three hours ashore this time. But if it's possible ...,' he replied hesitatingly not wishing to quell her enthusiasm.

'But there will be other chances – we're going to repeat the same itinerary nineteen more times before we move on to the Greek Islands in September – so, anything we miss tomorrow ...,' she replied.

'Matheus was telling me that the best way for us to get there is to walk from the quayside where the ship will be berthed – beside a mountain he says.'

'How far is it to the old city then?'

'About three miles – otherwise we would have to wait ages for a local bus – and the ship's shuttle buses will be full with guests early-on.'

'What about a taxi?' Amy suggested.

'We could try, but with three thousand guests, the queues are going to be long. The only consolation is that the shuttle buses will be almost empty by the time we need to get back to the ship, so we'll be able to …'

They never did finish their conversation as they were suddenly interrupted by a commotion. A noisy rabble of crew members, headed by Matheus, their friend, was coming towards them, then began surrounding the two newly-weds.

'Hey, Mr. and Mrs Eden, we were looking for you!' announced Matheus with a huge grin 'We have a surprise for you!'

One of the Filipino waiters in the assembled crowd, held a battered acoustic guitar which he started to play. They all began singing *Grow Old with You* by Adam Sandler.

'Thank you, all,' Charles announced, genuinely moved that some of the crew had made an effort to mark their wedding day with a song.

'That's not all. The real surprise is yet to come!' replied Matheus.

Then the little group, still singing, escorted the newly-weds along the open deck and through two sets of double-doors which led through to the bar where the fortnightly crew party was in full-swing. As soon as they arrived there were loud cheers as Charles and Amy joined-in the merrymaking. What had begun as an unassuming and discreet wedding ceremony earlier in the day had turned-into a full-blown celebration with over two hundred staff and crew members dancing the night away. It was like having a huge family around them to share their special occasion.

Afterwards, back in their cabin tired and exhausted from the day's events, they had made love. Charles looked at his new wife with a feeling of tenderness and wanting always to be there for her.

'You know I meant every word I said at the wedding – about being there to listen, comfort and support you, whatever our lives may bring.'

'And *you* know that I meant every word about giving you my love and friendship – and cherishing you always,' she replied with one of her beaming smiles. 'But just now, Mr. Eden, we need to get some sleep if we're to rise early in the morning for that three mile walk to Old Debrovnik!'

'There's no-one else on Earth for me,' were his last words before they both fell asleep exhausted.

They were at the start of a new phase in their lives, looking forward to a future together with brighter skies ahead. Neither of them was aware of the storm clouds gathering over the horizon, ready to wreak havoc on their hopes and dreams.

Chapter 36

His flight had been delayed for two hours at Schiphol Airport. It gave Lord Crawthorne plenty of time to think about the events of the day as he nursed a Glenfiddich in the departure lounge.

George Crawthorne had been milling-over Mr. Gs warnings. Firstly, there was Laetitia, the regular prostie that he visited whenever he went over to Amsterdam – usually seeing her before picking-up a consignment to smuggle back to the UK. He thought of her now, touting for business in her little booth in Oudekerksplein 2, the little street in the heart of the red-light district; near to the coffee shop where he'd had the meeting that afternoon. Laetitia, a Romanian girl with beautiful long, fair hair and sparkling blue eyes. It was George's custom to liaise with her around noon – the start of her working day when she was fresh and clean. Only, today, she hadn't been there, posing in her window. Instead, he'd settled for an African girl with large breasts – but he'd found her to be a sullen cow – not like Laetitia who always told him what a nice man he was – then he'd give her a generous tip and she would smile gratefully.

He hoped that Mr. G had been bluffing: he hated to think that Laetitia had been disfigured as a warning to him. But surely, that wouldn't make sense to these people? Laetitia was a high earner: putting her out of business would affect their profits. After all, they owned her – she was their property.

George decided that it would be foolish to return to Amsterdam anytime soon but he would speak nicely to a few ex-schoolpals in the House of Lords next week – offer a few favours and ask them to visit Laetitia – then report back. There was nothing altruistic in his motives – he just wanted to know whether his favourite Amsterdam commodity would still be ready and available to him if he braved-it enough to return to the great city. However, one thing was certain: he wouldn't be going back to collect any more diamonds. After tonight, that phase in his life would be well and truly over – despite anything that Mr. G might say.

As passengers started boarding the Boeing 737 bound for Gatwick Lord Crawthorne started to wonder whether there was any chance that Mr. G and his cronies would deliberately set him up to be apprehended by customs officers? It would only take one anonymous phone call and the game would be up. If caught, the diamonds would, of course, be confiscated and he'd be expected to recompense the organisation for the loss of the goods – as well as enduring a hefty jail sentence to boot – and at his age, he'd never see the light of day again. At least, not outside of prison. It was a depressing thought. He pressed the button above his seat, activating a panel light, alerting the cabin crew that he wanted something. He was travelling business class.

'Can I help you, Lord Crawthorne?'

'I'd like a scotch – on the rocks – make it a double, please.'

'Certainly sir.'

Five minutes later, he was savouring the lilting peppery sweetness of the whisky, drifting through a bitter warmth as it washed over his tongue. Already he was feeling better. He held it in his mouth, gums tingling: then swallowed slowly, feeling the heat up the back of his throat which then bloomed in his chest. He licked his lips with his tongue. He felt like he was tasting a soft-sweet, warm ember. His cheeks flushed just a little.

Pressing the button again, he ordered another drink: this time glugging-it back, leaving his head swimming, feeling heavy. His eyelids slipped a little lower as he started to relax, lips tingling. The nagging pain in his groin now felt duller and he began to nod-off.

Later, after the short one hour and fifteen-minute flight, George found himself on the long walk from the gate to passport control. He was exhausted after his turbulent day: it felt as though someone had thrown grit in his eyes and his legs were reluctant to keep-up with the rest of the exiting passengers. But eventually, he joined the end of a slow-moving queue and readied himself for the passport check, suddenly finding himself perspiring. For once, Lord George Edward Crawthorne was feeling nervous.

However, using the automatic self-service identity checker, he was relieved to find that the barrier allowed him through straight away without any hassle and he then headed towards the final hurdle: the customs hall, conscious that he was carrying a velvet bag containing around fifty thousand pounds-worth of diamonds tucked into his underpants.

Now feeling more at ease, George followed other passengers as they entered the section for EU citizens only; then through the green channel – *nothing to declare.* As was often the case, there were no customs officers in-sight, although he was more than aware that monitoring cameras would be tracking anyone of interest. He also knew that, even passing through this area unchallenged, there was always a chance of being apprehended at any stage of his exit from the airport, including the car park.

Once out of the arrivals lounge George took the elevator and across the bridge, finding his black Range Rover where he'd parked it earlier that day. As usual, he took out the burner phone hidden underneath the driver's seat and texted a number to say that he'd arrived. Although his contact would have been tracking the time of the plane's landing at Gatwick, the text message was the signal that all had gone well in passing through customs unscathed – it meant that George had made it to his car and that he would be at the meeting point in Brighton, in just over thirty minutes' time. The two-hour delay at Schiphol had served him well for avoiding the earlier traffic congestion which always snarled-up the main arterial roads in the South of England.

It was now a little past ten o'clock and Lord Crawthorne found himself having to concentrate hard as he drove southwards down the M23, then shortly joining-up with the A23 in drizzly rain: maybe it hadn't been such a good idea to have that whisky knowing that he would be driving to the rendezvous and then back home. He guessed that he was a little past the limit and needed to keep a steady hand on the wheel just in case some ambitious young police patrol officers were looking-out for someone to pull-over.

Parking in the usual place, adjacent to a small recreation ground near the centre of town, George waited for the exchange of goods to take place. After ten minutes, he heard a motorbike approaching. Shortly afterwards, as expected, there was a double thump on the roof of his black Land Rover.

Winding-down the car window, he passed-over the velvet bag wrapped in plastic, from inside his trousers. A leather gloved hand took the bag and George, used to this routine, watched a helmeted figure in his rear-view mirror making a cursory inspection of the contents by torchlight.

It's nearly over, he thought. *Soon I'll be home with Isabela, a large glass of scotch in my hand. Then I can start planning how to finally quit this game. There's no way that I'm going to do this anymore. For God's sake, I'm nearly eighty!*

Shortly afterwards there was another thump on the roof: the signal that the money was about to be passed through the open window. However, this was the point when everything suddenly went badly wrong. For, instead of setting eyes on the expected large A4 envelope full of banknotes, George felt the muzzle of a Makarov pistol being pushed against his head. He didn't hear the click of the trigger, releasing one single 9.3mm bullet, but he did feel the excruciating burning sensation just before the blood began pouring out of his mouth and down his back. Then nothing.

Mad Ronnie Howell wasn't stupid. He'd read all the signals and he realised that he could no longer rely on Lord George Edward Crawthorne, 15th Baron Crawthorne. He couldn't take anything the old man said at face value – George was a player who'd now served his purpose: and now the removal men had been called in. The organisation could not risk allowing Lord Crawthorne to live and have him blabbing to the authorities: he had become a liability.

For Lord George Crawthorne, diamonds were no longer the smuggler's best friend.

Chapter 37

It wasn't until a day later that Charles was summoned to the bridge of the cruise ship *The Sovereign Pearl* to take an emergency call from his mother, Helen Eden, daughter of Lord Crawthorne. Charles was in emotional turmoil, stunned by the news: his grandfather, who he had spoken to so recently, had been shot – in his car – in a Brighton car park. The news had rocked the family.

Back in West Sussex there had been a media frenzy with film crews and journalists camping-out on the grass verges outside The Knapp, the Crawthornes' residence in Aldwick Bay.

Albert Warnford was in his element, loving the opportunities that had arisen for him to become the centre of attention in this tragedy. Firstly, he had attempted to woo the press by sending-out Kathy with trays of tea and biscuits; then availing himself to be interviewed, answering their many questions about his deceased neighbour.

'Can you tell us about your relationship with Lord Crawthorne?' One curious journalist ventured.

'Yes, we had a lot in common: animal welfare in particular. We were both passionate about wildlife.' Albert had decided to adopt a caring, considerate and co-operative stance – he knew that would look good on television.

'And when did you last speak to him?' The journalist thrust a microphone in the direction of this wizened old gent, who was so willing to give his version of life next door to the famous Lord and Lady Crawthorne.

'Probably about a week ago. He was asking my advice about our boundary fence.' He did not mention that he had been harassing George and that the peer would have happily strangled his next-door neighbour given half-a-chance.

'Can you think of why anyone would want to murder him?' called-out Shane Montgomery, a veteran reporter from a national newspaper. He wore his signature sheepskin coat and a trilby.

'I have no idea,' replied Albert honestly. 'I did hear about allegations which were made against him when he went to stay at his former home recently.'

'You mean Crawthorne Hall?'

'Yes. I was there – at the hotel – shortly after he'd visited. I heard there was a serious problem between him and a female member of staff.'

'Oh? Montgomery's bushy, caterpillar-like eyebrows twitched as he jotted-down the details. 'Anything else you can tell us Albert?'

I know that Lord Crawthorne – I always called him George – went abroad on business from time-to-time. Like everyone else I can only speculate that there may have been some connection to his murder – especially as he'd just arrived back from Amsterdam on that same evening.'

After several more meaningless questions and plenty of banal answers from Albert, the media interest in him started to wane so he decided to hit them hard with an announcement that he had planned. Something that they could not ignore.

'By the way.' He spoke deliberately and with a degree of pomposity. 'I am organising a night vigil in honour of my friend and neighbour Lord George Crawthorne to take place exactly one week after the murder. It will be held from ten o'clock on the evening of Monday 3rd June.'

'Where will it take place, Albert?'

'On the private Aldwick Bay beach. I'd like to ask anyone in attendance to bring a candle. We'll be having a bonfire and maybe even a barbeque.' Albert, the self-appointed, arrogant busybody was making-it-up as he spoke. 'I will be having Who Shot George T-shirts printed which will be on sale. Also, I'll be bringing along a selection of music. Then we'll have a two minutes' silence at eleven o'clock. I hope as many of your viewers as possible will be able to come along and lend their support.' With that he returned indoors, hoping to have made enough impact to merit some kind of coverage on national television. He was not disappointed.

Next door, Lady Crawthorne, totally distraught, was being comforted by her daughter and son-in-law. The police, too, including the family liaison officer, were in attendance. They had been talking-through the events of the past twenty-four hours and had decided to go ahead with an imminent public appeal – to be televised – in the hope that members of the public might come forward with information.

'Of course, I'm happy to put up a reward,' offered Lady Crawthorne. 'I'll do anything I can to help you apprehend George's killer.'

Two detectives were sitting side-by-side on the leather chesterfield settee. One, Detective Constable O'Brien was in his mid-forties with thinning hair. He had a large frame underneath a loose-fitting coat. His companion, Detective Sergeant Ian Horvarth, was a little younger but more smartly dressed in a tailored suit.

'Can you think of anyone who may have had a motive to harm your late husband, Lady Crawthorne?' ventured Horvarth.

'It's true to say that he could be controversial – he spoke his mind and, like a lot of people in public life, no doubt had his enemies. I can't think of anyone specifically and he didn't mention to me any concerns – although it's true to say that I wasn't privy to his business dealings.' She paused.

'So, no-one comes to mind?' prompted Detective Constable O'Brien.

Isabela started to shake her head – and then a sudden thought struck her.

'There was one person who caused my late husband a lot of grief – always complaining. It's a neighbour of ours who seems rather unbalanced – my husband was convinced of him being mentally ill – very unstable …'

'And what is the name of this neighbour?' began DS Horvarth with interest.

Just then they were rudely interrupted by an announcement on the television, which was blaring-away in the adjacent room. Everyone froze as they heard the severe tones of Albert Warnford, the self-appointed neighbourhood meddler, addressing the media:

'I am organising a night vigil … Who Shot George T-Shirts … barbeque … two minutes' silence …'

'How dare he enter our family grief like that! The impudence of the man!' Helen Crawthorne was furious.

'Shall I go and have a word with him?' suggested her husband, Richard. As a solicitor he realised that Albert was not doing anything illegal. However, his insensitivity to what the Cawthornes were going through at this time together with his lack of tact and decorum was almost unbelievable and the next-door neighbour needed to be taken to task for his unwanted interference.

'Not just now, but thank you, Richard,' said Lady Isabela Crawthorne quietly. 'I think it best that we finish talking to the police so that they can get on quickly with their investigation. We can deal with Albert Warnford later.'

*

Despite the family's protestations, the night vigil went ahead without their permission, Albert Warnford, a law unto himself, ignoring their requests to cancel the plans. Richard Eden, Lord Crawthorne's son-in-law had considered taking out a court injunction, but Isabela caved-in and resigned herself to the event taking place – albeit without the family. Exhausted after the frenetic police and press activity during the days following her husband's murder, Lady Isabela Crawthorne had succumbed to pressure to go and stay with her daughter and son-in-law for a week or so until she felt more able to cope back at *The Knapp* along with all the painful memories.

And so it was that on the first Saturday of June, a crowd of just over thirty people, mostly local residents, gathered together around a fire which had been lit near to the burnt-out beach chalets on Aldwick Bay's private beach. Natasha, Albert Warnford's daughter was organising T-shirt sales from a small table to one side but there was little uptake as, most of those present, were reviled by the idea of walking around with *Who Shot George?* emblazoned upon their persons. There was little appetite, too, for the barbequed burgers on-sale, courtesy of Kathy Warnford; nor indeed, the hot drinks on this warm sultry summer's evening.

After a clumsy start, accompanied by Albert's inappropriate choice of music – an instrumental version of Paul McCartney's *Live and Let Die,* the informal ceremony took-on a sombre quality as one-by-one, people who had either known Lord Crawthorne personally or wished to contribute to the sentiments, approached the little podium which had been set-up a little way from the fire. Microphone in-hand they took it in turns to say their piece.

'His murder has just rocked the residents of this quiet bay,' announced one neighbour. 'I lived in South London for thirty-two years and it's like something you'd expect there but not in this part of the world. I hope they catch whoever it is soon.'

'God bless Lord Crawthorne. It's a very, very sad time,' commented another.

'I'm thinking why? Why? It's just so terrible. God bless his family and all the people he's left behind,' said a third person in the semi-darkness, candle held in one hand.

This was followed by a slight, nervous figure coming up to the podium.

'And you are?' enquired Albert rudely through the public address system as though she was an intruder.

'Hello, my name is Sylvia and I'm the housekeeper for Lord and Lady Crawthorne,' she began hesitatingly. 'The family are unable to be here personally tonight as they are still too distressed to face the public. However, they asked me to read a message.' Sylvia was accompanied by her husband who shone a torch on the piece of paper which she held in her shaking hand.

'We have been shocked and saddened by the death of Lord George Edward Crawthorne a dedicated husband and father who diligently set-about his work both in and out of the House of Lords. The family is working hard with the police to discover the perpetrator of this crime. Hopefully, he or she will soon be apprehended. Meanwhile, we would like to reiterate advice given by police to residents that they should tell family and friends where they are going and how long they will be before leaving the house. A criminal is still at large and we need to be vigilant and keep safe. Thank you.'

The two minutes' silence was a sombre moment for the well-wishers as they stood there, on the shingly beach with the sea lapping against the shore, each holding a lighted candle, absorbed in their own thoughts. Afterwards, neighbours chatted around the now dying fire, subdued music still playing in the background as Albert Warnford and his family began packing-up the many unsold T-shirts, extinguishing the barbeque and retrieving litter which had been discarded on the beach. At that point, two men approached Albert from the shadows.

'Excuse me? Mr. Warnford?' enquired DS Horvarth.

'Yes. But I'm a bit busy at the moment. I can't stop to talk,' Albert said abruptly, trying to brush them away like flies.

'Detective Sergeant Horvarth.'

'And Detective Constable O'Brien,' added the larger man. They both flashed their warrant cards.

'Well?' Albert spat out. He was unimpressed and unintimidated. 'I suppose it's about me organising this vigil. Some people are so ungrateful – I thought I was doing the family a favour.'

Not if you haven't the decency to even ask their permission, you insensitive bastard! People like you don't possess real dignity! thought O'Brien. But he kept his own counsel.

'No, it's on a different matter,' stated Horvarth matter-of-factly.

'Like what?' Albert was puzzled.

'Like, what were you doing on the evening of Monday the twenty seventh of May at around eleven o'clock in the evening?'

Albert was speechless – bewildered, shocked and dismayed. Surely, he wasn't a suspect?

'We heard you quarrelled a lot,' O'Brien added. 'And is it true that you keep a black motorcycle in your garage? If so, we'd like to take a look at it – if that isn't too much trouble Mr. Warnford?' There was a hint of sarcasm in his tone.

Albert, like all bullies when cornered, suddenly became compliant, finding it in himself to be civil for the first time that evening.

'One moment please.' He then called over to his wife. 'Kathy, can you and Natasha finish-off here. I have to show these gentlemen something.'

Kathy was bewildered, but she nodded – more out of habit, used to being at her husband's beck and call. *You go,* she thought. *I'm used to always clearing-up your mess after you, anyway.* Then with the sound of shingle scrunching underfoot echoing vaguely in the night, Albert reluctantly accompanied the two detectives along the beach and up the little side-alley leading to his house – and the garage where he kept his beloved motorbike.

The full-moon sat high in the sky generating an eerie light which permeated over the rippling sea. As Kathy Warnford continued packing-up for the night, helped by her daughter, she happened to glance over at the burnt-out shell of the Crawthorne's old beach chalet.

Gasping as she took in the sight of a figure standing there amongst the charred remains of the wooden building, Kathy could see a young woman. And in her arms, she held a baby. But something was not right. There was a look of anguish and panic on her face as she raised her head and stared back at Kathy.

'Mum, are you alright?' asked Natasha.

Kathy just stared, motionless, pointing towards the beach chalet remains and the creepy woman still standing there – at this time of night, holding her child. Maybe it was one of the homeless people who seemed to frequent the area at this time of year in the hope of finding shelter and generosity?

Natasha Warnford followed her gaze. 'Mum. What are you looking at? There's nothing there.' She was puzzled – and a little worried. Her mother had been acting strangely for the past few weeks now – ever since her wedding anniversary.

Kathy looked again at the figure standing there, staring back, looking as though a hand had been put down her throat, pulling-out her heart.

Chapter 38

The police had made little progress in their inquiries into the very violent and deliberate murder of Lord Crawthorne in a Brighton car park. Their first imperative was to find-out exactly what had happened that evening.

So far, they had established, using CCTV and road surveillance footage that George's black Range Rover had arrived at the recreation park at ten thirty-three precisely on the evening of Monday 27th May 2013. Shortly afterwards, a black Suzuki GSF 1250 Bandit motorcycle was picked-up by a road camera: the rider wore black leathers and matching full-face helmet, thought to be a Viper V170. A dog walker had heard a motorbike enter the car park at around that time and, when later interviewed, said that he'd heard a loud bang but hadn't gone to investigate. Cameras had again picked-up the motorcycle at four minutes past midnight, this time heading northwards on the A24 in the direction of Dorking. The number plate had been obscured.

There remained many unanswered questions. Firstly, they had been unable to establish a motive. Secondly, they could not understand – yet – why Lord Crawthorne should decide to stop-off in an out-of-the-way car park in Brighton on his way back from Gatwick to Aldwick Bay – it simply did not make sense at this stage. They had eliminated the neighbour, Albert Warnford from their enquiries and the focus of the investigation had now shifted to tracking the victim's movements in Amsterdam earlier that day: the Dutch police were co-operating and Interpol had been alerted. Nearer to home, the West Sussex police were currently looking through hours of CCTV footage to try to establish whether Lord Crawthorne had used the remote car park on any previous occasions: especially on the dates when he had flown back from Amsterdam.

Meanwhile, the coroner, having received the pathologist's report from the post-mortem had recorded the cause of death as being a fracture of the skull as a result of a gunshot wound. He had issued a burial order although a date for an inquest had been arranged to look at the full circumstances of the death.

*

The funeral had been a small, quiet, family affair. Richard Eden had taken charge of the arrangements on behalf of his mother-in-law Lady Crawthorne. Thinking outside the box, he'd used a new local undertaking firm by the name of comparethecoffin.com. Isabela, in the bleakness of her grief, had specifically requested a low-key event at the nearby parish church in Pagham, followed by a burial. Now in pieces without George to lean-on, she had opted for a small family gathering. Unable to face-up to a wake, she had told well-meaning friends and acquaintances that there would be a church service sometime later in the summer to celebrate her husband's life – with a reception afterwards: he'd have liked that.

The police family liaison officer had been very supportive throughout the time following George's untimely and tragic death. She had told the Press in no uncertain terms that they were to respect the family's wishes and to keep well away from the funeral – especially after local coverage in *The Chichester Times* which had revealed details and speculation about the shooting. The editor had received a reprimand after allowing an article to be published about an ongoing investigation which could give unwanted information to the wrong people, including the perpetrator. The liaison officer had also arranged for an undercover detective to be present at the funeral in case any persons of interest turned-up. In the event, they needn't have bothered.

Chapter 39

Passing-by the magnificent market cross in the small ancient Roman city of Chichester, Isabela and Helen then headed down West Street and past the cathedral until they came upon a tatty three-storied Georgian building next-door to an old warehouse. They gave their names to the severe-looking receptionist with the grey bun and judging eyes peering over half-moon spectacles. She asked them to step into the heartless waiting-room; old copies of magazines stacked high, mismatched chairs lining the walls like strangers; layers of dust conspicuously accumulating in corners.

'Ah! Lady Crawthorne and Mrs Eden, I'm Jasper Jacobs one of the partners here.' The paunchy, middle-aged solicitor with his thinning head of hair, proffered a clammy hand to each of them, which they shook out of politeness. 'I'm pleased you could make it – especially after the funeral being only yesterday. Do follow me.' He led them up creaky, carpetless stairs and then through a doorway. 'Mind your step.'

They found themselves in a small, cluttered room overlooking the front of the building with the cathedral towering above the roofs of distant houses.

'We thought it best to get all the formalities out of the way as soon as possible,' began Helen, referring to the reading of the will – their purpose for today's visit to the solicitor's office.

'Quite so,' Jasper Jacobs replied, looking with piercing blue eyes over his half-rimmed glasses. Isabela Crawthorne sensed an air of judgement about his demeanour. 'Please sit down both of you.'

They did as he asked.

'We've hunted at home for a copy of my husband's will – but he never told me where it was kept,' commented Isabela, hoping that the solicitor might shed some light on the matter.

'That's because I was under strict instructions to keep the original copy of the will here. We also keep copies in our secure storage facility – it's a precaution in case of fire and such like. I will, naturally, give you a copy of your husband's will before you leave today Lady Crawthorne, but I wanted to go over some of the contents with you first. That's why I've called you in to see me.'

Lady Isabela Crawthorne looked puzzled and her daughter Helen, too, wondered what the mystery was all about. Why not just hand it over and let them be on their way – unless it was a way of squeezing money out of a rich old widow – solicitors' time cost money. Helen, like her father, had always been one of life's cynics.

Jasper Jacobs retrieved a number of papers from a file and looked at his two new clients.

'Basically, Lady Crawthorne and Mrs Eden, I have been entrusted with looking after Lord Crawthorne's affairs now that he is deceased: it will involve liquidating some of his assets – certain stocks and shares – in order that invested monies are readily available to you – placed in a number of bank accounts. An accountant has also been appointed – Mr. Brian Braithwaite: I'm afraid he couldn't be here today. We are the executors to the will, with a duty to ensure that your husband's wishes are fulfilled.' He looked purposefully at Isabela.

'Go on,' said Helen, a little impatiently.

'This,' Jacobs held up a clipped wadge of papers, 'embodies the main part of the will – of which I will read the salient parts.'

'Thank you.' This from Isabela.

'And as I said earlier,' he continued, 'I'll hand over to you a copy – and other relevant financial information.' He paused and looked at each of his visitors to give them a chance to ask questions or to comment on what he had told them – but they both sat there blankly waiting for him to divulge the contents of George's last will and testament.

'I will read from Section Four which says, quote … *I leave the whole of my Residuary Estate to my wife Lady Isabela Crawthorne …*'

There was a tangible sigh of relief from Isabela – George had never discussed these matters with her. However, she was aware that her late husband had always accused her of having no money sense. She had half-expected the solicitor to announce that Lord Crawthorne's wealth had been put into trust for her. But here he was, announcing that George had left her the whole of his Residuary Estate. She wondered when she could go out and start spending some of it. She always loved squandering money – retail therapy was one of her favourite pastimes.

The solicitor was aware of Isabela's reaction. Her body language said it all: she could scarcely contain her delight at hearing that George had been generous to her in his will. Jacobs felt that he should clarify the situation before continuing to read further.

'Yes, Lady Crawthorne, the whole of his Residuary Estate – that means, what is left after any other bequests together with legal and other expenses such as funeral costs.'

'Please read on, Mr. Jacobs. I assume you are about to tell us about the other beneficiaries?' Isabela replied glancing furtively at her daughter. She now wished that she had asked Helen's husband, Richard, along to this meeting: after all, he was a solicitor. Unfortunately, he was busy in court for most of the week, so they'd decided to go ahead without him. After all, what could be so difficult about sitting listening to the reading of a will?

'Yes, Lady Crawthorne, there are, of course, other beneficiaries.' He read on, repeating the first part again, just for clarification.

'*I leave the whole of my Residuary Estate to my wife Lady Isabela ... with the exception of a sum of five hundred thousand pounds for my daughter Helen Eden together with all my personal effects to include my two Rolex watches, four gold rings and a velvet pouch of gemstones, held in a security box by Jacobs and Jacobs Solicitors. She may use her discretion to pass any of these items to my much-loved son-in-law Richard.*'

'Well, I'm overwhelmed – glad that my father remembered me in his will.' Helen, a genuinely modest and generous-hearted woman sat quietly in a purple upholstered armchair next to her mother, who appeared to be pleased for her daughter.

He continued reading. '*In addition, I am leaving fifty thousand pounds each to any grandchildren who are alive at the time of my death.*'

'That's Charles. He is the *only* grandchild,' commented Helen, Charles' mother.

'Quite so,' agreed the solicitor. Then he added, 'Of course, the will has to go through probate before we can start putting everything in motion.' He continued as before. '*I bequeath forty thousand pounds to the Crawthorne Hall Hotel towards a project to enhance the grounds. This is conditional upon allowing excavation of the kitchen gardens in the vicinity of the apple tree: an undertaking to be co-ordinated by my grandson, Charles. The purpose of this is to clear the good name of the family in respect of the rumoured murder which supposedly took place in the mid-seventies. A crime said to have taken place in what is now Room 13. There has been speculation for many years that there is a body buried near the tree and my wish is to prove this to be a false and wicked lie designed to discredit the Crawthornes.*'

Lady Crawthorne and Helen, having heard what they needed to know, now started getting-up to leave.

'Oh, I haven't quite finished I'm afraid. There's another part that I need to read – still from Section Four.'

Jacobs paused. 'Oh, yes, here it is … *Also, I leave a Cartier diamond necklace together with matching earrings and bracelet to my wonderful former personal assistant Sheila.*'

Isabela's face suddenly turned fierce and dark with the memory of her husband and his extra-marital affairs that had plagued their marriage – she would have left George years ago, but was too comfortable with the lavish lifestyle that he had provided through his vast wealth and family connections.

'*The jewellery has been lodged in the same security box as the gold rings and gemstones, held by my solicitors Jacobs and Jacobs.*' Having finished reading this section he looked-up at his disconcerted visitors.

'Is there anything that I can do to challenge the will?' enquired Lady Crawthorne hanging-on to a modicum of civility. Underneath, she was seething with hate and disgust for Lord George Crawthorne's lover and mistress – to whom he had bequeathed such items of great value.

'That is always possible Lady Crawthorne, but I would advise you that you would be unlikely to win. Lord Crawthorne was of sound mind – also, you might risk losing your own share of the will if there was a successful counter-challenge.'

Isabela held her peace.

'Then there is one final bequest,' he continued, reading once again from Section Four of the will. '*I leave five hundred thousand pounds together with my beloved Horizon Elegance 20 entry-level yacht to Frances Amelia Hughes …*'

'Who the hell is she?' interrupted Isabela with a flash of shock and irritation. She sat stone-still as though a ghost had passed-through her. There was a strange, wry expression on her face as though a realisation had suddenly dawned on her.

'Who is she, Mr. Jacobs,' repeated Helen indignantly, almost as shocked as her mother. Why would Lord Crawthorne, her father, leave money and a valuable asset to someone neither of them had ever heard of? She glanced sideways at Lady Crawthorne who was starting to turn purple as anger welled-up in her bosom.

'Well, I must say, that is a question I was about to ask *you*, too,' Jacobs replied, scrutinising firstly Helen, then her mother, 'because I have no idea who she is. I need to locate her as one of the benefactors of your father's will.'

Chapter 40

To: Amy
From: Mum
Date: Wednesday, July 3, 2013 15:58:10 EST
Subject: Venice

Hi Amy,
I was totally shocked by your news – your marriage – I saw the wedding photos on Facebook.

Something has happened that I need to talk to you about. I know that we haven't been getting along for some time, but I really need to speak to you – urgently.

Can we meet in Venice next time your ship is in Port?

Love (always), Mum x

To: Mum
From: Amy
Date: Thursday, July 4, 2013 16:32:07 EST
Subject: Venice

Hi Mum,

It would have been nice for you to congratulate us on our wedding – but no, not you. We didn't tell you because you don't like Charles. Anyway, he's my husband now so – *tough.*

I don't know whether I really want to see you. However, my husband has swapped shifts with me so that I can meet you in Venice, as requested. The ship docks early morning on Tuesday 8th July. I can meet you for an hour – if you suggest a time and place, I'll be there provided that nothing unforeseen occurs on the cruise – norovirus outbreak, staff illnesses, engine failure etc. etc. My first duty is to the ship. Amy x

To: Amy
From: Mum
Date: Thursday, July 4, 2013 19:47:23 EST
Subject: Venice

Hi Amy,

We've booked a hotel room for three nights – outskirts of Venice as couldn't get anything nearer to the city centre. Suggest meeting at eleven o'clock next Tuesday 8th July in the museum café in St. Mark's Square. It is quieter in there than most other cafes in Venice, tucked away on the first floor of the Royal Palace of Venice, in the reception area adjacent to the bookshop and the museum ticket office. We should be able to talk there away from crowds.

Text me if you have any problem finding it or if you need to change the timing.

It's important, so please don't cancel.

Look forward to seeing you.

Love (as always), Mum x

To: Mum
From: Amy
Date: Friday, July 5, 2013 23:02:17 EST
Subject: Venice

Hi Mum,

Will text you if any problems – otherwise will see you in the museum café.

Amy x

Chapter 41

Amy's mum sat waiting nervously for her estranged daughter, wondering whether they would still be on speaking terms by the time they left the café.

'Where's Harry?' Amy had just arrived – ten minutes late. She'd taken the *People Mover* – a type of shuttle train – from the San Basilio Cruise Terminal into the centre of Venice and then caught a number two water-bus from Ferrovia Station to St. Mark's Square. As always, Venice was seething with tourists and she'd had to wait longer than expected in the queues for tickets.

'I needed to see you alone, so he's gone over to Murano to see a glass-making demonstration – we're meeting up later for a gondola ride.'

'Lucky you.'

'I like your hair – it suits you. You're looking well,' said her mum encouragingly.

Maybe married life suits me? Amy thought sarcastically. But she kept her own counsel, not wanting to start an argument. Instead, she looked around her, noticing that, just as her mum had predicted, the café was fairly empty of customers. Then, feeling hot and sweaty after her walk she decided that she needed to freshen-up a bit.

'Is there a toilet in here?' she asked.

'It's through that door over there, down about six steps. I'll order drinks. Coffee?'

'A macchiato for me, please.'

Amy disappeared while her mum hailed a waitress. She was seated on a table for two beside a window with spectacular views over St. Mark's Square.

*

'Well, Mum. What's so urgent that you need to come seven hundred miles by air to see me? You know that I have only about one hour to spare – then I have to go?'

'I have something important to tell you – I'm sorry, darling.'

'About what? And why are you apologising?' Amy was bemused.

Sheila just sat there, seemingly trying to find the right words. She hardly knew where to begin. Amy was becoming impatient.

'Just spit-it-out for goodness' sake, Mum.'

'I'm sorry – I'm a coward,' began her mum. 'I'd give anything not to have to tell you this – something I should have told you years ago – about your real father. But I kept putting it off. You stopped asking about him, so I didn't say any more.'

'I've always been curious – of course I have,' replied Amy. 'But whenever I broached the subject, you always avoided answering my questions – I assumed my real dad was a mass murderer or something – someone so bad that it was best for me not to know about him. So, I blotted-him out, like I didn't have a real dad, only an empty space inside me.'

'It's nothing like that,' continued her mum. 'I wanted to spare Harry's feelings.'

'Well, as far as I'm concerned, Harry is my dad – he's always been there for me. I don't care about my real father any more. He never showed any interest in me.'

'That's just it, Amy. He did – show a lot of interest in you and was aware of every step you made as you grew-up.'

'So why did you never let me meet him?'

'Because it was a condition set by Harry.'

'Mum, I really do not understand any of this. Will you just level with me? Just speak in plain English – I'm not in the mood for riddles.'

'Okay. Your dad, Harry, has always been impotent. We were unable to have children and I was desperate to have a baby. Then my boss – took a fancy to me. I was his personal assistant at the time and we talked about personal things – his wife hated sex. So, we made an agreement to – shall we say – help each other out.'

Mum, that's disgusting!'

'No. I loved Harry – but our marriage would have died a death if I hadn't been able to have a child. So, it was agreed. Then, when you were born, Harry doted on you and we had a happy family life.'

'*But*? Mum, there's always a *but* – *a*nd I can tell that there's more to it than you're letting-on.'

'My boss and I found we had a chemistry together. He made me feel like a real woman – we carried-on seeing each other. He wouldn't leave his wife and I didn't want to leave Harry.'

'Did Harry know about your affair?'

'Yes. He put-up with it rather than end our marriage.

'That was very noble of him.' She felt a tinge of sadness.

'He knew that my boss could give me something that I needed,' continued Sheila. 'Something that he was unable to provide.'

'Sounds a bit too clinical to me. Dad – Harry – must have been crazy. He should have walked-out – you two-timing cow!' Amy was becoming angrier by the minute, thinking about her dad and what he must have suffered. 'May I ask for how long this affair lasted?'

'You really don't want to know, darling.'

'Don't you dare fucking-well tell me what I do or don't want to know, Mum. Just answer the fucking question or I swear I'm out of here.' She looked around her in the café, wondering whether to storm-off.

'Okay. Our affair lasted twenty-five years – on and off.'

'WHAT! You mean throughout my life you had been seeing my real father and not telling me who he was. You bitch!'

'You did know him, honey – when you were a little girl. He used to come and take us out sometimes. But when you started growing-up he stopped visiting you in case you realized his true identity.'

Amy suddenly paled with shock. 'Oh my God, mum. It's not who I think it is? Surely not?'

'I'm afraid it is,' replied Sheila. 'You knew your real father as Uncle Georgie.'

'So why tell me now – twenty-four years too late?' Her anger was rising in her once more.

'Because your father is dead. George was murdered six weeks ago. He was better known as Lord George Crawthorne, 15th Baron Crawthorne.'

Chapter 42

It was five-thirty and, after the mandatory safety drill, the ship was finally on its way with its three thousand newly embarked guests. The enormous *Sovereign Pearl*, over three hundred and forty metres in length – longer than the Eiffel Tower is high – edged slowly out of the San Basilio Cruise Terminal and then headed serenely and majestically along the huge canal towards the sea. The decks were crammed with passengers looking out over the magical floating city of Venice as they began their journey towards Bari, their first port of call.

Charles hadn't seen Amy since she'd arrived back. Embarkation day was always hectic from early afternoon and she had gone straight back to work: ensuring that the senior supervisory stewards had checked-off the cabins on each floor before they were made available for the new guests.

He had grabbed a half-hour break before starting-back on his split shift: he would be assisting the maître d'hôtel with seating for dinner tonight. There were three main restaurants onboard: *The Ritz*, which was set-out like a traditional top-class English hotel dining room; *The Janeiro,* which had a South American theme to the décor and a more informal ambience; and finally, *The Rialto,* decorated in the Italian tradition. All three main restaurants offered the same menu, but passengers often wanted to make changes to their allocated restaurant or table: most often demanding a table for two rather than share a larger table with strangers for eight days.

Charles had decided to go up on to deck 14 to watch as the *Sovereign Pearl* sailed steadily on course towards the Adriatic Sea, past crumbling, sumptuous and serene palazzi that clung to the banks along the way. From this vantage point he could take in a panoramic view of the whole of the old city with its Baroque architecture dominating the skyline. He could see ancient piazzas – public squares – and a network of tiny canals intrinsically woven around the buildings. Surely there was no other place on Earth like this: it was a magical moment for him – there was something beguiling about this city and he looked forward to coming back many times in the future, hoping that he would be able to spend time with his wife in Venice when they next docked.

It was at about that time that the ship rounded a corner and he could see the magnificent St. Mark's Square on his left surrounded on three sides by stately public buildings. On the fourth side, plain to see from his vantage point on the *Sovereign Pearl*, were the Basilica's riot of domes and arches and the soaring St. Mark's bell tower. He thought of Amy, who had met her mother there in the museum café earlier that day: he wondered what had been so urgent that Sheila Hughes had felt compelled to come all the way to Venice to talk to her only daughter.

*

Amy had debated how she was going to break the devastating news to Charles. In the end she'd decided to simply hand him the letter.

'My mother passed this on to me – unopened. It's from a firm of solicitors called Jacobs and Jacobs who are based in Chichester.'

'That's a coincidence,' he announced stating the obvious, 'Near where my grandad lives – *lived*,' he suddenly corrected himself. 'We never did get to see him before we left. I deeply regret now that I didn't make the effort. I was still cross with him for the way he behaved at the hotel.'

She made no comment. They were both sitting on one of the tiny beds in their cabin, shattered after the exhausting embarkation day – and her meeting with Sheila, her mother. They really needed to get to bed as they were scheduled to be up at six o'clock the following day ready for the first port day in the cruise itinerary. However, she doubted whether either of them would get much sleep anyway by the time they had both absorbed the implications of what she had learnt about herself – and Charles.

'Read it then Charles.'

He was staring at the envelope: it was addressed to *Miss Frances Amelia Hughes* and bore her parents' address. Amy hated her first name, so she had always been known as Amy by her friends and most of her family – the name being a derivation of Amelia.

Taking-out the letter, Charles started to scan it. 'Oh my God, Amy. I don't understand. This is madness!'

'That's what I thought at first.'

He resumed reading, this time giving the letter his full attention.

Dear Miss Hughes,
Re: The last will and testament of Lord George Edward Crawthorne

Charles wondered why she should have ben sent a letter from a solicitor relating to his grandfather's will. It simply did not make any sense. Besides which, Amy was rarely addressed as Frances. He continued to read:

We have been instructed to contact you regarding the will of the late Lord George Edward Crawthorne, 15th Baron Crawthorne, your father.
Having traced your mother's address in Dorking we took the liberty of phoning Mrs Sheila Hughes to ask whether she would ensure that this letter reaches you safely. We have told her nothing of the contents other than that it concerns the will. It should reach you unopened.

In essence, Miss Hughes, you have been named as a beneficiary in the estate of your father: we are obliged to tell you that, bearing in mind your love of boating, Lord Crawthorne has bequeathed to you his Horizon Elegance 20 entry-level yacht together with a sum of five hundred thousand pounds, both of which will be made over to you after probate.

We understand that you are currently working abroad, so would request that you contact us by phone or email to confirm safe receipt of this letter and so that we can establish the best ways of communicating in the future, as there will be various legal documents that you will need to complete relating to your inheritance.

We trust that we will hear from you at your earliest convenience.

Yours sincerely,

Jasper Jacobs

For Messrs. Jacobs and Jacobs Solicitors

Chapter 43

'So where do we start?' Amy asked Charles after he had finished reading the letter.

'How about telling me what your mum said to you today?' He had a horrible feeling of unreality as though this was just a bad dream happening to someone else. Amy's mum had a lot to answer for – in more ways than one.

Amy repeated what Sheila had told her about her long-term affair with George Crawthorne – how it had started and why.

'She told me that George Crawthorne, your grandad, was a good man – at least in her eyes. My mum can't see that *she's* the dodgy one. She even lied about my parentage for twenty years. It's only when I left university that she told me my dad, the person who brought me up, wasn't my real father. She lied to me by omission and I hate her for it. I remember this uncle who used to turn up from time to time in Dorking when I was young – she called him Uncle Georgie but said he was a friend of the family. I usually found him there when I got back from primary school on his way out – I often wondered just what the connection was as no-one else ever mentioned him.'

'Did your dad have an idea that she was having an affair?'

'It turned-out that my dad knew what had happened but decided to grin and bear it: bring up another man's child rather than lose my mother – the bitch.'

Suddenly the full implications of what they had been told started to hit-home with Charles. Amy was already feeling sick to the core. She had been able to mull it all over for several hours and was ahead of her husband.

Charles, like a drunkard suddenly sobering-up to bad news, had started to put the pieces together and he didn't like what he was seeing. The whole situation stank.

'It's all starting to make sense now,' he began queasily. 'Your mother not accepting me – her hostility – trying to dissuade us from being together. She knew all along.' He shook his head distractedly.

'She had always known of the existence of Lord Crawthorne's grandson. How could she *not* know – he was famous for goodness' sake. But as her lover, she took more than a passing interest in his family.'

'So that's why she started being cold towards me when we met at the Grand Regent Hotel on my birthday?' Charles cast his memory back to that evening and some of the questions that Sheila Hughes had asked him.

'Do you remember that everything was going well until my mum started quizzing you?'

'How could I forget? She started stone-walling me and I wondered what I'd done to offend her.'

'She confessed to it all when I met her at St. Mark's Square. You had told her that you went to Essex University and that you were brought up in Chichester. Then, I put my proverbial foot in it by telling her that your grandfather used to live at Crawthorne Hall before selling-up to the hotel chain.'

'Yes, I remember you saying that I was Lord Crawthorne's grandson!'

'And then they looked at each other in a curious way – my mum and Harry,' she recounted.

'I thought that was a bit spooky,' chirped-in Charles.

Amy continued. 'My mum told me that she phoned your grandfather afterwards – and that's why he came to see you at the hotel – that time he made an indecent pass at Penny.'

'The pervert. Who says you shouldn't speak ill of the dead? He was a dirty old man, pure and simple, whether or not he was a titled peer of the realm,' commented Charles matter-of-factly.

'That's my father you're talking about!' She meant it as a joke – and he realised that.

'As you know, he tried to persuade me not to stay with you, suggesting that I should be playing the field at my age.'

'And you told him to sling his hook – that it was none of his business. I remember you telling me about it.'

'So, the old bugger's left you a fortune!' Charles poured himself a glass of water. 'Would you like one?'

'Thanks.'

'What will you do with the boat?'

'I really don't know, Charles. Of course, I'd love to have it – travel around Europe in it, maybe. But I don't know that I could sustain the costs long-term. Maybe I'll keep it for a season and then sell it on. But anyway, that's the least of our problems. We have to deal with the elephant in the room. We both know what it is but neither of us is facing up to it.'

'I don't know so much about an elephant – I'd say it's more like a bloody great whale in here that we're pretending not to see.'

'Well?' Her eyes were brimming with tears, which welled-up and then began streaming down her face. He'd never seen her looking so sad. There was a pause. Silence, apart from the cabin's air conditioner and the melancholy boom of a foghorn out at sea.

'We need to talk this through until we can find a solution,' said Charles, feeling suddenly scared and tired at the same time. 'Everyone needs to talk.'

'No, everyone needs to cry. Certainly, I do.' Biting her lip, she placed her head in her hands, wishing things were different, but knowing that they never could be.

'I'm so sorry,' was all he could say at that moment. 'Today's news has royally screwed us.'

'It's not our fault Charles. We fell in love. I don't know whether I ever want to speak to my mum again after all her deceit. How could she have kept this from me for so long? I feel so hurt and totally betrayed.'

'I know all that, but it's not addressing the main issue. I love you so much, my darling Amy.' His eyes were moistening. He put his arm around her and held her close.

'But is love enough to get us through this? My mother spelt it out to me today. I'm your aunt – your mother's half-sister and you are my nephew. My real father is your grandfather. It's against the law for us to marry – so it means our wedding's a sham. We can't be together as husband and wife.'

It was two o'clock in the morning. They had no energy left to continue with this. It was not something that could be resolved with the flip of a switch – how could they suddenly make everything better unless the law suddenly changed?

Some things in life are worth fighting for and some are not. Charles and Amy were deeply in love – but also deeply shellshocked by the devastating news which had blown their whole future up in smoke.

Chapter 44

2014

Fast approaching the thirteenth anniversary of the terrorist attacks by Al-Qaeda against the United States on the morning of 11th September 2001, Heathrow Airport was on high alert.

Bob Bennett and Penny were queuing in the baggage check area when it happened. A dark-haired man had been pulled-aside for a body search, which he had resisted. Aged about thirty years old and dressed in jeans and a T-shirt he suddenly leapt over a counter. He was running, dodging through the sea of people, followed by two aviation security men dressed in black uniforms, each armed with Heckler & Koch MP5 submachine guns slung over their shoulders. After about forty metres he was slowed down by passengers pouring through from the luggage check-in area: at which point a third police officer from the operational command unit appeared, blocking his way. Little was said as they roughly grabbed hold of the man, pushing him face-down on to the floor before handcuffing and dragging him away through a side door.

Bob himself was travelling on a doctored passport and had been expecting a few hiccups along the way. Conscious that he had a criminal record for several counts of arson, he knew that there was little chance of being admitted into the United States – and achieving his dream of visiting The Big Apple – unless his forged documents were good enough to fool the authorities. In these days of hi-tech checks, he was also expecting border control to utilise fingerprint identification technology. So, he had paid big bucks to the best in the business, hoping that this would enable his entry into America.

It was obvious to Bob that security at Heathrow had been ratcheted-up to a high alert status, so when he and Penny finally joined the queue at Gate 37 to board their plane, it was no real surprise when a small American security man stepped over in their direction.

'Excuse me, sir. We're conducting spot-checks on this flight. I'm from the United States Department of Homeland Security.' He indicated his badge. 'How are you today?'

'Fine,' answered Bob hiding his nervousness behind a smile.

'May I ask you the purpose of your visit to the United States?' His ample moustache twitched as he spoke.

'I'm a tourist.' Bob answered politely.

'Are you travelling alone?' The man was ticking-off a checklist on his clipboard.

'No. I'm with my partner. She's waiting over there for me.' He pointed in the direction of Penny who had stopped at a rack of magazines and was selecting some reading material for the flight.

'May I see your passport?' Bob handed it over. The security man flicked-through the pages. 'Mr. Bennett?' Bob nodded.

Then, after several more seemingly meaningless questions, the passport was handed back to Bob, who felt relief wash through him.

'Have a good journey, sir. My colleague will need to look through your cabin luggage just before you board the plane.'

Although the authorities were obviously taking passengers' safety extremely seriously, Bob did wonder why his passport had needed to be scrutinised twice – had this truly been a spot-check or was he under some kind of suspicion? He was mulling this over as he re-joined Penny and they passed-by the second American security guy, seemingly without being noticed. Then, boarding the plane they took their seats in business class, making themselves comfortable ready for the seven hours and twenty-five minutes' journey to John F. Kennedy International Airport. It was then that they heard a commotion by the door.

'There he is!' The second American security guy, now panting and red-faced was pointing accusingly at Bob. He was accompanied by a male cabin steward who looked furious as he stepped onboard. The American, having no jurisdiction on the Boeing 787 Dreamliner, stayed where he was beside the door; passengers continued to push through, finding their seats.

'Oi you! Come with me!' bellowed the crimson-faced cabin steward with a swirl of outrage. He was on the warpath.

'Me?' Bob was amazed by the aggressive attitude.

'Yes, you. Come with me now. And bring your luggage with you.'

Bob had no choice. Humiliated in front of the other passengers he found himself being led-off the airliner. It reminded him of the times when, in the past, he had been arrested, remanded in custody, incarcerated and controlled by those in authority: often wearing handcuffs on those occasions. Bad memories came flooding back to him. This was not the treatment that he expected in his new, free, life: although there was no alternative at this moment but to comply.

Bob realised that if he complained or put up any resistance, the airport authorities could always prevent him from re-joining his flight. Led-out like a criminal, he soon found himself opening-up his cabin bag, which was then searched. This was followed by turning-out his pockets, placing various items into a plastic tray: keys, tissues, wallet, passport. One item that he always carried was concealed in a spring-loaded plastic container.

'What's that?' demanded the security man, as he chewed a piece of gum.

'My magnifying glass – I use it for reading small print?'

'Show me,' the American continued dubiously. To him it just looked like a slim, black plastic box – with a switch on the side.

Bob held it in his hand and pushed the automatic pop-up button on the side. The American pulled away sharply, instinctively covering his face with his arms, thinking that this passenger may have just triggered a bomb. Instead, Bob remained standing there, the magnifying glass now clearly in view.

By this time the Gate was closed and the aircraft was ready to leave. Bob felt slightly depressed imagining that his best friend Penny would soon be winging her way to the States while he was stuck here in this crummy passageway with the American security guy. However, five minutes later the man nodded to the still-waiting cabin steward who had so rudely ejected Bob from his seat. Then, escorted back on to the plane, he took his seat, now rather shaken-up. The door was promptly closed and the Dreamliner started taxiing along the runway amidst safety checks and emergency drills for passengers. Bob and Penny, now sitting more relaxed, clinked their glasses of champagne.

'Cheers!' They were on their way at last.

*

Bob knew that the last part of the journey was likely to be the most challenging. Queuing for over an hour to present themselves to United States Customs and Border Protection officers in JFK Airport, New York, Bob and Penny finally walked through the barrier. Even the fingerprint identification checks seemed to have been satisfactory. However, it wasn't long before they were approached by two plain-clothes security men and led away to a small interview room where Bob was once again made to hand over his passport and answer questions about himself. Penny remained outside the closed door.

'Have you ever been convicted of any crimes in the United Kingdom or any other country, Mr. Bennett?' asked the larger of the two men, a burly, beady-eyed individual. There was seriousness in his tone as he spoke, watching Bob Bennett unblinkingly.

'No, I haven't,' lied Bob. What else could he say?

There followed a barrage of questions: *Are you on any medication? Are you carrying anything banned in the United States? Did you pack your own bags?*

Finally, he was allowed to go and, joining Penny, the two of them hastened to the baggage reclaim area and then to the arrivals hall and out of the terminal to find their taxi. They laughed with relief as they read from the giant billboard opposite to the taxi-rank which said *WELCOME TO NEW YORK*. Bob Bennett, the ex-arsonist, had made it into America. Next stop: Times Square.

Chapter 45

A few days later, Bob and Penny were sitting in Junior's Diner, a celebrated eatery near the corner of Broadway and 45th Street. They were staying in a luxury suite in the nearby Marriott Marquis Hotel in Times Square but had heard that Juniors served-up a world-famous authentic New York Cheesecake and they had promised themselves to sample it for breakfast. A taxi driver had told them about it.

'You haven't really lived until you've had cheesecake at Juniors. Their cheesecake is as important to New Yorkers as the Brooklyn Dodgers ... the Fox Theatre ... Coney Island's famous mayors, presidents, Hall of Fame athletes, authors, singers, movie stars – many celebrities have travelled miles to Juniors for their cheesecake. You should try it.'

Bob and Amy were not disappointed. After consuming two large pieces of the famous cheesecake, they then went on to try the speciality pancakes with blueberries and whipped cream. Then they settled-down to make use of the free Wi-Fi – old habits died-hard for Bob Bennett the multi-millionaire. He opened his laptop and checked his emails – mostly trash – but there was something in his in-tray which grabbed his attention straight away.

'Talk about a blast from the proverbial past!' he said as he opened it with eagerness and anticipation.

It was an email from his friend Charles Eden. They had been keeping in touch since Bob had left the hotel and started on his world travels.

To: Bob
From: Charles
Date: Saturday, September 13, 2014 21:02:18 EST
Subject: Excavation of Crawthorne Hall kitchen gardens

Hi Bob,

I'm not sure which country you're in at the moment but wanted you to know about developments back at Crawthorne Hall.

As you know from my previous email, my grandfather Lord Crawthorne,

193

bequeathed a sum of money to the hotel – but it was conditional on being allowed to excavate the area around the apple tree. I know this is important to you so that you can lay to rest the story (true or false?) that your friend Paul told you before he died – witnessing a murder at the hands of my great grandfather.

Similarly, I want the Crawthorne name absolved and exonerated from wrong-doing. My grandfather George Crawthorne finally agreed to help me in this prior to his death and provided the means to accomplish this task.

Amy and I are currently back in the UK in-between contracts so I will be overseeing the excavation work which I have organised to take place on Wednesday 1st October. You are more than welcome to join us if you can.

Hopefully one of us will not be disappointed!

Take care. Charles.

Bob replied immediately.

To: Charles
From: Bob
Date: Sunday, September 14, 2014 13:02:18 EST
Subject: Excavation of Crawthorne Hall kitchen gardens

Hi Charles,

Thanks so much for keeping me in the loop. Penny and I are in New York – The Big Apple, shortly to fly to Los Angeles and Santa Monica. From there we're taking a cruise along the Mexican coast heading for the Panama Canal. We'll be in Guatemala on 1st October and, sadly, there's no way I can be at Crawthorne Hall without abandoning the itinerary.

So, apologies and, of course, I'll keep in touch by email. Please let me know if any news. Hopefully we will soon find out what really did (or didn't) happen in Room 13!

Your friend. Bob.

Chapter 46

There is something rather lovely about eating food sourced, at least in part, from your own garden.

Like many luxury hotels, Crawthorne Hall promoted its kitchen gardens: a place where much of the food on the menu could be grown. Guests could wander around the grounds, observing at first hand food that would be served up in the restaurants later that day, eating seasonally according to what was ripe to harvest. There was a team of gardeners, responsible for tending the crops and another team of pickers who would deliver the fresh produce to the kitchens.

Right now, the two teams had gathered near to the large Bramley apple tree with its ripening fruit, which was located in one corner of the walled kitchen gardens. This serene area within the grounds of Crawthorne Hall and close to the East wing of the house had remained unchanged for many years. Based on a classic Victorian design it had two cross paths bounded by a perimeter walkway, producing four central beds and a series of borders at the base of the surrounding walls. The central beds were the main growing areas for annual crops and operated on a four-year rotation of potatoes, brassicas (cabbage family), legumes (pea family) and salads and root crops. The potato quarter was manured and double-dug each year as it moved around the rotation. The wall borders accommodated perennial crops with soft fruit in the westernmost; asparagus, rhubarb, seakale, and globe artichoke in the easterly; and auriculas, lily of the valley and cordon currants and gooseberries in the southern.

The warm, South facing border was reserved for bringing-on early spring crops: heat lovers like herbs for summer, then late crops in the autumn. This central flower border was a feature of the original Victorian Garden layout at Crawthorne Hall which had been established in the mid-nineteenth century. In Summer, this area was full of scarlet crocosmia, orange dahlia and yellow kniphofia but now, with the onset of autumn, there was little colour apart from the changing hue of leaves.

Charles Eden, his unshaven face raw from the biting wind, stood anxiously watching the proceedings. The two gardening teams took-up picks and shovels and began to dig in a five-metre radius of the apple tree.

It was thought that mechanical diggers could cause too much damage to anything which lay buried; and also, to the roots of the old apple tree. Charles was accompanied by Colin Howard, the General Manager.

'It's good to have you back, Charles. So, where's Amy today?' Colin, hands in pockets, stood huddled in his capacious double-breasted peacoat jacket with the collar pulled-up. He shivered exaggeratedly.

'Amy opted to visit her mother in Dorking. It was a bit cold and blowy for her to stand around here all day.'

'A pity. I'd have liked to have seen her – maybe another time before you re-join your ship?' As he spoke, the wispy wind caught him in the face for an instant. He carried on with the conversation, brown hair, peppered with grey, now dishevelled. So, have you learnt anything in the cruise industry that you didn't already know from working here?'

Charles thought for a moment before replying. 'Only that really rich people have avocado on their toast rather than bacon and eggs!' He was joking.

They both laughed.

'By the way, once you two have had enough of sailing on the high seas, you know there is always a job awaiting you here at Crawthorne Hall.' Colin said it with an effortless calm.

Charles was taken by surprise. He had left under a cloud after the way his grandfather had behaved so abysmally towards Penny: he had been made to feel responsible and guilty at the time. 'That is very reassuring, I'll mention it to my wife!' They had retained their married status, shrugging-off the initial shock about the illegality of their union, deciding that life would go on: ignoring the archaic, nonsensical laws which they felt were no longer relevant to the modern age. Few people had realised that Charles and Amy were blood-related and that their marriage was really null and void.

'Yes, you know my proverbial door is always open to you,' added Colin reassuringly.

'Thank you.'

The two men had positioned themselves a little way from the diggers, near to the rubbish burning area in the far corner, from where they watched the proceedings.

'I hope they find something soon,' uttered Colin, who seemed to be in a talkative mood. 'It's as bloody cold as a witch's tit out here today. A pity it's not rubbish burning day: we could do with some heat.'

As the work around the Bramley apple tree continued, a sprinkling of rubbernecking guests hovered close to the diggers while others watched surreptitiously from their guestrooms. A rumour had been deliberately put-about that Roman treasure was thought to be buried on the site: this was thought to sound much better than advertising the exhumation of a suspected dead body.

It had taken some persuading to arrange for the excavation but the hotel directors had found the sweetener of Lord Crawthorne's bequest to be appealing enough to give the go-ahead. Charles was footing the bill for the diggers. He was also paying for the services of Arnold Butterworth, a trained archaeologist and Professor Susan Wilkinson, a forensic anthropologist who was leading the dig. As time had gone on, this excavation had taken on the hard edge of an obsession for both Charles Eden and Bob Bennett. This was going to be their only chance to find out whether there was any truth in the story about what happened in Room 13. Was there really murder on that night after one of the remaining poker players was caught cheating? And if so, was his body really buried here? Hopefully they would soon know one way or another.

As the topsoil was removed, the two professionals sifted through the accumulating piles of debris in the hope of retrieving any environmental and trace evidence. Using trowels and brushes, they examined material remains: an old broken plastic comb, ceramic fragments and a plastic chocolate bar wrapper. Nothing unexpected or of great interest.

The digging continued through the day with piles of removed soil growing in size, along with an orderly network of trenches. However, it was not until mid-afternoon that Charles and Colin heard a shout from one of the diggers, followed by the sound of a whistle: the signal to stop work. Professor Wilkinson headed over to an area two metres west of the tree. Then, signalling to everyone to stand back, she bent-down into the pit and started to gently scrape away the soil from an imbedded object. Arnold Butterworth, the archaeologist, put down the mattock that he had been using to break up the hard ground, then joined his colleague.

'Carefully does it, Susan.'

'Don't worry,' replied the forensic anthropologist, 'I've seen plenty of these in my time. I'll just clear some more of the accumulated debris. Can you pass me one of the small brushes please?'

'Here,' Arnold passed her the tool. 'Can I help?'

'Thank you but I'd rather do this alone, Arnold. I need focus now.' She raised her voice a little. 'Everyone move-back a little more, please.'

She worked away for a few minutes. There was a general hush as the diggers hovered around, peering with curiosity in Professor Wilkinson's direction as she worked. Charles and Colin took this as their cue to join the others – judging by the kerfuffle, something had clearly happened to instigate this pause in the proceedings.

As they approached, the workers parted a little, making room for them around the shallow pit which had been dug. Charles could see in the now dimming light of day that Professor Susan Wilkinson was gently scraping and brushing away dirt from the object which had been discovered. As he stared harder, he suddenly recognised what it was. The crown of a skull was poking above the soil.

Chapter 47

Ronnie Howell, one of Britain's most wanted fugitives had been caught hiding naked in a panic room at his luxury Spanish villa.

It was three o'clock in the morning when more than forty armed police officers had been given the signal to launch a dawn raid on his home in Malaga. Ronnie, sharing his bed with Elaine Evans and his new playmate Julieta, had been alerted to the operation when several of the hunting dogs he kept in his garden started barking. Pint-sized Howell, convicted armed robber and diamond trafficker, had been on the run since 2008 when he had escaped from a Category C Resettlement prison in Surrey, England. He'd previously served time in a much more secure institution but the authorities had mistakenly assumed that he was unlikely to try to escape, having already served most of his sentence.

Suddenly pandemonium broke out with the sounds of crashing, smashing, thudding and shouting as the Spanish police gained entry to Ronnie's villa.

'Put your hands where we can see them. NOW!' shouted one of the senior green-uniformed Guardia Civil police officers in English, steadily aiming his SIG Sauer P226 pistol at Luca, chief bodyguard to Ronnie Howell. The bodyguard immediately complied.

'Kneel!' commanded the special operations officer abrasively. 'Now lie-down, face to floor.' Luca was handcuffed from behind. The senior officer then moved on to the kitchen leaving one of his team behind pointing his H&K MP-5 submachine gun at the floor near to where Luca now remained motionless.

Similar actions were taking place in various parts of the house with the three other bodyguards surrendering without a fight; the element of surprise having got the better of them. Meanwhile, Ronnie had slipped into the walnut wardrobe beside his bed. Pushing aside a row of shirts hanging on the lower rail, he opened the small hatch which led to his panic room: a secure space which had been deliberately designed for situations such as this. Elaine then hastily rearranged the clothes rack and closed the wardrobe door: just in time before three armed police officers burst into the room. Taken by surprise, they had expected to find Mad Ronnie Howell but instead had interrupted two naked females in bed caressing. The older woman met their gaze then smiled.

'And what can I do for you, boys?' she teased, brushing back her lank hair and sitting up to expose her bounteous breasts. She achieved the desired effect as the policemen blushed and relaxed the grip on their weapons. Meanwhile, Ronnie Howell was watching the action furiously from the CCTV camera monitors inside the panic room. He could not believe that his men had behaved so cowardly without a shot even being fired – leaving him here trapped like a rat in a hole. He hoped that Elaine's ploy would be enough to save his skin: but he had not reckoned on the two German Shepherd detection dogs which were soon sniffing away and scratching at the wardrobe door.

'Come out, Señor Howell. We know you are in there. There is no escape for you.'

Ronnie knew that if he surrendered, he would likely be sent to a crummy overcrowded Spanish prison awaiting extradition to Britain. Then it would be a hefty jail sentence for a string of serious offences and his part in international organised crime. Should he come-out, guns blazing, making his last stand – or should he take his chances with the legal system – get himself a good team of lawyers, grease the palms of a few prominent people, arrange to knobble the jury? It was amazing how effective bribery and intimidation could be in earning a reduced sentence. After all the killings that Ronnie had instigated, he had always been acquitted of murder when it came to trial.

Having made-up his mind, Ronnie tentatively opened the little hatch, leaving his Colt Python double-action handgun hidden in a little recess. He knew that the .357 magnum calibre revolver, if discovered, would link him to a number of unsolved murders. Then, still naked after his impromptu attempt to hide away from the visitors he crawled-out to be greeted by several weapons which were pointing in his direction. Finally succumbing to having his hands cuffed, he was at least grateful that one of the officers draped a blanket around him. Now a pathetic figure, Ronnie Howell, who headed up one of the biggest criminal organisations in Britain and Europe devoted to diamond trafficking, extortion, money laundering and murder was at last in police custody.

'You, Mr. Howell, are going away for a long, long time, my friend,' uttered the Guardia Civil Police senior officer cheerily. He smiled smugly underneath his generous black moustache.

'Be sure not to make promises you can't keep,' retorted Ronnie with composure. 'Assume nothing, believe everything.'

The policeman looked baffled, trying to make sense of Ronnie's jibe. He pulled a face that was a caricature of confusion.

Elaine and Julieta were no longer in the house when Ronnie was finally detained in such a humiliating fashion. The two women had been allowed to dress before being bundled into the back of a filthy police van and driven away for questioning.

It was not until the following morning that Elaine Evans fully realised the seriousness of her position when, being brought up from her dank cell, she found herself in a bleak interview room in a police station close to the central court in Madrid. The two Spanish arresting officers who had detained her in Ronnie's bedroom were both in attendance, together with an interpreter and the solicitor who had been drafted-in the previous evening. They had been joined by a fifth person: someone who she had not seen for two years.

'Hello, Mrs Evans, do you remember me, Detective Sergeant Tom Crompton – West Sussex CID?'

Elaine said nothing.

'Elaine,' he continued without preamble. 'In addition to the charges read out to you last night which are being made by the Spanish police in regard to your criminal activities in an organised crime group, I am here with a European Arrest Warrant. Apart from current criminal charges that have been made against you in the United Kingdom relating to fraud – which was followed by your absconding to evade justice – I am here specifically to charge you with the murder of your first husband, Callum McFinn in 2006 and of your second husband Gareth Evans in 2012. An application has gone forward for you to be transferred to a prison in the United Kingdom where you will be held pending trial. You do not have to say anything, but it may harm your defence if you do not mention when questioned something which you later rely on in court. Anything you do say may be given in evidence.'

Elaine continued to stay silent. However, even then a plan was forming in her mind. A way of wriggling-out of years of incarceration. She was looking for a deal.

Chapter 48

2019

Action may not bring happiness;
But there is no happiness without action
Benjamin Disraeli

The sun, hidden behind greying clouds, suddenly made an unexpected appearance on this warm but unsettled summer's afternoon. Bob Bennett sat in his car, now parked by the grand entrance to the hotel. He was ahead of schedule and so relaxed and waited, taking in the view of the beautiful grounds which acted as a backdrop to this idyllic location. He looked again at the huge thunderbolt-like crack across his windscreen, caused by flying aggregate on the road, dropped by a builder's truck as he had sped here earlier, anxious to be on-time. He was waiting for Penny to arrive.

Hearing tyres crunching through gravel, he looked into his wing mirror and recognised the approaching vehicle as it scraped to a halt behind him. Bob, dressed in a light beige suit, climbed out into the hot August heat, closing the door behind him.

'What's happened to your windscreen then?' Penny called, winding-down her window. She always noticed little details.

'My car had an argument with some rubble. I'll get it checked-out tomorrow.

Penny slowly emerged from her car wearing her newly-bought bluey-grey snake print shirt-dress.

'Wow! You look stunning.' Bob held both her hands in his.

'I'm glad you like it – I chose the boa design. It's made from a lightweight cotton mix – I thought it was a cool option for our stay at Crawthorne Hall as it's so hot today.'

'And your hair – it looks lovely, Penny.' He loved her long, coral-brown hair.

'That's what four hours in the hairdresser's looks like!' She smiled. 'But there's no chance of you catching me in the swimming pool tonight. You'll have to go on your own!'

'No worries, that was the last thing on my mind for tonight,' he replied with some ambiguity.

Bob and Penny entered the hotel lobby where they were shown to their room: their luggage arriving shortly afterwards.

They had spring-boarded into a full-blown relationship after that first time together in New York when they realised that they wanted to be more than just good friends – they desired each other. A whirlwind romance had begun amidst their busy lives. From there, Bob had fulfilled a lifetime dream: setting-up his own business which he'd called *Fire Away Ltd.* He specialised in the manufacture of high-quality fire alarms. With the backing of his millions, investing in the latest technology, the firm had now established a good reputation, turning a good annual profit. Penny had taken time-out to study and qualify as a chartered accountant, now directing the financial side of *Fire Away Ltd.* Gradually the scattered pieces of their lives had been brought together like a giant jigsaw puzzle, each part fitting into the rest of the picture until they had the beginnings of a new shared future together.

When Penny had first met Bob at Crawthorne Hall Hotel, she had taken an instant liking to him but had not found him physically attractive to her. They had started-off as best friends. Then, during their travels they had become close to each other, wanting more than just friendship. In the beginning marriage was never considered desirable by either of them … not until that cold weekend one February.

After being together for five years, Bob had arranged a surprise weekend away in Paris. They had spent the day travelling around by bus, taking in the sights and sounds of the famous city, stopping off in the fashionable Marais district; bowled over by the beautiful authentic architecture of Rue Cremieux. Later strolling down the cobbled streets of Montmartre they finally ended up at *Le Mur des Je t'aime,* the famous Wall of Love in the Jehan Rictus Garden Square. In the evening they had taken a night time gourmet river cruise along the River Seine and it was as they were passing the iconic flood-lit Eiffel Tower that Bob suddenly and impulsively felt that this was the woman he wanted to be with for the rest of his life.

'Can I tell you something, Penny?' He'd suddenly asked.

'You know you can say anything to me – so long as it's something nice!' she had teased.

'I wanted to tell you that you are not only my friend, but you are my favourite human being.' He hesitated. 'I know you're the only one I definitely want to share my life with.' There, it was out at last.

Penny had remained impassive, just staring at him, waiting for him to continue. It was difficult to read her body language although he thought he could detect a twinkle in her eye.

'I promise you no-one will work harder to make you happy,' Bob continued. 'I just want to be where you are.' Already he wondered whether he'd gone too far – been carried away by the moment, so he'd just blurted it out at last. 'Will you marry me?' But had he now gone and spoilt everything? Bob half-expect her to laugh with her funny little chuckle, turning it all into a joke. But that had not happened.

Instead, she had said, 'You have an intensely romantic character, Mr. Bennett! I see trouble ahead.'

'Well?' he had ventured, rather more bravely this time.

'Yes, Bob. Of course, the answer is yes! I've been waiting for this moment for the past two years!'

Then, a year ago they had married – and here they were today, having returned to the place which, for a time, had become the landscape of their lives. Crawthorne Hall, where they first met. Now they were here again, having returned to celebrate their first wedding anniversary.

Bizarrely, they had deliberately booked Room 13 for their night's stay. Bob had never been superstitious. If there were such things as ghosts, he had never had any problems with them here at Crawthorne Hall. In a way, Room 13 held happy memories for him as it was the incident between Lord Crawthorne and Penny which had really launched a deep friendship, turning into love and marriage.

As for Mrs Penny Bennett, she did believe in the supernatural world and had noticed a pattern in the goings-on in Room 13 when she had worked at the hotel. It always seemed to her that bad people who stayed in the room, often ended-up with some misadventure: she remembered Albert Warnford's disastrous stay. Then there was Lord George Crawthorne – now dead. She remembered one disgruntled guest who had been consistently rude to staff – on the way home on a foggy morning his car had veered-off the road into a tree. A local newspaper report had claimed that, on his way to hospital he kept repeating over and over again that he'd looked in his mirror and seen a veiled woman with a baby sitting on the back seat: he claimed that she'd tapped him on the shoulder just before the accident.

On the other hand, there were numerous stories of other guests who had enjoyed happy stays in the infamous room. One woman had claimed to have been awoken in the early hours by a burning smell. She'd had an urge to phone her daughter in Sydney, Australia where it was early afternoon. The ringing of the phone, which was in the kitchen at the time, had alerted her to an unattended chip pan which had just started to ignite.

Penny also remembered an Egyptian guest staying in Room 13, whose passport had mysteriously gone missing. By the time it had been found he'd missed his flight. During his stay at the hotel in 2013 he'd told Penny that he was planning to take his wife on a surprise hot air balloon flight for her birthday when he returned home. But he didn't make it back to Egypt in time. The hot air balloon crashed: lucky for him, but not the nineteen other passengers who lost their lives. A fire had developed in the basket due to a leak in the balloon's gas fuel system, causing the balloon to deflate mid-air and crash to the ground. Penny had read about it in the papers – and she had wondered.

On another occasion a well-known novelist had deliberately asked to stay in Room 13 where he had happily spent two weeks finishing-off his latest book – a spine-tingling thriller. It had rapidly become a best seller and he had returned to Crawthorne Hall several times for inspiration in writing other books.

In her mind, Penny was convinced that good things as well as bad occurred in Room 13. She realised that her husband Bob didn't believe in supernatural happenings. However, whether it was at Crawthorne Hall or elsewhere on their travels she had noticed something slightly uncanny about Bob: he often seemed to be around when strange, inexplicable things occurred – whether for good or for bad. Sometimes she wondered whether he was a kind of conduit, unknowingly passing-on the vibes. She'd never mentioned it as he'd have told her she was going mad.

Their anniversary meal was taking place in the atmospheric Cromwellian Dining Room set in the underground vaults of the great house – an area that had, apparently been created by royalist prisoners during the English Civil War. Lord Crawthorne, 4rd Baron Crawthorne had been a supporter of Cromwell's parliamentarians and had helped to defeat the King's army at the Battle of Muster Green, then using enemy captives for slave labour at Crawthorne Hall. Like his father, he had been a cruel man and the prisoners had been treated harshly, many dying within the vaults.

Ironically, with its hidden chambers and recesses, there was a certain romantic appeal in this venue, steeped in history, together with its ghosts of the past: a unique place for celebrating special occasions. The candle-lit restaurant was half-full, being a Monday. The other diners were exclusively couples, who talked in quiet, subdued tones while gentle music played through speakers in the background. Although the Bennetts had spent many hours in this place in their previous working lives at Crawthorne Hall Hotel, they had never eaten here as guests and were looking forward to the novelty of the occasion.

'So, Bob, how was your day? You didn't tell me.' Penny sat opposite, the tiny flame of the candle flickering away, shadows dancing on Bob's face.

'You really don't want to know. It's not the best subject to discuss during our wedding anniversary celebration.'

Bob, now a respectable and successful businessman, had wanted to give something back to Society – partly motivated by a certain guilt over his misdemeanours in the past. So, he had decided to try to do something to improve the prison service. As a former inmate in a number of Her Majesty's establishments he had first-hand knowledge of bad practices – like slopping-out and prisoners cooped-up in tiny cells for twenty-three hours a day at times. He had once taken part in a prison riot to protest about poor conditions, although this had resulted in failure with the authorities ignoring the prisoners, rounding-up the ringleaders and meting-out draconian punishments.

However, Bob was now in a position to help and there was an appetite for change in Society – so he had joined the Independent Monitoring Board, known as the IMB, working as a volunteer three times a month. He would visit prisons, monitoring day-to-day life, ensuring that proper standards of care and decency were maintained. This position gave him unrestricted access to nearby prisons and immigration detention centres at any time. He could talk to any prisoner or detainee, out of sight and hearing of a members of staff if necessary.

'Go on,' insisted Penny. 'I'm interested.'

'As you know, I was up in Winchester today, looking at what was going-on in the kitchens, workshops and accommodation blocks. Spoke to a number of prisoners, as usual. Of course, they're always cagey about making complaints in case the screws get to hear about it.'

'Do you ever divulge that you've been inside?'

'No. But they know. They can always tell. People like them and people like me – we are the wrecked people.'

'I know you're still haunted by bad memories, Bob. So, how was it?'

'I always have that feeling of dread when I visit – like I'm going to wake-up and find I'm still an inmate. I'm always glad to get out into the fresh air afterwards. But I know that I can make things better – to make a difference – and that's what keeps me going back. It's rewarding emotionally.'

The wine waiter came along just at that moment and topped-up their champagne flutes before breezing-off again.

'Anyway,' continued Bob, now changing the subject. 'Happy Anniversary, Darling. Thanks for making me so happy. I knew something good could happen one day. I spent my life looking for you.'

'Likewise. It's been an amazing journey with you since we left this hotel. Cheers!' They clinked glasses.

'It's a bit like coming back as conquering heroes – returning as valued guests,' mused Bob.

'I'm glad we chose Crawthorne Hall for our first anniversary,' Penny added, looking at him with her beautiful shining eyes.

'Even staying in Room 13?'

'*Especially* as we're staying in Room 13,' she replied. 'I think I actually have a soft-spot for that room – despite a few bad experiences there in the past.'

They had finished their meal and were on the verge of going up to bed when Penny brought up something that had often been on Bob's mind over the years.

'It's a pity they never found a body, Bob. I mean, apart from the remains of a dead badger during the excavation of the kitchen gardens.'

'In a way, it's a good thing. It means that maybe no-one was murdered after all. I'd say that's something to celebrate, my lovely.'

'But, you know, Bob,' she ventured. 'That evening all those years ago in the Baronial Room – when I watched the hen party with the Ouija board. I was convinced that there was something uncanny going-on.'

'You and your supernatural!' Bob smiled affectionately. 'I remember you telling me that the spirit said he was called Lucky and that he'd been shot.'

'That's right.'

'I didn't know badgers could talk – or spell,' he said facetiously thinking of the glass moving around the Ouija board. 'I still think they were faking the whole thing just to put the frighteners on the bride-to-be!'

'If that's the case, then they were heartless cows,' she replied. 'But then, there was your cell-mate Paul Marsh who said he'd seen someone being shot when he was a boy – and thought his dad, the head gardener had been made to bury the body under the apple tree.'

'Only, when the excavation finally took place, all that could be found was the dead badger – complete with skull. That discovery was the end of the road as far as the Poker-Game Murder went. Maybe my cell mate, Paul, made it up after all? Just for the sympathy vote. You can never trust a jailbird.' He gave a funny sardonic smile.

'Personally, I still believe there was something uncanny about that Ouija board session,' she said after a pause. 'Once I was dusting the books in the old library in the West wing and came across a section containing various esoteric tomes on magic and other things.'

'Like what?'

'Like astrology, the paranormal, dream interpretation – oh, and there was something on extrasensory perception.' She raked her memory. 'There were a few books about mysticism and the occult, too – that's where I found stuff about using Ouija boards. I got the impression that someone in the Crawthorne dynasty must have had an interest in those subjects – otherwise, why buy the books?'

'Maybe we'll never know,' commented Bob. He was suddenly aware that his planned romantic evening had more or less gone up in smoke in favour of all this speculation about the supernatural. Looking at his watch he decided to change the subject. 'Come on, Penny, let's get to bed!'

'Good idea!'

'By the way.'

'Yes?'

'Happy Anniversary, again.' They kissed.

After all the talk about shootings, seances and dead badgers they had half-expected to have a bad night's sleep. However, once they were back in Room 13, they were focused on each other, enjoying just being together, in the moment. Bob and Penny drifted-off seemingly into a deep sleep, not stirring until the morning when they were awakened by a knock at the door announcing that Room Service and breakfast had arrived.

Room 13 was set-out in exactly the same was as it had always been since the opening of the hotel. Beautifully furnished and designed with its antiques, including an art nouveau statue of a scantily clad woman, the suite had been kitted-out to a high standard. The bespoke wallpaper had been designed by Belinda, the original interior designer. *The Kiss* print by the artist Gustav Klimt, still took pride of place and remained a prominent feature opposite the bed.

A little later, sitting at the low, round table in the recess after breakfast, Bob was browsing through the book which Penny had given him as part of his first wedding anniversary present. Penny was luxuriating in the en-suite jacuzzi as he browsed through the pages of *Great British Hotels and Gardens*. It was a newly published book illustrating how estates owned by nobility had fallen into disrepair, then risen from the ashes and restored to their former glory – but now being turned into luxury hotels rather than remaining as ancestral homes. Penny had chosen this due to its inclusion of Crawthorne Hall. It seemed fitting to give him a present featuring the place where they were now spending their anniversary.

As he glanced at the *now and then* photos something started to unsettle Bob, but he was unable to pinpoint exactly what was wrong. Holding the book in his hands he stood and looked out of the room's East wing window from where he could view the kitchen gardens to one side of the building. Just then Penny's mobile rang.

'Don't worry, Bob, I'll get it.' Penny had just emerged from the bathroom, her long, brown hair held-up with a small towel around her head. She wore one of the hotel's white flannel robes. 'Hello?' she noticed that there was no number displayed on her phone. As she listened, she was aware only of static. Then, without warning she felt a sharp burning sensation suddenly surge up on to her damp hand causing her to drop the phone. Bob looked up.

'Are you alright, Darling?'

'I got a shock from my phone. It must be my wet hand,' she replied, her face now ashen.

Bob looked puzzled – he'd never heard of anyone suffering an electric shock from a mobile phone. Stooping down to pick it up from the floor where it sat face-down, he glanced at the logo on the back of the casing. It was then that everything suddenly made sense. He realised what it was in the photos of the kitchen gardens that had been nagging away in his mind. Deep inside, he felt that, at last he was tantalisingly close to finding out what really happened in Room 13.

'That's a little creepy,' was all that he could think of saying.

The logo on the phone was in the shape of an apple.

Chapter 49

'Tonight's the night.'

Elaine nodded knowingly. After serving four years of her sentence, she had requested a transfer to somewhere nearer home, hoping to be placed in a lower grade institution. Bob Bennett had delivered the message to Elaine Evans personally during one of his IMB visits to the large Middlesex prison where she was being held. An old lag who had once provided Bob with forged work documents, had contacted him recently, asking him to locate Elaine and pass on the message. He couldn't refuse as he owed a favour. After all, it had been those forged documents which had enabled him to secure his job at Crawthorne Hall Hotel which, in turn, had transformed his life from a homeless vagrant and ex-con to the millionaire and successful businessman that he had now become. Judging by Elaine's reaction, she was expecting this message – maybe there was going to be an attempt to spring her from custody?

After being extradited to the UK and spending eighteen months on remand, Elaine had finally been convicted on two counts of manslaughter in relation to her deceased husbands. The more serious charges of murder had been dropped. She had escaped prosecution for fraud and a string of other offences. This had all been part of a deal hammered-out by her legal team in exchange for information relating to the criminal activities of Ronnie Howell.

He, in turn, had escaped many of the serious charges against him through plea bargaining, bribery and nobbling the jury. As one of the most feared and revered organised criminals in the country – the brains behind international diamond smuggling, extortion, drugs and people trafficking, he had finally pleaded guilty to *conspiracy to laundering income from crime*, for which he was now serving a seven- year sentence. His campaign of violence and intimidation, including the murder of anyone who got in his way, had been all-but ignored in the trial.

By rights Ronnie Howell should have been awarded several life sentences: in the event he had escaped justice with a bare minimal custodial sentence bearing in mind the severity of his crimes. On sentencing, Judge Patricia Braithwaite had described him as a criminal with a fertile, cunning and imaginative mind capable of sophisticated, complex and dishonest manipulation. He took that as a compliment.

'Come on, Evans. Get dressed and gather your things together. You're moving out of here tonight – just in time for Christmas. Do you understand? Answer Yes or No.' The huge, burly female prison officer stood intimidatingly close, leering at Elaine as she got out of bed and started to dress.

'Yes.' Elaine knew better than to ask questions. Her cell-mate, Jade, remained still, adopting the foetal position on her side as she lay on the top bunk pretending to be asleep.

'You have five minutes,' added the second prison officer. Do you understand? Answer Yes or No.' She thrust a large black bin liner at Elaine.

'Yes.' Elaine exhaled heavily. She had a splitting headache and could do without the gestapo hassling her like this. She started to bundle her personal effects into the bag. Even though Bob Bennett had tipped-her-off earlier, she was puzzled that she had not been summoned to the wing office to be formally informed of her transfer to another prison.

Within thirty minutes after being checked-out, she found herself in a small compartment the size of a toilet cubicle, inside a white prison van run by a private contractor. Despite the stench, which reminded her of an unwashed armpit, Elaine smiled smugly to herself, knowing that this mode of transport was far less secure than the official prison three-ton trucks that were often used. She heard other prisoners being loaded and then a long delay before the wheels started rolling and they began their bumpy, uncomfortable, monotonous journey to goodness knows where. She could hear the sound of the heavy, pounding December rain bombarding the van's roof like nails tearing through the sky.

Sitting on the hard moulded plastic bench inside the tiny compartment, she tried looking out of the tinted widow, squinting at the road, but there was little more than darkness to be seen, as night had set-in some hours before. Instead, she caught sight of her reflection in the glass, her brown hair now unkempt, uncombed and stringy. She shifted uncomfortably, feeling hot and stiff in the middle, then folded her arms rigidly across her chest, bracing herself as the ride became bumpier. It seemed as though they were now travelling across countryside, away from the main roads. She could just make out the shapes of passing fences in the night.

After an hour it happened. The van suddenly braked sharply. Headlights illuminated the road. She could see shadowy trees and then the sound of car doors slamming – and shouting. Something heavy started thumping on the side. There was the sound of breaking glass and screaming as a sledge hammer systematically struck the tinted windows. Then more shouting from outside.

'Elaine. Elaine Evans.' She could make-out the figure of a huge man. She knew by his posture that it was Luca, Ronnie Howell's sidekick.

'Yeah, I'm here,' she called through the newly broken glass with the welcome fresh air gushing through. She could now see Luca more clearly by the light of the headlights. He was dressed in red and donning a long white beard.

'She's in this one,' he called to the others.

Elaine heard more glass being shattered – this time at the front of the van – presumably the windscreen.

'Get out,' commanded Luca growling in a coarse voice at the prison officers. 'Now open the fucking doors or this blade cuts you. Got it? I won't tell you again.' This was followed by the sound of the external security door being opened. Then heavy footsteps in the tight passageway inside the prison van.

Elaine smirked as her door was released. Clambering out, she was led towards a silver Volkswagen Scirocco by Luca. She was installed on the rear seat while Luca joined the driver at the front. Two more men, also wearing Santa Claus costumes, punched the prison guards to the ground before joining Elaine in the back of the car. They sped-off down the lane, narrowly missing the driver of the prison van who was now running-off into woodland.

'Have a Crappy Christmas,' Luca shouted-out at the retreating prison officer, who disappeared from sight, fearing for his life. The other three men in the car laughed loudly.

After several miles, they stopped-off in a picnic area tucked out-of-sight of the main road where they switched to a black Mercedes. Then continuing with their journey, they carried on, now at a leisurely pace, leaving the Scirocco, a burning blaze illuminating the night.

Chapter 50

Elaine's euphoria at being sprung from the prison van, quickly evaporated. Sandwiched between two men, both dressed in Santa outfits, in the rear of the Mercedes, had been amusing at the beginning. However, a feeling of dread began to twist in her gut: she wasn't quite sure why she sensed that there was something awry.

'Thanks guys! Freedom again!' Her upbeat words masked the fear that had suddenly descended. The men remained silent, ignoring her words.

'Where are we headed, I could do with a pee!' Again, they said nothing. The smallest of the four men turned his head briefly in her direction before staring ahead at the road once more.

'This is it. Next left,' he said with a New York accent.

They turned-off down an unmade track, finally grinding to a halt outside a barn which sat in a haze of mist, lit-up by the car's headlights.

'This is your new home, Elaine,' announced the driver, now pulling-off his red hat and fake Santa beard. In the dim light she could see that he was, perhaps in his thirties with long dark hair – quite attractive, she thought. The others followed suit, also pulling-off their hats and beards, although she could not easily make-out their facial features in the semi-darkness. Elaine breathed a little easier now that the men were unmasked. Maybe it was prison life that had caused her to feel suspicious of her rescuers – that's what being banged-up did to you. Never trusting anyone as far as you could throw them.

'So, what's with the Santa costumes?' she asked.

'Ronnie said to wear disguises – we thought we'd adopt a festive theme,' replied the small man with the American accent.

'Yo! Ho! Ho!' added Luca.

With rain still pelting-down, they stumbled over the muddy, wet ground towards the door of the barn, directed only by faint torchlight.

'Hurry up, it's freezing my bollocks off out here,' called-out one of Elaine's rescuers.

'In here, Elaine,' said the American man, pulling open one of the large wooden doors. He struck a match, lighting-up an oil lamp on the floor beside the threshold. 'Please take a seat.'

Illuminated by the soft glow of the lamp, a solitary black plastic desk chair with rips in the upholstery awaited in the middle of the vast space. There was no other furniture or any home comforts – it was as though the party did not intend staying here for any great length of time.

'No, I'd rather stand,' answered Elaine supressing a shiver, her legs now wobbly with fear. Everything was wrong with this set-up. She felt like a goldfish in a small pond surrounded by sharks.

'I said, sit,' repeated the little American man, still quietly but now more insistently. The three others stood at a slight distance, watching the entertainment. Elaine, trembling inside, complied; her body now cold with dread as a hand gun was pulled-out. Her eyes widened with alarm.

'What is this all about?' she said, anxiety eclipsing her thoughts. 'Why have you brought me here?'

'Too many questions – and too little time, Elaine,' replied the little American man. 'We needed to deliver a Christmas present from Ronnie – and a message.'

'Oh?' Fear fluttered in Elaine's stomach. She suddenly realised what was happening – this was not about being freed from jail – it was about being punished. But what had they in mind? She fought a rising panic. Frown lines deepened on her lips.

Taking out his mobile phone from one of the side pockets in his leather bomber jacket, the young driver started to film the proceedings.

'Yes, Ronnie says that he doesn't take kindly to bitches ratting on him,' continued the small American man. 'You upset him very much when you grassed him up in order to save your own skin – those reduced sentences of yours. Mr. Howell needs to make an example of anyone who thinks they can betray him. But he has a soft spot for you, Elaine.'

'And I have a soft spot for him,' she lied. Maybe they were just putting-on the frighteners to teach her a lesson. With a bit of luck, they would be out of here soon – her included. She started to imagine them taking her to some sort of safehouse – she could do with a nice bath and a stiff drink.

'Yes,' continued the American man. 'Ronnie asked us to make it quick. You won't suffer for long.'

With that, one of the men came from behind, roughly grabbing both her arms.

'Ow! That hurts!'

Elaine heard the sound of duct tape being peeled-off a roll before it was used to bind her hands together behind her back. Then, it was wound around her torso, fixing her to the back of the chair so that she was unable to stand.

With sudden realisation, tears began to well-up, in her eyes, streaming down her cheeks. Furiously blinking, Elaine's face became a mixture of shock and confusion as she felt the barrel of a gun pressed firmly against the back of her head. With her greasy brown head of hair fixed down, she waited for the inevitable – the penalty for betraying Ronnie Howell.

However, there was no gun shot. Instead, the little American man spoke one last time to Elaine, this time in a whisper.'

'Ronnie wanted you to know that you're a nothing – a loser – a turkey. So, he decided to treat you like one. Very appropriate at this time of year. Now keep still, bitch.'

All of a sudden, she felt something being deftly pulled-over her head from behind.

'He's chosen a large-sized turkey oven bag,' the little man explained with a smile that Elaine could not see as he continued to ramble-on. 'Mainly because it fits all size heads, big and small.'

Another sound of duct tape could be heard as it was being pulled from its roll before being wound tightly around her neck. Elaine desperately struggling to breathe, started thrashing-about in the chair, panicking and gasping for breath; the plastic seemingly sticking to her mouth and nostrils as she tried to inhale. The level of deadly carbon-dioxide in the bag was now rapidly building-up by the second.

'You're honoured Elaine,' the little man continued conversationally. 'This was the preferred method of Mafia execution for snitches like you in the Brooklyn of my youth – in those days we used plastic trash bags. Goodbye Elaine – and Happy Holiday!'

By now, Elaine was twitching around. As she steadily suffocated through lack of air, she began to pass-out. Violent desperate struggling gave way to passive, slower movements, her mind starting to wander as she began to black-out. She faded into unconsciousness without ever uttering another sound, finally dying from the induced asphyxiation. For a moment the men stood staring in complete deafening silence, waiting to be sure that she was definitely dead.

'Okay, she's gone,' the American guy checked her pulse and breathing then looked at his watch. 'Send the footage to Ronnie, pronto,' he ordered. 'Come on, we're out of here. We have a boat to catch.'

Ten minutes later, a black Mercedes saloon car was heading through the colourless landscape, still shrouded by wintry darkness, towards Harwich International Port. This time, the car contained only four men – all tourists enroute for the Hook of Holland and then Amsterdam.

Later, as they waited patiently for the car ferry, three fire crews had arrived to extinguish a fierce blaze in a remote Essex barn near Colchester. The police had initially thought it had been started by youths, but that was before the charred remains of a body had been discovered early the following morning. It was still sitting in an upright position, now fused by melted plastic, in what had once been a black desk chair.

Relaxing in his high security cell, Mad Ronnie Howell watched the snuff film once again before uploading-it on to the internet. *Treacherous cow,* he thought nonchalantly, *she had it coming to her – needed to be taught a lesson – an example had to be made. No-one snitches on Ronnie Howell and gets away with it!* Looking forward to the day ahead, Ronnie breathed a sigh of relief that this particular problem had been resolved once and for all. Word would soon get around about Elaine's demise and with it, his reputation remained intact.

Ronnie Howell had retained his position – top man in his firm and top-dog of F-Wing – for now.

Chapter 51

2020

'Do something, for God's sake, do something!'

Sitting frozen on the upright wooden wishbone chair, Penny was unable to move a muscle without a searing pain shooting through her being. She had fallen from a step-ladder at the *Fire Away* warehouse that afternoon and landed badly, hurting her back. Bob had been down at Crawthorne Hall organising yet another excavation of the kitchen gardens, hoping that his latest hunch would, at last, be rewarded with a definitive answer. Finding a dead body seemed as elusive as discovering the holy grail, but he was determined to follow every lead that he could, to exhaust every avenue until he discovered the truth.

'I'll call an ambulance.'

Penny was in a bad state, twisted and contorted in agony. He hated seeing her like this – he felt so helpless.

'There always seems to be a disaster following your attempts to unearth your elusive body!' Penny had long-ago given-up seriously believing in what she now considered a myth. However, she continued to support Bob in his commitment to solve the so-called mystery.

'So, are you saying that some supernatural force deliberately pushed you off a ladder just because I was hunting for a buried body eighty miles away?' he retorted with a smile. 'Talk about far-fetched!'

'Well, it seems coincidental that we're scheduled to go on our holiday of a lifetime tomorrow and I'm unable to move. It's almost as though we're not meant to go.'

She was right about her accident jeopardising their long-awaited holiday to Asia – they were supposed to be heading to China for their New Year celebrations, stopping-off in Bangkok, Ho Chi Minh City, Hong Kong, Nagasaki in Japan and South Korea along the way. Now they'd probably shelve their plans until the following year.

By now, Bob was on the phone. 'I need an ambulance for my wife … her name is Penny Bennett …'

After spending ten minutes answering questions – *What is your address? Can you give me a brief outline of the incident or current complaint? Describe the pain on a scale of 0 to 10?* Bob felt that he was getting nowhere.

'I'm sorry, but this is not regarded as an emergency. Can you bring her along to the hospital in your car?'

'I told you – my wife is literally unable to move.'

'How many steps can she walk?'

'She cannot move,' Bob repeated, with little patience.

'Please outline her past medical history and any current medications.'

It was obvious that the operator was reading from some kind of script – she'd probably quizzed dozens of people already that day and sounded bored. The questions seemed endless, as though she was trying to spin this out. He imagined many more would-be callers desperately hanging on to their phone sets waiting for her to answer – instead, she was wasting time with her inane questions. Bob realised that it was the system at fault rather than any one individual call centre advisor. He imagined people bleeding to death while they had to jump through the hoops necessary nowadays in order to have an ambulance sent to attend their emergencies. Just then, the phone suddenly went dead.

'What's happening?' Penny asked, still in agony.

'I've been cut-off.' He sighed and punched in 111, the alternative NHS number, hoping to have more luck this time – only to find himself being asked exactly the same questions as before.

Then, while he was still answering the questions – this time posed by the 111 operator – he noticed something. Flashing blue lights were coming down the road. The first operator must have sent an ambulance after all. He ended the phone call quickly, glad that, at last, his emergency call had been taken seriously and acted upon.

*

After the arrival of the paramedics, Penny had been stretchered into the ambulance and taken to the Accident and Emergency Department where she had been put on a morphine drip to stem the pain. It had been decided to keep her in overnight for observation, leaving Bob to return home. He took the opportunity to phone Charles Eden to update him on the latest developments at Crawthorne Hall.

'Hello Charles, how are you?'

'I'm fine – apart from the sub-zero temperatures up here!' Charles was now living near Edinburgh where he was a senior manager at a large, renowned hotel complete with its own first class golf course.

'I thought I'd let you know that excavations have recommenced in the kitchen gardens. I've suggested that Colin should contact you if anything is unearthed as I'm due to fly to Singapore late tomorrow night. I may be out of the loop for a while during the flights.'

'Okay, Bob. No worries.'

'Anyway, there is a chance that we'll be cancelling our holiday.'

'Oh? Why's that?'

'Penny's fallen from a ladder and hurt her back. She's spending the night in hospital.'

'I'm sorry to hear that.'

'Well, I'll let you know one way or another.'

Bob and Charles had never given-up hope of finding a body. They were on a mission and this had united them now for a number of years, despite disagreements on other issues – in particular, Bob and Penny were angry at the way in which his friend Charles had treated Amy. They felt that his attitude towards her had been abysmal – but Bob was not prepared to let this come between him and finding out the truth of what happened in Room 13.

When he and Penny had stayed at the hotel for their wedding anniversary the previous August, he had been trying to puzzle-out what it was in the *Great British Hotels and Gardens* book that had so unsettled him. Something just hadn't been right about the *Then and Now* photos of Crawthorne Hall Hotel gardens. It was only when Penny's phone fell to the floor with its apple logo blazoned on the back, that he realised what he had been missing. In one of the 1950s photographs, he could see not one, but two apple trees growing in the kitchen gardens.

Presumably the other one had been cut-down at some point – perhaps it was diseased? It had been growing in the opposite corner to its counterpart – in the part of the garden where Bob had spent so many hours when he had worked at Crawthorne Hall Hotel. The missing apple tree had once grown in what, for years, had been known as the burning area, where rubbish was incinerated every week – the same place where Bob had discovered the lottery ticket which had transformed his life.

Bob was determined to arrange to have the burning area excavated but, as before, this had proved tricky. The hotel directors had been reluctant to give their permission – they were afraid that if news leaked out about an eccentric ex-employee searching for a dead body in the hotel grounds, that this could seriously affect their star ratings and their reputation. However, Bob had finally negotiated a financial sweetener that they could not refuse and it had been agreed to allow the excavation to go ahead – but this time for a week in the January low-season. Bob, having already booked his holiday, hadn't been entirely happy with the date but it was a take-it-or-leave-it offer, so he had accepted.

Then, hiring the same gardening teams as before, under the careful supervision of Professor Susan Wilkinson, the forensic anthropologist who was leading the dig and Arnold Butterworth, the trained archaeologist, Bob had spent the day watching the progress as the diggers had started working. However, there had been nothing unearthed so far. They had six days left – which included an undertaking to reinstate the kitchen gardens within the timeframe.

By the end of the dig, Bob Bennett would either be seven thousand miles away in the Far East – or, if Penny was still in agony, they would cancel the holiday leaving him free to be at Crawthorne Hall. Bob really had no idea whether Penny would improve by morning. If he was a gambler, he'd say there was a fifty-fifty chance of either staying or going. He wouldn't bet on it.

Chapter 52

After spending a sleepless and uncomfortable night in the hospital, Penny was discharged and given a note for her doctor.

'At least I can walk a few steps now – that morphine in hospital worked wonders with numbing the pain,' she said optimistically once Bob had helped her into the car. 'Although it makes me feel very queasy,' she added.

They were on their way to see their family practitioner with the intention of asking for a letter to send to their travel insurer giving reasons for cancelling their holiday.

'I wonder if my doctor would prescribe more morphine for the pain?' Penny suggested.

'Why not ask?'

'Maybe he'd give me a month's supply – just in case we decide to go on that holiday after all!' she joked.

Then, arriving at the surgery around eleven o'clock with just one patient in the waiting room, they were surprised when the receptionist agreed to retrospectively add them to the tail-end of the morning's appointments list.

'How bad is the pain just now?' Doctor Niraj Patel asked Penny.

'Last night I would have given it a score of eleven out of ten.' She replied. 'But since the morphine started to kick-in I'd give it eight. It's still excruciating but at least I'm more mobile now.'

'That is still an extremely high level of pain, Mrs Bennett. And you say you were due to go on holiday tomorrow?'

'Yes, we should be packing right now.'

'Well,' replied Doctor Patel, 'I will naturally prepare a letter for your insurers, as requested.'

'Thank you.'

'It should be ready by noon tomorrow – I suggest you call first to check. Also, I'll make out a prescription for morphine, as requested.'

'Will it need to be injected?' asked Penny.

'No, this is oral morphine – to be taken by mouth. I'm prescribing several doses per day – up to a maximum of one hundred millilitres in twenty-four hours.'

'And if we do by any chance decide to go on our holiday, Doctor Patel?' Penny looked at him hopefully.

'I would not advise that Mrs Bennett. Who knows – you could end up being taken into emergency care anywhere on your travels – Vietnam or Thailand, for instance? You'd be gambling with your health – playing a lottery with your life in certain parts of Asia.' He sounded very downbeat as he printed-off the prescription, scrawling his signature at the bottom.

While Penny was weighing-up her options in the doctor's consulting room, Bob was sitting in the now-empty waiting room browsing through a day-old newspaper that he had found on the magazine rack. Still fascinated with anything related to fire, his attention was drawn to an article about a barn blaze in Essex just before Christmas. The charred remains of a body which had been strapped to a chair, had now been identified as Elaine Evans, forty-eight years old, who had escaped from a prison van shortly before her death.

'What's the matter, Bob?' Penny had just finished her appointment with Doctor Patel and was standing there in some discomfort, clutching her prescription in one hand. 'You've gone very pale,' she added.

'Oh, it's nothing. I've just realised that I discarded something,' he replied distractedly, now realising the full-meaning of his message *Tonight's the night* when he had visited Elaine in prison just before she was sprung from custody.

'What did you discard, Bob?'

'An old friend.' He handed-over the newspaper so that Penny could read the article.

'Oh my God. Elaine. The woman you were telling me about.'

'Well, we were friends of sorts once-upon-a-time. But we went our separate ways.'

'I'm glad you did, otherwise we may never have met!'

'And I'm so glad we did.' He got up from his seat and would have given her a big hug there and then, but thought better of it, knowing the pain that she was in. They headed home.

Later that day, having picked-up Penny's prescribed morphine, Bob was half-heartedly trying to dissuade her from any thoughts of embarking on a holiday. However, they both knew that, in their own minds they were determined to go ahead naively with their plans, not really taking-in the problems that could occur when they were thousands of miles away from home.

That night they had found themselves hurriedly packing, throwing clothes, medication and personal possessions into two large suitcases before setting-off in a taxi in the early hours, hoping that they had made the right decision after all. Bob never did collect the doctor's letter – by the time it was ready, they were sitting on a very uncomfortable thirteen-hour flight from London Heathrow: first stop Singapore.

Chapter 53

Drugged up to the eyeballs, Singapore was nothing more than a hazy memory for Penny. Hiring a wheelchair as planned, Bob had taken her to some of Singapore's most iconic tourist attractions including afternoon tea at the famous Raffles Hotel and a trip on the Singapore Flyer – the giant observation wheel with its breath-taking views over Marina Bay.

They had just returned to their hotel in Orchard Street after a visit to the botanical gardens on the second day of their stay. Bob, opening the door to their suite found a message in an envelope which had been shoved under the door.

MR. BENNETT, PLEASE PHONE CHARLES EDEN. URGENT.

He noticed that a red light was flashing on one of the telephones in the bedroom. Picking-up the receiver, a mechanical voice started speaking.

'You have one message, received at 14:18 today. BEEP.' Then he heard the voice of Charles.

'Hi Bob, it's Charles. They've found something. Ring me as soon as you can – day or night – and I'll fill you in with what I know so far. I'm heading down to Crawthorne Hall early tomorrow. Hope to hear from you soon.'

Picking-up the handset, Bob immediately punched-in Charles' number. He heard the ringing tone and assumed that it was about to be forwarded to the answerphone. Then all of a sudden, he heard Charles' voice at the other end of the line.

'Charles, is that you?'

'Hi Bob.'

'Sorry to phone you at this time. I've just picked-up your message.' Then he added, 'I guess it must be early morning now in the UK?'

'Yes, but I told you to phone asap.'

'So, what have they found?'

'There were skeletal remains in the kitchen gardens – underneath the burning area. Professor Susan Wilkinson, the forensic anthropologist, confirmed that they are human and called-in the police. Now there is frantic activity going-on around the burial site. It looks like we're sucking diesel at last, Bob!'

'Do they know whether it's a man or woman?' Sudden hope was blasting through Bob. He swallowed hard as he gripped the phone, waiting for Charles to answer.

'I've heard nothing more about the skeleton. I guess that they're examining the area for DNA and other evidence. The bones are probably still in situ. All I know is that a white police forensic tent has been erected and the area cordoned-off.'

'Not great for attracting guests to the hotel,' commented Bob.

'I wouldn't be surprised if it has the opposite effect. Some people have a morbid curiosity – finding human remains may actually increase bookings at Crawthorne Hall. Anyway, the jury's out on that one.'

'So, shall I fly back tomorrow?'

'To be honest, Bob, there's nothing you can do at the moment. It's different for me – Crawthorne Hall is my ancestral home. Questions will be asked and I want to be there to give my family's side of the story. I'll keep in touch by email to keep you in the loop.'

'Okay,' Bob felt slightly deflated. After all, it was he who had bankrolled the latest excavation attempt. However, he was pragmatic and realised that now the police were involved, the best he could do was to wait and see what they came up with – if anything.

Chapter 54

Albert Warnford watched curiously as a number of visitors descended on Lady Crawthorne's detached Georgian Grade II listed residence next door. Since the death of her husband, she had led a quiet life and it was unusual to have this many people turn-up – especially as he instantly recognised one of them, a detective who had once interviewed him in connection with the murder of Lord Crawthorne. Perhaps they had, at last, found the culprit? Albert's interest was piqued. He could hardly contain himself and wondered whether it was worth knocking on his neighbour's door – perhaps offering to clear fallen leaves from the pathway – it might lead to an invitation to join the party? Albert was always full of hope – and an over-inflated opinion of his own importance.

Charles Eden opened the door to find two police officers waiting in the porch.

'Good morning, sir. I'm Detective Chief Inspector Angelia Wilmot and this is my colleague Detective Inspector Ian Horvarth.' They flashed their warrant cards. 'May we come in?' There was an air of grim professional seriousness in their manner.

'Please do,' replied Charles, 'we've been expecting you. This way.' He led them up a flight of stairs and then introduced them to the family, assembled in the double-aspect first floor drawing room.

'What is this all about?' asked Isobela Crawthorne after the police detectives were seated, along with freshly-made coffee.

'Firstly, let me explain my role,' began Angelia Wilmot. 'I work in the major crime team in Sussex and am currently heading-up a cold case investigation named Operation Skellig. DI Horvarth has been seconded to help me in this investigation as he has worked with your family before. There could even be a tentative connection between this case and that of your husband, Lady Crawthorne.' She nodded at Horvarth. Both of them had recently been rewarded with promotional moves.

'Yes, I remember DI Horvarth – detective sergeant last time we met,' replied Isabela. 'You investigated my husband's murder,' she added looking at Horvath with a slight air of disapproval. Horvarth, who had opened a black notebook ready to jot-down any useful information, evaded

Lady Crawthorne's gaze, slightly embarrassed that the police had never been able to find enough evidence to convict Mad Ronnie Howell of the crime.

'Four days ago,' Wilmot continued, 'human skeletal remains were found in the grounds of your former home, Crawthorne Hall.' She turned towards Charles. 'I believe that you, Mr. Eden, were collaborating in having part of the kitchen gardens excavated, which led to the discovery of the bones. May I ask what prompted you to search the area?'

'I think I can answer that,' interrupted Helen Eden, Charles' mother. 'As you can imagine, there have always been tales of murder and mystery attached to Crawthorne Hall – that's no different to many other old historic family homes. When I was a child, I listened to all sorts of stories – some of them quite ghastly. Who knows whether there was ever any truth in them? Anyway, it was rumoured that a murder had taken place sometime in the 1970s and the body buried in the kitchen gardens.'

'My husband, Lord Crawthorne, and I were living in Hong Kong when this was supposed to have happened,' interjected Isabela.

'But why, Mr. Eden, did you decide to take the story so literally? What made you believe that there really was a buried body?'

'There were several reasons,' replied Charles.

'Tell them about your friend Bob Bennett,' prompted Richard Eden, Charles' father. He had been sitting in the corner next to his wife quietly listening to the proceedings.

'I worked at Crawthorne Hall as a manager when it first became a hotel. Bob Bennett, a member of our staff, claimed that he had known the son of the former head gardener.'

'The head gardener in the 1970s was a man by the name of Daniel Marsh,' added Isabela Crawthorne.

'Well, the son's name was Paul,' said Charles. 'He told Bob Bennett that he had witnessed a shooting in a room in the East wing. There had been a poker game going on and the winner had been accused of cheating.'

'Who made the accusation?' asked DI Horvarth.

'My grandfather, 14th Baron Crawthorne,' Helen Eden once again answered for her son.

'And the alleged shooting?' Horvarth continued.

'My father-in-law,' answered Lady Crawthorne. There was a lot more that she could have added, for Isabela knew far more than she was prepared to let-on. Twelve years earlier, while George Crawthorne had been gallivanting around with his women, gambling and trips over to Amsterdam, she had been helping to nurse her father-in-law in his last stages of dementia. He'd seemed mired in his own darkness and, as he lay dying, the old Lord Crawthorne had told her something – a secret which she was not prepared to share without more proof. In his delirious state, she remembered him ranting-on, firstly about a masked man in the room watching him, then shouting into thin-air at a man who he said was cheating at cards.

'I don't like to lose – nobody does,' the old Lord Crawthorne had repeated over and over again as he thrashed-about, calling-out a name several times. Isabela had never told a soul. She had never repeated that name to anyone – no-one would have believed her – they would have said she was out of her mind. Surely, he was mistaken in his delerium?

Lady Crawthorne decided not to break her silence of many years so she just sat passively listening to her grandson talking to the police. She was prepared to wait for proof and if none was forthcoming – then she would let sleeping dogs lie.

'Before my grandfather's death, I asked him to help me prove or disprove the story,' explained Charles. 'I'd never asked him for anything before and I was surprised that, in his will, he made provision for me to be able to investigate by excavating the site.'

'So how did this Bob Bennett become involved?' This from DS Horvarth.

'His friend Paul Marsh – the head gardener's son.' Horvarth nodded his head encouragingly. 'He'd experienced some bad things as a child growing-up at Crawthorne Hall – and in the end he committed suicide. It seems that he'd told Bob the story about the shooting shortly before he died. In turn, Bob Bennett took it upon himself to find out the truth of what had happened.'

'Do you know if Daniel Marsh, the head gardener is still alive?' continued Horvarth to nobody in particular.

'No, he died about thirty years ago,' interjected Lady Crawthorne. 'He collapsed in the grounds of Crawthorne Hall.'

'Oh?' Horvarth wondered whether there were any suspicious circumstances. He realised that it would be convenient to dispose of a murder witness to prevent them from squealing. Perhaps Daniel Marsh had met with an unexpected accident? However, he was wrong.

'Yes,' Lady Crawthorne elaborated. 'It was in the late eighties when he collapsed by the lake. It was an aneurism – a condition known as an aortic dissection. He died on his way to hospital.'

'And where is Bob Bennett now? We will need to speak to him at some point.' Angelia Wilmot looked expectantly at Charles.

'He's on holiday in the Far East – on a cruise at the moment – due back in early February. I can email him to get in touch when he returns?'

'That would be very helpful Mr. Eden,' she replied. 'So, tell me why it was decided to excavate the burning area on the other side of the garden.'

'It sounds silly,' replied Charles. 'Another employee at the hotel said that she witnessed a séance in our Baronial Room – it was really a drunken stunt at a hen party – but Penny, the member of staff, took it seriously. Something was said about a shooting and being buried under an apple tree. It seemed to me at the time as though the whole thing was probably rigged to scare the poor girl who was getting married. Anyway, Bob took it seriously, too. He discovered that there had once been an apple tree where the burning area is now situated. So, he arranged for the excavation. I, for my part, have supported him, for the reasons I gave earlier – I want to find the truth and hopefully clear the family name. In many ways I was hoping that a body – or skeleton for that matter – would not be found, as it would exonerate my great grandfather from foundless accusations.'

'Very laudable,' commented Horvarth, scribbling-away in his notebook.

The two detectives did not stay for long after that. They had heard everything that they needed to know – for now. They were due back for a team meeting when they would collect together all the evidence and information gathered so far before deciding on the next steps towards solving the case.

Richard Eden showed them down the stairs and to the front door. *The Knapp Goddess* still on the newel post as it had been when the Crawthornes first moved in, seemed to scowl at the visitors on their way out.

'So, is it a male or female skeleton?' Richard Eden asked casually.

'I'm afraid we cannot divulge that at this stage, Mr. Eden.'

He had expected them to say that. 'And had he or she been shot?'

'You know the answer to that, too, Mr. Eden. But it was a nice try.' Angelia Wilmot knew that Richard was a solicitor – just trying his luck. Richard smiled knowingly.

Once out on the doorstep, Chief Inspector Angelia Wilmot hesitated and then turned back to Richard.

'Oh. That reminds me. Just one more question, Mr. Eden. Your son told us that the gardener's son, Paul Marsh claimed to have witnessed a shooting in a room in the East wing of the house. We'll need to see that room. Do you know which one it is?'

'Yes,' he replied. 'It was Room 13.'

Chapter 55

When Charles Eden had called Bob in Singapore with the news about the skeletal remains being found at Crawthorne Hall, it was tempting to just capitulate: pack their bags and return home. After all, Bob was aching to see at first-hand what was going on. Penny, at that time still felt pain with every movement and it was starting to look as though they had made the wrong decision to travel to Singapore – how could they continue like this for another three weeks? It was beginning to look like a holiday from hell. But then they had a breakthrough – a lifeline – a way of salvaging something of their dreams.

Firstly, Charles had assured them that now the police had taken control, there was nothing useful that Bob could do except wait for the outcome of the investigation into the unearthed skeleton. Secondly, with the Chinese New Year it was difficult to find a flight with spare seats at short notice. So they decided to continue with their original plan of travelling to China on a cruise ship: a more sedate mode of travel than an aircraft. It would hopefully give Penny a chance to recuperate.

On their third day in Singapore, they had embarked on the *Pacific Celebration,* a mid-sized cruise ship with just over two thousand passengers onboard – mostly Chinese. It was here that they were introduced to Doctor Sang Ha Shin, a South Korean acupuncturist working on the ship, who convinced them that he could work wonders, reducing the pain dramatically by inserting his thin needles through Penny's skin at strategic points on her body. The treatment didn't come cheap but, Bob could afford it. By that stage Penny was prepared to try almost anything – and the idea of using a tried and tested ancient Chinese method administered by a qualified member of the ship's staff, was more than appealing. So, she signed-up for regular sessions interspersed with recovery days.

By the time they arrived in Bangkok on the sixth day of their adventure, Penny had become more mobile and the pain had lessened. She'd decided to give up on the morphine as it was making her feel ill, relying only on over-the-counter painkillers just to take the edge off her discomfort. For the first time, Bob and Penny started to enjoy their holiday, having fun racing around Bangkok in a tuk-tuk – an auto rickshaw – seeing the sights of the city. Then afterwards they had visited Wat Pho, the temple of the reclining Buddha before hitching a ride on their ship to their next destination: Ho Chi Minh City in Vietnam.

On the eleventh day, they reached Hong Kong and Penny was now mobile enough to catch a traditional Chinese junk boat around the harbour followed by a ride on the Peak Tram with its panoramic views over part of the city and its seascape. She felt that Doctor Sang Ha Shin was truly performing miracles by now. She still took her over-the counter painkillers as back-up although her two litres of morphine were now all but redundant and had been discarded along with her dirty washing in one of the suitcases.

During their cruise, Charles and Bob had kept-in touch daily by email, in much the same way as they had done six years earlier during the first excavation at Crawthorne Hall.

To: Bob
From: Charles
Date: Thursday, January 16, 2020 11:06:17 EST
Subject: Excavation of Crawthorne Hall kitchen garden

Hi Bob,

Still not much news apart from a police statement to the press revealing that the skeletal remains of a man were unearthed in the grounds of Crawthorne Hall. They say these have now been removed and taken to a laboratory for analyses and piecing back together. Nothing has been mentioned about cause of death. The investigation is being carried-out by a cold case unit from Sussex in collaboration with the National UK Missing Persons Unit. I've attached a copy of the press release.

Have spoken to the police and told them what we know about the alleged shooting in Room 13 and what your friend Paul Marsh said he'd witnessed. The detectives want to speak to you when you get back – but no hurry.

I'm now back in Bonnie Scotland – snowed-in at the hotel! Enjoy your time in South Korea – I hear Busan has a great fish market!

Best Regards
Charles

*

The Bennetts finally arrived in Beijing: only to find that many of the Chinese New Year Celebrations had been scaled-down or even cancelled. However, they managed to make the most of their time. On the second day they attempted to walk on part of the Great Wall of China – just outside Beijing. Being at a higher altitude than the city, it was noticeably much colder there with heavy snowfall. They managed less than a quarter of a mile before turning back as Penny was really struggling, especially with the number of steps involved.

Each day, Bob would return to their hotel and check his emails, hoping for news from Charles, but there was nothing new.

After a week, they managed to find an internal flight covering the seven hundred and fifty miles to Xian, the former capital of China. Dumping their belongings at a hotel, they had explored the walled city. The following day they had visited the Terracotta Warriors, supposedly created two thousand years previously to accompany the emperor into the afterlife.

Bob waited anxiously for news about the skeletal remains found at Crawthorne Hall, but still there was nothing. It seemed that the police were keeping a tight lid on it all, as though they were unwilling to make public their findings so far. Perhaps there was more to the story than just a disagreement during a poker game? Nevertheless, no matter how impatient Bob became, he had no alternative but to bide his time. As for Penny, she had little to say on the subject – she had enough problems of her own, still battling with the pain now that she was no longer receiving acupuncture; but unwilling to give-in to taking the morphine.

Returning back to Beijing, on the final day of their holiday, Bob and Penny found themselves joining the flow of tourists in Tiannamon Square as they zeroed-in on the gate over which Chairman Mao's large portrait beamed at all and sundry as they trudged through to the Forbidden City. Just like bath-water that accelerates and quickens before it finally disappears down the plug-hole, so the crowd condensed as it approached the giant vermilion gateway, seeping like sand through the waist of an hour glass.

Going with the flow, Bob, pushing Penny in a hired rickety old wheelchair with no brakes, passed through the archway, coming out into what seemed like a different world trapped in a time-warp of its own.

The Forbidden City, known officially as the Palace Museum, was the most impressive sight that they had seen during their seven days in Beijing.

Located in the centre of the vast metropolis it was nothing short of breath-taking with its rumoured nine thousand, nine hundred and ninety-nine rooms. At every gate and at every turn within the magnificent architectural complex they came upon yet another spectacular discovery. They had never seen nor experienced anything like it in their lives and at that moment they were glad that they had taken the difficult decision to go ahead with their travel plans – despite Penny's continued pain and discomfort.

Chapter 55

Back in Sussex, England, DCI Angelia Wilmot was sitting in Malling House, the headquarters of the Sussex Major Crime Team. She was briefing her boss Chief Superintendent Danny McFarlane on the investigation into the remains which had been discovered in the grounds of Crawthorne Hall.

'So, what have we got, so far, Angelia?' began McFarlane.

'As you know, guv, the scene evidence recovery group has now finished their work. Apart from the skeletal remains, various items associated with the deceased's clothing were recovered.' She handed over a list of the items, which he scrutinised.

'I see that a number plastic buttons were collected – but no remnants of clothing,' he observed.

'Indicating that the deceased wore clothes made from natural fibres – which rot – whereas the buttons stayed intact. Some of the smaller ones are consistent with those used in the manufacture of waistcoats.'

'Which could be worn by a male or female. Anything else?'

'The larger leather remnants as listed – are consistent with that used to make shoes but, as there was no plastic or rubber left in that area of the grave, it can be assumed that the soles were leather – probably an expensive make.'

'That's just supposition, as you well know at this stage, Angelia. We need to keep focusing on the evidence. I want to make sure we're not heading down a rabbit hole – making assumptions that lead us in the wrong direction.'

She sensed a slightly disapproving tone to his voice. McFarlane was old-school and had been resistant to appointing a woman as a chief inspector. She suspected that her Jamaican heritage was not entirely to his liking either. Angelia had come from humble beginnings – her parents coming to Britain in the early 1950s as part of the so-called Windrush generation. She had found it incredibly hard to make her mark in this male dominated profession with over ninety-percent from white ethnic backgrounds. Throughout her career she had constantly found herself having to prove her ability and competence over and above many of her colleagues.

McFarlane was a particularly tough cookie, quick to shoot her down in flames given half-a-chance. So, suitably admonished, Detective Chief Inspector Angelia Wilmot decided to choose her words a little more carefully to avoid any further criticism.

'Either way, guv, it is certain that the deceased was clothed – at least partially – when buried.'

'I see that the remains of braces were found.' He was now glancing through the photos that accompanied her list. 'What about the skeleton?'

'Sir, we received the rest of the lab results late yesterday. Following the Home Office post-mortem, it has been ascertained that cause of death was by exsanguination – blood loss. There was evidence of a bullet being shot into the thorax area which left distinct markers on the ribs with bone fractures indicating that the victim's heart was in the line of trajectory. However, a definitive statement about the damage to organs cannot be made in the absence of soft tissue.'

'Anything else?' asked McFarlane.

'Yes, Sir. One bullet was found near the skeletal remains. It comes from an old Webley Mk VI .455 calibre revolver. We haven't been able to trace the gun. They were military issue – man-stopping weapons effective at fifty yards. There was little chance of surviving a shot at point blank range – the victim would likely have died quickly.'

'And, like the post-mortem confirms, there would have been a significant loss of blood from the wounds at the scene of the crime,' McFarlane mused.

Angelia Wilmot handed-over a copy of the forensic report. 'You have all the information there, guv, together with the findings of Carl Geyer, forensic specialist adviser from the National Crime Agency, who has been working with us.'

'I see that the deceased was male and very tall – six feet four inches to be precise. Aged between twenty-five and forty-five,' he said as he scanned-through the findings. 'Carbon dating pinpoints the death around the mid-1970s.' He looked up expectantly. All very interesting, Angelia. Have you got anywhere with identifying the victim?'

'We're working with Yanna McIntosh, a missing persons advisor from the National Crime Agency. As you know, Sir, around one hundred thousand adults go missing in the UK every year – so we have a potential half a million persons to sift through.'

'But, Angelia … there's always a but …'

'Stating the blatantly obvious, Sir, we can whittle this down significantly using the forensic evidence.'

'So, what are you currently focusing on?' he asked, still scanning the forensic report.

'As you can see, the victim had brown hair and was from a white ethnic group.'

'Anything else that you see as particularly significant at this stage of the enquiry?' Chief Superintendent Danny McFarlane looked hopeful.

'Yes, there is, indeed, Sir. As you can see from the report, the victim had a broken nose at some point in his life. Yanna McIntosh is working on a match. Importantly, traces of silicone were found on that area of the skull indicating that he had undergone plastic surgery. So, we are looking into x-rays from private practitioners during that era.' Angelia was disappointed that her boss did not look overly impressed with this revelation.

McFarlane thought it probable that x-rays and plastic surgeons' records would have been destroyed after more than forty years, which explained his lack of enthusiasm.

'And DNA?' he added, almost looking bored now.

'Nothing to identify the victim, so far. We have spoken to members of the family and they are not able to help in identifying our mystery person. However, they have told us that in the 1970s there was a rumour about a shooting in one of the rooms in Crawthorne Hall – now used as guest accommodation. It was rumoured that after a disagreement in a poker game, one of the players was shot by the then Lord Crawthorne, fourteenth Baron Crawthorne. The body was said to have been buried in the kitchen gardens.'

'So, some truth in the story, but no direct evidence to link a perpetrator?'

'Correct, Sir. But here's the nub. Under the direction of Carl Geyer, the forensic specialist adviser, the room in question – now called Room 13 – was subjected to a thorough forensic examination. Although the house was substantially remodelled into a luxury hotel, the joists underneath the new flooring date back to Victorian times.'

'And how is that significant?'

Detective Chief Inspector Angelia Wilmot tried to hide her excitement. 'Because, Sir, that is where forensics found substantial deposits of human blood which had seeped into the woodwork. Some of the blood – but not all of it – match the DNA of the victim. So far, we have no conclusive evidence that he was murdered in Room 13 – but the presence of his blood is conclusive proof that he was in that room – and he was bleeding.'

For the first time during their meeting, Chief Superintendent Danny McFarlane became more animated.

'Well-done. Good work, Angelia,' he muttered.

'Thank you, Sir,' she replied.
'So, Angelia, what's next?'

*

Later that day, DCI Wilmot had just finished a briefing, updating her Operation Skellig team on the findings so far.

'Okay, everybody. I want you to continue your present lines of enquiry with the following exceptions. DS Carinale and DC Fernandez, you're going to team-up to further investigate the family and their connections – particularly in the mid-1970s. Apparently there were some wild parties at Crawthorne Hall: there must still be survivors of those heady days out there somewhere. I want you to locate anyone still living who was close to the old Lord Crawthorne – the 14th Baron. If there's any truth in this story about a shooting in what is now known as Room 13, there must have been witnesses. Also, there must have been collusion in trying to dispose of the body and in cleaning-up the mess. The old gardener and his son are both dead – but there must still be someone alive who knows something. Ultimately, we're trying to find the identity of someone who, forty-five years ago, was walking around alive and then, without warning, he was erased. Once we know that, then we can look into his associates – possible enemies who might have wanted to harm him?'

'Yes Ma'am.' This from Detective Sergeant Claudia Cardinale.

'Oh, and Claudia.'

'Yes, Ma'am.'

'Look into the world of gambling – who might have been playing poker on that night?'

'Will do, Ma'am.'

'Ian.' She was referring to DI Horvarth. 'Can you concentrate on forensics – particularly the forensic odontology – get a report on dental records and try to get a match. Also, I'm interested in the victim's broken nose – there are traces of a silicone nasal implant around the nose. Silicone doesn't easily biodegrade or decompose. The fact that we found it means that he had plastic surgery – there may still be records or x-rays. If so, I want them found.'

'Yes boss.'

'As for me, I'm going to chase-up Yanna McIntosh to see if we can narrow-down the number of missing persons who fit the profile. We're also expecting a Mr. Bob Bennett to return to the UK tomorrow – he's the guy who commissioned the second excavation. I'll get some uniforms to bring him in for questioning. Finally, good news in that Dr Fergus O'Brien at the Centre for Anatomy and Human Identification at the University of Dundee is, as we speak, producing a facial reconstruction image from the skull. Before long, we should have a rough idea of what the victim looked like. I'd like us to reconvene here in forty-eight hours' time: five o'clock Thursday – unless something of major significance turns up before then. After that there will be some kind of press statement – perhaps even appealing to the general public for information on any of our lines of enquiry. Any questions?'

There were none. However, a certain sense of optimism had started to take hold of Detective Chief Inspector Angelia Wilmot's cold-case team. There seemed to be a vague light at the end of the tunnel, although at this point, they still had no idea of exactly who ... or what had been unearthed.'

Chapter 57

Beijing Capital International Airport was in chaos with many flights having been cancelled, resulting in thousands of passengers finding themselves stranded. There seemed to be no-one available who could explain the reason for all the disruption. Bob and Penny found themselves queuing for two hours, eventually managing to re-book economy class seats on a different flight which was scheduled to leave eight hours later than originally planned. After finding a wheelchair and special assistance for Penny, they were finally fast-tracked through the airport ready to join their Boeing 777 flight bound for Heathrow, London.

Once the Gate was opened for the flight, tired and frustrated passengers started lunging forward, trying to get ahead. As is often human nature, there was a deluge of people pushing and shoving along the passageway to the aircraft. Penny noticed an elderly man in the queue a little way ahead, creeping along like a tortoise with his bald head and sagging jowls. Craning his neck, he seemed to urge each leg forwards with deliberate, precarious movements. Then suddenly, he was pushed aside by an over-zealous beefy individual in a baseball cap with the slogan *I'm a Terracotta Warrior* emblazoned on the front. He was clearly impatient to overtake the doddery old slow-walker who was getting under his feet.

The frail senior citizen lost his balance, falling to the ground before being helped-up by a few travellers near to him. He appeared to be on his own. Someone handed him a wodge of tissues to mop his brow, which seemed to bleed. However, ignoring the drama, Mr. Baseball Cap together with his partner, continued ahead, jostling through the other passengers.

The aircraft, once fully loaded, remained on the ground for some while. Bob and Penny had booked two seats together in a middle row of four. Next to him was the impatient man with the baseball cap who emanated an aroma of stale sweat. There was the distinct, strong, earthy scent of baijiu, the traditional Chinese liquor, on his breath as he fiddled with his headphones, looking for the correct socket, preparing to settle down to some in-flight entertainment. Then there was an announcement.

'Good morning. Welcome aboard. This is Mark James the Captain. Just updating you on our current position.'

'Oi Babs. Where's the socket for me f-ing headphones,' came a loud voice from the seat beside Bob. The man in the baseball hat was still fidgeting and unsettled, not really interested in any announcements from the cockpit.

'We are delaying take-off due to storms over parts of Russia,' continued the Captain over the PA system.

'Did ya hear that, Gaz. Stop fiddling for a moment.'

'We're expecting the current bad weather to pass over during the next thirty minutes after which we will be able to resume our schedule; hoping for a more comfortable journey,' Captain Mark James added. 'The crew will try to make up for lost time over the course of tonight's flight. That's all for now – I'll hand you over to our In-flight Service Manager, who will acquaint you with our onboard services.'

Despite the delays, Bob and Penny were pleased to feel some heat at last after enduring freezing conditions in China for the past week followed by a long wait in the draughty airport terminal building.

'All of a sudden it feels very hot,' commented Bob. 'Maybe it's the heat of all these people huddled together in here?' Penny looked at him, puzzled as she still felt perishing cold. 'How's your back?' he asked her.

'Let's just say that, amazingly we made it this far!'

'With the help of a wheelchair at Beijing International Airport. By the way, I checked with the special assistance people and there should be help waiting for us at Heathrow when we land.'

'So, just thirteen or so hours to go and we should be back in good old Blighty!'

It was another hour before the plane finally started taxiing along the runway. Taking-off from the airport, Beijing soon became an intricate grid of orange and white lights in the night sky.

Bob smiled to himself, glad to be on the way home at last – he was aching to find out what had happened back at Crawthorne Hall Hotel in his absence. Bob finally began to relax, thinking over some of his memories from the past few weeks. He and Penny had certainly lived through some eye-opening experiences and their time in Asia had surpassed their expectations. However, throughout the trip, they had been plagued by Penny's back problem. The acupuncture had eased so much of the pain and it had been rare for her to take her prescribed medication – which always made her feel sick anyway. So, she had stuck to the over-the-counter painkillers during their time in China.

It was an eventful journey. Once in the air, one passenger had claimed that his wallet had gone missing, insisting that it had been stolen. There had been an announcement from the cockpit requesting all passengers to search, telling them that they would not be allowed to leave the plane until it turned up.

'It's like telling children that they'll be punished unless someone owns up as the culprit!' laughed Penny.

But Bob seemed half-asleep and just grunted. Then, typically, half an hour later the owner of the wallet, getting up to use the lavatory, had found it wedged down beside his seat cushion. Another announcement over the public address system had informed passengers that the wallet had now been recovered.

Waking up from his drowsiness, Bob was aware of the hot, stuffy atmosphere in their section of the aircraft.

'Excuse me, can I have some water, please?' Bob, still sweltering, was feeling parched and quickly finished the bottle which was brought to him by one of the in-flight stewards.

*

After seven hours the aircraft started to go through turbulence and the passengers were asked to return to their seats and fasten seat belts. Then screaming started simultaneously as the aircraft shook violently, buffeted by angry winds. It felt as though the carrier would break up at any moment. Penny was reminded of the time she visited Alton Towers Theme Park during part of a hen party weekend. The women, much the worse for drink, had ended up on the infamous *Nemesis* ride. With its seven hundred and sixteen metres of terror involving corkscrews, zero-g rolls and vertical loops, there was a distinct similarity with what she and Bob were now experiencing. The main difference though was that the theme park's topsy turvy thriller *Nemesis*, lasted a mere one minute and twenty seconds, as opposed to the one hour and ten minutes of extreme turbulence so far endured on the home journey as they flew over Russia.

Eight hours into the flight there was a commotion about eleven seats further forward from the Bennetts. A flight attendant had responded to a passenger's call and was soon joined by colleagues who appeared to be administering first aid. Then, shortly afterwards there was an announcement over the public address system: this time from another member of the flight crew.

'Hello, this is Clive Dunning, the First Officer. May I have your attention please? I'd like to ask any doctors travelling onboard to please make themselves known to one of the cabin staff immediately. Thank you for your cooperation.'

Looking towards the front of their section of the plane, Bob could see a fourth person attending to a passenger sitting in an aisle seat near to the lavatories. Shortly afterwards, with assistance, a man was helped to his feet and escorted forwards up the gangway in the direction of the business class section of the aircraft. Bob recognised him as the frail old man who had fallen earlier when they had been boarding.

Mr. Baseball Cap, the man who had been responsible for barging the elderly chap was just coming round from his alcohol-induced slumber and was in time to catch a glimpse of the drama.

'Oi, Gaz,' his female companion nudged him. 'Did you see that? It's that old geezer oo got in yer way. Y'know, the one oo fell over when we woz boarding the plane.'

'Is that so? Hey, have you got anything I can take for this headache, Babs?'

'I fuckin' told yer not to keep drinkin' that sodden baijiu Chinese liquor crap dint I? But no, would you listen? Yer never listen t'me.'

'I take that as a no, then?' he said sarcastically.

She reluctantly scrabbled around in her handbag like a lucky dip, finally retrieving a new packet of strong painkillers.

'Ere why not take the 'ole lot while yer at it? It'll put you out of your misery permanently!' she laughed thinking this was funny.

Bob, sitting on the other side of them hoped that he and Penny would always love and cherish each other – for the rest of their lives – he would hate to end up like these two next to him. He looked at Penny beside him. She was now fast asleep. He reached up to adjust the air vent, feeling its coolness on his hot and sweaty face. He took out a tissue to wipe his brow.

Soon the turbulence started becoming increasingly more violent and Penny was wide awake once more. Bob felt nauseous and dizzy. Already the three hundred and sixty passengers had been instructed to fasten seatbelts and adopt the brace position. A reminder had been given about the use of life jackets, although it seemed unlikely that these would ever be needed if the plane ended up plummeting through the air at fifteen thousand feet. Then there was another announcement from the flight deck.

'This is Captain Mark James just updating you on our progress. With the continuing turbulence we have now received permission from the authorities in Poland to land at Warsaw Chopin Airport.'

Bob and Penny looked at each other quizzically. Somehow this didn't make sense.

'We will start our descent shortly,' continued the captain, 'and I will keep you informed nearer to our expected landing in around twelve minutes.'

Sitting in the very back row of seats, they were aware of the cabin crew strapping themselves into their own seats in the galley area behind. Concerned whisperings were being shared between two of the stewards. Suddenly there was a major judder and crashing noise accompanied by further screaming. Bob and Penny clutched hands as they felt the plane losing height. On the screen in front, they could see a map of their journey over Russia, through Belarus and into Poland air-space. As the plane lurched forwards, there was nothing either of them could do but wait for the worst to happen.

Some people believe in fate or in miracles. Bob was more a believer in inevitability – what will be, will be – and this was one such time when he just had to succumb to events – in the way he had throughout his adult life, just waiting to see how things turned-out, for better or worse. He felt sure that information was being withheld from the passengers, suspecting that some damage had been sustained to the aircraft as a result of the violent turbulence – maybe something had fallen-off? Maybe an engine or two were malfunctioning? Or was it a failure of the controls? Whatever it was, the plane continued to accelerate rapidly downward; both he and Penny continuing to hold hands tightly. Bob held his breath, anticipating the impact – perhaps there would just be nothingness? Perhaps they would be another statistic in the world's list of catastrophic aeroplane disasters – or even disappearances?

In less than a minute Bob's mind was crammed full of what-ifs and maybes. However, the one overriding thought in his mind was that he wanted to survive – and to be with Penny. There was still too much to live for.

Then, suddenly and unexpectedly, the aircraft started to level-off. It steadied its course – the turbulence was ebbing away in the distance and gradually, very slowly at first and then increasing in speed, the plane started to rise again. As it did so, a flight attendant appeared from one of the forward sections of the plane and spoke to his two colleagues sitting behind Bob, Penny and the other two passengers in their row. The conversation was quiet and muted, meant to be private, but the four people sitting in front could hear every word that was being spoken.

'He's gone,' whispered the new arrival in hushed tones.

'What, that lovely old man? You mean he died?'

'They took him up to business class where there's more space. He's been lying on the emergency recliner – but he passed – ten minutes ago. So, we don't need to land for emergency medical attention anymore. He's beyond that.'

'Oh my gosh.'

'So, it will be usual protocol for death in-flight. Make sure the others in your section are alerted.'

He disappeared back up towards the front of the plane, pulling curtains behind him as he passed through to the next section.

'Ay, Gaz, did yer 'ere that. The old codger's a goner!'

'Looked to me like ee woz on 'is way out anyway.'

'That's not nice, Gaz. Hey I wonder what they'll do with the body?'

'I 'eard they lock-em in the toilets to keep 'em away from the rest of the passengers.'

'Maybe they just strap 'em into a seat and cover 'em over?'

At that moment an overhead indicator light went off signalling that the passengers could now, at last undo their seatbelts. Mr. Baseball Cap pushed past his partner, jumping the queue for the toilets.

'What do you think they'll do with the body, Bob?'

'Well, for a start I know that they don't put it in the toilets – so he's wrong on that score – if rigor mortar sets-in they would have to take the plane apart to get him out again. I know they carry body bags, so I suppose he'd be placed in one of those. But it's anyone's guess as to where he would be stored.'

'Maybe it's one of those mysteries in life that we'll never get to know the answer to,' Penny replied resignedly.

As the passengers in the aft section of the plane started to relax a little, slowly recovering from what everyone had feared was going to be their own extinction half an hour earlier, they could hear Mr. Baseball Hat in the queue spreading the gossip about the old man.

'Yeah. We're sitting in the back row – we 'eard the stewards say 'es brown bread – dead. That's why we never landed in Poland – it 'ad nuffink to do wiv the turbulance why we were 'eaded there. They were tryin' to get 'im to 'ospital. I bet they've locked 'im in one of the toilets.'

Before long, the rumours were rife.

'There's a dead bloke in the toilets,' was the general consensus as the plane landed at Heathrow at seven o'clock on the first Wednesday of February.

*

The landing at Heathrow had not been straightforward. Blustery weather and high winds had preceded them, reaching Britain earlier that morning. They had remained in the air, circling the airport three times until finally, wind buffeting the aircraft once more the pilot attempted a landing – unsuccessfully. Then, on the second try, with the giant wings almost making contact with the runway as the carrier was twisted here and there like a giant corkscrew, they at last touched down on the runway. The plane braked and everyone onboard joined-in with spontaneous applause for the pilot and crew who had brought them to safety.

As they taxied to the gate, emergency vehicles with lights flashing approached the plane. There was an announcement asking everyone to remain in their seats but, at no time did they receive any details of the rumoured death. After about ten minutes there was activity around the parked ambulance. The double doors at the rear were opened and something was loaded inside. Then a flight attendant appeared in the rear section on the aircraft and pointed towards the back seats. He was speaking to a policeman who followed him along the passageway, stopping at Bob's row.

'Excuse me sir,' said the officer looking at the man wearing the Terracotta Warriors baseball hat. 'Can you come with me for a moment?'

'What for?' He was more surprised than rude or aggressive.

'I have a few questions to ask you.'

'What about?'

'Please, sir. Just come with me and I'll explain.'

Begrudgingly, the man started to move.

'Can I come with him?' His partner, who wasn't stupid, had an inkling about why Gaz was about to be questioned by the police.

'Yes, Madam, you can come along, too. It shouldn't take long.'

Shortly afterwards the emergency vehicles left and the passengers were allowed to finally disembark, weary after the traumas of the past nine hours.

'How are you feeling?' Penny asked, looking hard at her husband. He didn't seem quite right.

'I'm fine.'

'That's the standard Bob Bennett answer!' teased Penny. 'You never admit to feeling ill!'

Chapter 58

Landing at Heathrow they were disappointed to find that there was no special assistance waiting for them at the gate as they disembarked from the aircraft. While the bulk of the passengers set-off on the long walk to immigration, Bob found a wall-mounted telephone and contacted someone who assured him that a wheelchair was on its way. By the time it finally arrived twenty minutes later there were no other passengers in sight. Exhaustion now setting-in, both Bob and Penny were anxious that their taxi would soon be arriving at the airport – they would need to hurry to clear security and border control then pick-up their luggage in order to meet their driver within the agreed timeframe in the arrivals area. They knew that their car would only wait for a limited time before abandoning them for other booked customers.

Eventually, they found themselves heading towards the passport checkpoints, Penny being pushed in a wheelchair. Bob followed behind, feeling hot and dizzy; wishing that he, too, had someone to transport him around the terminal. Then, on approaching immigration, the wheelchair assistant asked for both their passports which she handed to a uniformed security officer dressed all in black with a hi viz yellow vest who was stationed at the special assistance gate. As they had experienced before at the other airports they had entered, the officer then scanned the passports under a machine.

It was at this point that everything suddenly started to go wrong because, instead of having their passports handed-back to them and being waved through, they were ushered into a separate, bleak little waiting area. Another stern-looking border force officer then approached them.

'Mr. Bob Bennett. I am confiscating your passport. We have reason to believe that you are carrying illegal substances into this country. Please be seated.' He disappeared-off behind a door with both the passports, leaving no explanation.

Bob, still feeling hot and flushed, now experienced a wave of panic wash through him. This was like something out of a television reality programme. Why had he been singled-out – and detained? He was a law-abiding citizen, always trying to make the right choices nowadays – so, why was he here in this small, barricaded area of Heathrow when he should be on his way to meeting their car? Yes, the taxi – he suddenly remembered that the driver would be wondering what had happened to the Bennetts.

'Hello. This is Bob Bennett.' He called the contact number on his phone.

'Yes. Hello Mr. Bennett. I'm waiting by the café in the arrivals hall.'

'I'm afraid we might be a little while. We've just been stopped at immigration.'

'Well, I'm afraid I can only wait for a maximum of an hour. I have other jobs.'

'I'll pay extra if you have to wait longer. Please can you ask the company to send another driver for your next job. I have a sick wife and need to get her home as soon as possible.'

'I'll see what I can do, Mr. Bennett.'

Half an hour later, Doug Macpherson, a burly, bald-headed border force officer together with his assistant Monica Kaminski, walked Bob and Penny to the luggage reclaim area where their cases had already been retrieved by another member of the security team. Penny was still firmly seated in the wheelchair, pushed by the special airport assistant.

'Mr. Bennett,' Macpherson addressed Bob. 'Can you confirm that this is your suitcase?' It was blue with a red strap.

'Yes, it is.'

Both cases were then placed on a trolley, wheeled to the customs area where Bob's was placed on a table.

'What is all this about?' Bob asked.

'I'm unable to disclose that, Mr.Bennett,' replied Macpherson.

'This isn't exactly the best ending to our dream holiday,' complained Penny from her wheelchair. 'It's turned into more of a nightmare for us now.'

'Did you pack your case yourself, sir?' enquired Monica Kaminski.

'Yes.'

'And are you carrying anything for anyone else?' she continued.

'No – although some of my wife's belongings are in my luggage – her medication and some personal items.'

Suddenly a feeling of dread came over Bob as he realised what he had just uttered. In that instant, for the first time since they'd embarked on their travels, he started to realise exactly what he had been carrying around the world with him. All this time, he had been so absorbed in worrying about Penny and the pain she was enduring, that he had failed to see what had been staring him in the face all the time – and now it was too late.

Twelve hours earlier, Bai Lipeng, a customs officer in Beijing airport had been patrolling behind the scenes with Marina, his veteran sniffer dog, when they'd come across a large blue suitcase with a red strap. It was moving along a conveyor belt at the time, joining other luggage bound for London, England. Marina had leapt-up on to the moving row of cases and instantly started digging and pawing at the offending object.

Her handler, Bai, dragged the suitcase to the floor and, as was the custom, scanned the barcode on its label, which gave him the details of its owner. Then, with the suitcase back on the conveyor belt he contacted border control at Heathrow Airport, tipping them off about the suspected drugs smuggler.

Bob Bennett shakily unlocked the suitcase.

'Thank you, Mr.Bennett, we'll take it from here.' The two border control officers had donned rubber gloves and they were now sifting through his case.

It didn't take long for them to discover two litre bottles of fluid – each with a label announcing MORPHINE (ORAL) UP TO 25ML PER DOSE 4 TIMES A DAY MAX 100ML IN 24 HOURS MRS PENNY BENNETT.

'What's this then?' asked Dough Macpherson, knowing the answer already.

'It's my medication,' answered Penny. 'For my back pain. But I stopped taking it as it made me ill. I've been having acupuncture instead: I can show you the receipts. So only used half a bottle of morphine.'

'We'll have to take these away for tests,' Macpherson replied. They rummaged through the rest of Bob's case, pulling out various items but coming upon nothing of further interest. Macpherson then started walking-off with the bottles leaving his colleague with the Bennetts.

'How long will it take?' Bob asked hopefully.

'Not long,' was the reply.

*

Fifteen minutes later Macpherson reappeared. He had something in his hand: it was Bob and Penny's passports.

'I have good news and bad news for you, Mr.Bennett,' announced Macpherson. 'The good news is that our tests have verified that you are travelling with prescribed morphine – not Class A heroin as was suspected by our Beijing customs colleagues. The bad news is that morphine is a banned substance in China.'

'I'm so sorry. I was unaware of that,' replied Bob honestly.

'Clearly Mr. Bennett, it is for you to make yourself aware of customs regulations in the countries that you visit. It is your responsibility and for your own safety. It is no excuse to apologise after the event. In China, possession of morphine is a punishable offence – you could have been jailed for carrying this amount. Also, I understand that you have travelled to Singapore: similar laws apply there, too. However, as this was prescribed in the UK and is legal here, we are content that we need to take this no further. Mr. and Mrs Bennett, you are free to go.'

Bob and Penny were both awash with relief as they finally climbed into the taxi which had waited nearly two hours: the driver was hoping for a generous tip.

'How was your trip?' He asked them over his shoulder on their way back home.

'Brilliant!' answered Penny. Bob wasn't feeling very talkative – exhaustion was creeping up on him and he just wanted to get home – and to bed. Still feeling hot and flushed, his throat was dry and he had no water. His head was spinning.

'So, you've just come in from China,' the driver continued. It was a statement rather than a question – he knew that the flight he'd waited for was inbound from Beijing.

'Yes,' said Penny. 'We were there for the Chinese New Year. It's a fantastic place! Lovely people!'

'So, you haven't heard the news then?' replied the driver obtusely.

'What news?'

'China isn't very popular in the UK at the moment – a number of Chinese restaurants have been attacked.'

Penny had no idea what he was talking about. Bob sat half-asleep by her side, not responding to any of the driver's banter.

'Why is that?' she asked.

'It's all over the newspapers,' he replied as he handed over his copy of *The Daily Mirror* which had been laying on the front passenger seat.

Picking up the paper she read the headline and scanned the rest of the page. The news sounded bad – it sounded very bad indeed.

Chapter 59

'I hear you had a run-in with the authorities at Heathrow?'

Bob Bennett was helping the police with their enquiries on a voluntary basis. He was now sitting in an interview suite in Lewes Police Station facing DI Ian Horvarth and DC Carl Fernandez. Detective Chief Inspector Angelia Wilmot was watching the proceedings on a monitor in an adjoining room.

'Can someone please tell me what this is all about?' He wondered whether they were going to try to pin something on him relating to the morphine that had been found in his suitcase.

'I see from your records that you have had a chequered past, Bob. Prison sentences for arson,' continued Horvarth.

'I've paid for my crimes and you know it.' Bob was feeling tired, tetchy and run-down, still suffering from jet lag. He just wanted to go home and sleep.

'Let me level with you, Bob. We're interested in your connection to the Crawthorne family. We have information to suggest that in 2010 you were a homeless vagrant wandering around the Chichester and Aldwick Bay area of West Sussex – my patch as it happens. Ring any bells?'

'It might do.'

'Around the same time that you absconded from Ford Open Prison – you must remember that. The same week as Lord Crawthorne had his beach chalet burnt down.' Horvarth scrutinised Bob.

'I really don't know what you're getting at. Look, I came here voluntarily, not to sit here waiting for the next punch to come my way.'

DC Fernandez interjected. 'Bob, we're a bit puzzled about your involvement with the Crawthornes – for some reason you seem to be drawn to the family. Please enlighten us.' Fernandez was the voice of reason.

'Look, you don't need to play the good-guy, bad-guy routine with me. It's all very simple. Yes, I was homeless and a job came up at Crawthorne Hall Hotel. It was a coincidence that an acquaintance of mine used to live there as a boy and told me a story about some bad experiences he had there. Yes, I was curious.'

'Are we talking about your friend Paul Marsh?' interrupted Inspector Horvarth.

'We weren't friends. He was my cell mate and, as such, I looked-out for him – that's all. He was a train wreck – vulnerable. I expect you know he killed himself?'

'And what did he tell you about a shooting in the East wing – in what is now called Room 13?' asked Fernandez.

'That he was in the room while two men were finishing a poker game.'

'When was this?'

Bob rummaged through his memory. 'He never told me a specific date although he said it happened when he was ten years old. Paul was born in 1964.'

'Carry on.' This from Horvarth, who now spoke in a slightly gentler tone of voice.

'Paul told me that the winner was accused of cheating. Apparently, it happened in the early hours one morning,' continued Bob.

'What was a ten-year-old doing at a poker game in the middle of the night?' Fernandez interjected in a doubtful tone. 'Surely he should have been tucked-up in bed?'

'I asked him the same question,' replied Bob. 'I think Paul was an abused child. On this occasion he was being used to fetch and carry drinks during the all-night gambling session.' Fernandez nodded his head satisfied with the explanation.

'So, what is alleged to have happened next – according to our Mr. Paul Marsh?' persisted DI Horvarth.

'He said a shot was fired and that blood splattered everywhere.'

'Did he say anything about the victim's appearance?' continued Horvarth.

'Only that he was smartly dressed – in a suit. Oh. He said the man had a moustache.'

Angelia Wilmot, watching on the CCTV monitor, could hardly contain her delight. This could be a game changer when it came to the facial reconstruction imaging.

'And did he mention the identity of the perpetrator?' asked Carl Fernandez.

'Paul said it was the old Lord Crawthorne.'

'And what did Paul Marsh tell you about what happened to the body?' added DI Horvarth.

'He was sent to fetch his dad, the head gardener.'

'In the early hours of the morning?' This from Fernandez.

'Yes. Paul said he stayed at home after that – in the head gardener's lodge. It was raining heavily and, in the morning, he noticed his dad's muddy boots. Then later that day, when he was passing through the kitchen gardens, he noticed a freshly dug mound of earth which hadn't been there the day before. It was near an apple tree.'

'Is there anything else you can tell us?' asked Fernandez.

'Only that, while working at the hotel I became more and more curious. So did my girlfriend Penny – who is now my wife. Also, Lord Crawthorne's grandson, Charles Eden became convinced that there might be some truth in the story. We started to delve into it – which led to the excavations. And that's it. I've been anxious to return to the UK to pick-up the threads. Find out whether the identity of the victim has been discovered. I've seen nothing on the internet while I've been away.'

Just then there was a knock on the door, which was answered by DI Horvarth. After a whispered conversation in the corridor outside, he gestured to DC Fernandez. They both left the room. A drably dressed female walked-in.

'Good afternoon, Mr. Bennett. My name is Detective Chief Inspector Angelia Wilmot. I'd like to thank you for coming in today and answering our questions. You have been most helpful.'

Bob was taken by surprised, being treated with a modicum of respect for the first time ever in his dealings with the police.

'Believe it or not, DCI Wilmot, I'm not your enemy – I'm on your side. I want to get to the bottom of this mystery – which is why I was prepared to bankroll the second excavation of the kitchen gardens at Crawthorne Hall Hotel. Which – by the way led to the discovery of the body.'

'We very much appreciate that. You have been very public spirited.'

'No. I did it for my ex-cell-mate, who ended up hanging himself because of his miserable life. Witnessing that shooting and other terrible things that happened to him as a boy, really messed him up. I did it for him.'

'Nevertheless, thank you.'

'I also have to say, that I came here voluntarily. I just returned from China late last night and feel very rough – I need to sleep. I wanted to help the enquiry. As a law-abiding citizen, I was not impressed with the rough treatment which I received from DI Horvarth.'

'Sorry about that. The trouble with hiring an Alsatian is that it tends to bite occasionally. That's our DI Horvarth for you. He has his uses,' she said conspiratorially.

'And his issues, it seems,' retorted Bob. He wasn't sure whether DCI Wilmot was humouring or patronising him.

'Anyway, thank you for your time, Mr. Bennett,' DCI Wilmot carried on pleasantly, ignoring the jibe.

'Perhaps DI Horvarth needs to go on a police training course on treating members of the public with more respect?' suggested Bob, still not finished with the subject of the detective inspector's interviewing technique.

Wilmot smiled knowingly. Horvarth had a reputation for being rude to people: especially colleagues. She wondered how he would react if he were told to attend a session on improving his manners.

Bob decided that this was the moment to ask the question that was uppermost in his mind. 'Anyway, moving on Detective Chief Inspector, can you tell me anything about the investigation? Have you identified the victim?'

'All I can say, Mr. Bennett, is that we now have enough evidence to take our investigation forwards although we will be making a public appeal soon – we believe that someone, somewhere knows something – and we want to hear from them – pronto. Sorry, I can't say more. You have been extremely helpful in what you have told my colleagues today and I am very grateful.'

With that, Bob was walked to an unmarked police car to be taken home.

'Oh and Mr. Bennett,' DCI Wilmot called as he was about to open the passenger door.' He turned and glanced over at her. 'I hope you manage to sleep-off your jet lag – it's a horrible feeling. Nice meeting you, sir.'

With that she disappeared back through the main entrance to the police station. From there she was going to head back to the cold-case unit for the next team briefing – and to share the piece of information that she hoped would be the long-awaited breakthrough needed to conclude the investigation.

Chapter 60

Two days after arriving home, Bob was feeling more tired than normal: going to bed early; feeling more exhausted than he had ever known. At first, he'd put it down to jetlag – but then it had progressively worsened, his legs had become excruciatingly painful.

He tried taking paracetamol, which made no difference. So, that is when he started taking Penny's morphine to quell the pain, which felt a bit like having a trapped nerve: he assumed that he must have twisted his back lifting luggage on and off trolleys and conveyor belts on their journey back to the UK. He'd also started to develop a cough – but it wasn't persistent.

Then, four days after arriving back from China Bob was overcome by an algid coldness: he began shivering uncontrollably, even sitting on the sofa with an electric blanket over him; which seemed to make no difference. So, he went up to bed, waking in the middle of the night in a fever: his body felt like it was on fire, his head pounding away. By morning he was vomiting profusely and wringing wet with sweat. It started to become difficult to breathe: and that is when Penny finally called the ambulance.

By the time they arrived forty-five minutes later, Bob was slipping in and out of consciousness. The paramedics, dressed in white plastic hazmat suits, put an oxygen mask on their patient and carried him out to the ambulance.

'Can I come with him?' asked Penny.

'Sorry, but you're not allowed in the ambulance – and Covid patients aren't allowed visitors.'

'So, is it Coronavirus then?' Penny was perplexed. She'd read the article that the taxi driver had given her – and he was right: the media was full of stories about it. So far, nearly three hundred people in the UK had tested positive for the virus: she hoped that Bob wasn't going to be another of the statistics.

'We can't be sure until he's tested in the hospital – but you said you'd recently come back from China?'

'Yes.'

'Then there's a high chance that he has Covid 19. It started in China.'

'In that case, will I be allowed to come to the hospital – in my own car – to be by his bedside?'

'Covid patients aren't permitted to have visitors: it's too contagious. My advice is to stay at home and phone the hospital for updates. If he tests negative, I expect you'll be able to come along to see your husband, but it will depend on the infection rate. You may need to be tested yourself, too.'

'But I'm fine – apart from a back injury.'

'Some people are asymptomatic – they have the virus but don't show symptoms. The hospital won't risk letting you near patients if there is any chance that you are carrying Covid 19. Sorry Mrs Bennett – you'll just have to take it up with the hospital. Call them.'

'As for us, we really need to get your husband into hospital as soon as possible.'

So, loading Bob into the back of the vehicle, the two paramedics closed the double back doors and sped on their way, blue lights flashing.

Penny had read that millions of people, just like her and Bob, had travelled to China for the country's Chinese New Year on 25th January, followed by the week of celebrations to welcome in the Year of the Metal Rat. When they had been staying in Beijing, they'd wondered why many of the planned events had been cancelled. It was only after they had arrived back in the UK that they had gleaned the full seriousness of the situation. For, during the month of February, after all the mingling, mixing and celebrating, the multitudes who had gathered in China had returned home to the countries in which they lived and worked; most carrying gifts and souvenirs for their loved ones. Some inadvertently carried Covid 19: known by many as Coronavirus, picked up from friends, families or travellers during their time away. Penny hoped that she and Bob were not amongst those who had been infected by the deadly virus.

Arriving at the hospital, Bob was one of many patients inside queuing ambulances which were waiting to off-load patients at the accident and emergency drop-off point. He lay there for three hours before he was finally eased into a wheelchair, vaguely aware of someone saying that there were no cubicles left for patients: the department was full to capacity. He closed his eyes, listening to everything around him: people rushing around, phones ringing, general commotion.

'I have to swab you for Covid-19,' a tall, dark-haired nurse announced at last.

She stuck a swab stick so far down Bob's throat that he was retching. Then, just as he was recovering, she did the same again: but this time up his nostrils. Then blood was taken for analysis and he was wheeled-off for a chest x-ray.

By this time Bob was feeling pummelled.

What the hell's going on? he thought as he waited for the verdict.

Then, twenty-five minutes later he received the news.

'Just to let you know,' announced a doctor as Bob waited patiently in a corridor; still seated in the wheelchair with the oxygen mask over his face. 'Your X-ray results have come back – you have pneumonia in the lungs and you'll have to continue to be on oxygen for 24/7. We'll find you a bed as soon as one becomes available.'

With that the doctor moved-on to other waiting patients.

Later, now in bed, sharing a bay with three others, there were nursing staff continually monitoring and keeping observations. Bob started to feel a heavy pain in his chest.

'I can't breathe.' He had lifted the oxygen mask with some effort in order to call out.

'Please Mr. Bennett, you must keep your mask on – otherwise it will be a lot worse.'

'It feels like I'm being compressed by slabs of concrete.'

'Sorry darling. That's the pneumonia attacking your lungs.' She injected something into his arm through the canula which had been applied earlier. 'Just some morphine to help you sleep.'

But then, added to his breathing difficulties, he started feeling violent stabbing pains in his stomach as though someone was gouging-out his insides with a rusty knife.

'I can't take this anymore. I can't carry on!'

Then delirium set-in.

*

He was unable to remember much of the first few days: just nurses coming in and out all the time; cleaners hovering around, disinfecting everything. He'd watch the staff – all working a minimum of a twelve-hour shift – many looking exhausted from the constant, punishing demands of their time, skills and attention. Most of the noise emanated from Bob ringing the bell and gasping for drinks of water: he was so weak that he could hardly utter the words 'bed pan'.

One night, an aged man in the opposite bed was screaming and writhing in agony for hours on end: then silence. The next morning the ward curtains were opened and Bob noticed that the bed was empty.

That was when Bob began to hallucinate: experiencing flashbacks of conversations he'd had in his life. In his mind he re-lived snatches of some of his nightmare moments. In his befuddled mind, he re-visited the horror of finding Paul Marsh hanged in their shared prison cell, his eyes bulging and his tongue protruding from the asphyxia and suffocation. He saw, once again, that swollen face; skin now with a purplish-bluish hue and pinpoint bleeds around his eyes. Then he was waking-up as a three-year-old finding the house ablaze, watching the fire take hold of his home with bangs and loud crackling, thick black smoke billowing out of the roof. As he stood there, a figure slowly emerged from the furnace, walking towards him. As it approached, he saw that it was a woman holding a limp, lifeless baby in her arms.

Bob Bennett tossed and turned in the hospital bed, letting out a scream. At one point he wondered whether he was dead or alive – did the flashbacks mean that he was transitioning to death? Was this Bob's life passing before him as he prepared to die? It was all so bizarre and surreal, as though the demons in his life were pulling him apart. Still looking into the blaze, he saw the figure of a man emerging, dressed in black velvet and wearing a mask. The stranger stood at a familiar-looking bedroom window watching imperturbably, then beckoning to Bob, who couldn't stop himself being pulled towards the dancing flames as they leapt and licked at their surrounds.

As Bob struggled for his life in the hospital, emergency crews were attending a blaze at Crawthorne Hall Hotel. The fire alarms, which had been recently installed by *Fire Away Ltd.,* had performed effectively enough, alerting the fire service, who soon brought the raging inferno under control. It had started in the East wing – apparently some kind of spontaneous combustion, completely destroying part of the building. The cause was unknown.

Back in the hospital, Bob's condition was finally considered bad enough to put him into an induced coma with one of the few available respirators. Then it was a matter of biding time; patiently waiting to see whether the cocktail of medicines that were being administered would start to make some difference. Maybe this would give Bob a chance to be eased-back into a state where he would once more be able to breathe for himself, unassisted by a machine?

He remained in this state for another five days with a nurse in attendance monitoring him at all times – but Penny, at home nervously stuck on a rollercoaster between optimism and pessimism, was still not allowed to be by his side.

*

The will to live is strong in everyone – almost impossible to destroy – but Bob, unconscious and unable to fight the virus anymore simply drifted away. His body lay there for nearly two hours before overstretched hospital staff, prioritising their attentions on saving the living, finally paid attention to his corpse; cleaning it and wrapping it in plastic like a parcel being packaged. Then they transferred it to a body bag, which was unceremoniously zipped-up.

'On the count of three: one … two … three …'

Then onto a metal trolley while a lemon-smelling disinfectant was sprayed on to the bed where he had lain for days. The body of Bob Bennett was then wheeled-down to the morgue and put into cold storage like a fetid piece of meat waiting to be discarded.

Chapter 61

The coffin, with its rounded ends, was woven from golden banana plant leaves. It sat upon a wooden Victorian hand-drawn cart with a cast iron frame – a garden feature which Bob and Penny had originally bought from an antiques auction in Chichester. He had always joked that the cart, a funeral bier, would be useful to carry him to his final resting place one day. She had decided to arrange for this to happen – he always liked to be different.

The country was in lockdown. The Covid-19 pandemic, sweeping across the world was now out of control and governments were desperately trying to find ways of abating the rate of infections. So, restrictions had been placed on the lives of everyone: restaurants and hotels had closed; only essential shops were allowed to open; massive queues were commonplace at supermarkets, with customers panic-buying, fearing a shortage of food. Social distancing, self-isolating and shielding from others had become the so-called new normal. Journeys were only to be made if absolutely essential and attendance at funerals was limited to a handful of close relatives only.

Bob had lost touch with his family years beforehand – they had turned their backs on him when he had been imprisoned for arson and later on the streets as a homeless beggar. He had never sought any reconciliation after he had turned his life around. Yes, he had plenty of friends – including Charles Eden, who now lived four hundred and fifty miles away in Scotland. However, under the circumstances it was not a good idea to travel anywhere unless absolutely necessary. So, Penny had taken the decision to say a final goodbye to Bob on her own.

Setting-off from the sustainability centre nestling under a canopy of broadleaf trees and a yew grove towards the natural burial site, two of the centre's staff pulled the wooden bier along a windy track through a sheep pasture, followed by Penny and Tim Fellows, the centre's funeral director. They donned thick outdoor clothing and waterproofs, wellington boots and hats to shield them from the gusty mid-April winds which whipped-up around them.

They trundled through a small meadow surrounded by large, billowing willow trees, branches hanging to the floor, wind whipping them lazily. The green sprouts and leaves on the tips of the branches dragged softly, skimming over the ground and swaying ever so slightly as they passed through into a partial woodland area. Penny could hear the faint sound of water and she knew that they were nearly at their destination: Bob's final resting place.

When they had married, Bob had told Penny that, if he were to die first, he wanted a natural burial. The thought of a full church service didn't really reflect him. He loved nature: he was fascinated by the changing seasons and loved walks through woodland and over sweeping open countryside. Living in Sussex for most of his life, he had spent many hours lost in his thoughts in the South Downs and Penny knew that this was the best place for Bob to be buried. He would have wanted this: to nurture the Earth as it had nurtured him.

Finally stopping beside yet another old willow tree – this one gnarled by the years, branches now dancing in the wind – she saw the shallow grave, dug in a little clearing with a pile of earth to one side; two attendants standing back discretely. She saw no birds flying in the small expanse of visible sky, yet a small nameless tune could be heard, the wind carrying it all around the trees.

To begin with they all stood there in silence, masks on faces and keeping a social distance from each other, still aware of the Covid-19 restrictions upon them all. Penny clutched a handful of flowers from their garden: mostly daffodils.

'Well, welcome Penny … and welcome, Bob,' began Tim Fellows. 'We're here today to say goodbye and to return Bob's body to the earth. Penny, you are welcome to lay flowers in the grave.'

She stepped over and did so, gently tossing a few of the daffodils into the shallow empty hole in the ground. Then Tim, the centre's director continued.

'Here in this peaceful place, at the opening to this natural grave, we prepare to give back to the earth so that you may become part of it all. We return to the nature loved, to the trees, the grasses, the little creatures and the elements of Mother Earth.'

Then, at that point, standing there under the willow tree, Penny played one of Bob's favourite songs on her mobile phone. It was called *Bends Like A Willow* and was sung by his favourite rock group. She felt that the words and sentiments were very apt for the occasion of her deceased husband's funeral.

There was no eulogy. Instead, the centre's staff approached the funeral bier and, each grasping one of the coffin's rope handles, gently lifted Bob over, placing him beside the hole. Then, attaching cords, they gradually lowered the coffin into the ground.

'You're still in my heart but you are free at last,' called out Penny, tears welling in her eyes. 'I wanted to tell you that. I'm so sorry you had to suffer like that.' She threw the rest of the flowers on top of the coffin thinking of Bob, who used to paint pictures of them spending their lives together – now there would be so many unfulfilled dreams.

'As we let you go now,' said Tim Fellows in a bold voice, 'borne into a deeper understanding, the dark earth will soon close its safe arms around you and you will become part of a greater embrace.' Then picking-up a shovel he handed it to Penny. 'Now it is time to close the grave.'

She took it and, digging into the pile beside the hole, threw some of the earth on top of the coffin. Then, ambling back along the track with Tim, she turned one more time in the direction of her husband's coffin, just as the staff got to work filling-in the rest of the grave.

Bob, now just an empty shell, no longer a person in pain and suffering, had headed-out of the world. Finally, he had moved on: hopefully to a better place.

Penny, tearful and distraught, was just about to drive home from the sustainability centre, glad to have finally stumbled through this terrible day when her mobile phone started to ring.

'Hello?'

'Hello. Mrs Bennett? This is DCI Wilmot. Is Mr. Bennett there? He hasn't answered my messages – the ones I left on his phone. I thought I'd try you. I have some news.'

'Didn't you know?'

'Sorry?' Wilmot sounded bewildered by the question.

'Bob. He passed. The Coronavirus – he succumbed to it.'

'Oh.' Wilmot was taken aback. 'I'm so sorry – I didn't realise he was in such a serious condition.'

'I've just buried him.' Tears were streaming down Penny's face.

'Again. I'm so, so, sorry. I expect the last thing you need right now is for me to call you. I can try later if that would be more timely – more appropriate. I'm sorry for your loss – your husband helped us so much in our inquiry. I thought I'd make a courtesy call to tell him the news. I've already phoned Lady Crawthorne.'

'May I ask exactly what this is about?'

'It concerns the human remains that your husband helped to find. Sorry – I realise that you don't want to hear about this now. My commiserations. I'll call again.' She was repeating herself, clearly embarrassed about her bad timing.

'No,' insisted Penny. 'Please tell me. Bob would have wanted to know as soon as possible – it meant so much to him.'

'Alright, Mrs Bennett. I can tell you that, confronted by the weight of evidence, we now have a one hundred percent identification of the victim. We know exactly who was buried in the kitchen gardens at Crawthorne Hall Hotel. We couldn't have done it without your husband's help. I wanted him to be one of the first to know … before it hits the news headlines tomorrow. We now know what happened in Room 13.'

Epilogue

She was once bright and bubbly – ambitious, even. She had dreams, and wants. Her smile would brighten up the room.

Yet, one day, she stopped. Smiles ceased to happen, or if they did, they looked so dead: there was no longer any shine in her deep brown lacklustre eyes when she smiled. It was like a plastic doll, eyes in a daze, distant. It was as if she was always somewhere else. Her head, perhaps? Or maybe a whole different world.

She didn't talk much anymore, either. Gradually becoming more reserved, she had distanced herself from others, fumbling for her words: it was as if she was afraid to utter a word. As if doing so would lead to punishment. She always seemed unsure of herself, insecure. Her body radiated the exact opposite of confidence in its aura.

Preferring to be alone, isolating herself in her house, she didn't talk to her friends much anymore, didn't dream her dreams anymore. She didn't want anything anymore; didn't participate in her old hobbies anymore. Her life went on but as though she were a statue wrapped in darkness.

Nothing mattered, because she felt hopeless. And the shine in her eyes never returned, the smiles never alive.

Amy sat in her comfortable four-bedroomed house in the historic village of Liphook in Hampshire. They had moved here after five years at sea – with a six months gap when she'd fulfilled her dream of sailing her own boat around parts of Europe, finally ending-up in the Bay of Kotor, Europe's southernmost fjords: playground of the rich and famous. Then, mooring in the marina near the beautiful town of Kotor in Montenegro she had delivered her prize possession; the Horizon Elegance 20 entry-level yacht, now named *Lucky Girl,* which had been left to her by her father, Lord George Edward Crawthorne, 15th Baron Crawthorne.

Back then, after deciding to stay living together – but no longer legally married as husband and wife, she and Charles had agreed to make it their priority to build a home together, settling for Liphook, a Hampshire village, on the old A3 road leading from London to Portsmouth. It had seemed ideally located providing good road and railway links with easy access to high calibre hotels so that they could continue in the hospitality

Tony Ashridge

industry once their time at sea was spent. It was also near enough to the sea so that Amy could continue with her sailing pursuits – albeit in a much smaller, more economical vessel. She had also discovered the nearby Frensham Ponds where she had enjoyed poodling around in her little dinghy.

She and Charles had been happy. That was, until their lives had been once more thrown into turmoil because of who they were. The storm clouds had finally broken: all the circumstances that surrounded their lives compounded what was possible for a continuing relationship. Indeed, Amy rarely smiled anymore.

Four years ago, she'd fallen pregnant. She and Charles had spent many hours debating what to do if their child had Downs' Syndrome. It was a possible consequence of their union together – with the joint DNA which they'd inherited.

'What do you think we should do if the baby has it?' Charles had broached the subject.

'A kid with Down's Syndrome isn't so different,' she'd replied. 'Life can be pretty normal.'

But then the cold reality had hit them after she'd had the amniocentesis – an amniotic fluid test to determine whether the baby had any chromosomal abnormalities. They had both awaited the result with nausea, apprehension and lurching anticipation.

'Your baby has tested positive,' the doctor had told them on the phone – no face-to-face chat in their case.

Their reaction to the news hadn't been as they had anticipated: the reality had been different to the perception. Slumped on the sofa, tears overflowing, and feeling like her world had just imploded, Amy knew that nothing would ever be the same again. She had woken into a new world, a world that was cold and harsh: entirely different from anything she had ever had to imagine for herself. She had to think about the future carefully and with clarity. Amy had a sense of soul-crushing hopelessness for what her daughter's life would be like; hopelessness for what the diagnosis meant to her as a parent; hopelessness for how different her family would look from the one she'd always planned. It was all changed forever by that call.

'Why doesn't someone throw some more heavy-duty crap at us?' Charles had moaned despondently. It seemed to him like just one hole after another. In truth, he didn't feel that he could face-up to bringing up a child with disabilities. He realised he was being cowardly and selfish.

264

'Will you support me if I decide to keep her?' Amy needed to know whether they were in this together – or whether he was looking for a get-out clause. He seemed to be hesitating. 'You must know how you feel,' she added.

'I know we both desperately want a child,' he said at last. 'You have to go with your gut feeling Amy – but just remember, we have to be prepared for all the demands that will come – and we'll be looking after her for the rest of our lives – also it'll mean no grandchildren.'

'So, no pressure on me then.' Amy had felt depressed and ashamed at her own misgivings.

'Then there will be all the good-intentioned well-meaning smiles.' Charles seemed to be becoming less supportive by the minute, as though he wanted to distance himself: to side-step the issue or maybe even to walk away from Amy and their baby. After that, he avoided talking about it, dissociating himself. Much remained unsaid, lying deep and cold under the surface of politeness. In the end, the very best he could do was to quietly crawl away.

That was four years ago.

But now, looking back on that moment, Amy no longer felt anxiety, sorrow and anger. She had different emotions – sometimes joy at seeing the little milestones that her daughter, Harriet, achieved. She sometimes smiled as she looked at those sparkling almond-shaped eyes that were the same colour as Charles' and that same captivating smile which could make her laugh. She would watch those small hands, quick to seek mischief and then sign for forgiveness. She was overwhelmed by love for her only child but she grieved for her marriage which had so sorely suffered, unable to take the strain any longer.

In the end Charles had locked his love away, shutting her out of his life. Once they had been good together; but that hadn't been enough to keep them together. Taking fright and taking flight, he had ended up spending more and more time away from home, eventually having an affair with the bookings' manager at his hotel. His betrayal had been the beginning of Amy's disenchantment. Then, to make matters worse, they'd married and moved up to Scotland. He rarely took the trouble to contact Amy or his daughter anymore.

Amy was sad and bitter about her life. She hugged her three-year old daughter. They were in this together now – for life.

Sighing heavily, she looked at the front page of the newspaper beside her on the sofa. More bad news about Coronavirus deaths with a national lockdown coming soon – yet another blow. She wondered how she would cope with more isolation in her life. Her doctor was worried about her mental health – and so was her mother Sheila Hughes and her half-sister, Helen Eden. At least she and Harriet had so far managed to stay safe from the virus – unlike poor Bob Bennett. She had liked Bob.

Amy turned over the page looking for other news – perhaps something good that was happening in the world. Surely it couldn't all be bad news?

It was then that she saw it. On page two – a headline about a discovery at Crawthorne Hall Hotel some weeks earlier. She read the article.

JOHN BINGHAM MYSTERY SOLVED AFTER 46 YEARS

Police have now identified the mystery man whose remains were unearthed at Crawthorne Hall Hotel earlier in the year. DNA, dental records and facial reconstruction technology were used to verify the identity together with x-rays from plastic surgery to his nose. Using radiocarbon dating and other information police were able to establish that he died in 1974. Examination of the skeletal remains revealed that the cause of death was a single gunshot wound to the thorax in the region of his heart.

Richard John Bingham disappeared after visiting friends in Uckfield, East Sussex in the early hours of Friday 8th November 1974.
Detective Chief Inspector Angelia Wilmot leading the investigation made the following statement:

'On 8th November 1974 an international manhunt began in search of Richard John Bingham, suspected of murdering his children's nanny the previous evening in London. She had been bludgeoned to death with a piece of lead piping. Bingham's estranged wife claimed that she had witnessed the murder, naming her husband as the perpetrator.

We have now established that on the same evening John Bingham left London, stopping-off in Uckfield before continuing his journey to Crawthorne Hall near Hailsham, some eleven miles further on. There he joined-in a game of poker in the East wing of the house. Bingham was well-known for high-stakes gambling and, as the card game drew to a close, there was an argument. He was accused of cheating and a shot was fired.

A detailed forensic examination of the room revealed a large amount of blood which had seeped-through the flooring and which gives an exact match to that of John Bingham. The human remains unearthed in the grounds of the hotel have also been conclusively identified as those of John Bingham.

We have concluded that John Bingham was murdered in what is now known as Room 13 and buried in the garden. There is no evidence to determine who fired the shot, only heresay.

On Friday 8th November 1974 Bingham's borrowed Ford Corsair was found in Newhaven, eighteen miles from Crawthorne Hall. We are convinced that there must have been collusion in the disposal of Bingham's body and the car.

Richard John Bingham was better known as Lord Lucan, 7th Earl Lucan – he was often called 'Lucky' by his friends.

The case is now closed.'

A NOTE FROM THE AUTHOR

Richard John Bingham, 7th Lord Lucan was born in 1934, disappeared on 8th November 1974 and was declared officially dead 3rd February 2016.

A keen poker player since serving in the Coldstream Guards in the 1950s, he was well-known for his gambling habits, eventually becoming a professional gambler, gaining the moniker 'Lucky Lucan.'

After his marriage broke down, his wife Veronica was awarded custody of the children, much to Lord Lucan's displeasure. It was on Thursday 7th November 1974 when he drove an old, dark, scruffy Ford Corsair to his wife's home in Belgrave Street, Belgravia, London, where the children's nanny was bludgeoned to death with a piece of bandaged lead pipe in the basement kitchen. Lady Lucan came down the stairs as he was placing the body into a canvas mailbag. She was then attacked and eventually escaped to a nearby pub.

Lucan phoned his mother to collect the children and later drove the Ford Corsair to Uckfield, East Sussex to visit friends. He left their house at around 1.15a.m. on Friday 8th November. He was never seen again.

Early on the Friday morning Sandra Rivett, the nanny, was pronounced dead. A bloodstained lead pipe was found on the floor at the scene of the murder. On searching Lord Lucan's home his passport was found in a drawer and his blue Mercedes-Benz car was parked outside. Later-on that day, the Ford Corsair was found in Newhaven (sixteen miles from Uckfield). Inside, a piece of lead pipe and a bottle of vodka were discovered.

Police divers searched the harbour, but found no body.

What Happened in Room 13 is a work of fiction – nobody knows what happened to Lord Lucan. Did he die or adopt a new identity? Throughout the years there have been many claimed sightings of Richard John Bingham.

On 16th June 1975 a full inquest declared that Sandra Rivett, the nanny, died from head injuries and that the criminal offence of her murder had been committed by Richard John Bingham, 7th Lord Lucan.

Acknowledgements

Due to the wide scope of settings, scenarios and characters in this book, there has been extensive research to ensure accuracy of detail and facts. I owe a huge debt to everyone who has helped by giving me information and answering my questions. Thank you to the many people who have furnished me with an insight into the workings and procedures inherent in their roles, particularly those health professionals from Queen Alexandra Hospital, Portsmouth and the Basingstoke and North Hampshire Hospital. Also, officers from Hampshire and West Midlands Constabularies.

To single out a few names in particular, thank you to Sue Gillet for the inspiration, support and advice which you gave me over time and your guidance in having this book published. A huge thank you to JB and MM for permission to use their poem The Kiss (1990) based on the painting of the same name by Gustac Klimt (1907 – 1908). Also, Siobhan, from Novotel in Coventry, Suzanne Clark (Salvation Army), Ian from Taylor Garnier, for the opportunity to visit a truly haunted house! Also, Natalie French (Poole Yacht Club) for talking through some of the intricacies of sailing; Bart at Hotel Swissotel Amsterdam and Rob from Beaulieu House, New Forest, England.

During my research I found great inspiration for the book from the Sustainability Centre (East Meon), Tylney Hall Hotel (Hook) and Wyvenhoe House Hotel (Colchester) – thanks to the students who told me about the management practices.

Thanks to the skill of the crew on that fateful Boeing 777 journey which inspired the air travel chapter – they never did finish explaining what happens to someone who passes during a flight – maybe there are some secrets best kept from nosy authors! Just a mention, also, to those staff at Alton Towers who took time out to explain the workings of the Nemesis ride.

On the travel front, thanks to the tourist information staff based in Amsterdam and Venice. In particular, thanks to Gail (New Forest

Tourism), Travel Wisconsin (Madison), Federica and Veronica (Venice local guides). My appreciation also goes to include numerous staff and crew members based with Royal Caribbean, Princess Cruises, Cunard and MSC Cruises.

As always, thank you to my partner, Siobhan, for the encouragement, support, patience and technical help during the writing of this book: also, for the gallons of tea and coffee that she provided during the writing of What Happened in Room 13.

FINALLY, THANK YOU TO THE REAL ROOM 13 IN A CERTAIN ABU DHABI HOTEL, UNITED ARAB EMIRATES, WHERE EVERYTHING SEEMED TO GO WRONG! ROOM 13 WAS WHERE IT ALL STARTED ...

About the Author

Tony Ashridge was born in Essex, then attended schools in Cheshire and Surrey before studying Art History and Education at the University of Warwick. As a teacher, he has lived and worked in various parts of England including the Midlands, Essex, London and finally Hampshire where he has settled for a quiet life in the country.

He has travelled widely throughout the world, often finding inspiration for his writing from incidents, characters and locations along the way.

070721

Printed in Great Britain
by Amazon